# The Forever Watch

DAVID RAMIREZ

# The Forever Watch

HODDER &
STOUGHTON

First published in Great Britain in 2014 by

Hodder & Stoughton
An Hachette UK company

1

Copyright © David Ramirez 2014

A CIP catalogue record for this title is available from the British Library

Hardback ISBN 978 1 444 78790 0
Trade Paperback ISBN 978 1 444 78789 4
Ebook ISBN 978 1 444 78787 0

Printed and bound by Clays Ltd, St Ives plc

Hodder & Stoughton policy is to use papers that are natural, renewable and recyclable
products and made from wood grown in sustainable forests. The logging and manufacturing processes are expected to conform to the environmental regulations of the
country of origin.

Hodder & Stoughton Ltd

London NW1 3BH

www.hodder.co.uk

*For Liza,*
*Who kept believing*

*And for my father,*
*Who never got to read this*

# The Forever Watch

FUNCTIONAL, SLIGHTLY UNCOMFORTABLE PLASTECH BEDSHEETS CLING WHERE the hospital gown exposes skin. The air is cool and dry against my face. My muscles feel heavy, cold, unwieldy. The air whispers through the vents, the devices beside me hum and buzz and beep. My eyelids are slow to open. Orange glimmers streak back and forth across my vision, as the Implant starts to pipe signals into the optic nerves.

Waking up has been odd since the last of the post-Duty surgeries were completed. The Doctors tell me that it is primarily due to the hibernation, and to a lesser degree, the medication altering the timing between the organic and inorganic parts of my brain.

Menus come alive, superimposed over my vision.

My mental commands, clicking through the options and windows and tabs, are sluggish. Despite the chemical interference, the Implant processes my thoughts, assists me in revving up the *touch* center of my mind. To my left, the curtains slide open, brightening the room further. Normally, I can do this without going through the interface, but I cannot muster the concentration right now.

It is the end of the week, the last day of my long, long "holiday." If my evaluation goes well, I can go home.

A thought about the time pulls up a display. There are hours yet.

Breakfast is on the table by the bed. Oatmeal, an apple, a biscuit, a packet of margarine, and a carton of soy milk. I could float it over and eat without getting up, but I've been on my back for too long. I force myself upright and swing my legs over. On my feet, the world sways, left and right. But it is not as bad as the first day I woke up after restorative surgery. Four days ago, even sitting up induced nausea.

Eating is a slow ordeal, each motion requiring my complete attention. My hands still shake. The milk sloshes when I raise it to my lips. A little trickles between my numb lips. I can barely taste the food. Is it the typical bland hospital food, or is it the meds?

An hour to eat and I am already tired, but I do not want to sleep. There is a rehab room where I could exercise for a bit. There is an inner courtyard garden where my fellow post-Duty patients are walking around in the sun, talking through what we've been through. I do not want to talk. I do not want to play cards with the other patients. I want out.

A few command pulses tap me into the Nth Web. My body is left behind a cramped desk, but I fly through the glittering mazes of dataspace, a world made of light and information. At my bookmarked sites, I look into what has been happening while I slept. There is little to catch up on. The weather is as expected. There are articles about performances in the theaters, and petty crime being on the decline, and the usual updates about the Noah's vital systems. All good, situation nominal.

A little more awake now, I open a music application and try to listen to Thelonius Monk. I cannot enjoy it; my emotions are still too dulled. I try an old movie about cowboys for two hours' worth of distraction. Shop for replacement parts for the coffee grinder I was not able to fix before I was picked up by the Breeding Center.

Knocking at the door. Old forms from another age. A lost world.

"Come in." My voice still startles me. Did I always sound like this?

"Afternoon, ma'am."

The orderly delivers lunch, picks up the breakfast tray. I notice a little cupcake on the corner, with a lit candle.

"Your last day, right?"

"Yes."

Baby face. Too young. He tries his best charming smile. "Maybe I'll see you around on the outside." Not very subtly, he messages me his ID along with my copy of the receipt for today's meals. In my head, the packet includes a little attachment. My. He is confident about his body. "Maybe." I wonder how many women give him a call afterward.

"Well. Bye then, Ms. Dempsey."

I don't want to eat any more. Should have gotten up earlier instead of putting off breakfast. I make myself eat the salad. I spear and consume every bit of lettuce and drink the last mouthful of chickenish broth. The Behavioralist will notice if I don't.

A hot shower makes me feel marginally more alive. Almost scalding hot. I try to enjoy the water crashing down on me, until the system automatically cuts it off when I have hit today's limit. A wireless transmission through the Implant authorizes a debit to my accounts, and I indulge in a half hour more, until my fingers and toes wrinkle up.

The hospital towels are coarse. In the mirror, there I am. Thinking of the past, and the device in my head.

Behind the wall constructed by the meds, emotions are boiling up, seeping through. I *need,* desperately. Need what? Maybe nothing. Maybe it's just neurotransmitters pinging off each other in my head. But real or not, despair is bubbling up through the artificial calm.

I resort to the one memory that has always been a comfort to me—that first moment after waking from the neural augmentation.

The neural Implant is a web of nanoscale threads spread through the brain. The bulk of it forms a dense network on the outer surface of the skull. Through an X-scanner, it looks like a flower, blooming from a stem rooted at the base of the brain close to the chiasma of the optic nerve, with silvery transmitter petals that open up over the skin of the face.

Pre-psi-tech, the closest analogue is working with a computer, which is still how pre-Implant children do their homework, access the Nth Web, entertain themselves. The Implant too is a computer, except that the control devices are not manipulated with the hands. The cpu is part of the brain, responding to thoughts rather than key presses and button clicks. Instead of being displayed with a monitor and speakers, the information is written into the mind and onto the senses. It is a constant passenger linking me to a larger world. Data, communications, and perfect memory recall all just a thought-command away.

There is a qualitative difference before the device is implanted, when memories are blurry and fluid, and after, when they become concrete and immutable. They can be accessed in slow motion or fast-forward, or searched with database queries. The stimuli of the senses are preserved in perfect slices with a clarity that will never diminish as the years separate me from them. The transition between merely human recall and enhanced experience is sudden.

Automatic scripts take over my bodily functions, lock my nerves, and prepare me for full reimmersion. I go back to that when, to that me.

I have my Implant!

Looking in the mirror, my eyes are itching and a little red, and I think I will cry.

Not that I was very pretty before the surgery, but I was hoping for something . . . *cuter* . . . than what I got on my face. There's too much chrome! I touch my reflection. There is a metallic eye drawn on my forehead. And under my eyes, following the edges of my cheekbones, are a pair of flattened triangles that start just to the sides of my nose and spread out toward my temples. My lips are just barely dusted with silver.

What does it—oh!

Just as I start to wonder, the interface opens up in my head. Menu bars and buttons light up across my field of view. I remember from the pre-op orientation that those are just symbols. It's the thought structure in my head that matters, the way the biological electrical pulses along the neurons talk to the hardware poking into the synapses in between.

Blurring flashes in my eyes, chaos, colors, pictures, text, sounds in my ears. The passenger is listening, but it doesn't know which of my thoughts to pay attention to, so it tries to respond to all of them.

"Think disciplined," Mala said to me, over and over, when I was growing up. "No stray thoughts. Keep the mind empty except for what you need."

A long, dizzy minute passes while I get a grip. Like everybody else, I have been drilled with meditation, visualization, and biofeedback, practice for keeping my thoughts from jumping all over the place. The interface steadies, and my vision clears.

The Implant receives my awkward, slow questions. It accesses the Noah's systems and informs me. Data pours into my head. One hand braces against the sink, and the other touches my reflection. Orange arrows appear and highlight the emitter-plates on my face.

The silver eye indicates that I have some talent for *reading* and the lips indicate *writing*. From the size and density of the exposed filaments, I only have enough for neural-programming on the Nth Web—no poking around in others' heads or making them do what I want.

The triangles on my cheekbones, which are bright and large, indicate that the majority of my talents lie in *touch*. I can reach out with my thoughts and manipulate objects without my hands. Ooh. My projected power-output suggests that I will be pretty strong. Lifting a car with my mind is not out of the question, if I have the correct amplifier to boost the signal. Oh! I'll be getting my first amplifier today. No more watching enviously while the older kids play crazy, physics-defying games—no-hands baseball, psycho-paintball, ultra-dodgeball . . .

The ugly pattern of chrome on my face is starting to seem a little less uncool.

Lastly, there is the bit I did not notice—a tiny, shining teardrop right in the corner of my left eye, which is correlated with *guessing*. I have just a little bit more intuition than most.

The red toothbrush in the mug to the side of the sink catches my eye. I squint at it and think hard at it, remembering my lessons. It starts dancing, makes a clinking sound as it whips from side to side against the ceramic. . . . This really, kind of, somewhat *rocks,* and as I manage to float the toothbrush to a jerky kind of hover in front of my face, maybe it's even the height of *boss.*

I think of all the funny words and phrases from the movies of lost Earth that Mala watches with me, but the ones I want are from before the Implant, and they're fuzzy and hang just at the tip of the tongue. It's centuries later, and just like everything else on the ship, the slang gets recycled too.

That was that, and this is this. The rest of my life.

The loss of concentration releases the toothbrush. It falls and clatters around the drain.

I focus on my face again. Maybe it's not so bad. The chrome brings the sepia and umber highlights out of the brown skin and makes my round face a little sharper, a bit more adult. The green eyes look brighter because the cheek-plates catch some of the light and reflect more of it onto my eyes at an angle, and it brings out the hint of orange-jade at the edges of the irises. Maybe it doesn't look too bad with the white-yellow hair either, makes the long waves seem less like generic blond and more like something with an exotic name, such as maize.

Someone is knocking on the door. I know, without a reason why, that it's Mala.

"Come in!"

It is. She stands behind me and puts her hands on my shoulders, bare in my patient's shift. Her palms are warm but her fingers are cool. She's smiling with her eyes but not with her mouth.

"You're growing up."

Then I am crying, and I don't know why, and she's crying and hugging me.

I trigger the cutout procedure, and my sensorium returns to now.

Here I am, in another hospital, looking in another mirror—only, I am thirty years old.

I know now why Mala was crying that day I was twelve and marveling over my new Implant and my shiny future. Because she would have to let go of me soon. Because I would forget her, too busy with training school and new friends and all the great things I would do with my talents, which put me squarely beyond the ninety-fifth percentile: one of the ship's elite, requiring earlier and more demanding training.

Life, she had told me, only went forward. But the Implant's memory features defy that. An idle thought relives a past moment as if it were the present. The distinction between yesterday and decades ago seems only a matter of semantics.

Now, I am not looking at my face. I am looking at my body.

It is as if nothing has changed between my going to sleep nine months ago, and my waking up today. Only Doctors with the strongest *healing* handle Breeding.

My arms and legs are smooth and wiry, the muscles not at all atrophied, despite the long period of inactivity. No scars or stretch marks cross my belly. My breasts are not particularly swollen or tender. I look down and cup the folds of my sex, and they are the same color, the inner lips the same size, and internally, when I clench, the muscles tighten around my fingers and the fit is snug.

It is as if I were never pregnant, as if I had not given birth mere days before.

I am crying, and the tears are hot. Mala is not here with me, and I do not want to see the Behavioralist waiting in the receiving room.

For women on the ship, Breeding is a duty and a privilege. Fertility is perfectly regulated. There are no slipups.

Perhaps there was with me. I am not supposed to feel any different now. It is supposed to be a long, paid vacation spent asleep. During that time, a woman's body is just a rented incubator. That's all. The baby may not even have been made with an egg from my ovaries. The father could be any of the thousands of male crewmen with favorable genetics.

Somehow, I know. Despite the lack of physical evidence, I know it in my body, in the flesh.

I have a baby out there.

Behind the meds, there is a longing to hold something tightly. There is a yawning cavity inside my body, which was filled and stretched, and now is empty.

I wash my face carefully and put on the patient's gown. Pink for a female—comfortable and warm. I bite down on the resentment of how much easier this is for male crew members. For them, Breeding Duty is a bit of awkwardness that can be done away with during a lunch break.

When I walk out and take my seat, the woman in the deep-green coat and spectacles processes me. She asks me the same questions I filled out on the form. I answer the same way. I smile and nod where appropriate.

But there is no deceiving a professional. The eye on her forehead is three times the size of her biological eyes, and the silver coat on her lips is solid, gleaming chrome. The circlet she wears glows green and gold and is actively drawing on the Noah's power. She *reads* me with the combined insight of centuries, empirically derived heuristics analyzing my posture and the muscle twitches on my face, as well as the mind-bond forged by her psychic ability and amplified by the circlet. Empathic and telepathic probes slide through my head with the delicacy and grace of a dancer prancing around onstage.

"Ms. Dempsey, it seems as if Dr. Harrison was a touch too conservative with the suppressors, that's all."

"Which means?"

"What you're feeling is just a by-product: traces from a slight amount of telepathic contact with the fetus. It's not supposed to happen, but no Breeding is exactly the same. Some embryos are stronger than others. It's nothing physical. Dr. Harrison assures me that your hormones have been rebalanced and stabilized."

"I see."

"No need to feel so anxious, Ms. Dempsey." She licks her lips and her fingers tap away at the black slab of crystal in her hand.

This Behavioralist is more practical than Dr. Harrison was. He liked to show off and gesture and point in midair.

The psi-tablet she uses is an interface device for accessing the ship's systems. Though everything can be done directly through the Implant, it takes continuous concentration and focus to do so—any misthought comes through as an error, can cause a typo in a document or slide in incongruous data, a flash of imagery, a scent, a taste. The psi-tab and larger hard-line desk terminals are easier to use for long durations, and for certain applications they can be endowed with stronger security than the sometimes leaky interface of discrete data packets passing between wetware and hardware.

"There we are. I've modified your prescription. The system will ping you with reminders when to take it. The orderly will administer a dose just before you are released. More will be in your mailbox in the morning. Be sure to follow the instructions."

She flips the faux-leather cover on her tablet closed and stands.

"Is that it?"

"Yes, that's it. You'll be expected back at work tomorrow. You are discharged." She pauses, looks to one side as she accesses the Network. "Yes, the paperwork has gone through. The Noah and humanity thank you for your service. When you check your account, you will see that the standard amount has been deposited."

A week of evaluations, and the Behavioralist never even told me her name! Typical.

I take a deep breath just as those tall, black heels are about to pass the threshold of the doorway. "Could I, perhaps, just have an image of him, or her? Just a static two-D?"

She looks back at me and purses her lips. "You were briefed, Ms. Dempsey. You know that is not permitted. I'll adjust the dosage a tick upward. Now, let's not speak further of this."

The urge to weep is strong. I fight it down. "Have you gone through this too?" She has gray hair, so by that age . . .

Those steel eyes soften. "Of course, Ms. Dempsey. Only postbirth Behavioralists see to Breeding patients. Go home. Take your meds. Buy something nice for yourself with the compensation package. You'll feel right as rain."

I try to imagine that it will be so. But still, I want to hold my child, just once. I hope the drugs help me forget soon.

## 2

As promised, the orderly comes by. Still smiling. Flirting. He holds my wrist rather familiarly with one hand and administers my last intravenous dose with the other.

*Call me,* he messages. Not mind-to-mind, as he has no telepathic talent, but through the standard messaging app preloaded on everyone's Implant.

To home then, by way of a ride in a long, sleek, white car. One last service provided for Breeders. The driver does not try to make small talk. Does he do this every day? What else does he do for BD Central? I could find out. It would take a few seconds. But everything seems to take so much effort. Just paying attention. Numb. The cityscape slides by in the windows. He stops, and here I am, at Torus—a ring-shaped building with clean, upper-class apartments for officers. Gray carpets, sterile steely lights, tastefully selected prints of ancient Earth art.

I could have afforded better years ago, but never got around to it. Moving would be inconvenient and I am set in my routines. But maybe it's time for a change; maybe that's what I'll do with the Breeding compensation. Put in the down payment for a lifetime rental on an actual house, in the same exclusive neighborhood where my friends live.

Up the elevator to the twelfth floor and I am swaying now, stumbling to my door. I have not done anything today but think and wait and I am exhausted.

I think the password to the lock, and there they are, laughing and cheering. They have glasses, they are eating, they are so close around me, touching my shoulder, my arm . . . They are very, very loud.

"Heya, D! So, what was it like?"

"Oh, come on! She was just asleep. It's not—"

"Give her some goddamn room!" Barrens's voice booms as he shoves them aside without a care for their complaining. He looks down at me and smiles what passes for his smile. Half snarl, it is harsh and a little cruel. "Eh. Hey. I told 'em a party wasn't a good idea, but—"

For a moment, we just stand there, him looking down and me looking up, for perhaps a little too long, while music and conversation pound the space around us.

"Come on, join in!" the others insist.

There are balloons of different colors. There is a cake with ten candles on it, surrounded by platters of steaming food. It's a carrot cake layered with enough sugared cream to induce diabetic shock. There is fettuccine with a cream sauce. There is tofu, breaded and delicately fried, seasoned with miso and spring onions. There is fresh bread, and an assortment of expensive cheeses. Most pricey of all, there is animal protein—an actual fish, steamed and stuffed and glazed with a sugary, peppery crust. In all, it represents resources that would cost an average crewman an entire month's income.

That is not a problem for Lyn and Marcus, who probably pushed the idea of this party to its completion.

Lyn is a project leader in Nth Web Development and Maintenance, one of the research arms of Information Security. And Marcus is the director of Water Management. It would not have taken much for them to convince Jazz, who loves any opportunity to party. She does research in High Energy Physics, but is not like the stiffs in her department.

Technically, as a City Planning Administrator, I am higher ranked and in a more direct line of command to one of the Ministers of the Council, but the internal hierarchies of the departments under the individual Ministries are not straightforward, and the three of them are all paid somewhat more than I am, though even I earn many times what the average crewman on the ship makes.

We met back in school, long before we qualified together for the Class V Training Center, the second-most-prestigious career-preparation track there is.

They are dressed in actual organic silk and cotton, wear shoes of leather, and have jewelry with real gold.

The rest of the less luxuriantly attired attendees are from our respective departments. Mostly young, ambitious kids a year out of their training groups, waiting for the opportunity to get ahead, get promoted, and replace us, and a few older officers who hit their ceiling and will never reach any higher.

My old schoolmates direct the evening's course and keep the social contract going. We chat about things that don't matter. They tell me about all the events

I missed out on while I was on Breeding Duty, and I cannot help thinking that for all the things they talk about, nothing has changed between before and the present. Nothing, but myself.

Then there is Barrens. Barrens does not fit in with the rest of us. He is at least half a foot taller than anyone else in the room, and broader too. His clothes are cheap plastech processed to look like a plain, white, stretch T-shirt, and denim pants, and functional black shoes. His complexion is pale and watery—too many night shifts, not enough simulated sun.

He is quiet after that first loud moment. The looks he gets from my other friends and our coworkers are curious, amused. Lots of arched brows.

Some murmuring.

"The guy with the medals?"

"Heard he got written up or something."

If I can hear it, Barrens, whose senses are sharp even when he isn't enhancing them with the Power, can hear it.

He doesn't offend easily. He just shakes his head and walks out to the balcony, a giant trying not to step on the normal-size people in his way. Out there, he starts puffing on his cigarettes, watching me through the glass.

I want to throw them all out. I do not.

They fill the air with conversation, about Web streams I've missed out on, old Earth movies being shown in the theaters, and minor improvements in the fidelity of the sky and weather simulation. They make me feel a little less empty. Everyone does his or her part, a show of caring. Of course the young ones from our respective departments are here more for the food, and for a chance to hang out with the superiors they depend upon for their quarterly performance evaluations and recommendations.

By midnight, the party has wound down and only the terrible three are left, with Barrens content to be an outsider, still puffing away on the balcony. The discussion becomes only marginally more personal. We talk about our school days, about bad dates and old drama and parties and sadistic teachers. The three take turns mentioning men they want to introduce me to.

"Come on, Hana," Lyn says. "You haven't dated anyone in years and years."

"I just like to focus on work."

"Yeah, that's exactly the problem. You need a man, dearie, to scratch that special itch. Isn't that right, Marcus?"

He laughs, puts up his open hands. "Leave me out of this one."

"Sure, just what services one can provide," Jazz says, leering; it looks wrong on her pixie face. Or maybe too right. "Come now. I've heard that most post-Duty women feel certain *urges* more than normal."

Do they? The entire evening, I have needed to fake my emotions. Since the higher dose kicked in, my head feels packed with sludgy treacle. I have to think about how I would normally feel in response to something instead of just feeling it. Desire is the furthest thing from my thoughts, and I suppose enough indifference or distaste shows on my face that they let it go, when they'd normally needle me about my lack of sex life for a bit longer.

Lyn smiles and pulls a bottle out of a bag. She waves her fingers and faint blue light outlines the cork as it pops free. She pours a glass for each of us.

The wine is a deep red. I've never liked wine.

Jazz takes a sip, points to the balcony with her little finger. Her ring has a bit of crystal on it that catches the light. "D, why's the goon even here?"

I never explained Barrens to the rest of my friends. We did not go to school together. We were not in any of the same child-rearing groups. We did not grow up in the same neighborhood.

"Please don't talk about him like that. Leon is more capable than you might think. He's a good guy."

"Oh, come on. How did you meet anyway?"

I just shake my head.

Marcus breaks open a deck of cards, and we make it through a few rounds of bridge. I imagine old people must spend nights like this, after they are Retired.

At last, they leave. Tomorrow is a workday, after all. And only Barrens is left.

He opens the glass door for me, and I join him out there.

"Did you eat anything at all?"

"Psh. Too rich for me anyway. Would just upset my stomach."

We stand side by side, elbows resting on the rail, and look up at the fake sky, with its fake moon and fake stars. Beyond the skyline of the tall crystal towers of Edo Section is a horizon. It is how the night might look back on Earth if it were not just a blasted wasteland, with a toxic atmosphere too thick for light to penetrate, and no one and nothing left alive to see it. Almost always a gentle breeze goes through the city, generated by carefully designed ventilation ducts behind the simulated sky, interacting with thermal radiation from the warmer street level. There are seasons too in the Habitat, also patterned after Earth.

The Noah has days and nights because humans evolved with all these things, with a sun, with a moon and stars, with weather and seasons, and biologically, we do not do so well without all these environmental signals related to the passage of time.

"How are you, Leon? I was surprised to see you."

"Enh, does a guy good to rub shoulders with his betters once in a while."

"How did you even find out about the party?" They would not have asked him to help or thought to invite him.

He shrugs. "I knew you would be released today. And even if they don't know me, I know your pals—you talk about them enough. Of course they were going to throw you a party."

"They are my friends, you know."

"Yes. I do."

For a moment, I touch his elbow. He always runs hot. "You're my friend too."

He takes a breath, "I don't really have friends. There's you, and a couple of guys from the force."

In that dim light, the shadows across Barrens's face deepened those craggy angles, make his expressions harsher. His jaw and temples are coated in chrome. A *bruiser,* Barrens is not just physically strong—his psionics lend themselves toward modifying his metabolism and biochemistry, as well as surrounding his body with raw psychokinetic energy. He can make himself faster and stronger, and he is utterly unstoppable.

I'd seen it before, when he tried to help me.

"How are you, Leon?"

It is on his mind too, which is why he is not meeting my eyes when his voice rumbles, "My transfer to Long Term Investigations finally came through. Funny. Years after I helped you out that one time, you know, with that thing, and they finally got around to it."

I close my eyes. Cold cases.

They don't get solved until the perpetrators die and their crimes are revealed when the dead implants are scanned. Police officers in that department do secretarial work and that's all. They file information and hide unsolved crimes from the system until they can be declared "solved" so that the utopian illusion is preserved. Hundred percent crime resolution is what everyone is led to believe is true, and it is, if only superficially.

For some, it would be a cushy job. An LTI Inspector does not have to go around on patrols, does not have to deal with even the minor risks of violent confrontations. But Barrens actually cares for people. It is part of his problem. He truly wants to help. It is a punitive assignment, for him.

That aspect of his nature is the reason we met.

My saying "I'm sorry" is not much comfort.

I am surprised by his grim smile. On him, that is an expression of pleasure.

"Don't be. Supposed to be a dead-end job, ya know. But there are opportunities, in LTI. If the likes of me could get some help."

I am tired. I just want to sleep. I want to dream fool's dreams about what my baby might be like. To wonder if, somehow, I might see him someday, just walking around, and know it is him. Is it a boy? It could be a girl. Instinct though, just a little of the tenuous link the Behavioralist talked about, nudges thoughts of a boy to me.

Or it's pure fantasy.

Barrens sees something of my mood. One great big mitt enfolds one of my hands, lets go too soon. "Look, I know you're having a tough time. I see people went through Breeding Duty. Some of them were never the same, after. Don't care what the propaganda folks say, I know it's rough. I do need your help, Dempsey, and I figure, you know—could give you something else to think about, something to put the emptiness out of your mind."

"For what, specifically?"

"Your magic on the Web. I've gotten good with what you've taught, but I need more."

Of course he would if he was tangling with the encryption and security of the LTI databases, which were definitely not for public access. Most of the crew of the Noah are not permitted to know that there is such a department. Navigating its security is another level from the simple neuralhacks I showed him for scripting special probes into the police database or digging through school records or property ownership.

"I . . ."

"I'm a fast learner. Said so yourself. You only have to show me once."

It's not as if he's calling in a favor. He's too much a gentleman, in his way, to expect me to pay him back. But there is this, between us: the darkest night of my life. I close my eyes. The memory slices through the meds, and for a moment I feel it all over again, raw and real.

I am twenty-eight years old. My back is bruised and scraped against the rough pavement of the alleyway. I ache, I'm torn between my legs. I am this close to vomiting.

A man I thought was my friend is pushing himself upright, away from me. The awful intrusion slides free and his . . . It trickles down. In my imagination, it burns like acid.

Senior Engineer Holmheim is gloating, he laughs at the hulking policeman pinned against the wall by his *touch*.

Holmheim raises his hand. It is covered with an engineer's work glove. He is not supposed to carry it off duty. It is a powerful telekinetic amplifier—with it, I could carve a building out of a tank of plastech myself, or crush it. I am rated at twice Holmheim's strength, and perhaps that is why he has chosen me for this. I am the department's fast-rising star, the youngest at my rank.

And I am a rule-follower. I did not have my professional amp with me. What I could do with the civilian-grade amp I did have on me was nothing to him; he burned it out the second I tried to resist.

So I cover myself with the torn bits of my dress and scream until my throat is raw and watch as Holmheim draws more energy from the grid. Blue streaks stream from his face emitters to the gauntlet, and the gauntlet is like a sun at the end of his arm. Telekinetic leakage kicks up the dirt around us, sends black flecks whirling up, sends papers and garbage from the garbage bin in the corner flying.

The massive cop grunts with the increased pressure. Holmheim is mind-pushing him into the wall with such force that the brick and mortar surface starts to crack, to cave in. It seems impossible that the huge man's ribs haven't shattered already.

"Shouldn't have messed with me! I'm mission-critical, you dumb Boy Scout! I can get away with anything!"

The fragments of the cop's shattered club rise into the air, shimmering with cobalt light. They fuse into a spear. It sticks the cop through the belly, punches through him into the wall with a steely crunch.

Holmheim is so pleased by this, he is getting hard again.

"Yeah, 'm dumb," the cop gasps out. The syllables slosh together in his bloody mouth. "But y'know . . . if miss'n-cr't'cal staff 'tack someun, ev'n 'f they n't punished f'that . . . well . . . fella can attack back."

"Oh, please. What can a nothing like you do? You're just a brawler with a badge!"

The cop snarls. It is a terrifying sound. His ribs are broken, and blood is gurgling up his throat. The badge on his breast starts to glow a bright, bright red. His already huge arms and legs seem to swell.

"Please! You gonna fight me, Boy Scout? You're practically a cripple already!"

Holmheim always likes to boast before the job is done.

One moment the cop is there, and then he is gone, just the bloody shaft left against the crater in the wall. There is a sound like thunder. Holmheim's face distorts, becomes a battered mess, his metal twisted and torn as he falls backward, away from the cop's extended fist.

The cop spits blood and snot and saliva, wipes his mouth. His speech clears up some, without psychokinetic force crushing in his chest.

"Idiot. Cops train for combat, not showing off. We get training no technical officer gets."

He bends over me. Before I have time to be scared of his size, he puts his blue uniform coat around me. It is warm and smells of cloves and cigarettes.

"I'm sorry." His voice is so deep, I can feel the vibrations in my chest as he tries, with endearing awkwardness, to calm me down. I am still shaking. He says, "Idiot's right. Not much punishment or anything while he's mission-critical. But that status isn't forever, and others are allowed to defend themselves, if they can."

"Y-you . . . You're bleeding, really bad," I get out.

Gently, he gets me to my feet. The heel on one of my shoes is torn off, and somehow that makes me feel even worse.

He holds a hand to his side. "'Snuthin'. Look, I called in the medics already. You wanna kick him? You know, before they get here?"

"What?"

"You wanna kick him? A few times maybe? You'll feel better, I promise."

Somehow, he makes me laugh. I do kick Holmheim. Just twice. But he'll ache down there much longer than I will. I sank my stupid, pointy shoe in deep.

My hand disappears in the cop's hand when we shake. He is that much larger, and I am not a small girl.

This is how our odd little friendship begins.


On the balcony, I move eyes from the simulated horizon and I'm looking up at Barrens. He is looking down at me.

He has moments when his features twist, make him seem like a small boy. I cannot say no to him.

I can still smell the odors of his gut wound, the blood leaking down his belly, and the garbage around us in the alleyway. He was hospitalized for weeks because of persistent infections.

So I sigh, and nod. I wonder how bad what he's asking will be, but maybe he's right. Maybe I need this. I don't know if I can just go back to the way things were.

Ah, I've forgotten how being around him makes me feel—standing this close, even tranquilized by the pills, something inside squeezes, just a little.

"Next Sunday, if you can sneak me into your office, let's see what we'll see."

Barrens smiles and passes me his cig. "Thank you, Hana." He so rarely says my name that way.

I take just one drag and choke a little before passing it back. I use my psi and play with the smoke I exhale. It gathers in the air in the shape of a bulldog, like from the documentaries of Earth, and it barks and runs circles around us, ghost-like.

"Nice," he murmurs.

He embraces me. Deep inside, past the fog, there is giddiness, desire, a wish that I could prod him into doing more. He's never done that before.

He does not say good-bye when he leaves.

Other than that hug, this is how it's always been with us. I might not see him for months, not a call or message, and then on a good day or an ordinary day or a particularly bad day when I'm remembering what I want to forget, he'll just be there. Distracting me with a request for some lessons on database queries, on programming, on analysis, or with a talk about freedom and responsibility, his rough voice quietly dropping a few hints, here and there, of the evils he sees.

And once in a while, I'll send him a message over the Nth Web, and we have coffee at a cheap café where nobody knows us, and I'll tell him about my day while he quietly vibrates in place, tense and anxious at first, slowly relaxing. He does not talk much about the simmering red inside of him, and I don't talk about my blues; we just sit together, sometimes listening quietly to the amateur jazz performers on the stage, and sometimes, our fingers touch, and we don't say "Bye."

I want to ask for more, and sometimes I'm even sure he does too.

**3**

ANOTHER EFFECT OF THE NEURAL IMPLANT IS THAT ONE NEVER OVERSLEEPS, unless one is seriously ill, or intoxicated. It is difficult to ignore an alarm clock inside your own skull: the internal timekeeper built into the Implant.

Despite not falling asleep until four in the morning, I wake up bright and early, with the spring dawn, from the Implant's firing off thoughts of *Wake up wake up wake up* that cut through sleep and dreams.

It's autopilot. Showering. Choosing the day's clothes out of the dustless, hermetically sealed closets. Picking out matching shoes. I take my medication. I go to work.

It still takes twenty-two minutes to get there. The same walk, the same bus ride. The team is the same too, except for the addition of a new trainee, Wong, who greets me a little too stiffly and politely. Ah, to get such respect from all my subordinates. How long will that fresh-faced awe last?

The big project I organized just before I received my summons for Breeding Duty—a new resource-tracking and analytics module—was completed in my absence. Going through the reports, it is clear that my assistant, Hennessy, has done a decent job while I was gone. The number of error reports has steadily dropped off, and at this point, 93.25 percent of user help requests can be handled by the system's agent programs, without need for human intervention.

He does not even seem to mind having a younger woman as his boss. That's rare. Also, not once has he attempted to glance down my blouse during meetings. I must remember to buy him a gift.

The first day of the rest of my life, the goal is to reassimilate into the living world. I tell myself that what happened to me is fading. I practice pretending everything is okay. I succeed in not thinking about that first waking moment, clutching my belly, knowing something is missing. Most of the time.

This is just another transition in life. Just another test. Everyone's life on the Noah is full of tests. My childhood had more of them than the average because, the better you perform, the more you can do, the more they push you to maximize what you might become.

This is not nearly so terrible as the third Track Determination Exams when I was fifteen. Wasn't it worse back then? Before the day I met Barrens, wasn't that the worst day of my life?


Fifteen minutes pas—seven! How did I manage to do that! I overslept, I—

Stayed up until five, studying. Did I misthink setting the alarm for the first time in three years? Shit, not even time to shower . . .

In a pajama top with winged hearts and striped jogging pants, running for the train. Eyes on me. Yeah, don't look at me, I'm busy, I'm a mess, I—

"Sorry! So sorry." I almost knock over this older guy in a suit. I almost trip, rushing down the escalator to the S-line platform.

Oh shit, oh shit, it's leaving, it's . . . left.

I have to take the bus. It is another fifteen minutes to run up to the stop.

The bus is crowded. It's shift transit hour, when the night workers leave and the day staff start. Sweat pouring down my face, from the run, from the growing anxiety as the bus seems to have to *stop at every fricking light.*

Finally here, the grim black octagon of the testing facility. And I'm late. I am so, so late.

They do let me in to take the TDE. But half of the time for the Data Structures exam went by before I even sat at the damn terminal.

I go through all the tricks to calm myself.

Eyes burning. I think the proctors are looking at me, why wouldn't they? Stupid tears.

The terminal locks to my Implant, shuts off access to the Nth Web, isolates me from every other student taking the test, and it begins. Every correct answer gets a harder question after, and every wrong one gets an easier follow-up, and there's no backtracking. Getting a max score in every exam is nearly impossible, but I've heard it's how kids get selected for Command Officer School, something I can't admit I've wanted for years, and why why why is it so hard to think?

The first questions should be trivial, they're about B-tree implementation. . . .
I've done practice tests for this a hundred times, and I can *feel* Lyn and Jazz and
Marcus staring at my back, feel them being worried for me.

They're only the exams that determine the path of the rest of our lives.

All the fiddly little differences between the different kinds of lists. Messing
with hash tables. Linking. Operations. Procedures. Abstract data types.

All right, I bombed the first test. Get a grip, Dempsey. Stop crying! There's
twenty-four hours more of exams ahead.

I didn't make COS. None of my friends did either. But I was wretched for a
good long while. I did not cry other than those first moments during Data
Structures, but it felt as if I should have. The terrible three took me out and got
me properly drunk in between bowls of ice cream. My first hangover was
that morning after, in Lyn's apartment, with the rest of them passed out
around the couch and the air smelling very much as if something excessive
happened the night before. It was not so bad really. The path of my life had
been set. The three of us ended up going to the same training facility, and
even if it was not on the path to a seat on the Noah's Bridge or a high rank in
one of the Ministries, it is still Type V training, the educational tier just under
that of the top officers on the ship.

Why do I care so much about a child I never saw, never touched? Women
are not supposed to get depressed over this. There was no time for a personal
connection. I was just an incubator. I wasn't even awake for the months my
womb was occupied.

It is not like the aberration that what had happened with Holmheim. That
secret trauma that's got nothing to do with normal life. Or maybe I can say
that now because Holmheim wasn't nearly so valuable as his pride led him to
believe and was discreetly *Adjusted,* those troublesome urges excised from his
brain, his creative centers subtly locked down by incidental damage, his future
prospects limited. Most of his coworkers probably did not notice the change in
him.

Just as mine never noticed the change in me, and I did change for all that I
was not Adjusted.

The ordinary drama of life on the Noah—messing up a test, Breeding Duty,
recovering from all that—is something every woman is supposed to handle.

I'm supposed to be stronger than this. Nobody but Barrens seems to understand that I'm having a tough time.

This is this, and that was that.

They glitter darkly, in the back of my thoughts, locked away. Subversive, dangerous desires, to hack my way through the system, find out what my baby looks like.

I consider voluntarily setting up a follow-up with that Behavioralist from the post-Duty evaluation. There is not supposed to be any stigma from psych counseling, but everyone knows those sessions go into one's career records, and an officer's emotional-stability score is a significant factor in being evaluated for future promotions.

After work, I watch streams on the Web. I watch the commercials. They let you taste, for just an instant, the sensation of having that product.

A few of them are for clothes or food or drinks or shoes. But most of the ads are selling memories themselves.

A memory can be shared with others for the sake of entertainment, or for educational purposes, or as testimony in the courts. They are bought and sold and spread on the Nth Web the way movies and music used to be when the net-working of computation was new. If a crewman cannot afford to pay for the awesome experience of a real steak, he can at least buy the memory of someone who can.

These days, the most desired of actors and actresses are not the most beautiful, or the most skilled. It is about authenticity. Success is about the emotional breadth of experience to move the minds of those who experience the scenarios one has acted through.

There is an ad for a memory from a rich Behavioralist with a cat.

I pay the fee and subscribe.

For two minutes, I live inside her head.

Minnow's fur is so soft. So soft. When I run the brush along his back, he arches against it and purrs. He is warm in my hands. He trusts me. I feel needed and loved, and content, kneeling on the plush velvety carpet, while I slide stroke after stroke of the stiff bristles against him.

He is worth every credit it takes to pay for his keep. He is beautiful. His coat shines, glossy black dusted with ash gray. The white patches on his feet make them look larger, softer. Being with him is the only bright moment in each day.

The warm euphoria slips a moment, to grays and gloom, but his tail thumps against the carpet demandingly, and as I resume my attentions, the world is a little less dark, and I immerse myself in pleasure.

I buy a dozen scenes from that vendor.

Behavioralists make the best memories. They have this different way of looking at the world. Their *reading* talents are so attuned that they work *not* to use them except when needed. This tight rein on one's thoughts changes the sensorium of experience. They dive into their own sense feedback and live from moment to moment, minds empty, to stop themselves from being tainted by the stray thoughts of others around them. This woman's memories of her cat are, except for the emotional content, more potent than any of my own true ones.

I think about whether it would be worth it to blow the entire twenty thousand cred from the Duty compensation on a cat.

Time doesn't stop for anyone.

Before I know it, it is Friday and it is as if I were never gone from the office.

Behind the tall tombstone walls at City Planning, the hours pass slowly, as if the mass of them drags at the fabric of space-time. Or maybe all workplaces are like this.

My head aches from the tedium of another report about water-reclamation efficiency. My team has been arguing with our superiors all morning about whether a newly developed purification protocol can justify the resources it will take to change the old one. The discussion is loaded with jargon and numbers and the occasional dramatic exaggeration.

Hennessy flails about as he exclaims, "Come on! Look at this graph!" The poor dear's voice gets shrill when he's excited. It makes him seem less competent than he actually is. "I mean, just look at it! If we do this, it's projected that we can support a thousand more people than we would be able to without it in a hundred years! That's a big difference, isn't it? It's huge! That's a, that's a—"

"That's an inflated figure that does not take into account all the added resource needs," Hester drones in response. She adds more data to the model, and the analysis shows that the net benefit is perhaps just a dozen humans more. "Is that worth risking the existing homeostasis figures?"

*Homeostasis.* That word enters these arguments all the time. Hester is good at her job. The old battle-ax is extremely risk averse, which is the way she should be.

"But it's these incremental improvements that—"

"All right, all right. It's time for a break. Let's reconvene in an hour. Getting testy in here. We are all on the same side."

I close my eyes and press my temples with my fingers, sliding them in slow circles.

"You all right, Dempsey?"

"I'm fine," I lie. I'm not reacting well to the medication. There is no nausea, no headache, no palpitations, but I feel dull, drained, as asleep as I am awake. "I'll just be at the rooftop garden, okay?"

I climb in a daze.

The breeze is better on the roof than at street level.

The bench is solid granite. It is reassuringly rough, and its structure is chaotic and imperfect and hand carved and lovely. The fountain in front of me sprays a fine, cool mist. The simulated sun warms my face. The wing-beats of a bee hovering in front of a flower steal me away, but not for long enough. Up in the garden's air, I force myself to recall my passion for what I do, to reach through the haze of imposed chemical calm.

I need to refocus. Remind myself that what I'm doing means something. That I'm not just a tiny cog in a machine.

Well, I am a tiny cog. But it is important just the same, being a little gear of the right mass with teeth of just the right size and shape.

Humanity does happen to be on the brink of extinction. How can any responsible human being be a slacker under these circumstances?

I entertain myself with an old game I programmed into my head when I was twenty, a newly minted underling of City Planning.

It starts with just me. Just all the little things I do, talking, filing reports, crunching numbers. It pulls back and diagrams, circuitlike, the web of interactions between us all, the relationships of food, water, and air, supply and demand, crops and livestock, sustainability and consumption.

Then it pulls back to the beginning, with the Noah leaving newly destroyed Earth, carrying the best and brightest of those who remain. We do not know what destroyed Earth. Information Security tells us it does not matter anyway.

Pull on one person here, push there. Maybe that individual makes life a bit better or a bit worse. Arrows going between each person-node change, bright colors representing positive interactions, dark ones symbolizing the negative.

It is playing an instrument, watching the web of lights play out while trying to improve scores of efficiency and productivity and limiting social unrest and misery. Each touch consumes energy, so one can only influence so many at a time. As the game plays out, new features unlock, productivity-improving entertainments for the masses, sports centers, parks, nature biomes, research projects for fanciful inventions from my childhood.

Sometimes there are accidents, disasters and crises, fires, meteorite strikes on the hull. Entropy steadily eats away all resources. Sections of the ship are closed and used as spare parts to keep the rest going.

The lives of the crew are the most precious resource of course—even as the population contracts, the player has to try to maintain genetic diversity, just as the Breeding Department does on the ship. Too little diversity and random routines create diseases or obstacles that the population is not adaptable enough to handle.

If one does well, the ship, the Noah, makes it to the new world, and trumpets blare and fireworks light up a new sky. If one does poorly, too few survivors make it to Canaan to propagate the species, or the ship does not make it at all.

I play the game for a few minutes. It is absorbing and simple and easy. My real job is much the same, but with the complications of working with people who just refuse to see eye-to-eye, and with all those bad moods and irrational jealousies and turf wars. And criminals too.

The people part of the equation is what makes real life so much harder than my simulation.

The journey from Earth to here has taken 346 years, still less than a third of the way.

All that is left of the human species is hurtling through space at relativistic velocity, living for the journey, in the hope that our descendants will make it.

I give up on the game. Even facing away from the playground, I cannot stop listening to a little girl yelling at a little boy for getting dirt on her new shoes. Their tinny voices raise beads of sweat on the back of my neck. They crack my cool, medicated detachment.

Those kids must be here on a field trip. Keepers are granted access to show children the different job tracks they might enter when they are older. Keepers are professionals—theirs is a full-time position, raising the young, preparing them for the rest of their lives. I don't want to, but I watch them. They look happy together, the boy and the girl. A man leans against the rooftop rail, smiling quietly to himself as he ticks off items on his psi-tablet, probably a Keeper's regular behavioral report, while his partner hums softly, unpacking a picnic basket.

They look perfect together.

I have a duty, and it is not to an abstract ideal, but to them, and everyone that comes after.

So I work, there, on the bench. I lock out my senses, connect my Implant wirelessly into the office access point, and blaze through summaries and abstracts of reports, journal articles, anything that might help with the proposal. Hopeless. Nothing relevant, or it's too far off to be feasible. It is no great disaster if we do not succeed in pushing the project through today, but it is not progress either, and the waste of the resources we have put in, the hours of labor and analysis, the simulations and meetings, well. Waste is a terrible thing in the confines of a closed system.

Then I remember Jazz mentioning something, back at the party. One of the guys she wanted to introduce me to, also working at the High Energy Labs. Savelyev. Brilliant, she said. And not too proud to work on marginal improvements in efficiency instead of grand, hopelessly abstract theory.

I put a call in through the system and almost hope he doesn't answer.

*Jacob Savelyev here.*

Translated into data and back over the system, his thoughts taste small and neat, fastidious, exacting.

I try my warmest. *Hello, Dr. Savelyev. This is Hana Dempsey? We have a mutual friend named Jazz. She was telling me about something you've been working on that I think could help us out here in City Planning.* I stick a little image of me at the end of the transmitted thought, smiling.

The fellow is acerbic and impatient and it takes an embarrassing fifteen minutes to get him to understand that, apart from any ideas he may have that I'm flirting with him during office hours, we actually have a mutual professional interest that can help us both.

When he gets it, Jazz turns out to be right. He is brilliant. With the personal put aside for the moment, it takes a mere five minutes of harmonious data interchange for us to both get something we want.

Though I do have to remind him I'm not a physicist when he starts sending complex 3-D images of the effects of his proposed injection protocols on the psionic field in the reactor vessels, accompanied by a truly dizzying matrix of equations and quantum control-theory analysis that I can understand just enough to know I don't really understand it at all. It's all brilliant flashes of light to me, with the shape of the blazing toroid of energy twisting just a little differently from before, minute changes in the topological space.

It's the conclusion from his paper that I need, and the statistics comparing his results to the current standard operating procedures.

*Ah, of course, of course, Administrator Dempsey. May I call you Hana? Here are the five graphs you will want to show, and then throw a page of my equations at them anyway for shock value.*

I can see his self-image leaking through in the messages. A shy, small smile, on a person who is a little too brilliant and has difficulty relating to others.

*Thank you, Dr. Savelyev. You've saved my team from wasting quite a lot of work. Yes, you can call me Hana.*

*Well, Hana. Ah. I'm sure any nudge from the Ministry of the Interior will help me on my side in Energy.*

We finish our discussion just in time. I tweak the data even as I sink back into my senses and rise from the bench. And I do not have to promise to have a date with him or anything else. He concludes with his thanks and farewells, and already I can feel him pulling back into the cold shell of his expertise and mind.

It would not have been a terrible thing to go out with him. And it might have gotten my friends to ease up on my dating situation. He seems nice, even. So much like the archetype that everyone thinks I should be going out with.

If I didn't already want someone else.

My footsteps are loud against the stairs. The rail along the spiraling steps is embossed with orchids. In the meeting room Hennessy feels my positivity, relaxes into his chair beside mine.

*You have something. You got something done over lunch.*

*Yes.*

*That's why you're the boss.*

"You want to address the Board, Administrator Dempsey?"

"My team is confident in our figures. But we understand the Board's position. I suggest a compromise. HEL also has a proposal in the pipe. Separately, the improvements seem negligible when considering the risk-benefit ratio, but packaged together with ours, the graph changes." A wave of my fingers, and the displays hovering in our brains are updated with new numbers, the line lifting ever so slightly. "A contact at High Energy assures me that they can deploy in three months. By then, my group can add 0.012 percent efficiency to our proposed protocol."

The murmurs of approval would have had me giddy and bouncing in my seat, once. At least for a while I can smile without its feeling entirely faked.

But I am not thinking of Savelyev, or Jazz, or this little victory over bureaucratic inertia. I am already thinking of the coming weekend with Barrens. The days in between could not end fast enough.

# 4

Sunday morning, before dawn, I am awake, yawning. I swallow the last of the watermelon-seed-size, cherry-red pills with relief. Tomorrow, the world will be a touch brighter, perhaps. I will be closer to normal, closer to my old self. Since going on the meds, my dreams have been mechanical and dry, just repetitions of fragments of the days, sitting in front of a terminal and tapping away, coding simulation parameters. Sometimes, boring pieces from puberty, sitting in class and absorbing a lecture. Nothing like the vibrant, strange lives that I am used to living in my sleep. Where are my lunar oceans, my winged unicorns?

By tonight, the last of the drugs will have dissipated, and maybe when my dreams crack the fog of the mundane again, I can kick my growing addiction to purchased memories. Too much Minnow the cat.

Barrens's timing has always been good. He messages me that he's at my door just as I finish dressing.

The pads of my fingers slide along the slick, heavy material of the police coat spread out on my bed. It is night blue, a deep shade, depths-of-the-ocean blue. The buttons are gold-plated. Silver tassels are braided together and highlight the right lapel, and on the left breast pocket, a thick, triangular shield of office is emblazoned with a trio of stars and the crest of Earth's moon. It is a combat amplifier, and when I touch it, it hums as it harmonizes with my brain waves.

The nameplate engraved above the badge indicates its owner, Miyaki Miura.

"You didn't steal this from your coworker, did you?" I call out to the kitchen. The penalty for losing a mainline amplifier is steep.

"Naw, naw. She owes me a favor. Anyway, she's on leave for a week. Taking a vacation, you know, going camping in the biome reserve on the top floor of the vertical farm. Damn fine coffee you've got, Dempsey."

I thrust an arm into the double-breasted greatcoat and pull it on. The sleeves are a little short, but the shoulders feel cavernously loose. Miyaki is shorter than me, but broader in the shoulders, probably a *bruiser* like Barrens. I hope he isn't lying about her willingly loaning me her uniform and shield. It is easy to picture a diminutive, sprightly goddess with rose lightning around her fist taking a swing at me.

In the mirror, I am a child again, playing at cops and robbers. I cannot remember when I first realized that the cops could also be the robbers, and that some of the bad guys were beyond the reach of justice, so it must have been before I got the Implant. How did I learn that particular life lesson? It is not something my Keeper, Mala, would have taught me by choice.

I take a deep breath and step out of my bedroom. "How do I look?"

"Ha! You're a cutie. City Planning ought to have uniforms."

The lug can make me smile.

He slurps the last dregs of coffee and his face is a bit slack, the muscles loose as he savors the little bit of bliss he's allowing himself. Barrens never lets himself taste my "elite's food" as he calls it, but he can't resist my coffee.

I check over the signal routines between the amplifier and my Implant. I can see Barrens's heavy-handed but effective hacks. He's gotten a lot better. It is certainly more than adequate to fool the security checkpoints beyond the public areas of a police precinct.

"Now." He claps those meaty paws together. "Ready to do some good?"

His forehead is knotted up, and the skin around his eyes tightens. He looks ready for battle, a gladiator out of his time, and my smile becomes a grin. More Inspectors should be like Barrens. Sincere, fiery, true.

"Okay!" My hands come up in a bad caricature of a boxer's ready stance, and I jab at Barrens's shoulder. "Let's do it!"

Our bootheels click against the checkered tiles. Then we walk down flight after flight of steps, designed to mimic the look and feel of bare concrete. I suppose the police-precinct interior decorators feel that it is supposed to look functional and minimalistic and professional, or perhaps they've watched too many Earth movies. Motes of dust catch the sterile, white light from the illuminated strips along the center of the ceiling, murky, translucent rays through the darkness.

"It's ugly and poorly ventilated. Got personality down here though, doesn't it?"

We enter through an unlabeled doorway. It could just as well be the entrance to a broom closet.

Instead, the room is dim and airless, and far, far larger than I expected, even with the privileged information I have from City Planning. The single hall is nearly large enough to fit the rest of the entire building. Row after row of shelves dominate the space, laden with bar-coded boxes. Barrens walks me to his desk and system terminal in the corner. The finish of umber, ocher, sepia, and sienna streaks, meant to look something like wood, has peeled off in long, dirty flakes. It clashes with the perfectly smooth, achromatic slab in the center.

He offers me an ancient chair. The vinyl creaks when I sink into the cushions. I stretch out my arms and pop my knuckles and wake up the hard-line terminal. Function keys light up in rows over the interface surface, which feeds the displays directly to my implants, superimposing the command prompt and some general-purpose frames over my eyesight.

"Okay, Leon. What exactly do you need? You wouldn't tell me anything beforehand, so I just brushed up on some general skills."

He paces back and forth. His ruddy lips part several times, but he does not speak, and he paces some more. I let him work through his thoughts. The chair squeaks as I swivel it back and forth, watching him.

Finally, he clears his throat. "I just don't got enough to list down the specifics I gotta learn how to do. I'm sorry, I should have asked before taking you down here—"

Easy, big guy. "You know I don't mind. Take your time."

"Look. Look, I do have something specific I want to do. But it's best to show you, first. If you want to see it."

"See what?"

"A memory." He looks over his shoulder at the door, as if he expects someone to knock on it and barge in. Licks his lips. "Mine."

"Well, let's have it."

He holds up a hand. "It's, ah, pretty rough. And I don't know what it means. It could get you Adjusted, if we get caught."

A deep breath. "What's in it?"

"It's . . . It's a mystery. About my mentor in the force. A violent end that's been hidden away, hidden even from a Long Term Investigations cold file."

"Hidden?"

"Ah, you know how it works, Dempsey. Detectives don't do any detecting anymore. We just rely on the perfect memories from witness Implants. The most we do is some poking around through documents, forensic accounting, that kinda junk. A real mystery? It just comes here to LTI to sleep until the perp dies and his memories go in the database. Cal's death, it's not even in LTI. He was just listed as a Retirement."

Something hidden beyond a department that is already about hiding away unpleasant things from the system? It either falls under the purview of Information Security, which has the real authority beneath the Ship's Central Council, or it's been hidden by an elite neuralhack of the highest skill.

I place both hands on the desk terminal. "Is this an ISec matter, Leon?"

He clears his throat. "ISec is at least involved in hiding it."

ISec. It does so many things. It handles the testing of all children. After all, those tests determine the kind of crewman a child can be. A janitor. An engineer. An artist. An officer. Testing determines who you are, which determines what you can know. ISec chooses school curricula, chooses what history is, controls the culture of society. What books and movies and plays and music are permissible, and what are on the Proscribed List—just knowing that such a list exists is only permitted for those of my rank and above.

ISec also, of course, handles the security of the Nth Web. What news is fit to be known by the public, and what concentric circles going inward of fewer and fewer individuals are allowed to know of certain truths that must be kept secret. ISec's visible and invisible influence lies everywhere throughout every crewman's life.

The Central Council, the leadership of the Noah, is composed of the Ministers of Information, Health, Energy, the Interior, and Peace, and a single Ship's Captain who is selected from one of the five, along with the support staff beneath them: an Executive Officer and the handful of secretive navigators and pilots that actually fly the ship. Ostensibly, the five Ministers are equals, but for all that Information is the smallest Ministry in terms of staff, it commands the most resources and is allocated the smartest and most capable of each generation's children.

And from the first captain to the present, they have all been ISec. More than this, each has been the Commander of the Enforcers.

The Ministry of Information controls the Enforcers, the ship's most power-ful combat officers. I think of those most elite of the elites, ISec's best field op-eratives, black-clad soldier-scientists who had to have scored at the top tenth of a percentile throughout childhood and training, and shiver.

"Are we going to have Enforcers after us, Leon?"

"Can't say for sure that we won't."

We stare at each other for just a second. We could have our brains wiped, get ourselves Adjusted until we're just living automata carrying out Behavioralist-implanted routines and programming for the rest of our lives, deeper and worse than what was done to Holmheim.

"I'll look." Maybe I should not. I have achieved the vaunted status of mission-critical, but Barrens just looks so serious. I have no illusions about my place in City Planning, just one of the administrative departments under the Ministry of the Interior.

He is nervous, and the man that I know is afraid of absolutely nothing. Bar-rens has commendations for all sorts of reckless feats he does not show anyone, which I know about because I was curious and used my position to get access to his records.

When he was on the streets, he was always first in. He has smashed through a wall into a burning building to get out a single trapped resident, charged right into the teeth of a cross fire of TK-fired projectiles from a dozen Psyn-dealers to get to a downed officer, and more. If someone needs help, he does not wait for backup. If there was danger, he was always the one blasting in the door or busting a hole down from the roof.

So, seeing him blinking rapidly, sweat trickling down his neck, and dark spots spreading across his gunmetal shirt—all this gives me pause.

It is not as if he saved my life. Holmheim would not have killed me, and Barrens did not reach me quickly enough to stop the rape. It is the realization that I am rationalizing down the trauma, the shame, just to excuse myself from this that gets me to repeat, louder, "I'll look."

He retrieves a psi-tablet from the inner pocket of his coat. "Burned out the wireless access before I put the memory on there and encrypted it. Only some-one holding this tablet can get the thing out, and . . ." He lowers it to the desk before me. "Anyhow, the password is . . ." He pauses, thinks to me, *Blossom,* and not just the word, but an accompanying flash of thought, the connection from my name to the word in Japanese, the shape of the characters, the sound in his throat, to a scent he has in mind.

Do I really smell that good to him? Normally that would get a blush out of me, but the nerves are getting to me, the talk of ISec and Enforcers and Adjustments.

"Leon"—my fingers pause just before they make contact with the glossy platinum casing—"what am I going to see?"

"That's the thing, little missy." Barrens is pacing again. "I was the guy that experienced it, and I've looked at it much as I can stand, an' I still don't know what I saw."

Deep breath, and my hands make contact. I get to the file before I scare myself any more than I have.


Damned noisy neighbors partying. It is so loud, he cannot hear himself thinking.

It is not at all like Callahan to take so long answering his door.

He knocks again. He tries calling by Implant-to-Implant link. He knows Callahan is in there. They were just talking an hour ago; the guy was saying how he wasn't feeling well.

His gut says to go, so he goes. No badge on him, but he doesn't need an amp to bust doors.

One kick. Two kicks. Crazy coot—gets himself a fancy elite's door and locks when he's got nothing worth stealing. Three kicks, and the doorframe shatters around the three separate dead bolts.

"Cal! You okay, man?"

Then the smell. Awful smell. Like nothing else. The air rushing out is sweltering hot, humid.

He sees blood streaks and pools.

He ought to dial the precinct first and request backup and wait. He never does that. He crouches low, picks up a bottle by the neck. That's enough weapon for a lunkhead such as himself. He calls up his animal instead.

Roaring in his head. Raging mad, mad to smash things, mad to break somebody. He is quiet, he is wolf, he lets the dark place take the wheel. Follows the droplets and pools and trickles. Like packets of ketchup have exploded all over the place. His boot slides in a pool, and the primal beast snarls at him. Careless! The colors all bleed to red and black, adrenaline, and his psi setting him glowing in sangria and carmine.

Nostrils flaring.

He is It and It is he, but he is in the background, watching and thinking, analyzing the way they're taught to in cop school, while the wolf prowls and moves, teeth bared.

Takes in the details even while moving. Half-eaten bean burger on the kitchen counter. In the hallway are bloody bits, flat swatches of stuff. He only guesses at what they are because of old movies and TV shows, 'cause nothing like this is covered in training, nothing. Torn scraps of human skin. Index finger, first knuckle. All the toes of a left foot. Grayish slab; last time he saw he was at the high-end butcher's, thinking about buying liver, something fancy to cook for Dempsey. Bits of bone even, as if something was taking Callahan to pieces while Cal was trying to crawl away.

Ain't nothing like he has ever imagined.

Wolf is looking left and looking right. It's confused. Sniffing. Tasting the air. Nobody else around.

They reach the bedroom together, and he lets the beast go and falls to his knees. Most of what is left is spread out on the bed, which is soaked in it. Piece of the jaw with a tooth. An eyeball. Oatmeal-looking thing's got to be brain, with the little tinfoil spiderweb of neural Implant poking out of it. A short, pink loop of intestine. Creamy globules of fat. Striated shreds of muscle. Even the bones, even the bones are chopped up; the largest is a few inches long. Most of the stuff that was once his friend is reduced to small particles, a paste, mash. It was like a vast, crude sausage were torn open over the bed.

The smell, agh, it's crawling up his nose and down his lungs and into his head through his ears.

Perverse shit, his stomach is growling, 'cause he was gonna grab something with Cal. He can only think of that butcher shop, the machines in the back, the grinders . . .

When I come to, I've bitten bloody arcs into Barrens's hand. My head is on his lap. He is humming something, a song. I forget the words, but it is about the sea, and islands, the wind.

He notices and blinks down at me. His shirt is torn. Bloody scratches are on his face.

"Told you it was gonna be bad."

When I sit upright, he holds a handkerchief out to me, and I wipe my face clean of snot and tears and sp___ "___sn't that bad."

He barks a choppy laugh.

Terrible as it was, the content of the memory was not the cause of my violent reaction. The way he sees the world is disjointed in a way I have never felt with any other memory transfer. He has two sets of memories on top of each other. All the time. The part of him that is the cop, the man, experiences the world dully, senses diminished, vision almost color-blind as he peers at everything and tries to make sense of it. The beast or the wolf, it is all senses and raw emotion, awareness of his own body, textures of the cloth against his skin, scents in the nose, the press of air currents against his skin.

I went mad, scratching and clawing and screaming, not because of secondhand trauma, but because a little of his wolf took me over, for however many minutes it took me to get free of it. It was a nightmare I could not wake from, with something else moving my body, seeing through my eyes.

He sees it on my face before I can turn away and hide it. What did he see there? I can tell it hurts him. "Oh." He shies back. "I get it. I'm . . . uh . . . Sorry. I was hoping . . . I wanted to tell you, but couldn't figure out how."

This is why he's never asked before, what's kept him behind a wall.

He looks smaller somehow, and it tugs at me. He is ashamed of scaring me. "It's not like—"

"Guess you're wondering how I've not been Adjusted yet. When a Behavioralist *reads* me, the part that's animal knows. It spreads itself thin in the attic, in the basement, deep where nobody goes."

Several deep breaths of the musty air. I can taste his blood in my mouth.

"Are you going to call them in on me, Hana?" He looks sad, and faded, childishly disappointed and witheringly aged. This is why he has never been in a relationship, why he never lets anyone close.

"No! No."

We've known each other for years, and I was always wondering why he seemed afraid. And now, I know.

Lick my lips. Put my hands on his rocky hooks. Another step puts my face against his chest. "I was just surprised."

"Yeah. Surprised." He feels big and solid against me, but his presence is tight, his voice like glass. "I shoulda warned you more."

His chin is on top of my head. His arm goes round me; it's like being hugged by a brick wall. He is frightening and safe, a protector and a savage. I have never met anyone else so alone.

"Can you be okay with this? With me?" He shakes as if he can't believe I'm still here, and I get it, that for all that he worries about getting caught and getting Adjusted, what he was frightened of was what my reaction would be to him.

"It's okay. Listen to me, really listen to me." I pull back and look him in the eye and whisper, "I trust you, Leon." *And you can trust me.*

We do not get any work done that day. Mostly, we sit next to each other in silence. Sometimes, we talk. He tells me about growing up, all these fights, the many times he was this close to getting Adjusted. I tell him about Holmheim, about how, once, I thought I loved him. He talks about Callahan, his teacher at the academy, the only reason he was able to graduate. Callahan found out about his other side, taught him how to discipline and channel it. I tell him about my recent splurge on experiences of this woman pampering a dumb, lazy cat named Minnow. He goes on about Callahan's fascination with the strange, with the out-of-place, and how a hobby of looking into urban legends and rumors on the Nth Web grew into an obsession that got the old man willingly transferred to Long Term Investigations, the better to look into these imperfections in the system. I tell Barrens about being another of those women he's known, devastated and emptied out by Breeding Duty, just holding it together and pretending.

"All these stories heard by a friend of a friend, someone going missing. And they call them Mincemeat stories 'cause that's all they find. I never took him serious, you know? And then whatever he or it was *got him*."

The way he says it causes me to shiver. Yes, there is this between us, and there is also that, a mystery of blood, a secret that should not be.

"This thing's gotten in my head, and there's no way I'm letting it go," I say with a confidence that is not, that shakes and quivers. "Anyway. So. What I'm saying is I'm with you."

He pulls me close again, and I forget feeling scared. He talks into my hair, soft, shy. It feels so good, the way he holds me, the raw need, desire thrumming in that power, a waterfall standing still in midair.

"You're a fine woman, Administrator Dempsey. I . . . like you."

I squeeze him back, and my arms don't go all the way around that massive, barrel torso. "I like you too."

Eventually, we have dinner together. I walk him to his little coffin-size apartment and stay the night.

## 5

HE IS GONE WHEN I WAKE.

The neural Implant superimposes a blinking light onto my field of vision, just visible out of the corner of my eye. A message for me. I focus on it and sub-vocalize the command to open it, and there is the thought unfolding. I feel Barrens's lips on my cheek, his voice in my ears, apologizing for having to leave for an early shift. He has also left some files for me to look at, when I have the time. A thick envelope is on the pillow next to me. I take it with me.

It is a thirty-minute train ride back to my own high-rise unit. The rush-hour crowd pays me no attention, but I imagine that they are all looking at me, and when I shift my feet from side to side, balancing as the monorail curves, a delicious remnant of an ache is down there, and my cheeks are aflame. I imagine their eyes on me, wondering where this policewoman with a badly fitting overcoat is going, and what she was up to the night before.

There is no respite yet even when I reach the building. A woman with thick ankles and a flower-print bag as big as my torso eyes me in the elevator and, after taking a barely audible sniff, backs away, gently redirecting the children in her care behind her. She gives me a look that would set the hair on the back of my head on fire, if she had the talent for it.

I should have showered first. I pretend not to hear the kids asking questions. The girl is just old enough to have a knowing smile on her face, reflected off the elevator console.

When I am finally in my rooms, I lean against my door, drop Barrens's package, press my hands to my face, and hold in the squeak that wants to pop out.

There is no time to think and cogitate and savor and blush and giggle. I rush through my shower and the brushing of my teeth and the rest of the morning rites that typically consume an hour, completing them in a quarter of that time. I am already late.

I message Hennessy that I will not be there quite yet, and to begin the morning briefing himself.

My team does not give me curious looks or ask inconvenient questions when I finally join them. The discussion about how many more hours of computation time we can get from the City Planning mainframe continues smoothly. An hour is spent around the additional material Dr. Savelyev from High Energy has sent over to the office.

By the time lunch rolls around, I believe that nobody has noticed anything. Which is right when Hennessy joins me in my cube and offers to exchange half his homemade sandwich with half of my mass-production cafeteria number.

I accept. He is quite the crafter of food eaten with the hands. Sushi, rolls, appetizers, wraps. He makes great big platters of them for workplace parties, and there are never leftovers.

"Your hair was wet when you came in," he notes. "And you smell different today."

"I did not have time to dry it is all. And, hey, James Hennessy, how do you know what I normally smell like?"

I am staring right into his face, trying to ignore the great big metal eye peering into my soul. He cannot *read* me truly without a Behavioralist's circlet, but his native talent adds a depth of perception that is more than natural. I pull up all the random memories of Minnow and of my schoolmates to the front of my head that I can manage.

"It is impolite to try to peek into your boss's head," I warn.

He is grinning. Insufferably. "You got laid."

"James!" There is just no way he can know that.

"I have a knack for this sort of thing. Not a terribly useful manifestation of psionics, I know"—his fingers splay across his chest—"but I am never wrong."

"Hennessy, it is none of your business. Don't you dare."

"Oh, come on," he gushes. "Talk to me and I swear I won't betray your confidence. But if I'm just guessing, I have no obligation to you not to speculate out loud."

I cannot help it. I am sure that I am bright red from my forehead to my neck, even through the darker pigmentation of my skin.

"My life is not that interesting."

"Please. The team is full of stiffs." His hand flicks sideways, as if shooing away flies. "Except for our fresh new trainee, who is still idealistic and so very young, they're all ambitious blokes that just want to get ahead in the system and get bigger paychecks. I don't get how people can live like that. Come on, my dear." He sits on my desk and gleefully rubs his palms together. "What is he like? Is he any good?"

It is three hundred years past the end of the world and Eugenics has still not bred the instinct to gossip out of us. We are doomed as a species, I guess.

His sandwich is good. Spicy and sweet. Peppers, romaine, bean sprouts, tofu, rye bread, teriyaki sauce. He watches patiently while I try to get some bit of the prim and proper back, chewing and frowning, and trying hard to squint at him fiercely.

"Oh, do give it up, just a bit? I haven't been with anyone in, oh, forever."

"Go buy a memory or something then. I'm the private sort, James. Why would that have changed in the years you've known me?"

Hennessy does an excellent sniff of disdain. It is the high art of expressing contempt, without being gauche. No juvenile eye-rolling for him. It is all in the hundred little details of his posture and the twist of his lip, even the way his heel swings back and forth from the knee crossed over the other. "I do not believe in the veracity of borrowed memories. I'll give you the rest of my lunch."

"But you do in idle gossip? And, no! That's not suitable compensation!"

"I am merely trying to live vicariously the way people used to, before one could just buy the emotion and mood and experience one wants. Anyway, you can't tell me you don't want to share, a little bit. Look, I'll make your lunch every day for a week. Now, let's start small, or not. How big is he?"

The blush is back and then some. Power of suggestion. I am this close to pulling up the memory. Instead I just think about it, just one step removed from thinking it.

Apparently, that is bad enough.

"Wow, that good, huh? You should see the look on your face."

I shake my head. I refuse to be wheedled into talking to anyone about this. "James, out!"

"Fine then. But just so you know, I will wear you down eventually."

Blue light haloes around the pens that levitate out of the case next to my papers. They point at him and lurch forward threateningly. "Out!"

He does go, finally. His parting shot: "Just so you know, your eyes totally glazed over."

Despite myself, I am grinning. Ah, damn it. Jazz has a great number of dirty lines she might say to describe this moment, and my state of mind. How much of it is Leon and me, and how much of it is the pendulum of my brain chemistry's swinging the other way after coming off those disgusting cherry-red pills?

It is disturbing to be so pleased just a day after watching the memory of a crime scene. Or is that just the biological imperative, the desire to feel close in the face of death? I am a little creeped out at myself because even that thought is not enough to keep me entirely from considering last night.

What might be waiting for me back in my room, in the thick plastech envelope, does not make me feel any less alive.

Work, you, work!

I shelter myself behind all the mechanical tasks there are to being in City Planning. There are always more reports to go through, to correct, to evaluate. I autopilot through the paperwork, fingers tapping away at my desk terminal, while using *touch* to build a replica of the pyramids out of paper clips and pencils.

Even with all data and records existing in digital form, some departments still insist on physical-paper prints. And why not, I suppose, when nearly all paper is actually made of plastech and printing on it or erasing it or recycling it is as simple as using a moment's concentration of psi.

I drift and float in that space where the busywork is just a thread, fiddling with the paper clips a second, and then the rest of my mind slips to the past.


Face is hot. Am I walking funny? Surely I'm walking funny, along the red-tiled corridors of the Practical Psionics Quad.

In the Waxmere Auditorium, named after the first captain of the Noah, we sit in concentric tiers that descend down to the surly-faced *touch* instructor, Salvador, who goes on and on about the properties of plastech and how we can use psi to work wonders with it, to change its color, density, thermal and electromagnetic properties, durability, elasticity . . . almost anything the mind can imagine. The structure of the Noah, the Dome around the Habitat, the buildings we live in, the furniture we sit on, our tablets, the cars, the buses, the trains, are all made out of plastech; endlessly recyclable, its adaptability is only limited by the mind.

He spends a good half hour talking about the history of plastech, and a few of our classmates have started to nod off. By now, all of us are messing around with the brick of plastech at each of our desks.

I'm a bit embarrassed to see that I've daydreamed up a knight in shining armor, with a horse, a lance, and everything, taking shape in front of me.

A message from Lyn. *Why are you sleepwalking through today? Was the date that good?* I can feel her smirking amusement.

Was it me or was it him? I thought of lying and replying that it was fantastic and we were up all night.

*It was . . . okay.*

*Just okay? You did stay at—*

*Well, yes. We did. It was . . . weird, that's all. Just okay.*

From the books and the stories, and even the few illicit memories I've watched so shamefacedly with Jazz and Lyn, it ought to have been so much more. It can be so much more, I hope. Sex the first time and all the thinking about it that goes on before and after is more trouble than it's worth.

Finally Salvador winds down the lecture part of the class. He snaps his fingers and the gray plastech brick on the stage worktable floats up to his hand.

"It's easy to play with plastech. A child can do it and make a chair, a toy, or a dollhouse.

"In order to be in this class, Advanced Psychokinetic Engineering 133, you are all at least in the ninetieth percentile of *touch* talent. This means that you aren't going to be making furniture. You aren't going to be making clothes. Should you pass this class, that means you should be capable of synthesizing the most infinitesimal of nanocircuitry, or of building a vertical farm with a thousand floors, all with the power of thought, an amplifier to tap into the ship's power, and some raw plastech.

"On this first day, you are all to do something you *think* would be simple, but isn't. You are all to manufacture a single strut, just like this."

His wrist amplifier just barely gives of a flicker of blue; Salvador is extremely efficient. Glowing when using psionics is impressive, but it's actually a sign of waste energy, raw psi exciting the electrons in the air. The gray brick melts and flows and becomes a simple cylinder one meter long and a centimeter thick.

"Doesn't look like much, does it?"

He takes hold of one end, and we all nearly jump out of our seats when he smashes it into the worktable, which splits in half despite being a meter thick. Quite the stunt; not many engineers have both the psychokinesis of *touch* and the psychometabolic manipulation of a *bruiser*.

"This strut can withstand a load measured in tons. It can deflect five centimeters without fatiguing. It is not electrically conductive, and it has to maintain its strength at a temperature as hot as the surface of a yellow star. Why?

"Because struts like this go into the ship's reactor assemblies, ladies and gentlemen.

"Should one of you ever be trusted with something so critical as the Noah's engines or her reactors, what do you think might happen if a moment's idle thought results in a tiny, undetectable defect in one of these components, or one of any of the millions of parts that will need maintaining over our thousand-year voyage?"

I shrink into my seat as he glares at us. It feels as if he were glaring exactly at me, but I'm sure we all feel like that.

"Miss Dempsey! Come down and reshape yon knight into one of these, and it shall be the first to go under today's stress tests. Let's see if you belong here, or if you should be transferred to"—Salvador paused—"an *Arts* program." He has a fantastic sneer. Potent. I feel all of four inches tall. On my Implant, I call up the relevant equations for stress and deflection and try to figure out just how dense the strut needs to be and what polymeric arrangements we studied recently in Materials Science grant the most strength.

I shape my plastech, and as I walk down to the stage and to the ominously huge piece of machinery at the back designed to apply force to an object until it breaks, I try to show no fear.


I can't help smiling. Mine was the only strut that didn't shatter.

In the time it took me to get through a stack of inventory reports, my pyramid has reached its peak of a mere four inches. But it is yellowed, has the consistency and density of old limestone, and is carved through with a thousand tiny lines to give a hint of all those blocks that made up the original.

I was at the top of APE 133, and when we graduated, Salvador shook my hand and told me I ought to apply to City Planning.

At the end of the day I and my coworkers stream out the heavy doors under the watchful gazes of gargoyles rescued from some cathedral in France or Germany before it was destroyed. Down the stone steps, a great big fellow in a blue coat is standing off to one side. He is walking, back and forth, and the flowers in his hand are plastech, like most everything else, and he is so very, very much larger-than-life. He draws every eye when he sees me, and a smile is on his toothy, massive mug as he walks up to me and shyly offers me sunflowers and daisies and a rose.

"Heya."

If I could, I would crawl into his coat and hide. I just take his arm and resign myself to my whole team giving me the nth degree tomorrow. At least they look more amused than disapproving. I can only wince at the thought of what Jazz, Lyn, and Marcus will say.

Barrens's face smooths over as he examines mine. "Did I make a mistake, coming here?" The life in his voice fades, just a bit.

There is no racial discrimination anymore in our great shipborne civilization. But there will always be the human instinct of *us and them,* only now it's based on test metrics and on rank and the sort of job one is able to qualify for. It's a caste system justified by science. I tighten my hand around his arm. "It's not their business anyway!" I stand on tiptoe and the big lug is just too damned tall. I have to reach up and pull his face down, to be able to brush my lips against his. "Come on. Let's get some bean-dogs on the way home." I try hard to ignore Hennessy and the buzzing of the rest of the team behind us asking him for details.


After a light dinner of dogs on buns with mustard and ketchup, and a stilted hour of awkward chitchat, sitting on my expensive, cream-colored couch, watching news streams on the main viewer in my living room, I can't take it anymore.

"Oh, this is ridiculous."

"Wha—"

I sweep my hands to the sides.

The buttons on his shirt slide open all at once, as does the buckle on his pants. As do the buttons on my sundress, from my neck to the hem.

This time is better than the first. Neither of us is afraid anymore.

"This Callahan of yours was really something."

It is midnight and Barrens is in my kitchen cooking us a second dinner. Whatever he is making smells good. A hint of onions and garlic, something sweet, cumin. Basil.

"Yes, he was. Kept me put together. My Keepers didn't know how to handle me. I was always . . . well . . . rough. Violent. Got mad all the time, no knowing why."

The package has two items. Another tablet with the wireless burned out—this an older model. So I guess it was Callahan that taught Barrens that trick. The rest is a thick folder with physical printouts. Pictures. Tables. Names. Locations. All reconstructed from partially destroyed information. It was labeled "The Mincemeat File."

"Dinner number two is served." He tugs me to the table, obviously proud of the spread. "Now, lay it on me."

We talk while we eat. First is a fragrant bowl of rice noodles. The broth is peppery enough to get tears out of me. I love it.

"There are only pieces here."

The data on the tablet too has many missing parts for each entry. I skim through it yet again while he talks about the man that's become part of the case he was chasing.

"Yeah. After he got injured and stuck behind a desk, Cal had more time for his hobbies. You know how it is, desk cops are just clerks. When he got bored enough, he asked for a transfer to LTI and got it because of, enh, 'previous meritorious conduct.'

"When he had more time to actually try to find files to match to his collection of Mincemeat stories and general weirdness, Cal noticed that a case's entire logs and files, trees and clusters, vanished after he matched it up with one specific Mincemeat tale, about a Keeper named Sullivan coming to his baby's locked room and finding . . . you know. *It*. Pieces. That story was different because it had a lot of concrete details, a date, a time, names.

"The commands were from nowhere. The only evidence that baby ever existed was just the memory in his head. How could a baby disappearing be covered up as a *Retirement*? A death by accident or disease would take faking autopsy reports, medical records, documents signed by so many Doctors. So it was deleted instead.

"Cal decided that since he wasn't in an ISec holding cell yet, it meant that it was something that happened all the time, not just in response to his querying the system."

That is not quite so. Information Security propaganda would have everyone believe that they are always watching, but while past societies had the problem of not having enough surveillance, the opposite is so on the Noah. There is simply too much data on everyone, and filtering it to find what is important is not a straightforward task.

The Ministry of Information is the smallest Ministry, so they have to automate as much as possible. For the wrong reasons, Callahan was right to think that it was the result of programs being triggered, and not the work of a living gray-coat agent. Long Term Investigations is still a police department, under the Ministry of Peace, and even though it is maintained due to Information Security's regulations, it is a lower priority to them, just as it is a lower priority to the police. A real ISec officer might look at a collation of reports from their monitoring programs once every few months.

Callahan's next step was done with enough skill to keep from catching the attention of ISec. If they had noticed him, he would have been interrogated and Adjusted, though ISec doesn't keep long-term prisoners the way urban legend says.

He put a hack in place, monitoring LTI's isolated-case database. Every time one of these deletion commands went into the system, his little monitoring app would register it and start to copy it even as it was deleted, then reconstruct the incomplete data with probabilistic guesswork.

Great chunks are still missing, but already a terrible pattern can be discerned. People are being erased from the system. As if they had never been born. Others have had their files modified, evidence of falsified Retirements.

Whoever was doing this was, at the least, trained by Information Security. I am a gifted neuralhack, but I do not have that kind of skill. It is impressive that Callahan was able to get even this much, suggesting he too was better at this than I am.

"I won't be able to help you the way you're asking." I never felt the need to try to impress Barrens. I am glad this has not changed, despite the change in, well, whatever it is we have got. It is easy to admit to him that while I'm the best neuralhack in City Planning, Information Security is at a different level from me.

His head droops. "So, I'm on my own on this?"

"I didn't say that, Leon. I think there are less obvious ways I can help."

I am not without certain skills. My intuition has, over the years, become attuned to ferreting out trends and patterns. While ISec can erase the records of these people, it's against policy to erase an individual just like that from the memories of all the coworkers and ex-classmates and neighbors they knew. Each of these vanished victims had a home. They bought food and furniture and clothes. They each left the subtle imprint of what they browsed and bought and said on the Nth Web.

The subject might have been deleted from the records, but deleting everything around a subject? In the Noah's databases, every entry corresponds to so much data, which in turn is associated with other entries in other databases. A person's being deleted means deleting his educational history, his employment records, his health records, every single purchase he ever made, every e-mail he received or sent—and such a cascading deletion in turn creates more inconsistencies in the vast, unified system of the Nth Web. That is what we can search for. From there, we can talk to the people that actually knew them, find the memories that are not so simple to erase.

"Ah, I get it. You can do stuff like check about which departments had to fill in empty positions all of a sudden."

I nod. "That's the idea. Let me see if I can cobble something together that can find them the long way around."

I start to lay out the specifications of what we'll need for Barrens. Lyn would think it a waste of time, but I know he can get this and find details I'd miss.

It would have to be semiautonomous, this program, and capable of some degree of evaluation. It would be even better if it could self-modify its parameters as it improved its own search criteria. And it would have to be distributed—a small load on multiple Analytical Nodes is less noticeable than a heavy draw on a single node.

The electronic hardware of the ship is incredibly powerful, each node a quantum supercomputer; the network of all the ship's nodes that formed the backbone of the Nth Web made it a vast digital universe.

For this task, a population of simpler self-optimizing agent programs would be much more efficient than a single large program.

"You can guess what the other benefit is, right?"

"Okay," he says, tilting his head over the drawings on the napkins between us. It's just simplified schematics of what the network of nodes resembles, and a cloud of dots representing the swarm of programs I mean to code. He gnaws a bit on the corner of his lip. "And if it is a bunch of programs spread across the nodes instead of a single program in one place running queries all over the place, it's harder to trace."

"That's right." I lean over and press my lips to the side of his jaw. "Don't chew your lips. They peel and get bloody."

"I'll try. Well. Your idea sounds good to me."

It has been a long time since I have had to create something—my position is mostly administrative, aside from the rare optimization improvements we try to develop. I find my enthusiasm growing, despite the morbid subject of Barrens's quest.

I slurp down my last noodle and skim through the entries on the tablet. Even with only fragments of file information, a tremendous volume of data is here. "Callahan must have been working on this for a long time."

Barrens serves platters of salad next. Apple slices, cherry tomatoes, spinach, with a dressing of honey, oil, and vinegar. Steaming scoops of couscous on the sides.

"Cal told me about this only a couple years ago. He wanted to pass it on because he was being Retired soon." There is a loose leaf in the folder, with messy handwriting scrawled diagonally, creeping up left to right. "He thought it's a single killer. Someone from ISec, or someone protected by ISec."

The files at the front of the folder are chilling. Half of someone's family name labeling a picture of a crime scene that looks just like Barrens's memory, just blood and gore spilled out across a room. The last page of a medical examiner's report about the amount of psi energy it would take to cause this level of catastrophic damage. Other reports about remains that went missing from the morgue. But other files look less like pieces of police records and more like oral histories and short stories. They have other labels: "Tunnel Snipes," "Conspiracy Theories," "Alien Origins," "Hidden Histories."

"What's this other stuff?"

"Hmm? Oh. The other stuff Cal liked to collect, you know. Like I said, he was into weird things. Stories about beasts in the sewers and maintenance tunnels. Alien conspiracies. Passed on his calling to me, huh? Wonder if he foresaw it."

A picture slides out of the folder.

"Whoa." It is in black and white. A massive blob of light and shadow is in the distance at the end of a shaft. Simian. Irregular. It has two arms and two legs, but they look asymmetric, wrong. It could be a man . . . maybe. It is actually more disturbing than the clinical image of a Mincemeat victim on an ME's table. The gore on the slab is abstract, a specimen, but the image of the thing in the darkness pricks the imagination, gets the mind trying to fill in the pieces.

"Tunnel Snipe A5. Printout from the memory of some engineer replacing a sewage valve. Lots of them have stories about the weird down there. Maybe it's the fumes."

He stands up one last time to retrieve dessert, which is a single, large bowl of roasted sweet potatoes and syrup.

"Maybe pause on this? It's not right to have dessert and be talking shop."

I do my best half-lidded, smoky-eyed look. I'm sure I'm doing it wrong, but he still smiles and pulls me onto his lap. It's fair, I guess, since even I'll admit that his smile looks mostly like a snarl. We lift pieces of the soft, starchy stuff to each other's lips. We are both licking our fingers at the end of it. Each other's fingers. I'm blushing and sighing, from the things his off hand is doing. We stopped talking a while ago, and thoughts of killers and myths and coding fade away.

My body drifts along a river; it curves and curls and there are moments of roars and periods of soft, gurgling sighs. It feels different under the moonlight, even if the moonlight is composed of infinitesimally small pixels on a vast dome outside the window. My lips are swollen with kissing and on my tongue is the thick taste of loving. My skin is a desert and the sand is shifting with each slow breeze, with each fingertip touch.

His hands are so large, all rocky ridges and plateaus of calluses, in places rough as sandpaper and in others smooth like worn marble. He is unlike any other I have shared this experience with, so much more real and vital than the pretty ones, the slender ones, the ones who seem half-occupied with some distant image of themselves even as we are coupling.

The night is long, sometimes we sleep and sometimes we wake, and over and over we sail a little farther together on that mysterious waterway.

Less afraid and more sure each time, we try more in pleasing and being pleased. We both use psychic talents, he to enhance and control his already prodigious stamina, and perhaps the better to take in my responses by smell and touch and taste, and I to guess just where I might reach out and touch with ethereal fingers of the mind and how better to angle this or that, or to guess the many subtle ways I can change the way those soft, yielding other muscles clasp at him.

I could wonder what we are to each other, he and I. I could think and re-think and overthink what is emotion and what is merely a synthesis of the spurts of hormones and chemicals in the brain.

There is what is. I try things I've never been brave enough to, and he takes me in ways I've never before permitted.

He has seen me at my moment of deepest shame, grimy and befouled and betrayed in an alleyway. I alone have met the other self he keeps inside, the savage hunter, brutal and unrefined, as well as the small boy that has never felt as if he belonged.

He moves inside of me, and I hold him when he is gentle and the man, and he holds me down when he is It and primal, and these moments come one after the other and sometimes at the same time, and when I am biting his hand bloody so as not to scream, it is in pleasure and with desire. At his slowest and kindest it still brings me to yelps and gasps, for he is larger and thicker than I thought men could get at all, and when It is taking me with the force and speed of an avalanche, marking me with his teeth and his claws, we howl together, flushed and breathless.

In those moments I am drifting from wakefulness, I can only hope we do not get one of Barrens's colleagues knocking on my door about noise complaints. It strikes me that the entire day today, not once did I think of Minnow the cat, and I fall asleep, probably more pleased than I ought to be.

# 6

CREATING THE DATA-MINING SWARM IS NOT TOO HARD. IT NEEDS SEARCH functions, secure access protocols, statistical tools, some plug-in modularity, and some machine learning to optimize performance over time. It will mostly be a fancy search engine that will trawl public forums and sites, and penetrate the secure data archives accessible with Callahan's hacks, and other databases as bypasses are found to get to them. I discard the most robust of the evolutionary algorithm techniques and re-implement what I have gotten to work before in my class projects. I build it around a loosely coupled neural net of particles that can alter the weights of the communications between each individual subunit, and a simplified algorithm that will allow the swarm limited self-modification over how each unit evaluates search parameters and how each tags retrieved data for assembly by the collective. The function for testing the swarm's output is fitted to Callahan's trove of files, and can itself be tweaked with new results. Coding it takes two weekends, since most of the module functions are code blocks I've recycled, or from the toolkits of Barrens's mentor.

Debugging the little monsters takes a month.

Barrens helps with the testing on an isolated server I've built, a computational cube that's just a stack of tablets wired together for more power. He has a knack for putting in just the right mix of inputs and training data to crash the thing. I teach him about the program as I add in a more robust set of debugging functions—when this thing starts to get going, we'll probably need them for future fixes.

Finally, when a week straight of his putting it through its paces fails to crash it, it's probably stable enough to use. We'll still need to modify it as we go along, but it's good enough. Now I just need to tap into the rebellious youth

Lyn and I pretended to have when we were kids, to make sure that the spread of my artificial infection is as untraceable as can be.

Lyn was always the better programmer. It's why she gets paid so much to be in Information Security. She did not have the temperament and physicality to make it as a field agent, but she is one of the best neuralhacks under Research and Development, and not just Network Administration.

At seventeen, I learned my best tricks from her. It is also when we discovered some of the peculiarities of the Nth Web architecture.

The false dawn has begun to slip up at the edge of the false sky, its red-gold light cutting through the shadows in an alleyway between the Londinium Center for Fine Arts and the Museum of Ethics, revealing two girls in tan jumpsuits and boots and gloves and face masks climbing into and out of the recycling bins.

I'm sweating, and breathing hard, and it's not from the physical effort or from the smell.

*Could you look any more anxious, Hana? Calm down. We're just students rooting through the junk for a project.*

We think our thoughts directly to each other, telepathically. It is sloppier and more difficult than using the Implant to send e-messages to each other, but this way, there is no record of the messages going from Implant to the Web and to Implant. Nobody hears our thoughts but us, and no record exists but in our memories.

*I'm nervous, okay? You should be nervous too. If you get written up, you're never getting into ISec.*

*Sure I could. We're just exploring the system—nothing malicious intended.* Lyn gives me her brightest, most confident grin. *It's even true.*

Standing knee-deep inside a blue garbage bin full of dusty coils of wiring and a variety of shattered appliances and electronics, I finally spot a cracked black slab of crystal. My student amplifier glimmers to life.

"Found one."

Lyn hops out of the adjacent garbage bin, calls out, "Don't shatter another one!"

"It happened once, okay? Lighten up."

I don't need the amp to lift such a light mass up into the air, but I need the practice of regulating the extra power available through the grid. My talent's been going through its last surge of growth, and while it makes big jobs easier, I had to relearn how to handle delicate objects.

My control is mostly back to normal. The hours of juggling eggs with my mind at night has restored my fine mental control, but it still takes more focus than I'm used to.

So, yes, I pulverized the first tablet we found this morning. Too excited, maybe, or worried that any moment someone in a uniform with a loud voice is going to walk up to us and ask exactly what we think we're doing. The next two tablets we found had chemical contamination in the circuitry and could not be made functional without completely deconstructing them back into raw plastech and resynthesizing the circuits.

This one is perfect. A wave of my hands, and the screen flickers. Lots of static. This part I can do better than Lyn. She's a better programmer, but is mediocre with plastech manipulation and fabrication.

I think-tap the small app I customized into my amplifier. It draws on my talent, and under the loose guidance of my thoughts, the program slides psychic tendrils through the circuits, finding the loose connections, repairing them. It takes twenty minutes, and then I directly flare some more power and fuse the cracks on the casing.

"Almost brand-new."

"Great!" Lyn almost snatches it from me in her haste. "Did you remember to burn out the transmitter?"

I didn't actually.

"Of course I did." Surreptitiously, I send a last telekinetic spike of energy into the device and melt the wireless components as I was supposed to.

She grins at me. She probably felt the surge through her fingers. "Suuuure you did. Let's get going."

I can't help shaking my head. "You are way too enthusiastic about getting into the sewers."

"Hush now. Do your thing, muscles!"

I take a deep breath. A manhole is right in the alley. Now, I need to draw some real power from the grid—lifting the two-hundred-kilo armored disk out of the way is more than I can do without an amplifier. A few blue sparks of waste energy ripple around the edges.

"Wahoo!" Without a beat of hesitation, she drops down into the darkness. Lyn has some *bruiser* in her; not enough that she could have a combat role, but she can dance with preternatural grace and has no fear of a five-meter drop.

Gingerly, I climb down the ladder, then lower the access door back over us with a clang. In the darkness, the utility lights on our shoulder pads and belts automatically come on, drawing on our psi to light the way.

For all her bluster about not being afraid, Lyn is the one who insists on our attempting our experiments only through an untraceable tablet wired into a maintenance port in the sewers. She is the one who taught me about the curious phenomenon of dangling IDs—code identifiers for individuals who don't seem to exist anywhere in the system. Every person who has ever lived on the ship has a unique ident code; when one dies, the code is supposed to be locked out of the system.

But in her restless, sleepless nights of exploring the Nth Web, Lyn found active identifiers that don't belong to anyone. We had thought they were just a myth.

The air down here is fetid and sour, but not toxic. We try not to look at the things floating in the ankle-deep water.

She plugs a jury-rigged adaptor cable into the centimeter-wide, triangular maintenance port and plugs the other, tiny needle end into our refurbished hand-held terminal. "Testing and . . . it works."

Something bumps my calf and I hold in a shriek.

"Lyn, I swear, if a rat climbs up my pants, I am going to murder you." I shiver a little in the hot, humid shaft.

"I'll treat you to lunch at that crepe place you like every day until you're sick of it if that happens, okay? Now, what have we here?"

Both of us have our hands on the tablet. She leads now because she is the better neuralhack, but I ghost along behind her, watch as she runs her custom-made masking algorithm, which sets up a subnet of proxies scattered around the hardware network of Analytical Nodes upon which the Nth Web runs.

Finally, she starts trying out one ident code after the other, logging them into the system through a maze of accesses that would take hours for any system monitors to notice.

"Huh. They all work. They . . . they all work."

The bemused expression leaves Lyn's face, and she's not smiling anymore.

Perhaps she's finally thinking through what it might mean.

"How can so many of them work?" Now, her cheeks are starting to redden. She is upset. "I figured maybe a couple of them would. But we've gone thirty-two for thirty-two."

"Let me have a turn, all right?"

I imagine that Lyn is thinking furiously about why so many vulnerabilities are slipping through the cracks of the Nth Web's security.

But I also have some experiments I want to run. Now that we don't have to worry about tripping an unauthorized-access alert that can trace to our real identities, what I want to learn most of all is just how big the Nth Web is.

I plug in my apps, which start to use a special data signal I found while messing with a buggy Nth Web protocol assignment. It is a code for a data packet that ignores security between the nodes and accesses the hardware directly. The only thing the signal does is cause one Analytical Node to ping all adjacent nodes, which then send an echo back to the source. Limited as it is, no student should have access to something like this.

My program sends out these special pings from the nodes closest to our access point, measures the delay it takes for each reply, then accesses the next ring of nodes to send a new set of signals. In this way, it slowly constructs a map of how the nodes are connected. Then it's my turn to think that surely something is very, very wrong. The map is the way I imagine it to be, at first. Then, as more pings go out and more nodes answer, it keeps growing, and growing. From dozens of points of light, it becomes thousands, then tens of thousands. There are so many connections to display and so many echoes returning that the limited processor in the tablet slows to a halt, freezes completely.

"What in the . . . How can there possibly be so many nodes on the ship? There's . . . there's thousands of times the computational power we could possibly need for every function, and ninety-nine percent of it is just dormant, with no program processes running on them."

Lyn frowns. Down here in the dark, both of us have found something we would have been happier not knowing. All our lives, we have been told that we have to conserve resources for the long, long journey to our new home. So why would more computers than we are supposed to have power to run be built into the Noah? "If the system is that large, that could explain why so many dangling ident codes slip through the garbage-collection programs. They must get copied back onto some of those redundant systems, and maybe it takes ages to propagate the sweeps."

I try to think of reasons why. "Perhaps all those extra nodes are needed for something. Maybe for when the Noah reaches Canaan?"

Lyn unplugs the tablet and carefully and thoroughly smashes it under a glowing, psi-enhanced kick. She lets the pieces float away.

"I just changed my mind. I think, very strongly, that we should forget this."
Her voice is grave, and the words are slow.

Yeah. All right.

It doesn't feel like a joke anymore, the stories we tell each other late at night, of overcurious students being taken away by gray-uniformed officers only to return dazed, unable to remember quite what their class project was. And of course, there are stories of those who never return at all.

How much more is there to the ship that people are not supposed to know?

Lyn and I eventually spoke of those discoveries again years later and laughed at ourselves. As we were promoted through the ranks, we convinced ourselves that what seemed like vast and dangerous secrets were ordinary redundancies built into the system, and functions of bureaucratic red tape such as the LTI database, which we wanted to think was the source of the dangling IDs. That the ghost ident codes belonged to individuals who were temporarily taken out of the system, unsolved murder victims hidden away in the LTI databases indefinitely or until their killer dies and his revealed memories "solve" the crime, at which point the records are restored to the larger system. But I don't think so anymore.

Back then, it had seemed like the sign of something bigger than Lyn and me, something terrifying. Something that could get Information Security appearing at our door late at night.

That cold fear creeps up my spine again as I consider what Mincemeat could be. Killer? Monster?

Lyn's method of masking system access still works. With it, my data-miner begins to infect its way across the nodes of the Noah. I take an untraceable tablet I restored out of a junk pile, wire it into a maintenance port behind the Moskva Mathematika Center, run a masking function through proxies and a dangling-ID log-in, and upload the first piece of the swarm. It starts in the Statistical Research Center's cluster of Analytical Nodes, where its multiple threads, even if someone notices them, could be mistaken for a statistical probe through the databases. From there, it replicates onto adjacent Analytical Nodes, into the financial system, health records, employment records, and further and further out across the ship.

After another week of waiting and wondering, the first useful data retrievals start coming in. I am eager to do something other than refine my program and comb through Callahan's trove and stare at the image of Barrens's weblike map of the victims and possible relationships and the possible profile of a killer that might do this. It's more question marks than anything else. Another month goes by before we have a new lead to chase down.

The human element of detecting is not without boredom either.

I waste an hour going back and forth along the West Twelfth Park on foot, trying to find a person of interest I have dug up on my very own. It feels as if the bronze statues of the historic explorers of Earth are mocking me with their far-off gazes and optimistic poses. James Cook, in particular, regards me, brows tilted just so, his eyes simultaneously knowing and condescending. I have passed his green-tinged statue three times.

I promise myself that when the opportunity arises, I will have Cook's statue relocated to some lightless corner of one of the museum archives.

Finding my man would be easier if I had messaged the man first and actually made an appointment. The small weed of anxiety has grown larger. I avoid leaving tracks in the system as much as I can.

I do my deep-searches anonymously on public terminals, mask my accesses and queries with false trails to other nodes throughout the system. I change my pattern of purchasing groceries, no longer always picking them up from the same vendor each time. I let Barrens do his watchdog best. Just in case.

These worries arise more easily at night, or in the dark office of Long Term Investigations. Walking through the park under the bright daytime skyscape fades the misty fears, until I think of how Mincemeat might have found and eliminated Callahan, a canny veteran gifted with both *bruiser* and *touch* talents.

"Seen Cal spar with Enforcers and give them a run for their money," Barrens once said. "Take a real monster to do that to Cal so quick, without a fight that would tear up the whole apartment block."

Bees buzz in the air. Lavender blossoms along the pebble-textured paths through the park. Gold and orange and silver carp swim idly through the streams connecting the ponds spread out through the park. Oak trees dapple the grass with the shadows of the leaves. Children are everywhere. Some sit and laugh at the sight of a fuzzy Welsh corgi scampering and barking, and a few particularly lucky ones pet it and giggle when it licks them. It must belong to a whole team from some department—no one individual can afford a dog, other than the department chiefs and higher-ups in the chain, the ones who own actual houses as individuals, rather than renting. If any one of those top-class officers were out here in the park, an ominous escort of black-armored Enforcers would be keeping an eye on everyone around.

Finally, I spot the man I am looking for. Keepers are required to bring the children in their care out for "fresh air" and greenery a minimum number of hours of the day depending on the child's age, and this is the closest park or garden to his residence.

He is young, for a Keeper. Just twenty years old, still a bit coltish and lean, not yet come into the weight he looks as if he will put on later. His mix of looks calls to mind long-lost regions of the Mediterranean—dark hair, olive skin, sharp features. He gently rocks a baby carriage, singing something without words, slow and soothing. He has no permanent partner anymore, just a rotating series of substitutes—this, and the drop in his household leisure spending, is what drew the attention of my AI probes.

Today, he is alone, and he looks somewhat lost and unsure compared to the other Keepers, who are all older than him, watching their assigned charges, all working in pairs carefully selected for balancing personalities and psychological traits. He keeps checking his psi-tablet, as if looking through a guidebook. He stands up, checks his watch, sits again. His eyes are tired, and his ocher Keeper's apron is rumpled and spattered with globs of myriad yellow and brown hues.

"Hello? Mr. Gorovsky, right?"

"Um. Yes. Apollo." He shakes my hand. His fingers are soft, his grip is rather limp. It does not match his listed profile.

"My name is Hana. I'm here to ask how you've been doing since your partner's Retirement."

He looks askance at me. Not at all subtly, he is noting the emitter pattern of my Implant. "Um, you don't look like a Behavioralist."

"I'm not." I try to work my smile a little more, with teeth, and try to front-load my subconscious with happy, neutral thoughts of trends and graphs and statistical equations. "I am conducting a preliminary study on the cost-effectiveness of the Behavioralists' child-rearing protocols. Naturally, I am relying on your discretion—the bureau would be displeased about a lowly number cruncher trying to grade them."

His face eases into a melancholy smile. "Since you're not with *them,* maybe I'll be willing to talk. I too will rely on your secrecy. I could get in trouble, you know." His sighs are short and pinched and frequent, as though compressed out of him bit by bit. "I already am, kind of."

"How so?" I have a spare tablet out and a stylus, and I'm projecting my best, trustworthy self, the facial manifestations and posture from back when I was a student interviewing random subjects in the field for a school report.

I have on my old clothes from then too—a blouse that is, perhaps, too tight across the chest now, and a skirt that was not as short then as it has become. I have youthful, flirty, cherry-shaped earrings dangling and swinging, and my hair is pulled back in a ponytail. Put together, I had hoped it might take a few years off my appearance, or at least distract this young fellow out of his caution. Barrens had been rather amused at my go-getter fashion choices and said so, before I took off on the day's venture.

Maybe it was working, or maybe it would not have made a difference. Gorovsky seems to have been waiting for a chance to unburden himself because I barely have to prompt him to get a flood of complaints and woe-is-me.

"If only they did not retire Sasha so soon! It is overwhelming, doing this alone when I am still learning. The substitutes, they mean well, but since they are rotated through, there isn't a chance to bond." He goes on. The baby keeps waking him up at odd hours. He forgets which formula to use at which time of day. He makes mistakes balancing the protein profile of the milk. "It would not be so terrible if I was just allowed to message Sasha to, you know, ask for advice, to get a pep talk. That sort of thing. But contact with Retirees is prohibited for everybody.

"What's worse is I had no chance to prepare for her Retirement. Behavioralist Central just tells me I must have missed the notice. And in a week, I am being assigned two more babies to raise. . . . I don't know if I can do this alone!"

The bell in the bell tower rings, announcing that it is noon.

White-walled compounds open their gates, releasing children seven to nine years old from their morning classes, and they amble along the roads and paths back to their homes, where their Keepers are waiting for them. The noon sun is high overhead and warmer; it makes the brilliant blue-glazed tiles atop the pagodas of the archways and towers of the school centers glitter like the sea.

In the distance, the towering black cubes of the vertical farms hiss as hundreds of exterior panels close or open as needed to get the proper amount of light on the various crops being raised within them and to regulate the humidity and the temperature. Green cracks appear and disappear across the black surfaces, and white mist and foam sprays out of the different-salinity ocean, lake, and river tanks on the fishery floors. I can hear a few of the other Keepers in the park explaining this to their wards, and about how all our food is raised in those buildings.

Gorovsky is still unburdening. "My requests for a new permanent partner just get automated responses. I don't understand at all—everyone else tells me that a Keeper's Retirement is planned for months ahead, so that there's no problem getting children prepped, and so that a proper replacement can be phased in. Sasha was gone so quick, and the baby, little Zaide here, does not sleep soundly without her."

Zaide starts to cry and Gorovsky pops in and cradles him carefully, rocking him and murmuring soothing syllables statistically determined to calm a majority of babies. He focuses power, a pale green glow around his silvery lips, and *writes* sleep onto the baby until it takes effect and he can return the boy to the carriage.

"Does he need a diaper change? Is he hungry?"

Gorovsky sighs and shakes his head. "No, and no. I think it's because I mentioned, you know, that name. He is bright, and very sociable. I think he will be quite the *reader*—he formed the bond with, well, with her, very quickly."

"Tell me about her last few weeks. Was there anything strange at that time?"

He is puzzled. "Strange?"

"Was there perhaps an unannounced evaluation? Was there anyone new that joined your circle, and then left just as she did?"

Those chrome lips twist. "You think central was watching us and found something . . . wrong . . . with her?"

"I'm not suggesting—"

"Because that would just, just be so unfair! Sasha"—with that, the baby was awake and crying again, and Gorovsky had him up in his arms once more— "Sasha was good to me, and to Zaide. She was so devoted! She did everything like the manuals and our training suggest. It is not her fault her crèche-sister got sick. She just did what any crèche-mate would do, helping out. She didn't spend that many hours away from us." His eyes roll back in their sockets. The baby wakes again, upset as Gorovsky goes stiff and unresponsive.

Is this a mistake? Should Barrens be asking the questions?

Gorovsky returns from his memory scan. "No, I'm sorry, there was nothing out of the ordinary. I wish there was. Maybe I would understand it better if there was some reason. One Tuesday, Sasha went out to pick up our allocation of protein powders. And she never came back. Just a message from Central telling us that she was Retired on schedule as previously announced. Retired! She's only been a Keeper for a year. I wish I could just talk to her. . . ."

He is crying, and the Keepers around us look on incredulously. I take Zaide from him and warble out a few, clumsy notes. The boy places both hands on my jaw and peers up at me. It is like being tested. I suppose Zaide does not disapprove too much, as he does calm down, eventually, curling up in my arms.

A weight is inside me, sinking deeper. I remember again the hollowness. It is not something Barrens can fill, however much affection he gives me.

Long minutes pass, but Gorovsky does recover himself before another Keeper can approach and offer assistance. He takes Zaide back and sighs and kisses the boy.

"You would have made a decent Keeper yourself," Gorovsky says to me, and now I am the one grappling with my emotions. That is exactly the worst thing he could have said.

We talk some more about this and that and nothing, and for the form of it, I get some numbers out of him about how many hours Sasha spent at which locations, about how Zaide's metrics charted before her "Retirement" and how the little devil is testing now.

It has not been a waste of time, but I wanted more than this. The urge to stamp my feet and vanish into a memory of a cat that loves playing in boxes strikes. It is not nothing. This man's grief, his misery, is as real as my own. He just does not know all there is to know, all the things that might make it worse.

Would it help him if he knew that it was possible Sasha died a violent, gruesome end?

I am getting all twisted up inside. Are we fooling ourselves, seeing more than there is to see? Self-important, ordinary people who want to believe we see a deeper reality than there is? But Barrens's memory is real, and the legend of Mincemeat in the dark reaches of the Nth Web has been around since before Callahan's death. I believe in this society; I have to, it is the only human society left. I cannot have it be tainted by the thought of some twisted creature preying on us with impunity.

The park's gardeners tromp out for their midday duties. They are low-level *touch* talents, men and women in brown with passable telekinesis but not much of a head for anything. So they spend the majority of their productive lives wearing dun jumpsuits and pushing amplifier carts along, using their power with nearly automated scripts that others programmed for them. In their wake, grass is automatically cut with a dim crackle and gathered up in the holding bags on their carts, together with dead leaves and assorted litter from inconsiderate crewmates. The carts also scan the soil and surrounding plants and trees and, as required, deposit micro-pellets that maintain the desired soil chemistry. Once a week the gardeners wear backpacks with trimmer amplifiers to touch up the bushes and prune the trees, and once in a while, they plant seedlings.

TKs of slightly greater ability work in the vertical farms.

I drift along, thinking of those men and women working the farms, barely paying attention to Gorovsky by the time I wrap up my first interrogation and leave the park.

Twenty minutes later, Barrens slides through the crowd to my side when I am halfway up Yamato 3Street.

"Great chowder place at the corner, partner."

"You look cheery."

"Every piece is another piece of the puzzle. Not all that was useless, right?" Just most of it. "Chowder? With clams?"

He laughs and puts an arm around me. "With some imagination, guess you can tell that the bits of compressed bean curd are supposed to taste clam-ish. It's good anyway, creamy, thick. Didn't really think you'd get talk about some mysterious, scary guy following his Keeper partner around, did you?"

No, but I hoped for it. My grumbling amuses Barrens, changes the character of his smile, but from the way the other customers in the little corner restaurant back away from us, this expression looks even more dangerous on him than his default, stony impassiveness. This is the patient side of him, the waiting predator, scenting out the prey's trail. While I think about whatever this is out there, possibly only days or weeks away from vanishing someone else, Barrens keeps his mind on what it is we can do next. He does not get distracted by what we have no control over.

We have chowder and it is good. A crackle of false thunder carries through the air, and rushing, we make it back to his place just as the rain starts to pour.

His apartment is part of a complex of tiny sleeping chambers. The kitchens, showers, and locker rooms are shared facilities.

The wind sweeps the rain in waves that splash hard against the lone porthole in his coffin apartment that looks out on the city. It calms my frustrations, as do the hours Barrens spends at my side, sometimes touching, sometimes kissing, mostly just listening to the tinny voices and old classics on his half-size Nth Web terminal.

To watch through that lone window in his private space, I have to stay on my knees. There is not enough room to stand. For a giant such as Barrens, it must feel like a cage, terribly constricting. But he never seems to mind, and when we spend the night together, he prefers the confines of this cell to my spacious quarters. It is cozy here, I guess.

While he sleeps, I watch the lights of the city for a while, ghostly through the mist, blurred, bright streaks of supply trucks and a few private cars along the aerial bridges flying from tall tower to tall tower. The granaries and warehouses next to the dark, hulking cubes of the vertical farms are slender towers of gossamer webs climbing up to the top of the dome, birdlike, the wings around the globular storage eggs actually part of the transport system that delivers the raw produce to the factories in the underlevels, and to the markets across the Habitat. Red and yellow spotlights stretch out into the darkness, proximity indicators to warn off the ever-present Enforcers that flit across the city skies in their glowing flight rigs, watching for who knew what, always watching. I see a handful of them shoot to the horizon, burning fireflies plunging into the dark mouth of the distant air-lock gate that leads to the far sections of the Habitat. The larger, dragonfly-like ornithopter rigs of the police patrols, slower, less agile, try to follow. It starts to rain again.

"Wonder where they're going in such a hurry?"

Barrens stirs and turns onto his belly, murmurs something about a fire. He winces and twitches and bares his teeth.

Under his threadbare blankets, it is warm enough for me, curled up against him, and I suppose that it is not the worst way for my first day of "detective work" to end. But I feel a little guilty being content. How many other Apollos are out there, wondering why someone important to them vanished?

I think of what it would be like if I lost Barrens now, never knowing for sure what happened to him. I grab hold of a tree-trunk arm and hang on, suddenly afraid, and sleep is a long time coming.

It's always stories. A friend of a friend. Third-hand mention of the people who are "disappeared" by ISec. But I know it happens. I know the facilities exist; I've seen the power requirements for them. Much more than Mincemeat, I am afraid of those faceless figures in the gray coats.

## 7

THE FIRST DOWNPOUR MARKS THE FADE OF SUMMER INTO FALL. WEATHER protocols modify the lighting, heating, and humidifying procedures through the Habitat sections. It rains every evening, a product of water vapor collected at the condensers at the top of the Dome, and augmented with the condensate from the ponds, streams, lakes, and micro-oceans of the fisheries and biomes. It helps keep the air flowing through large spaces of the Dome, as well as washing the surfaces of the buildings free of the accumulated dust and salts. The luminosity of the sky is reduced during the shortened daylight hours, and to compensate, "interior" lighting is increased.

At City Planning, everything is constantly changing, yet nothing changes. Hennessy still pokes fun at me and tries to bribe me with food. Stephen Wong, trainee, still confuses form F-33A with F-33E and makes up for such occasional mistakes with youthful enthusiasm. Julia still complains to me about how lazy Nestor is in documenting the project proposal they have been working on forever. Charles and Antonia continue their on-again, off-again almost-relationship. Lita, Erica, and Manuel still drink too much on the weekends and come in red-eyed and hungover on Mondays. Hester Merced, our tier supervisor, still looms over the whole department with her powers of approving or disapproving. It is all forgettably ordinary, the minor disagreements and fights. There are always more meetings about equilibrium and efficiency and proposals and different cliques trying to one-up each other.

Though it has won approval, the new procedure for water treatment is still winding its way through the bureaucracy. Resources from elsewhere have to be freed up for it. Schedules need to be designed. Marcus is in Water Management and won't have any say in it until it is time for implementation, but already he spends at least an hour a week going through the procedure and looking for possible conflicts that might arise from parallel processes in the system that also deal with the same variables.

My job is made up of these small details, finding them, analyzing them, managing them.

That was almost my whole world before Breeding Duty punched me loose from the Hana-shaped hole I fit into.

When we are together, Barrens is as sweet to me as he can be. I guess we will always draw odd looks when we are out together, but I've stopped caring.

My officemates still don't understand. Except for Hennessy, who gives me these knowing grins and asks me if my man is as savage in bed as he looks. The rest look at me with disbelief when their eyes catch the static 2-D image of his face on my desk, snarling his best, fiercest smile.

Beyond work, there is the quest for Mincemeat.

My distributed program spreads and grows. It accumulates probable and improbable matches, and Barrens and I check through them, one by one. He is quickly picking up how to create subgroups in the swarm and specialize them to search for other possibilities, other signs of data manipulation. He finds the data-mining swarm fascinating and calls it Hunter, talks to it as he puts in his own little coding tweaks. Both of us are still required to put in our normal levels of performance at our respective jobs.

We interview others. We find little we did not already know. A grind of weeks passing with little progress. A few moments of tension when we find others on the Web, collectors of hideous things, who sell us Mincemeat memories of a few who have come across the death scenes and are willing to find more for us. They change their access regularly and are nearly as hard to find as we are, on the Web. They promise us more, if we have the money. Creepy people who like to experience real horror for fun, with names like Ms. Smoke or Mr. Paper.

They sell us a handful of real memories, too unbearably vivid and bloody to be faked. But the meta-details embedded in the data are confusing and impossible, spanning too much time. All I can do is enter the new parameters into the targeting for Hunter and see how it refines the search.

Barrens can tell that I need a break from this. He tells me not to be impatient, reminds me that Callahan spent years to accumulate what he had. It is not as if Barrens expected Mincemeat to be found in the confines of a two-hour movie.

His birthday approaches, and we decide on a picnic.

Still, the urge is consuming. I need to be doing something important, something larger than myself. I try to fine-tune my data-miner during every free moment. The midnight before our date, Barrens stares at me tapping away at the desk terminal in my miniature office at the apartment. He picks me up out of the chair, ignoring my protests, and carries me on his shoulder.

"I want my present, I do. Drop that tablet and close off your developer kit already."

"What if I don't?"

"You'll get a spanking, you will." He gets a little shriek out of me when he claps his hand against my butt.

"I give, I give!"

And I do. I give quite a lot.

I can't quite help myself though. When he falls asleep, I go back to my terminal and tablet and fiddle with the code some more. I fall asleep there.

In the morning, Barrens groans when I insist that we do an update/download while we are out. "Fine! But you're not analyzing nothing until *after* my birthday."

We pack up the food and he tries to keep me talking about other things. Even on the train, though, I end up talking about my program with him, in our heads, over Implant-to-Implant messaging. I would prefer a mind-to-mind link, but Barrens doesn't have any *reading* at all, and my talents aren't enough to sustain a telepathic connection with one who has none. We keep it up all the way to the Forest biome.

It is a five-kilometer hike through wooded hills to the picnic area. Each biome is only a square kilometer; the trail I insist on twists and turns along the hills. He suggests that we take the bus to the other biome entrance, right next to the barbecues and the benches and cabins, but I feel ambitious. I want to make this worth it for him.

In minutes, I am reduced to huffing and gasping, and he smirks just a little bit as he takes my backpack and carries it along with his own.

Looking at the sky, and tall redwoods leaning over us, it seems almost easy to forget that we are on a ship. Pebbles and bugs and things are underfoot. Sometimes, birds call to each other in the distance. Illusory mountains rise at the illusory horizon, tall, imposing peaks copied from the Rockies. The air smells alive, much more so than outside in the Habitat. I can tell Barrens loves it; it is his first time in one of the preserves.

He keeps looking at everything all around us, and every once in a while he crouches low and crumbles a little dirt between his fingers. This is disgustingly easy for him; he could probably jump and swing from tree to tree all the way through and he wouldn't be breathing hard.

*Remember, wash hands before eat—*

"Hana, doll, you're breathing so hard you can't message me straight anymore. Chill."

*Helps distract from the walk.*

"Shit!" I stumble on a tree root, and he manages not to laugh.

When we finally get out of the forest, I fling myself onto the soft, manicured grass of the picnic area, wiggle my toes in my hiking boots, and sigh. I'll be sore later.

Barrens lowers himself next to me and opens up our packs. His eyes are bright. There is a tension to him too. A part of him that probably wants to run amuck through the forest, burn off thousands of calories, find something to chase and hunt and kill and bring back to cook.

"Thanks, Hana. This is . . . this is nice."

Hopefully, he never looks up how much today's permit costs or he'll say it's way too much to spend on him.

Ah. A hard-line socket off the path! I hop up and set up the tablet.

He sprawls out on his back and I sit cross-legged next to him. A yellowed leaf drifts down from the tree giving us some shade, and I brush it out of his wiry hair.

An ordinary couple having a picnic in the park on a Sunday morning. Nobody would look at us and think we are engaged in anything of questionable legality. I hope.

While we relax and take in the breeze and the sun, the tablet continues its download from the search program and uploads parameter modifications. The wireless transmitter of the device is burned out; hence the cables snaking through the grass, plugged into a port next to one of the many trails cutting through the biome. Usually, these ports scattered through the ship are used only by the maintenance crews, but anyone may use them.

Once again, I use the tricks Lyn and I figured out together. A program masks my access through the intermediary of a functioning ghost-ident code and a maze of proxies hiding the data accesses across dozens of Analytical Nodes spread out across the ship.

"What were you thinking about?"

"Just remembering when we were kids. I guess it was more fun for me than you. . . ."

"Ah, it wasn't that bad. I was huge even then. Not too many people messed with me, and the few who did gave me some fun fights."

I can't imagine bonding with my friends over fists and bruises.

Looking down, I glance at the status of the running applications on the tablet in my hands. This one was reacquired from an architect-in-training for the same price as a decent pair of running shoes. I met with him over blini in Café Moskva, a dainty little store under the shadow of the replica of St. Basil's Cathedral. No names needed, just one of thousands of goods sold over the Web, arranged by anonymous posting on a junk-exchange forum.

As a graduate under Dr. Salvador's APE 133, I could synthesize one directly from raw plastech, but it's hardly worth the hours of intricate psychokinetic circuit-tuning it would take to do so, as I would also have to configure and program it. Repairing this one took fifteen minutes.

I plug updates into the data-miner swarm, watch them propagate through the pieces. My snooping application creeps across the chatter, building associative trees around the absence of individuals taken off-system. The population changes and grows. The swarm downloads new entries into the local database in the tablet.

Right now, I am not supposed to be thinking about a killer in the dark.

I scoot closer to Barrens and bend close. My lips are just short of his, and as he rises to kiss me, I lean back so that his mouth can chase mine.

"Happy birthday, Leon."

He bites just a bit, just hinting. Desires, emotions. The language of all the different ways he holds my hand. It is a lovely, lazy day. We could be on Earth, under a real sky, listening to the sound of the brook splashing its way through its rocky course.

He looks at me. What does he see in me when he gives me that stare that sparks that curious internal quivering.

"Happy birthday to me, yep."

In Barrens's eyes, there is a hunger. Is it for me alone? Or would he look this way at any other woman who could love him?

I like to think psychic abilities would not help answer that, though the Behavioralists surely have endless relevant studies about peer-bonding, relationships, and intimacy. If we both had strong *reading* talents, we would never have to wonder; we could commune, sharing thoughts directly, and not through the interface of signals from Implant to Implant. Jazz talked about a relationship she had like that, and how quickly it became awful and boring. The fantasy of completely sharing oneself with another is better kept a fantasy, she told me— the reality is full of endless little annoyances at random thoughts and feelings, plus the rather disturbing sense of losing oneself, of the dissolution of identity.

That deep sadness is still there, buried. I want him to hold me tight, to fill me up and help me forget. I fantasize about his consciousness and mine smashing together, unifying, mutual destruction, completion. I'll settle for the heat of his great big paw on my thigh, the memory of last night, the sweet, lingering ache of the flesh, his toothy, contented grin.

The sun is bright, and the autumn foliage is molten fire and gold. The breeze picks up, a surge resulting from many factors: vents opening and closing between the Habitat and the biome preserves. Red, yellow, and brown leaves take flight for a moment. More heating elements come online to simulate the sun climbing higher into the sky. Children in the distance run through the flight of fall colors.

A cold sandwich is the start of a satisfying weight in my belly. We share a plastic tub of macaroni salad. For the rest of the afternoon, our kisses will probably taste like the figs we have for dessert. I delete the signals in the corner of my vision, messages from Jazz and Lyn and Marcus, subtle and not-so-subtle criticism of this thing growing between Barrens and me.

Friends care and friends judge; how much worse if they knew about this awful mystery we share? Would they be horrified, or would they admire it? Wouldn't it be good for the ship to stop these deaths? Somewhere out there, Apollo Gorovsky is wheeling about a child, struggling to provide it with adequate care, missing half of the team assigned to raise the boy. And there are others. How many more?

"Hey. You're pretty lousy at this taking-a-break thing," Barrens murmurs. "We're still on holiday." He pulls me down and it's nice, lying against this great big beast, my rock, a wall against uncertainty. His fingers are almost too large to lace into mine. The slow rumble of his heartbeat against me, the breath of his huge lungs, soothes me. His is the scent of primal things, soil and trees and grass and sea. I could sleep like this. I let myself ease into it, slipping away.

The tablet beeps. It is done syncing, and I pull out the plug, wrap the cables.

*Let's take a walk. Or maybe ride one of those boats in the pond.*

*Sure. Don't blame me if we fall in the water though. I'm . . . pretty heavy. Little boats tilt,* he warns.

It's warmer than average, for an autumn-cycle day. In my professional capacity, I know it means that one of the maintenance teams has screwed up a thermal-management protocol. But off duty, it is a fine afternoon to risk messing about in a boat.


We do fall in the water—and laugh about it. It is good that psi-tablets are water resistant. We get back in the boat and mess about on the water some more.

The sun sets, and it is time to go home.

The walk to the train is damp even with my TK drawing the water out of our clothes and hair. We pass by a stand selling fresh pierogi and fill up our emptied picnic basket with them for dinner. From another stall, we obtain a half dozen fragrant loaves of sourdough.

"I'm going to get fat with all this rich stuff yer buying." There is that awkward, shy grin.

*Don't be like that.*

Because theirs is the only talent that is closely tied to metabolism, *bruisers* fuel their powers with more than psi-energy from the grid. Barrens burns through four thousand or more calories in a single workout at the gym each morning. If he has to participate in a combat operation, he can burn ten thousand in moments. More than half of his income goes to pay for food, even with the supplementary ration chits given to *bruisers*.

It would be easier to smile back if it did not bring to mind the enormous disparity between our incomes. I know he does not mind. Consciously, anyway.

A part of the male brain still says he should provide for his female.

In battles between pride and practicality though, well—when we share meals or go out together, I pay. And if future interactions with the collectors on the forums are necessary, it will be my money too.

It's a worthier cause than blowing my Breeding Duty comp on a pet. Or a weeklong biome vacation at a beach.

We are at my apartment, tonight. I insisted because I was not in the mood to use the communal shower at Barrens's. And this way, while he is in there, I can join him and wash his back. It still makes me a bit giddy, feeling that awesome, iron-hard flesh under the soapy skin. His back is so broad, I feel positively tiny as I work my little washcloth in circles across it. He smells good.

Then there is dinner. We eat our evening walk's spoils. We reminisce. I serve up awkward stories about first dates at the academy. And the weird social hierarchies and passive-aggressive conflicts. He talks about the fights he got into at his school, the rivalries, the few friends he found at the end of a day's battle with his fists. The biggest scandal in my class was a plagiarized research assignment. In his, it was two students overdosing on Psyn and trashing the gym.

His stories are better than mine. It is funny to see him concentrate so when it is my turn. We peer into each other's pasts through our words. We could share the memories directly, of course. But we don't.

We drift to sleep on the couch, listening to slow, dreamy blues.

At midnight, we wake up simultaneously. And share a look. Our agreed-upon break is over. Time to get back to the hunt.

I sit up a little straighter. My will demands it, and my bag opens. The tablet flies up and out and into my outstretched hand. In the kitchen, fifteen feet away, a jar lid unscrews itself and coffee floats up into the percolator.

We both hold on to the tablet's conductive frame and dive in.

"I got the forums and rumor threads and stuff, like usual." I can feel him grimace. "Another message from the weirdos. No new Mincemeat memories for sale, but they do have an encounter with the monsters in the tunnels. I said no thanks, for now."

It is hard enough dealing with the awful immediacy of the memories we do have, the cloying smells, and in the case of one unlucky witness who tripped and fell, the sick feel of offal under the fingertips. I get enough nightmares as is without adding encounters of strange creatures running around in the sewers into the curse of the Implant's perfect memories.

I skim through the results of the file-deletion searches. This is our usual division of labor.

Nothing stands out, or rather, too many things stand out.

Does my methodology have some fundamental flaw? With today's results, even after the parameter refinement of the black-market memories, there are thousands too many. There are disappearances from too long ago to have been caused by one man. False positives—if they were all correct, they would indicate a trail of death going back too many decades. The killer would have had to have started as a little kid and would by now be a withered, old man over a hundred. It has to mean that the program is failing to differentiate between the normal dangling ident codes that Lyn and I decided were due to innocuous garbage-collection programs or bureaucratic issues, and real disappearances.

We are still on my couch, in my room, on the twelfth floor of the Torus building. Our minds are far apart, in different digital landscapes, but still we are just a thought, a word, apart.

"Sure they're false positives?"

"Leon, the alternative is that the Mincemeat killer is immortal."

"Maybe there's not just one. Maybe . . ."

"What?"

He scowls. "Ya won't take me serious."

"I will."

Well, I do not after all. His idea of a Council-sponsored program for getting rid of undesirables among the crew? It would explain some things, but "they don't need some special assassination group. They can already Adjust anyone they consider dangerous, erase his memories outright."

"Maybe Adjustment don't work perfect all the time. Maybe this is for when it doesn't."

I take a deep breath and let it go. Like many of the theories Barrens comes up with, we cannot make conclusions about this one way or another until we have more data. He tends to think up things that disturb me.

What event in his childhood, what shortcoming by his Keepers, sabotaged his education? He is so much more than the test records in his file.

All the same, his latest theory does not feel right. Would this not draw more attention just from the sheer brutality? Why would assassins use such methods? On the other hand, nearly everything about these deaths has been successfully hidden so far, so maybe they're just that good. But why? And why those people?

"I know already, I know what you're thinking. But maybe it's for dealing with people who are getting too close to ISec's precious secrets."

No.

"Look, it's just an idea. I told you it's too early. But you must admit that the Ministry of Information is crazy paranoid about its secrets. Couldn't you see them deciding that coming too close to something forbidden justifies anything?"

"Hana, they lie to us every day. The lies are different depending on the crewman's rank. Maybe even whoever old man captains the ship doesn't know the whole truth. The truths we are taught are different depending on how we test in school. There are books everyone can read, books some people can read, and books that nobody is allowed to read; all determined by the Ministry of Information.

"We don't even know what the exact disaster on Earth was, and that's the biggest event in human history."

I clear my throat. "Well."

The problem is, he's not wrong. And I don't want to think that. I know ISec is more than Lyn's desk job and dealing with the data network and checking the validity of the testing procedures of children. Or there would be no need for the Enforcers, black-armored figures with both incredible psychic talents and brutal training to maximize what genetics they have.

I know that they have unchecked powers to detain, interrogate, and Adjust nearly anyone.

"What in the . . ." The couch cushions shift with Barrens's weight as he leans forward, frowning. "Hana, something's . . ." He sucks in a breath.

I minimize my internal display windows and look at the external on the tablet. The device flickers, lines of black-and-white static cut through the orderly lists and charts.

"I didn't just screw somethin' up, did I?"

"No, I don't . . ." We both stiffen up.

"Are you," he gasps, "you seeing this?"

The safe-wall built into the handheld is pierced; the contaminating data just goes right past it as if it were not there.

It is more than data, it is a telepathic reverberation buried in the electronic signal. Its echo resonates in the mind, picked up as if the neural Implant were an antenna.

Information creeps into my Implant and from Implant to brain. Crackling interference in my ears, numbness in the extremities. It is more than a data recording, but not quite a memory. Other stimuli that are not real ghost through me. I focus, I concentrate on the beating of my heart, the pulse of the blood in my veins, and trigger the security routines in the Implant. Program commands cascade in and out from metal to organic brain and back across the synapses.

Barrens scoots closer. His hand swallows up mine. *Hana, don't fight it.*

I can see his unfocused eyes darting wildly from side to side, up and down. *It could be dangerous. Some leftover neural virus that the program found.*

*It's important. It's . . . You have to see it.*

Another deep breath. *All right.*

———

I am a passenger along for a ride in someone else's skull. It is jerky and disorienting, not the smooth dive into a warm sea I am used to.

There is a sky above me. I feel it. The love for her own sky.

But it looks nothing like the blue skies from lost Earth I know through movies and paintings and textbooks and documentaries. Distantly, I am aware of my heart beating faster.

Corruption. That is what occurs to me at first. The sensory impressions of a memory that has been damaged. I stay aware of myself, keep from sinking fully into the experience. The eyes do not see right, the smell of the air is not foul, but off somehow, and the skin . . . The body itself feels wrong, different.

Turns the focal point of her awareness. Raises her arm in greeting.

Dizzying explosion of mental exchange, at thought densities that are beyond human.

The thoughts are indecipherable, the strangest music in the mind, sensations, feelings, ideas flashing in the darkness like dying stars.

The arm is a glossy grayish-blue. As is the flesh of everyone around her.

Sleek and sinuous. They have twofold symmetry: two arms and two legs and distinct left and right sides, and a front and a back. And that is where any similarity in appearance to humanity ends. Tall, wiry, and lean, their thin coils of muscle anchor at strange angles around their joints. The feet have no toes and they also have no fingers. The long, narrow faces are so unlike anything else I have seen that it takes a moment of forever to take in the sight. The bulging foreheads are proportionately larger than ours, and there is no hair to frame the shapes of the faces. They have no eyes, though depressions above their cheeks imply some vestigial remnants that could have been eyes in some ancestral species. Psychic sight provides the visuals. There are but the tiniest slits for nostrils. And their mouths are narrow, with small, flattened teeth.

Startlingly, they have the same, silvery emitter plates on their faces that we do.

My mind keeps attempting to impose human proportions and musculature onto the experience, and of course it fails, just as it fails to properly interpret the senses and thoughts of a mind that is nothing like my own.

They are strange to look upon but not ugly. There is a beauty to their smiles, which use fewer muscles than ours. Their clothes are simple in cut but radiate in colors the human eye does not see. They glide upon glowing currents of psi, willowy and graceful.

A second dawn, and a second sun rises into an incarnadine sky.

Her companion approaches. Their arms stop short of touching, but fingers of energy entwine, and that dense mental language roars, the music of an orchestra, so many layered threads of communication and melody, beats and hums and trills. There is something like warmth. There is something like love, but more than that, there is a profound, aching sadness, a sorrow that is quiet and mournful and all the colors of regret.

Those suns cast their light past the ridge of a vast hollow in the ground below them. Floating above, tiny blue birds. Others like themselves flit across a gigantic structure taking shape within a scaffolding of titanic energies.

I recognize that outline.

The vision cuts out there. Dissolves into static and snow.

Barrens and I come out of it and say nothing for a long time. We sink into the seat cushions. Less traumatizing than another Mincemeat memory, this is far more disturbing.

He takes a rumpled handkerchief out of his pocket and slowly dabs at my tears.

"That was the Noah, wasn't it?"

I swallow and clear my throat. "Maybe."

But if it was, then Noah was certainly not the name the Builders would have given to this ship.

Impossibly large, there in its cradle. The sweep of those wings as they were formed from tons upon tons of plastech, the mighty reactor vessels being packed together in the rear, artificial mountains . . .

It is worse for me than for Barrens. Since Callahan, he's not trusted the Council propaganda indoctrinated in all of us. That is not me. For me, this hunt has been out of curiosity and my obligation to and affection for him, and of course I want to do something only I can do, but I still had my faith, my beliefs in what I knew to be real.

I consider other possibilities. That it is a hoax. A prank left by clever young geniuses floating through the Nth Web. Or a failed entertainment project by an imaginative director.

It explains too many things. It explains why our research and development has been so slow on the Noah, despite eugenics programs selecting for improved intelligence and abilities. We find it difficult to improve on any of the technologies of the ship and our implants and amplifiers; we have only adapted

them. We still do not use more than a tiny fraction of the ship's computing potential, we still have not touched the limits of the vast spaces of the Nth Web.
Even the Implant technology in our heads—surely there is so much more it
could be used for. All our improvements have been in the realm of programming, all software, or the usage optimization of existing equipment. No hardware. Little to no progress at all in the pure sciences; physics, math, chemistry,
and biology have been at a standstill, and not because of the limited resources
and population on the ship.

The dormant nodes Lyn and I found are unused because we don't know
how to use them all. Possibly, the alien reactors powering everything simply
don't have as much fuel as they did during the time of the Builders, or maybe
we use them too poorly to make the most of them. The Nth Web, our clumsy
human programming running on top of the alien hardware, is just a façade. All
the inefficiencies, all the cracks in the system, are because it is not a human system we built ourselves, but something bigger than us, something we do not
fully understand.

Perhaps it is all humanity can do to get the Builders' technologies to work.

I feel Barrens's lips slide across my cheek, warm where they press against my
bare skin, cool where it contacts my emitter face plates. We are together, but
we are alone in our heads.

Why hide the history of the Builders? Why conceal the origins of the ship?
I have to stop. Where will my questions lead if I do not? Older questions then,
why we had to leave Earth at all. What was the catastrophe that destroyed our
home? Was it really destroyed? Just where are we going?

I talk and talk and talk about what it could all mean. Barrens just sits next to
me, listening, breathing.

When I have run over the same ideas for the third time, he pulls me onto his
lap, says slowly, "Mincemeat has nothing to do with the Builders though."

"Well . . . no. Perhaps they died before the ship even reached Earth. Or maybe
there are some still alive, being kept by the Central Council? Maybe—"

His paw enfolds mine. Warm, hard, it slows the unraveling tangle, the threads
of possibility spooling out in my head.

"For me," he rumbles, chest against my back, "this is still about people dying. It is a big deal, Hana, I know it is. But it is too big for the likes of me, when
all I want to do is hunt down whoever killed my friend."

A brief flare of anger dies out as fast as it flashes through me. Of course. Unless it has to do with these deaths, it is just a distraction to Barrens. For all that

he loved spending today relaxing with me, it is the hunt that brought us together, and it is the hunt that matters most. Whatever reasons Information Security has for keeping the Builders and the origin of the ship a secret, they are huge and vast and far in the past. But individuals are still being vanished, and our files on Mincemeat continue to grow.

The Hunter swarm is still finding more incidents that look like the work of Callahan's killer.

"Although . . . ," Barrens murmurs, frowning. "Nah. Never mind."

We lie in the darkness, waiting for sleep that does not come.

## 8

I ADD MORE SECURITY FEATURES TO MY MINER OF THE NTH WEB: BETTER PRO-
tocols to quarantine suspicious data. Barrens is not concerned about what the
pieces of Builder programming could do to it, but I am. It still grows and creeps
through the Analytical Nodes of the ship, churning through deleted and missing data.

Barrens keeps focused on what is in front of us, and not this great big mess
of secrets hanging over history. He is still a cop looking for a killer. I'm still just
a bureaucrat with some shortcuts through the system. I tell myself that the
ship's construction's occurring someplace else and being done by others does
not affect us. It does not affect the mission.

Ah, but it does.

A stolen moment on the rooftop of his precinct, overlooking Stern-2, one
of the four arteries cutting a straight path all the way through the dense mass of
construction in the Habitat Dome. Eight lanes wide, with ramps coming up off
the center, rising up to the threadlike ribbons above the city. All the police, fire,
and emergency-response centers are located close to one of these ramps, the
better to quickly send a force to any location they are needed in a city that is
vertical as much as it is horizontal.

Not much rain scheduled for today, but here and there throughout the Dome,
microclimates arise due to airflow and temperature pockets, and up here on the
roof, there is wind and mist and fog. His arm around my shoulders feels warm,
even through the layers of our coats.

"It doesn't feel like a *Hunter* to me."

He laughs quietly when I tell him that. "Too quirky to be *Hunter*? Could be you're right. I think there's a lot more we could be using it for. The right name will come."

Yes, there is the potential for so much more. Barrens would know, as he is expanding its functions. Occasionally, when I sample a cross section of the pieces of the swarm to see how its code is changing, the feel and response of some of the subunits has been tailored by another influence. I made this for him in the first place. I do not mind if he does his own customization, his own additions.

"It won't affect the primary search negatively, will it?"

"No. It's a population of semiautonomous programs—it would take a catastrophe to crash it now. Change it too much and you'll just have created an offshoot population, your own little horde."

"Gotcha."

He lets go of me to light a cigarette, puffs a slow stream out into the cold air. Our shoulders still touch, and I like to think I can still feel him even through that slight contact.

"I wish you wouldn't smoke." Even though most of the harmful chemicals are neutralized by catalysts integrated into the filter and throughout the substance of the cig, I just don't like how it smells. Well. Sometimes I don't like it, and sometimes the scent is comforting.

"Yeah, sorry. Been cutting down though, haven't I?"

He has. "What are you adding to the data-miner, Leon?"

"Stuff. There's some other things I want to find. And I've got this idea, you see. I'll tell you about it. I will. Right now, there's not enough to it."

"Can't you tell me now?"

He purses his lips just so around the cig. "Nah. I mean, right now, we'll just end up fighting about it."

Barrens goes on, "I'll say something about how it can't be just one guy anymore, there's got to be a bigger cover-up, and then you'll bang down the statistics and your higher clearance know-how and I'll just stand there like a lump of smolderin' coal and you'll get that look on your face and say sorry, and it will be like we'll pretend not to have talked about it."

Or he'll bring up how my bosses have lied to me about the Builders, so what else are they lying about, and then he'll be the one seeing that I feel hurt, whispering a quiet apology.

It has gone that way before, just as he says. Neither of us want to fight about questions that have no answers.

I shake off thoughts of how his cheeks and forehead turn bright red when he is passionate about something. I put aside his voice, at times too loud, at times too soft, and the restlessness of his hands when the ideas seem too big for his body. Our discussions about Mincemeat have grown heated; his theories growing wilder as I become more determined to shoot holes in them.

I am still stunned by the enormous deception about the ship. Why cut the others out of our history? Why make up human inventors for all these alien innovations? An entire false origin of the life-changing technologies on the ship has been made up and taught to us. The ship is not human. Plastech and the Implants are also from the Builders. Nearly everything about our way of life exists as a mask built on top of what *they* brought to us from the stars.

He sees something more than I do.

Barrens struggles to tie it together, convoluted strings of intuitive jumps. Theories about fundamental wrongs with the whole society, and Mincemeat and hiding the Builders, are all tied together, and those are the fights where we get uncomfortably loud. The virtual board inside his head that he shows to me has grown and grown, a space with all these pictures and ideas and files pinned into place and linked together with thread. Monsters in the tunnels, Breeding Duty, the Builders, secret deaths, early Retirements, Mincemeat. He is much more aggressive now, with his theories that either Mincemeat is a man operating with the tolerance of the Central Council, or is an entire secret function of Information Security. The question marks from earlier are still there, but now he has theories bolded out under them; too many of them.

Am I in denial? This other stuff with aliens, with the secrets held by the ship's Council, surely that has nothing to do with this. And I still refuse to believe that Mincemeat is a state-sponsored execution program. It just doesn't make sense that way. Too wasteful. And why such a gruesome means to do it?

Those particularly bad fights only happened twice.

Maybe this is what old-time marriage was like, knowing when *not* to talk about something anymore, and just accepting what's there.

"I'll tell you when there's something to it. Don't like arguing with ya, Dempsey. I . . . I like us best when we're quiet together."

I do too. "When will I see you next?"

He bends low, brushes his lips across the spot behind my ear. "A week, tops."

Then he escorts me down to the lobby, and I leave to go back to my office, and he watches me until I get on the right bus.

———

I worry when he is gone for a week or more. Though he is supposed to be a desk jockey, he still gets requested for pacification missions targeting turf wars between Psyn-dealers.

When such violent encounters occur, all police staff in that section of the Habitat get called in for support, especially those with such a wealth of combat experience as Barrens. The damage and injuries from these incidents are reported to the public as accidents and equipment failure. But I know, because of the forms that pass through my office beforehand from the police requesting special dispensation to draw "tactical yield" levels of power from the grid.

There is not a lot of crime on the ship. But even with surveillance technology the likes of which was beyond the dreams of the most paranoid authoritarian government on old Earth, with mind readers and data aggregrators and data-miners, the Psyn trade has proven impossible to stamp out.

Over the years, I have approved dozens of drug-prevention programs. And every Keeper is expected to inculcate the dangers of illicit substances to their charges and, above all, to warn them of Psyn.

Other drugs heighten pleasure, produce altered states, sometimes resulting in psychosis. But most of the damage they cause is internal.

The official origin of Psyn is that some kids came up with it in a school laboratory for a project a hundred years ago. The unofficial story, which is limited to the police and to officers in other Ministries of my rank and above, is that it was an attempt by the Ministry of Energy to augment the ship's fuel supplies by boosting the psionic abilities of test subjects to the point that they did not need amplifiers drawing on the power of the grid. An enzyme cocktail extracted from the pulverized amygdalae cloned from the strongest psychics of the first generation of the ship's crew from centuries before, and reprogrammed nanomachines based on the ones that are used to form the neural Implant, Psyn works by creating a feedback loop between the Implant and brain, allowing the power to build continuously, briefly creating inside the skull the quantum signature of the ship's psionic reactors. That's what the reports say, though the equations are beyond me.

What I know is that it works. It is Power, Power to avoid the destiny one's tests results can limit life to.

Power is addictive, and the psychic enhancement that Psyn grants has made it the only illegal drug that anyone risks Adjustment for. Every pleasure can be had in a legally obtained memory, for a price. But much more so than in any previous society, Power is money. A few precious milliliters of Psyn and a man of average *touch* can smash through a meter of hardened armor, without an amplifier. In school, in training, or at work, an undetectable drop in the blood can enhance one's performance for any psi-related task. On the edge of success and promotion or failure and punishment, the temptation for that little extra something is understandable.

The cost is a steady loss of self-control, growing paranoia, eventual psychosis.

Psyn can not only cause twisted dreams and nightmares of the first order, it can boost psionic ability enough to alter physical reality. To manifest nightmares and make them real. Even in those who react positively to Psyn, dangers are produced by the euphoria of power. Psyn-users often imagine themselves to be gods.

I try not to imagine Barrens smashing through a wall, where await a dozen mentally disturbed, violent individuals dizzy with their drug-boosted powers, waiting for a chance to show what they can do without society's expectations and rules holding them back.

Each day, I watch out for the damage reports, the accidents that these encounters are hidden as.

The week goes by and it is a relief when Barrens finally messages me that they've wrapped up another raid, that he's safe, and *would it be okay if I come by tonight?*

Most the time we are together, it is just how we like it. Quiet in each other's presence, talking softly, or working, or touching, or sleeping.

The work he does not tell me about does not bother me. We are our own selves still.

But when he receives a message in the middle of the night that springs him to wakefulness and he prepares to depart to do who knows what, dressed in ordinary civilian clothes and not his police blues, I am unhappy.

"I want to know, Leon. I've checked the rules—they can't pull you for another operation for at least a whole week. You're up to something else."

He pauses at my door, hand on the knob, shoulders wider than the doorframe, massive and imposing, an unreal figure, too large for the enclosed spaces of the ship. He looked most right when we were hiking through the false wilderness. He is meant for a larger world than the Noah.

"You're in enough hot water helping me with Mr. Mincemeat."

"With all the regs my programming is breaking, one more bit of something I'm not supposed to know won't affect how much Adjusting I'd get. Just tell me what else you're also working on."

He turns, and a kiss silences me for a long, tingling moment. His growing familiarity with what sets my nerves afire is blessing and curse.

He winks as he leaves. "Tell you soon. I'm close. Got a gift for you. Truth."

"I'll keep a pot on for you."

He gives me that savage grin. "Thanks. Shouldn't take too long." Which means he might be back at four in the morning.

When he leaves, I do fire up the coffee machine.

But I'm not waiting. I put on my own nightgear. A heavy coat that hides my curves, and a self-defense amplifier. Hard-capped boots. I put up my hair and hide it under a hat.

I go out too. I do not sleep well anyway, unless I have my beast next to me.


I choose a different location each time when I use a public-access terminal. A lightweight application I programmed into my tablet makes a semi-random selection, controlled with a series of parameters including ease of transportation and safety.

Tonight, chance has determined that I am to take a bus to the shopping district at the heart of the McKinley Section.

The rain is the drummer and all the Habitat the drum. Water percusses all those differently textured, different densities of plastech that compose the roads, the buildings, and my umbrella. It raises a soft, whispering rhythm as I walk to the closest stop for the E1 line.

The bus sighs when it stops, a bright yellow animal on six narrow wheels. It is all aerodynamic curves and shine, covered with subliminal ads for a performance being put on by some band that is popular with the school-age bracket. As I enter, the ads ping my Implant, playing samples of their thumping music, opening a frame in my eyesight showing the slick-skinned, bare-chested youths yowling onstage, while a sea of young faces chant their adoration. I would have found those young boys deliciously pretty, once. I close the streams and flag them as spam.

The bus driver yawns, sees me without looking, and nods sleepily in acknowledgment. It is empty at this hour, and I choose a seat in the middle.

The city lights slide by as the bus hums and rolls. Its engine is a limited amplifier under control of the driver. The wheel in his hands does not steer and the pedals at his feet connect to nothing—they are physical representations of mental commands to focus his concentration. His mind propels the vehicle forward, controls the steering and the braking, and in his eyesight, the roadways are lit up and highlighted and labeled by the bus software.

The bus tilts back as it glides up the steep on-ramp to the port-to-starboard 5 highway. The narrow roads going up and down through the city are glassy threads in the night. Other vehicles I see in farther parts of the section glimmer as they go up and down and along the skyways so far above the ground level, the elevated roads so thin they are almost invisible in the distance.

Soon, one of the great air locks yawns before the bus. The walls dividing the Habitat sections are thirty meters of specially processed, high-density plas-tech. In the event of a major accident, such as a relativistic velocity meteorite punching a hole through the hull, the city sections can be isolated in a tenth of a second.

I wonder how often the gates are tested. They have never been used.

*Far as you know,* Barrens would say.

Shut it, you. You're not even here and you're making me paranoid.


When I enter the access-terminal shop, the manager barely looks at me. Have humans gotten quieter, because of our technologies, because of being able to live in our heads and replay whatever, whenever? I am surrounded by two dozen men and women of different ages and backgrounds and we are, each of us, alone.

The heart of the Londinium shopping district is also the primary financial center for the Habitat, where Economic Management, another department under the Ministry of the Interior, monitors all production, consumption, pricing, and salary allocation. In the square kilometer just outside the door is the greatest concentration of skyscrapers and high-end stores.

I touch the bot fragments of the Hunter swarm lurking on the various forums of lonely, sleepless people on the ship, and they return bits of interesting conversations.

Most of these threads I just copy automatically, to screen through later. Teenagers talking about stories their Keepers tell to scare them, of monsters in the sewers, of a dreaded killer monitoring the Web for potential victims.

Wait. What?

*Mincemeat killings have always been around,* posted malta194x.

What is this?

Behind my closed lids, my eyes flicker up and down as I scan a particular thread of postings and replies. They keep using *Mincemeat* as a term. And there are static 2-D pictures. Gruesome images of the sort I have seen before. Different dates. Uploaded by different users.

I unfold the structure of the thread deeper and deeper, examining post after post. One forum name appears the most: jaegercal.

He asks, "What could explain the level of damage in these images?" He asks if there are broader implications. He asks others to help him build a timeline. Other posters mock him. Call him a nutter if they're from Londinium or *atama ga kurutteru* if they're from Nippon Re-creationists or a Don Quixote if they were trained in the Arts and Literature Preservation Program. But some are serious contributors and mention specific names, supposed victims that died ten years before, thirty years before. Longer.

MalthusMarx declares, "This whole thing is ridiculous, because it means Mincemeat's kills number in excess of a hundred. Information Security might hide such a thing, but the Council would never allow so many killings, something that disrupts the balance of the ship."

And jaegercal replies, "Does that not imply that it is something more than just one killer?"

CactusRose concurs. And adds, "Your suspicion is that all Mincemeat Deaths are being covered up as early Retirements, but are not early Retirements anomalies in the first place? Maybe the question is not how many early Retirements are Mincemeat victims, but whether all early Retirements are."

The thread explodes into a whirlwind. It comes down, mostly, to jaegercal, who becomes the de facto moderator for these posters. And CactusRose, who alarms me with cutting insights that egg on the mass of them into considering darker and darker possibilities.

I set Hunter to search for jaegercal. Because I know the feel of that writing. Immediately, there are more hits, also in these low-population channels, the unmonitored regions of the Nth Web where the criminal element sometimes does its business. These areas on the periphery are ghost zones on low-use Analytical Nodes that come fully online only when additional processing power is needed. There are so very many of them, and the Nth Web is gigantic in the first place, too big for the finite resources of the Ministries to watch everything.

Traces suggest that jaegercal has also been active in forums about alien conspiracies. And about . . . Breeding Duty?

A few moments to find the ident code and comparing it to the memory of the first table of dangling IDs we found, and there it is. That long alphanumeric string was one of the first dozen that Leon and I found together.

It doesn't have to be him. But the way he writes is the way I hear him talking, and I know it's him.

Oh, Leonard, what are you doing?

I run traces on that name. It is a relief to see them dead-end. At least he's been careful.

How long, I wonder, before these forums are deleted, and the less cautious participants brought to the attention of Information Security? Or will they slip through the cracks, just like all the dangling ident codes floating through the system?

I download the contents of those forums and flash the local history of the terminal.

Around me, other night owls play games on the system and mess around with their friends, doing things they do not want their Keepers to catch them at.

I exit the public-terminal shop, get on another bus, and sit in the rear.

It's packed. An offset shift is ending, and another is beginning. Officemates and maintenance workers talk about their stiff necks and aching feet and joke about all the sex they're not getting, or about how hot this one girl is, except she's gay.

A few of them look at me, and not with that casual weight of physical interest, but with concern. A deep breath, and I steady my expression. Placid. Empty.

Barrens wants to protect me to the extent that he can. That includes keeping me out of things he can do on his own. Ah, but it stings. I want him to need me more. I want him to tell me everything, the way I've been telling him everything.

My will pages through the menus. Starts music playing in my thoughts. The application in my hand streams mournful torch songs with wailing saxophones, and women with voices that throb with implied hurt.

I hope he doesn't read too much into the words of those crazies.

A deep breath, a sigh.

I'm not a sappy teenager, and it isn't as if he's cheating on me.

I'll get it out of him. I won't ambush him when I get home. But he'd better talk to me about it on his own by New Year's. I resolve to not be so defensive when he comes to me with what he's found, to think into logic that which he does through intuition. All along, I've been getting deeper and it was always my choice.

# 9

My dreams take a dark turn.

I suppose they should have much sooner, with all the work Barrens and I are putting in. Memories of gory ends. Always thinking about this killer, these disappearing victims.

When Barrens is not around, I wake up with my pillow and my face wet with tears.

I wish I could just get it out of my system. It is different, remembering while inside a dream. The quality of the recollection is still perfect, but the subconscious mind interprets it, stretches and shrinks it, distorts time sense, degrades some aspects and heightens others.

It was all getting chased through the darkness, some terrible, silent, immense shape lumbering after me. One recurring dream stands out though. Just myself, giving birth, while another me watches. A younger me.

When Barrens is with me, he shakes me awake before the worst of it. When he is there, the nightmares are less frequent in the first place. Tonight, I wake to his heavy paw shaking me.

That awful one again. Birth, blood, my child being taken from me. While something that looks like me, but isn't, watches. Watches.

"You guard me even in my sleep, huh?"

He yawns and rumbles something like "Course," before turning on his other side and drifting back to sleep. "Course I do."

It's 4:27 a.m. by my internal clock. Not worth trying to go back to sleep, not with how long it will take my heart to stop racing. Might as well get ready for the workday. Have breakfast.

A hot shower, and I check over my most recent scan of the Hunter.

Barrens must be working hard on his programming skills because the complexity he's adding is impressive. New modules are coming online, particles in the swarm that do other things, not just for evaluating other kinds of information, but communications functionality, secure data sharing.

One omelet for each of us just takes me a few minutes. His breakfast is supplemented with a giant glass of the thick, generic protein/grain slush that is the free staple food provided to everyone on the ship. He has a heavy workout scheduled this evening and will need a ton of calories to fuel him.

He lumbers out of bed and showers.

Cheese and red onion and egg, hot in my mouth. I scan a translucent window of text in my vision while eating. Hovering between my plate and my face, the neural Implant's internal display shows today's news. More articles about the coming holidays, schedule changes, weather changes. Output results of the vertical farms are always portrayed as positive—shortfalls never make it to the news. Something about a fire in the textile district of Moskva Section. Is that a genuine accident report, or a cover-up for something else?

It's not my place to know. I would have accepted that, once.

I never repeated that night where I checked on Barrens's activities using other ident codes. I told myself I wouldn't ask until he was ready. But if he wants me to stop just blindly accepting what ISec says is proper . . .

It's not nagging. It isn't. "Hey, you. Been putting a lot of work in growing our baby?"

"Mrraaagr. Backscatter. Signal stuff. Routing," he mumbles. "Dijkstra. You know. *Stuff*. Been looking for ways to hide information as Network background noise."

"What are the comms for?"

He blinks, wakes up a little at the tone of my voice. Really looks at me. "I'm almost there," he says softly. "I will tell you, and it will be soon."

"You better."

"I will." He pauses.

Barren's fingers turn my face gently. Ah. Wow. It is a long, lingering kiss, while another hand slides up from my waist, under my shirt. So hard, those hands, and rough; it still surprises me how gentle they can be. He pulls a moan out of me.

A little breathless now. "Good morning to you too."

He grins. Pleased with himself. He drops into the other chair, which creaks with his weight. He savors each bite of the eggs, grimaces, and bolts down the cheap stuff. I like to watch him eat. He is not sloppy or disgusting. But food vanishes in front of him. Heaping spoonfuls, chewed rapidly, neatly, swallowed down. And he is always appreciative.

Another slow kiss after we're done.

"Unless you're going to take the morning off," I get out, "you'd better stop that."

His grin is boyish. "Yeah, yeah."

"What time will you be by?"

"I don't know. I'll message you."

We leave together and split up at the street.

By the time I reach City Planning, I suspect I still have a somewhat dazed smile on my face. I'd best not be thinking about those smoldering kisses where Hennessy can peer at me and do his best impression of a Behavioralist. His teasing gibes are playful, but they can be sharp and too perceptive. I ought to put my foot down and remind him that I'm his superior . . . but I do like him. And he is quite good at what he does.

It says something about society that the most exciting thing in the office to gossip about is the boss's love life.

"They think he's beneath you, that's all," Hennessy remarks as he drops off another packet of proposals. "That makes it juicier. Now, now, don't get upset."

"I'm not upset." I am upset.

"It's not what I think. I think he's been good for you. You've looked a lot more alive. Since the two of you got together. But you know, the whole society is built around metrics, test scores, assigning every person like pegs to their holes. When people see you together, and it's obvious there's a, ah, rank gap . . . People wonder about what the two of you have in common, what you do together, and such."

Rank gap!

"James, I've been letting this go for too long. It's one thing if it's you. But the rest of the team . . . Get them focused on their work. Cool off talk about Barrens and me, okay? Or the worst offenders will find themselves buried in the secretarial pool."

He raises his hands in surrender. "I'll warn them."

The next proposals to come in front of me are subjected to my most vicious evaluation, with endless corrections and brutal comments. So there.

Barrens comes at lunch, a great big presence in my doorway. To everyone else, his face probably looks its usual fierce and focused best. But to me, the nervous anxiety is plain. He is worried.

He almost lifts me out of my chair and hugs me too tightly.

*Leon! Not in the office!* He lets me push back a bit, though his hands stay on my shoulders.

"You're okay," he whispers. "Anything, ah. Anything odd happen around here lately?"

"No. What's this about?"

"Let's take a walk. The bean-dog stand down the block's got a special today, two for one."

I ought to be annoyed. He is almost dragging me. People are staring. But there is such fear on his face. Fear for me. Every once in a while, he pauses, glows with psi for a second, cranes his neck and inhales, long and deep. He leads me to the plaza two blocks away from the monolithic cube of City Planning. A large fountain in the middle is festooned with baroque statues, marble figures of imposing, muscular angels and fat, little cherubs. And we keep walking.

*What is it?*

*Someone is onto us.*

"What?"

My knees want to give way. A thousand terrors spark and come alive, and I clamp down on them hard, pasting a mask of calm on my face, even as my heart seems to grow determined to escape out of my chest.

Barrens takes a breath to compose himself. He sends me brief flashes of memory.

*Bruisers,* when they use their talent, also have enhanced senses. But I do not have his training. And since I have to keep walking by his side, I can only do a partial immersion, so the contents are further removed from me. All I can tell is that they are brief moments several seconds long. One was from that day he was watching me interview Gorovsky. The others have him standing at various locations, neck craned, looking around. Standing at a sidewalk. The chowder place we like. *What do you want me to see?*

*There's a scent! A scent keeps repeating. I didn't think anything of it at first, but this morning, I smelled it again while doing my run. It just clicked in my head. Someone is closing in on us.*

The concentration required to form Implant-to-Implant messages distracts me from panicking. Staves off the formless anxiety skittering up my spine. In my imagination, there is already a thin man in ISec grays on our heels.

We walk and talk on the move. Sometimes we talk out loud and sometimes we message each other in our heads.

The major streets of the Habitat tend to be oriented in concentric loops from the smallest ring road in the heart of the Dome to Circle-zero, the twelve-lane highway just inside the Dome. Most of the lesser streets are a grid of straight lines with names indicating which section that stretch of road is in, and either a number, indicating a port-to-starboard orientation, or a letter, which means the road runs along the length of the ship. Some of the roads are at Deck-zero, the street level of the Habitat, some rise up into the sky, and some descend into the underside of the Habitat.

Only the top few hundred officers of the ship are allowed to have private vehicles. The rest of the crew in their tens of thousands walk, take the bus, take the train, ride bicycles. Around us, men and women in practical steel or slate or coal business attire or uniform jumpsuits laugh on their way to get food.

For an hour we zigzag along the Thames Streets. From the picturesque little, apple-tree-lined, pseudo-cobblestone Thames 3 Street to the four-lane Thames F Street with its midrange retail clothing stores. The mannequins in false silk and suede wave to us as we turn onto the 5, lined with small office buildings, mostly subcenters for accounting and ship-inventory management— three-floor, gray cubelets that report to City Planning. We walk the bridge over a picturesque stream called the Thames, ever so much smaller than the real one was. We pass corner pubs and little shops with replicas of precious authentic antiques preserved in nonreactive-gas vessels under nondamaging low-energy light. Soon, we reach the ring road Thames Central, set around an arc-shaped public-access park.

Along the little brick footpaths under the sun or under the shade of trees in autumn foliage, we wonder if we need to run, while we talk as if it is still we who are the hunters.

"If this stranger is following us based on our Web accesses, which I am pretty sure is nearly impossible, then he would be appearing at the places from which we have logged in with the dangling IDs—locations that are far apart, and which we do not use more than once. Or he could have traced it to us directly, in which case he would already know exactly who we are."

"Can't be," Barrens says. "Can't." He sends me a map of the city, with points lit up indicating where he's come across the stranger's scent. This individual, and Barrens is sure that it is an individual male, is somehow tracking us physically, from location to location.

*How? Could a* bruiser *scent-track us like that?*

Barrens shakes his head. *No. Even when we use the talent, we're no bloodhounds. And even specially bred dogs can only track scent trails that are several days old. This guy's appearing at places we were at a month before or more. I can't figure out how he's doing it.*

"Are you sure it's just one man?"

"Yeah, I'm sure." *I've searched my Implant plenty, trying to cross-index scents. Only this guy appears repeatedly, and he only started showing after we started. He's not from my precinct, he doesn't work at City Planning, he's never been around your friends.*

There is at least the relief that it is not Information Security. Or we would already be in their custody

Could it happen by random chance? I could run the odds in my head, based on population concentrations and City Planning studies on crew residence and job location. Probabilities won't give me an answer one way or another.

I choose to have faith in Barrens's instinct. Unfortunately, there is no crew database identification category for *scent*!

He lets out a grim chuckle when I complain about this. *You can certainly propose it to the database guys above me. I'm sure you could make a very convincing study.*

A thought strikes me, and I shiver. *Leon. Did you detect this scent when Callahan died?*

*I didn't have an amplifier on me that day.*

Around us, ordinary men and women in business attire are finishing up their coffees and sandwiches and cigarettes. The younger kids are done with classes for the day; a handful of girls and boys play around the fountain, splashing each other with telekinetic bursts. It is a beautiful day in the fall, bright and cool, pleasant as only Hennessy's best could program into the simulation parameters.

*Do you think it's Mincemeat?*

*I don't know what to think.*

Too soon, we have to return to work.

He pleads with me. He never does that. "Please. Just be careful, okay?"

"I will." *Leon. It's you who needs to watch yourself. He's closer to finding you than me. I can take care of myself.*

I want to protest that I can take care of myself too. Shit. I don't even always keep my civilian self-defense bracelet on me. Something I will change immediately.

He gives me a fierce, almost angry kiss, right as we reach the base of the steps leading up to my ugly, gray office building. A sigh escapes me; it would be just that kind of day someone from my team would be looking out through the right window exactly at this moment.

"Wait for me later. I'll take you home."

"Okay."

We let go and walk away from each other. Both looking over our shoulders.


The rest of my workday would be a total waste if I let it. I indulge in just fifteen minutes of this. My head buzzing with possibilities. Petrified in my chair. My eyes note the reports in front of me, but I just cannot take them in. All the while, my team is quietly doing their thing, *too quietly,* which means they are all chatting with each other Implant to Implant, probably about what looks like a fight between Barrens and me.

Then I shake it off, put it aside. I need to work, so I work. Mala's mental tricks shunt aside emotion, grant me clarity and focus and emptiness. I open five files at once; they float over the desk, visible only to me, as I pull out the paper reports and begin to cross-reference them with the live data in the Nth Web.

Finally, the day is done. Barrens and I meet up, ignoring, once again, my coworkers' curious gazes, and go to my place.

"No," I tell him.

His face goes all tight. "Gotta find him first. Before he finds us."

"And I'm doing it with you."

"Hana . . ."

"No, Leon." I am scared for him too. He is not going to take all the risk and try to keep me safe.

Our arms are crossed as we stare each other down. The words get stuck in his throat, and he is about to think his argument at me, but I cheat and throw all my feelings at him. Everything I'm feeling. For him.

One last time, he tries to order me, "Just do as I say, you crazy broad!"

I focus psi at the carpet under my feet, convert the plastech, lift myself up on a growing footstool until my eyes are even with his.

"You. Are. Not. Going. Without. Me."

He throws his hands up and stalks off to the balcony. Lights a cig, puffs away.

I sink into the couch in my living room, trying hard to push away the urge to shiver.

After Barrens burns through half a pack, I see him let out a massive sigh, his great shoulders deflating. He comes back in.

"This is the deal. You do what I say to stay safe. And when I think I'm getting close, I will let you know, and if it ain't impossible, I'll take you with."


When Barrens and I began our foray into the hidden, I was cavalier in response to his safety concerns.

Now, it no longer feels so paranoid. I accept his desire to shadow me on my way to and from work to watch for others watching for me. Every evening, he reminds me to check my tablet for worms or spybots. He screens my apartment for listening devices and more subtle psionic recorders while I sleep—I know because I have seen the detection gear in his duffel bag in the morning.

I find myself noticing every stranger in City Planning, wondering whether he or she belongs, afraid I'll be caught looking. Among the many hundreds of individuals that I pass every day, is there one with a violent secret, a destructive urge that, for some reason, is indulged by the Noah's Central Council?

After two days, Barrens introduces me to Officer Miyaki Miura.

The diner is small, open only late at night and on weekends. The décor is 1950s Americana. Prints of those old petrol-burning cars and trucks. Black and whites of the famous actresses from the movies not on the ISec proscribed list. The owners are workers at the vertical farm who run this restaurant as a hobby. Between the overhead for rent and the expenses for their supplies, their culinary skills allow them a price scale that probably just allows them to eat a slightly better class of food. Denser synthetic meat. A slightly richer blend of margarine. A milk substitute that is almost like real milk.

She is there before us, stands when we enter. Officer Miura is a broad-shouldered woman with a delicate face. Porcelain cheeks, and bright gems for eyes and lips. She is diminutive, petite even with the bulk of the blue Inspector's overcoat. It is one I have seen before. I know her of course, though we have never met before today. I know her from combat briefings and after-action reports I have dipped into, and when Barrens would toss and turn at my side in the midst of nightmares, it is her name he muttered. She is the other woman closest to Barrens. A sister in battle, who has bled for him and whom he has bled for too.

She is as intimidating as I imagined she would be.

"Um. Hello."

"Hi."

We shake hands. I am taller, but her hand is larger than mine. It is steel under the glove, tense, all carefully controlled power. I wonder if all field peace officers have this coiled-spring tension in all their movements. Perhaps it is a by-product of their training, just as the dreamy-eyed, distracted looks that afflict me are a by-product of mine, an indicator of the multithreaded thought trances analysts maintain through most of the working day. She openly eyes me up and down. What does she see in me? I've wanted to meet her for a while, curious about this other woman in Barrens's life, the only other who knows about his beast. But I am not happy to meet like this, with his saddling her with my safety.

"Sorry about this."

"Don't be sorry. The big lug just cares about you is all. He's a worrier."

Barrens's glower is particularly fierce. "When I'm not around, you gotta protect her, Miya."

"Okay already." She rolls her eyes. "Nothing's going to happen, Barrens."

The booths are designed for parties of four. She has one bench all to herself and slouches to take up all that space. She is languid, at ease, but her eyes are still sharp, flickering around the diner, examining every person who enters and leaves.

Crammed together on the opposite bench, Barrens and I barely fit. It might be easier if I sat on his lap. Barrens has been with me long enough that I have grown accustomed to how much larger he is than the average; eating out is always a reminder.

We have a short, quick meal together, us three. Tofu burgers and fried yam chips. Ice cream that is more natural than artificial. We chat about everything except for why Barrens wants her to be my part-time bodyguard.

Then Officer Miura cocks her head to one side, as those who receive a direct message often do. She has to go. "Assignment and all. Good to meet you, Ms. Dempsey. I'll be by in the morning at seven."

I am to never go anywhere alone. He practically moves into my apartment, except for nights when we are both at his. He changes the locks on our doors and has me reinforce the hinges with a special telekinetic processing that makes them more resistant to TK manipulation. I don't know what good that will do, considering how Mincemeat got to Callahan through a thick door triple-bolted from the inside.

Miyaki Miura is faintly amused when it's her turn to keep an eye on me. She knows about our looking into Callahan's death, but not the scope of it, or how many other similar deaths there have been. Mostly, she talks about the old days, about being Barrens's partner through police academy and their first years in the force. Sometimes, she complains about her low income, and how much money she has to spend on food. She complains about the Psyn rings that have been spreading throughout the Habitat, kids riding the highs of enhanced psychic ability at the cost of burned-out brain cells and psychosis.

Unlike Barrens, she does not much care about politics and history, which is a relief. I get more than enough of that with Leon.

When he was shunted to Long Term Investigations, she got a promotion. And rates a police car. It's an interesting change, the mornings and evenings when she drives me around. I rank a private-vehicle permit, but anything more substantial than a bicycle is ridiculously pricey, and I live close to a train station and multiple bus stops.

Like Hennessy, Miyaki has no problems with getting a little too personal. "So, Miss Dempsey. What's he like in bed, our great big beastly friend?" Her smile is wicked.

"Uh." Stammering, I try to turn it around. "You don't know?"

"It never worked out between me and him. We're just not each other's type. Actually, before you, I didn't think there was anyone, man or woman, who was his type."

That heats up my cheeks more than her too informative tales about her multitude of boyfriends.

Miyaki turns the wheel. The narrow wedge of the car whispers around a corner. She is careful and aware of all our surroundings. Like Barrens, she does not need *reading* talents to get a read on people.

"You are the only one he's ever fallen for," she says, something sad and happy in her voice. "There have been others. But you know him. He's different inside from how he seems. They never lasted."

"I like you together. And he's a good friend to me. Which is the only reason I'm humoring this current bout of looniness."

She drops me off at my apartment and stays long enough to watch me unlock the building's outer door and enter.

The days pass without incident. Maybe it is just a coincidence. Maybe we are getting too deep into this. Are we at the point where we're scaring ourselves, looking for shadows where there aren't any?

Barrens, of course, has no doubts. We spend every night talking about our stranger. About what we can do to catch him first.

He is out there. He is closing in on us every day.

# 10

THE BEST IDEA WE COME UP WITH IS TO KEEP VISITING THE LOCATIONS OUR
stalker has already tracked us to. It seems too passive to me, and what's worse is
we can't just stake out all these locations on our own. We still have our jobs. At
most we can make a map of locations where Barrens has scented our man and
the dates he's done so, then try to rotate through those locations when we can
go there, mostly after our workdays are over and weekends.

It is dependent on chance for so many reasons. Barrens can't just stand
there with his amplifier continuously activated. The calorie burn would be
enormous—he'd have to eat enough for a normal person's daily intake of calories for each half hour with the amp on even the lowest power draw. So he has to
use an app that automatically turns it on for a few seconds out of every minute.

The strobing effect on his senses gives him a constant headache.

Barrens wants to do it on his own and keep me safe and far away. Nuts to
that.

"You're not leaving me behind for anything," I keep having to tell him
every time before we leave to follow the strange, not-quite random pattern of
the stranger's scent.

Weeks pass like this, and my nerves tighten up with the passing days, until
the occasional evening when I can't take it anymore and force Barrens to take a
break with me. To attend a jazz concert. To go dancing. To just watch an old
movie.

But we always return to this. Standing with Barrens in an alley next to the
chowder place, or at this train station or that one, or in the park where I met
Gorovsky, we watch people come and go. Is it this guy, or that guy? Wondering if it's Mincemeat. And if it is, what would a monster look like?

In the meantime, my program still spreads and searches throughout the Web. I can't understand how there can be so many Mincemeat vanishings; I'm sure they must be false positives, just as Barrens is sure they are not.

If we happen across him, will Barrens smell him first? Or will he detect us first, through whatever means the stranger has managed to find us?

Friday evening and I couldn't get out of it. The terrible three insisted and dragged me out to the paintball course. They also invited half of our graduating class from school. At least only thirty came.

"Didn't you miss this?" Jazz laughs while glowing globs of paint fly overhead.

We're crouched behind my hastily erected barrier; just a mound of earth three feet high.

The course is a maze. The rules are that anyone can use one of the guns, or use *touch*, but not both, and no amplifiers.

She shrieks and ducks as a hail of blue spheres curves around my wall, necessitating some impressive and desperate tumbling to avoid the splatter.

Down the range, Lyn laughs at us. "Come on, D, do your thing!"

"Ooooh, that's it now." Jazz glows. Without an amp, her touch of *bruiser* is still substantial enough to give her performance at the edge of human ability—enough for a nine-second hundred-meter dash. She ducks and dives, a demented ballerina laughing as she *touch*-flings paintballs from her waist belt right back at Lyn.

I am *not* in the mood to be running around playing at battle.

But they are my friends, and I'm being mopey and it's not fair to them. "Hey, wait for me!"

I don't have any *bruiser*'s psychometabolism at all, so compared to Jazz, I move in slow motion. But I do have the strongest *touch* talents of anybody in today's game, and as I charge like a snail behind Jazz, I keep pulling up earthen barriers an inch thick to block incoming fire. They're paintballs—it doesn't take much of a wall to stop them.

Then I make like the artillery and send the other group squealing in retreat as, still jogging forward, I fling up my hands and fire up half my pack of paintballs all at once. The red blobs blur and chase the enemy as they run. I scatter half a dozen of Marcus's Water Department buddies and Lyn's team from Nth Web R&D in about five seconds. When I lose sight of my targets, I have enough control to stop the projectiles without crushing them, then retarget and shoot them again.

"That is totally unfair," Jazz says admiringly, laughing. "I'm suddenly remembering why we stopped playing paintball halfway through school."

Marcus yells from the bottom of a ditch, out of sight, but I saw him jumping in and guessed right at his position when I sent half a dozen blurs his way. He always sits still too long after taking cover. "Son of a bitch! I just got my hair done!" He stands, shaking his fists in Lyn's general direction, in a bunker that serves as their side's base. "You just *had* to get her going!"

Now I'm laughing too. "Hey, you wake up the dragon, you get the fire, baby!"

For a couple of hours, we're kids again.


It is Saturday, the night just after I played at chasing and being chased by my friends.

And now, Barrens and I are not playing, at all. We are stalking even as we are being stalked.

It is a cold night. There are no stars tonight, just thick clouds, a haze reflecting the glow from the city.

I see him before Barrens smells him.

A slender man in a long coat, with a hat. I notice him because, as he walks along the sidewalk, he keeps stopping, and . . . touching things. Lampposts. The handles to the doors into the buildings. He does not seem drunk. He is not swaying or stumbling. Sometimes, he just brushes those long, slender fingers against an object. Sometimes he stays with his hands on something for ten minutes at a time.

He passes without turning to look at the opposite side of the street, where we are. Under the bright circle of a streetlamp, his face is astonishingly young. He looks like a teenager. This . . . this can't possibly be our killer. Can it? If it is . . . the dates of so many of our hits are wildly off.

*Don't follow close.*

Barrens glides out of the alleyway. Glides. It seems impossible someone so large can walk so quietly. His badge is on the inside of his coat; only a little bit of its red glow leaks as he moves. He crosses over to where our quarry is.

I take a deep, deep breath of the frosty air. When Barrens is half a block away, I follow too.

*Crap. He practically already found me.*

Haltingly, the stranger is making his way toward the South Edo Precinct. Barrens's station.

At every street corner, the slender figure touches the post for the pedestrian lights, the transmission boxes that project ads into the neural Implants of everyone that passes.

When the stranger passes the next alley, Barrens pours it on. Each step covers several feet. In an instant, Barrens is there.

His arm comes around from behind, clamps tight against the smaller man's face. A second more, and both of them vanish into the gap between two shophouses that are closed for the evening.

Even if the street had not been empty, I wonder if anyone would have noticed.

I walk the rest of the distance, quick as I can.

When I get there, Barrens has the boy hoisted up against a wall. His huge paw is clamped tight against the other's neck. Both the kid's hands don't as much as budge the steel pillar that is Barrens's arm.

"You're going to tell us who you are," Barrens growls. "And how you found us."

Wide-eyed, red-faced, the boy croaks something out.

"What was that?"

Gasping, the boy repeats himself. "I . . . juh-just . . . w'nted . . . ta . . . know . . ." Panicked, he broadcasts to both of us; he has more *writing* talent than I do and pushes a flood of murky images and thoughts at us telepathically, rather than through Implant messaging. Most of it is too unfocused to understand, but there is a single, clear image.

It is the inside of a coffin apartment. And it is covered in blood, bone fragments, offal.

His mind's voice screams at us, *Want to know! Want to know!*

*Leon . . . put him down. He . . . he's like you. Like us.*


"Joe. Joe November. Everybody calls me Bullet though, on account of this stupid haircut back in school. Hair's different now, but the name stuck." His voice is still a raspy whisper. He keeps massaging his throat. "Dude. I wasn't fighting back or nothing. Did you have to grab me so hard?"

Barrens keeps a steady, cold gaze on him as he sips his bourbon. He says nothing, content to let me do the talking.

I start to apologize. "Sorry, Joe, but—"

"Bullet, ma'am. Nobody's called me Joe since my Keeper." He manages this small smile. The dimples make me want to pinch his cheeks.

*Bullet then. We had to be careful. You might've been dangerous.*

"Yeah, yeah. Fine. Nothing permanent."

We have the corner booth in the very back of the smoky establishment just a few blocks down from the precinct. It's another of Barrens's cop hangouts. Particularly cheap fake-wood paneling covers everything. Lots of static 2-D pictures are on the walls, of groups of police officers eating together. The dates go back to the first generation of the Noah's crew. The bar and the tables up front are occupied by half a dozen off-duty blue coats complaining loudly at the display feed hanging from the ceiling. On it, the sports news is covering Edo Section's baseball league, which has been saddled with a scandal: the pitcher of the top team has been accused of wearing a concealed amplifier during games.

Nobody is paying attention to us, except for Officer Miura, sitting at the near end of the bar, giving us the occasional, curious glance. Mostly though, she keeps her eyes down on her tablet. I can hear her groaning loudly about the particulars of a case report she is struggling to fill out.

Bullet takes a swig of beer and grimaces. "So. Um. What's next?"

I can't help tilting my head this way and that and peering at him. "How old are you?"

He fidgets, mumbles, "Twenty-seven. It's just genetics."

His face is small and round like a mouse's. Apple-cheeked and skinny and awkward as if he might be all of fourteen. Thick, dark curls, girlish eyes with long lashes. I like him. He shouldn't be mixed up with all this. But we have something dark and serious between the three of us.

"You first," Barrens rumbles.

Bullet stares at him, then me.

*My story starts probably like yours does. No. Uh. First I need to explain . . .*

"Take your time. We got all night."

*I'm a Keeper Certification Examiner. Ah. No, that's not where I should start either.*

His hands start shaking. Biting his lip, he pulls them in, clenches them against his pants.

*Let's begin with this.* He shows it to us again. A vision that is familiar, gruesome, terrible. Sasha. In pieces.

He tells us of the fluctuating ratings of Apollo Gorovsky. Of how he did not usually personally involve himself in the test results of Keepers, but found himself interested because of the unusual circumstances around Gorovsky's partner's early Retirement, just as they had been assigned a child to raise.

*Sasha and Apollo were just starting out. She hadn't even finished moving out of her solo apartment. Weeks after Keeper Gorovsky started his repeated requests for a new, permanent partner, I went to her old place and . . .*

Bullet falters then. He orders and consumes another beer before he continues. *The thing is, I have this extra talent, you know? Or, you probably don't know.*

He yelps as I lean across the table, staring at a cluster of silver emitter plates. On his palms.

"Psychometry!" I whisper, intrigued. "That's how you found us."

This rare talent does not serve much purpose on the ship. It does not help in building or growing things, it does not help people understand themselves, and with the perfect memories given to everyone by neural Implants, it rarely helps even in police investigations, which are mostly about documentation and collecting the right memory from the right witness.

Bullet explains that it is like playing back someone else's memory, except that it is a memory of an object or place, instead of something living. How strange that must be, feeling the psychic imprint of events through inanimate things. The stronger one is, the clearer the vision, and the farther back one sees. It is uncommon in the first place, and those that have it rarely see beyond five minutes. Bullet's talent is extremely strong; sometimes when he touches something, he has flashes that go back months or years. Sometimes a complete vision lasts long moments; sometimes it is merely a feel, a vibration, a taste.

*There are no amps for psychometry, so I don't have much control. I only get the strongest impressions most of the time. But when I touched Sasha's clean, empty room, it went crazy. It's like I was there. Just after she was torn apart.*

He was overwhelmed of course.

The vision began to consume him.

*I visited Gorovsky. Touched everything in the apartment. And what would you know, on one of little Zaide's jumpers, a vibe. Someone who touched Zaide also was exposed to a similar, terrible memory.*

He saw a day in a park. A woman with dark skin, in a blouse that was a little tighter than it had to be and a skirt that showed off, in his opinion, a truly fine set of legs.

I'm pretty sure Bullet did not mean to share that observation in his thoughts. He's maybe drinking more than he is used to.

Barrens smirks at that point, leans to whisper in my ear. "I told ya it was a great outfit. You should wear it more."

I guess by this point, even Barrens's suspicious nature is satisfied that the kid isn't dangerous. I should stop thinking of him like that. He is almost the same age as I am.

In front of us, Bullet's eyes are a little glazed over. "Oops. Sorry, ma'am."

"John, the little guy's had enough," Barrens says, waving off the next round. "Best bring him some water. Or coffee."

Bullet presses his hands against the table. "I'm fine," he says, a little too loudly. He steadies himself. Breathes. Continues. The look on his face.

Barrens's smile is gone. "Hey. It's okay."

*The questions you were asking Gorovsky. I knew you were trying to figure it out.*

The problem was, facial recognition databases are off-limits to a mere Keeper Examiner. And for a name, all he had was Hana. He did not even know if it was my real first name. So, slowly, over many, many nights, Bullet wandered from place to place, waiting for uncontrolled flashes of his talent to clue him in to where to go next. Feeling for the terrible echo of the memories Barrens and I carry around, glimpses of him and me. I think of those long, long hours, his walking, wandering, bending low to touch this or that, at night, when there aren't too many people who can see him.

"Next thing I know"—he belches—" 'scuse me. Next thing I know, I'm in an alley being lifted up by—wazzit? From a movie—King Kong."

Bullet's eyes narrow, and suddenly he looks fierce and focused as he reaches out and puts a hand on Barrens. He looks at me too. His face becomes older, tormented.

*Driving you mad, seeing it every night. The blood smell. In your dreams. I see it on you, that terrible, psychic taint. Let me join you. It's worse for me. That girl! I can't sleep anymore! I can help. I found you, didn't it?*

His eyes tear up. He starts to go to pieces, just barely holds it together.

*Her pain is inside me. Please. Please let me help.*

## 11

The end of another Earth calendar year is upon us.

In Edo Section, along the street to Torus, the violet blossoms of the hydrangea shrubs were gone before I noticed them. Everyone's wearing heavier coats, and soon there is the magic that the younger kids look forward to year-round.

The heaters throughout the Dome are turned low and, in some cases, shut down completely for maintenance. Condensers and precipitators continue to function, and at night there is snow. Never more than the streetsweeps can handle, but enough to grace the buildings and streetlamps and parks and gardens with clean, soft white. It smooths away the hard corners and adds curves to the straight lines and edges.

City Planning and Management teams go throughout the city, dolling up the buildings and towers with festive strings of red and green lights, and sprays of decorative gold color. Subliminal thought-packets emanate from transmitters embedded everywhere, filling the ears with old holiday music and songs, from times and places gone by.

On Sundays, there are parades, centered around the floats built by the children and teenagers, and featuring them singing and dancing, and laughing, as the thousands of adult crew members watch, gorging themselves on an emotional abundance and confluent aura of joy. These memories have to last until the next year, and we all need as much as we can get. The sight of these smiling little merrymakers, still free of worry, is a promise of hope. Yule is an official celebration aboard the Noah. The traditions are good for morale, and if they cause a short-term drop in productivity, studies from a century before with generations of crew that did without holidays and their associated socializing and leisure activities show they were significantly less orderly and efficient in the long term.

Miyaki no longer plays bodyguard for me when Leon isn't around, and Joe November, the boyish young Examiner nicknamed Bullet, has joined us in our dark hobby.

What he provides is the opposite of the sort of thing I and my program do. With his psychometry, he can visit the places I find that are candidates for where a Mincemeat victim was found. He can touch the evidence stashes Barrens finds in the Long Term Investigations warehouse that correspond to my search results. What I find in the virtual realm of dataspace, Bullet can link to physical reality. So, I do not see Bullet much. He is a decent programmer, but the best contribution he can make is at Barrens's side, evaluating and tracking down the leads I find.

Tonight, we meet at Stoney's, a dive bar just outside the posh High 3 Street area, where the pricier nightclubs of Londinium are clustered. The air is thick with smoke and flavored just slightly with vomit, and the seats are peeling. But it's also loud and crowded with young twentysomethings who have just finished their qualifying exams, the last tests that validate their skills before they begin their internship phase at whatever Ministry track they have been funneled into.

With the loud music and all this emotion in the air, it is hard to eavesdrop on any one conversation, and even the most skilled Behavioralist would be unable to pick out more than the slightest fragment of individual thought from the dense chaos of kids, singing, dancing, laughing, crying, celebrating, commiserating, hooking up, breaking up.

We crowd around a tiny table at the edge of the impromptu dance floor.

"It's progress, right? Kind of."

At least there is more data for all of us to look through and input into refining the Monster.

The Monster is what we're currently calling my swarm of programs, as it is no longer a small, sleek hunter ferreting out specific pieces of information, but a multiheaded mess. Though each single copy of the program is still relatively simple, there are now many versions of each, and the whole is becoming more complex at a faster rate than I expected.

"Monster is good. We're using a Monster to find one," Barrens says.

I'm surprised my design hasn't collapsed from all the shifts happening inside the subgroups of the swarm.

"Hey, you know how it goes. If ain't broke . . ."

"The weird thing is, it's working better than ever." Inefficiencies should be accumulating and slowing down its rate of improvement, but perhaps the alien might of the Analytical Nodes is so great that wasted cycles are not so noticeable.

Barrens shrugs. "I can do the tricks ya teach me, Dempsey, but the theory stuff is not for the likes of me. Anyway, we're moving now. Finding more, and doing it faster."

Yet, even though we have more data, we aren't actually getting closer to what Mincemeat *is*.

Beyond the physical brutality of what happens to the victims, I am disconcerted by the *lack* of a pattern to the physical locations of these deaths. Bullet has touched the places where they fell, and Mincemeat struck them down in their homes, in their offices, in restaurant bathrooms, in lonely maintenance shafts. How can there be no witnesses for so long? How can this be happening all over the ship?

"You know what I think about that," Barrens rumbles, as he adds more locations to our map of the deaths across the ship.

The clustering is random, a cloud of blood red lights hovering between us, superimposed on a glowing wire-frame diagram. The shared sight augments our vision through a program we made together, loaded on our Implants. While I load up the tables of search results from the data-miner and Barrens does the mapping, Bullet ticks them off, either with an X for a strikeout or a skull for a real victim.

We talk, sometimes out loud, sometimes through our Implants.

"It's not one man."

Barrens's instinct is still to blame the Ministries of the ship. I have my own fears, my own suspicious, creeping worries in the dark.

"It could be one man, if he had a *talent* that can act remotely."

Leon gnaws on his lip. "Dunno, Dempsey. What's more crazy, you think?" He pauses for the mental shift to his Implant. *That there's a shipwide conspiracy of killers acting above the law, or that there's some nut job with Power like nothing any kid's ever tested positive for? A Power that can kill violently through a locked door, without needing line of sight even.*

Bullet says softly, "There is still not enough data either way, and there are still all the possibilities we haven't even thought of yet."

A Certification Examiner for Keepers, Joe "Bullet" November actually works under the Ministry of Information. Understandably, he does not want to think that some terrible conspiracy involves people who might be his friends, people he trained with and hung out with and graduated with and has known for years. He wants to think the best of people. The existence of the Mincemeat deaths has shaken his comfortable existence. What terrible secrets are out there to justify this if this has Ministry sanction?

Like Barrens, he doesn't care about the Builders the way I do when I show him the memory of the creatures forming the Noah out of plastech under an alien sky.

More than anyone else I know, Bullet mixes spoken speech and Implant messages and direct telepathy. In one moment, he thinks to us, *Aliens behind the crazy tech of this ship that nobody could really explain to us in school?* Without missing a beat, he says out loud, "Well. It just figures." Then he shifts to the Implant to take advantage of being able to attach emotional data from his memories to these silent words in a neat, enclosed bubble: *Mincemeat, people dying in secret, the others left behind who are never allowed to know—that wrecks me.*

I stir round and round the peanuts in the little dish in front of me. Our new friend is looking more solid and steady than that night he found us, red-eyed, exhausted. Maybe it's the knowledge that he is not alone in this. He has never broken down since that first night.

He looks naturally cheerful, but is just a little bit thinner every time I see him, the shadows under his eyes just a little deeper. Psychometry could be a fun trick in school, around friends. But touching things involved in violence and blood? I think of him walking in all those places, twitching, shuddering when he has to take in psychic impressions by touch, feeling the raw pain, the confused terror.

"Don't worry about it. I wish I could do more."

"You're doing plenty, something that Hana and I can't. You can differentiate the false positives the Monster finds on the Web from legitimate incidents and fill in details that just aren't in the Network at all."

"Look," Bullet says. *I refuse to believe it is Ministry-sponsored assassination.*

"Why?"

He sighs and drinks his beer, which went flat twenty minutes ago. His hands start to shake as he lowers the glass to the table, and Bullet *writes* his latest find into our minds. Three nights ago, a little girl in the bathroom at Edo Primary School. There is the impression of confusion, terror, blood.

And pain that leaves me gasping and Barrens gripping the table's edge so hard, it creaks, close to breaking.

"Probably," Bullet says, after giving us some minutes to collect ourselves, "there must have been some major cleaning up afterwards, because when I asked her classmates, they all thought she'd been transferred to another district school." *Why would anyone assassinate a child? What could she have possibly done? And then the cleanup cost includes Adjustments of other children?*

He swallows down the last of his beer, emptying half the stein in one long, endless swallow.

Barrens is silent. This is not the first child Mincemeat victim we've found—Callahan's files had Keeper Sullivan's locked-room mystery. But it's the first one confirmed by someone else using another method. It's not just data or possibly distorted memories recovered by my program anymore, not with the terrible sense impressions Bullet can draw from the scene of a death.

Oh, that's not enough to convince my suspicious bear, my watchful lion. I don't have to read his mind to know his thoughts, that maybe the child read the wrong book or was exposed to the wrong memory by a careless Keeper. He thinks the Ministries will not stop at anything if they believe they are justified.

And I, I ache inside, remembering, wondering about the child I will never know. Yes. How can anyone justify killing a child when so few people are left at all?

How many more will die like this? Can we really do anything?

Bullet leaves after that. For now, we're done syncing up our map of death.


In between these sessions, there is work and meeting friends and everything that is normal life.

The Yule festivities rise to their annual apex, with caroling kids, grand parties, and snow festivals with ice-carving contests in the parks.

I talk Barrens into accompanying me to the party at the new home that Lyn and Marcus just qualified for. I feel guilty. I haven't been seeing my other friends nearly enough.

"Do I have to wear this? Why am I going anyway?"

"They all know I'm with you. I don't see the point of hiding."

"They don't like me."

"And you don't like them. But you do like me, and I like them too."

His scowl is playful and deserves a pinch on the cheek. "Ow. What was that for?"

"Just because."

I rise up on my toes and pull his head down to brush my lips against his jaw.

A tug settles Barrens's tie into place. The black onyx suit I have purchased for him fits well and shows off his trim waist, thick chest and back, and the breadth of his shoulders. He still looks more like a gangster from an Earth 2-D movie about the 1920s than any sort of gentleman, but I would not want him to look anything other than a little dangerous.

Now I check myself in the mirror.

"Why do women do that?" he asks.

"What?"

"Look yourself down like there's some problem needs fixing. You're better than fine."

These opportunities for style and vanity, pleasure and luxury, have value too, brief moments to set aside thoughts of keeping our ark going through the black emptiness.

The sheath dress is bone white and is a stark contrast with the deep brown of my skin, of which rather a lot is showing, as it is sleeveless, nearly backless, and reveals perhaps too much of that bothersome cleft up top that draws so much attention from the male of the species. It falls to the knees but has a slit along one thigh that goes higher than I am comfortable with. The shoes are the same shade of white as the silk and have heels that will have me tottering and swaying and leaning for support against Barrens quite often, I am sure.

Still, it pleases me, the way he cannot help looking. I can feel his eyes linger as they trace their way up from my ankles and calves, up to the curves of my thighs and hips. That stare is a spotlight on the bare curve of my back, and his hand feels like fire when it brushes against my shoulder blade.

Now, a kiss at the nape, and maybe I should not have put my hair up because I know Barrens will be doing that all evening, and each time he does, I can feel the burst of those troublesome chemicals that send tingles sliding down my back, into my belly, and lower.

"Behave."

"Aww. Don't get the point of dressing like that when it's always 'behave.'"

"I've read that visual temptation, frustration, and the delay of gratification," I explain to him, smiling up at his reflection, "have interesting effects on later amorous encounters."

His chuckle could be the bark of an enormous dog. I've grown fond of it anyway.

I dab color onto my lips—a sheen of candy pink that glitters when the light hits it at certain angles. I do not like it, but it is a gift from Jazz and she will be pleased to see it on me, even if she pretends not to notice.

Marcus's gifts, lapis-lazuli stars, hover in telekinetic fields a preset distance from the studs in my ears. Slowly rotating and tumbling, free-floating, they draw on my natural field of psi energy.

Just a touch more of the silvery perfume that is from Lyn. The top notes are light and sweet shades of apples, fading to a heart of crushed grass. I cannot detect the base notes, but on the card that came with the blue crystal bottle, it assures me that the fragrance will linger and call to mind the sea. Not that any memories are floating around anywhere from someone who has actually smelled the sea. If they exist at all, they are locked down with the deepest security.

"Okay?"

"Okay." I hold out my arms, and he puts my new beige overcoat on me. The little silver-scale clutch bag is heavy in one hand, and his calloused paw grasps the other. Time to go.

Lyn and Marcus now reside in one of the few hundred private homes in the Habitat.

These dwellings are always filled by the top officers of the Noah, expensive money-sinks to rebalance the credits of the closed economy.

Only residents and on-duty crew with assignments for that area are permitted to carry amplifiers of any kind in these areas. Traffic is carefully screened before being permitted through. We show my psi-tablet displaying the encrypted invitation codes for myself and one guest over and over to the zealous police staff assigned exclusively to this zone.

We disembark at a cobblestone path winding up a grassy hill.

A low wall made to look like white-plastered stone surrounds the compound. A three-story pagoda rises from the center of it, gleaming white, except for the glazed tiles on the roof tiers, which are stained cobalt, ultramarine, and midnight. A garden is tucked into the narrow spaces between the house-proper and the walls. Screens of cherry trees, bushes, bamboo stands, pseudo-granite rocks, faux-stone lamps, and water basins are positioned to give the illusion of space. With the light dusting of snow left from the night before, it looks like a fairy-tale cake.

Theirs is not the tallest or largest tower in the neighborhood, or even along the street, but it is a show of wealth beyond what most of the crew even realize is available in the Habitat.

The sight of all this gets a scowl out of my man. A thundercloud of disapproval is gathering over him. When we walk through the gates, I dig an elbow into Barrens's side and send him an Implant-to-Implant message: *No arguments about class and privilege tonight.*

His expression eases into something like a smile. *You're sure adding a lot to your tab for tonight.*

A hand-squeeze shows that I know it. I like him this way too, and shiver when he takes my coat off and takes it to the cloakroom branching off the entryway.

I give my greetings for the both of us as we move in the semi-random paths of social Brownian motion. The other guests compliment my hair or my dress and do not know exactly what to say of my partner. Around these tiny, graceful ladies and the slender, foppish men, Barrens is huge and solid and imposing. When I introduce him, reactions range from curiosity and "What exciting work that must be!" to a sort of baffled, unspoken "What did you say?" Barrens is a sport and answers as sincerely as he can, talking about the many weeks of boredom in between those few moments of terror when he might actually have to inflict violence on somebody.

My dearest ones—Jazz, Lyn, and Marcus—embrace me. They are frostier with Barrens. The corner of Lyn's eye twitches at the sight of Barrens, though Marcus does shake his hand.

"Merry Yule."

"Ah. Merry Yule," Barrens stammers. He flushes at the turn of their eyes, and the notch under his Adam's apple stands out.

"I love what you've done with the place!" I exclaim desperately. I loathe the words as they escape my lips.

At least it gets them talking about the many hours of work and the expense of their décor. I get them to talk about their clothes, new acquisitions, the latest fashions.

"From Corona and Black's." Jazz twirls proudly to display hers, the material swirling, showing off her gleaming, tanned thighs, her sculpted abdomen.

Marcus nods. "We bought them together."

Jazz and Lyn are both wearing fairy dresses of gossamer silk and beads of glass. Marcus is in a toga inspired by the style of ancient Rome, crisp and white and scarlet, eagle brooches of gold flying above his shoulders, a crown of oak leaves hovering over his blond curls. Their outfits are held up and draped artfully upon their figures by means of *touch* routines, much like my floating ear-rings. A disruptive burst of psionic energy would leave them naked, the strips and ribbons and sheets fluttering away. Jazz is in blues and whites, ice and win-ter, and Lyn is all summer flame, with burnished steel bangles for one arm and copper for the other. Pagan goddesses to the left and right of a man who could be Caesar.

They walk and sit as if posing for a catalog. Marcus struts somewhere be-tween a peacock and a general, and the two women sway their hips in an exag-gerated fashion that sets their bosoms bouncing with each step, and their hair flouncing from side to side.

*Dempsey. Is there something wrong with your buddies?*

*There are memories that go with the clothes. So they can show them off right.*

Other guests demand their attention and they leave us to mingle.

A large field emanation propagates from the transmitter in the ceiling of the party room, broadcasting music into the mind, all violins and flutes, and the light voices of children.

The hall is not normally this large. Marcus temporarily removed the walls separating the dining room from the living room, and the addition of mirrored surfaces to most of the support pillars and weight-bearing walls to expand the illusion of space was probably Lyn's work. Garlands hang from the ceiling, cheery branches from pine trees and ornaments of crystal and gold. It will be recycled by the end of the week, but for now, it is magical. The hall is dominated by the open hearth in the center under a ceiling chimney, with an extravagantly large Yule log burning bright and fragrant.

Around the log are tables laden with self-heating trays of foods that are only affordable because of the annual culls of the livestock and fisheries. The steam and the scent of the rich volatiles from the pork and mutton fat in the dishes is heady, dizzying.

It is too much for Barrens. The perfumes from the guests around us, the smoke from the fire, the spices, and the meat are overwhelming. The tightness to his mouth has nothing to do with feeling offended.

"It's okay," I murmur to him. "Take a walk around their garden, or hang out on the veranda. You're not the only one who finds this a bit much. You've got better odds of making acquaintances out there."

"I—sorry, Hana—"

"Hush. I'll bring you a cup of mead later, maybe figs and bread and cheese." A kiss eases his anxieties of disappointing me, and he departs with a smile.

"Finally sent the oaf off?" Jazz places a glass of wine in my hand. The bubbles sparkle. "Have one of these. It's glorious. Wish we could have Yule every week."

"I wish you wouldn't say that."

"Is he really who you're shacking up with?" Marcus asks, frowning.

Lyn completes that thought: "You could do so much better!"

Was I like them before? I want to think I always valued every citizen of the Noah.

I try to divert us to the safer, blander topic of our jobs, and what the higher-ups want out of us next year. That only gets them talking about how difficult our work is, the combination of genes for psychic talents, intelligence, discipline, all the rubbish needed to qualify for our positions. It is still about "our place" in society.

Maybe this was a mistake, but I cannot give up my past and my friends just to have Barrens. I should not have to choose.

"It's his schlong, isn't it?" Jazz asks, grinning. "Does he do you good, my dear? I've heard it hurts, when it's too large."

"Guys that huge usually don't have the equipment to match," Marcus protests.

They are only this crude when Barrens is what they are talking about.

Why fight it? I will do what I wish. I still love them, but I am not letting anyone shame me out of what I have found.

"Barrens," I declare, "has a penis worth every one of my past lovers put together. He is good to me and gets me good and wet and ready and has me screaming every time."

My hands go out just so and my fingers curl. "His dimensions are exactly thus."

All three of them are bright red now.

They all take long sips from their glasses, ignoring the shocked stares from the guests in earshot. Hennessy is looking right at me and whistling and clapping.

A little more quietly: "Barrens cooks for me and takes care of me. He does not make fun of me when I buy memories of this old lady's cat. He cheered me up after Breeding Duty. He was kind to me when I needed it." I switch to whispering by Implant-to-Implant multicast. *And not once did he ever make me feel shamed after I was raped.*

"Wha—"

They get in each other's way verbally. I never told them. Immediately, there is that guilt. They'll guess it's Holmheim—that guy they liked so much. Whom I just stopped bringing around.

Hennessy is my savior then. He may not have been a target of my foolish words, but that relationship intuition of his tells him that I just did something I am not ready to deal with. He slides in, glib and polished, his gold-trimmed frock coat dazzling by the firelight, and he tugs me away, gushing, "Hey, hey! Come, darling, now you simply must tell me more about all this magnificent fucking you're getting."

My throat is all closed up and I am hot from forehead down to the small of the back.

"Hana—I have to be able to call you Hana during Yule, right? Is there any chance at all I could borrow one of these illicit memories of yours? I promise I won't even share it with the girls on the team. I'll just talk about it and make them jealous, yes? I would dearly love to know how that mega-cock you were talking about feels. . . ." His eyes cross as he oohs in imagined ecstasy.

Hennessy has me laughing, even as I dab at my eyes. "If you keep me company while I cool off and then when I apologize to my friends and help me keep Barrens out of the discussion for the rest of the evening," I get out, "I just might let you have a memory."

"Glorious! I knew I would get lucky attending this party instead of the stuffy one at Hester's."



"Something happen while I was outside sports-talking with the nongirlie men?"

Back at my place, we stand on the balcony behind a barrier of laminar-flow air, kept moving by background threads running on the neural Implants of all the residents. I extend my arms forward, catch the flakes of snow falling beyond the heated current, and touch the cold.

"Oh, just them being them. We amused my assistant, anyway. You know, Hennessy."

"Oh. He, uh. Makes me uncomfortable. Has this look on his face when he sees me."

"Leon, he's one of my few friends that likes you and approves of us."

Barrens's mouth is hot and wet on my neck. His hands slide the straps of my dress off my shoulders. The cloth falls away, pools at my feet.

"Okay. My apologies to him next time. Tell him he's a prince."

"Ahnnnnnh . . ." Bites on the nape, on my shoulder. His thigh eases my legs apart. "Not here, please . . ."

Those hands start doing what they do. Getting hard to think.

"Got to take off early. Should start squaring up your tab already . . ."

"Wouldn't . . . nuh . . . want to let . . . debts . . . linger."

With the alcohol and the emotional balancing act of the evening, I didn't notice the sad tenderness with which he made love to me.

In the middle of the night, I stir long enough to see him sitting at the edge of the bed. He looks down at his tablet. I can't see his face well enough.

"Leon?" Loose, languid, I yawn.

Another kiss. Softer. The softest. "'S nothing. You go back to sleep."

I should have paid attention. I should have asked what he saw.

## 12

I WAKE UP ALONE, IN A TANGLE OF CARPET AND BLANKETS AND CLOTHES, A bleak sun looking down at me. Perhaps we overdo it a little, the change of light levels with winter.

An envelope with a card is on the low crystal table in the living room. It is handmade paper, the fibers coarse and distinct under my fingertips.

On the card, Leon has written, in his cramped, irregular scrawl, *Happy Yule, my love.*

The eighteen-digit alphanumeric code is an ident number.

*The date and the time-stamp match up with the end of your Breeding Duty.* His hand trembled there. *M for male. Last three digits match the last three digits of your ID. I don't know for sure. But this is probably your son.*

*I am sorry.*

*The places I have to go, what I have to do next, things cannot stay the same, and I must choose if I will fight or give it up and pretend everything is fine.*

*The people I've been talking to. They've found something. Something I can't ignore. Mincemeat is not one man. Bullet was right too, though. It's not about execution. There is too much now, to ignore.*

*I choose to fight. You know I can't choose to do anything else.*

*And others, less friendly types, I think, have started to close in on who I am, on the Web.*

*I need for you to stay safe, Hana. I've endangered you enough.*

*I have never known happiness, till there was you.*

*Good-bye.*

I send out countless messages. I beg. There are no replies.

When I message Bullet and get no replies from him either, I feel particularly awful.

Really, Leon? You left me behind and took the kid with you?

There is no stopping myself from going to his precinct. And waiting. I don't know how long I would have waited out there, in one of the cramped little chairs in the lobby. But Miyaki Miura spots me and marches out.

"He's a fuckin' idiot. Listen, don't come round here, don't go to his place. Go home, do your usual thing. Wait for me."

Three days drift by in a haze of numbers and reports and proposals and revisions of proposals. The nights crawl by. I am always cold. Numb. I feel almost as bad as when I was on my post–Breeding Duty meds. As though there were a barrier between me and what I feel.

At work, my face is a storm cloud and nobody questions my black mood.

Nothing tastes good anymore. I force myself to finish off an apple at lunch and take the elevator back to my floor.

Hennessy catches my arm at the door to our department. "Chief? There's someone waiting for you. Umm, she looks kind of scary."

"Good afternoon, Officer Miura."

"Hi, Dempsey."

She steps into my office. "He's gone and cocked it up something terrible, Dempsey."

"Hana. Just Hana."

Her smile is brittle, her eyes dart around, taking in who is watching us. "Miyaki. No, um. Then, you can call me Miya. You're only the second allowed to."

I wave my hands, using *touch* to lower the blinds over all the clear glass that lets me keep an eye on my team when I please, but also lets them keep an eye on me. I also close the blinds on the windows looking out on the street below.

"So."

Deep breath. Crossing my arms across my chest does not calm me, but if my hands are holding on to something, they will not shake. "He's really missing," I say.

"Yes."

"What will you do?"

We each examine the face of the other. Do I look soft and weak to her, as all elites seemed to Barrens? Insecurity pecks at the back of my skull. It has no place here.

*He's got a storage unit rented in the warehouse districts. "Inherited" it, sort of, from*
*Cal. I want you to come with me.*

*Right now?*

*I don't know how many people know about it. Maybe it's already too late to retrieve*
*whatever the dumbass hid in there. Maybe not.*

If I close my eyes, I will lose myself in the way he held me, that first evening, after Breeding Duty, at that ghastly party. I will think of his voice like a
bear's roar and the heat of his smell and the toothy smile on his craggy face that
is a snarl to everyone else. I pull on my coat. It feels heavier than it should. My
shoulders are stiff, and I know it is from worrying. My bag is heavy in my
hand—why even bring that? A neural Implant multicast informs the team that
I will be out for the rest of the day.

"Let's go."

And we are gone, my officemates looking after us, curious, but not curious
enough to stop what they are doing.

"James, you're in charge for a bit."

"Wha—? Chief, there's—"

We are gone.

We watch each other, though we pretend not to, examining each other's reflection.

I've been in her car about a dozen times, but I never paid much attention to
it before. A lean, narrow wedge with three wheels, it is large enough to seat one
passenger up front just behind the driver. In the rear is a padded, armored cap-
sule with shackles and straps for a single prisoner.

She drives smoothly, carefully. She stops at every light and sign, signals before each turn, checks her mirrors before changing lanes, and stays at the speed
limit. Not at all like the other police captains I have seen, zooming along reck-
lessly just because they can.

"Did he leave you a note too?"

"You got a note? It must be love then. No. He just stopped showing at work.
And when I went to his place—" She swallows. Clears her throat.

"Yes?"

"Gray coats. I got one look at them and just kept walking."

How did they find out? We were so careful. I suppose everyone thinks he is
too careful to get caught, until he is.

"I know he got out."

How can she be so sure?

"Trust me. If they had caught him there, there would have been a fight. They'd never take him in without wrecking the place."

Another deep breath. I've had to take so many in the past few minutes. Did I think I was feeling drugged and removed from my emotions again? I wish I were because I am terribly afraid right now, and only the thought of Miya's disapproving glare holds back my panic.

"Will they come for me too? Interrogate me?"

"Information Security can't be seen just talking to every person in Barrens's life. Most likely, they've already checked you out and haven't found anything yet. If there was something, they'd have already taken you."

Small comfort. "Now he's vanished himself. He was so excited, said he found something, a real breakthrough."

Wait. The timing.

My lists . . . I try to recall where that particular psi-tablet was, with the latest reports from my botnet. I do an internal memory search for that interface device. Flashing through the images, I see myself setting it down on the nightstand next to my bed, just before I started getting dressed for the party. The next time I walked into that room was after reading Barrens's note, with me crying as I throw myself into bed. That tablet, with both the newest data-crawl results and my latest tweaks to my data-miner code, is gone.

Barrens has it.

I guess that was just one of the things he was working on, with the Monster. The program had changed so much. He was looking into Breeding Duty because of me. Or did he find out through some of the contacts he made, creeping through the wastes of the Nth Web, in the forums and on the boards that pop up for one night and then vanish, the better to protect everyone's identity? Or perhaps one of the collectors of illicit memories. Maybe somewhere out there, some pervert Breeding Duty Doctor is selling memories of births.

How did ISec find him out, but not me? It has to be through these other projects of his, or these other people on the Web, the things he never brought me in on.

Miyaki is right. He must have left nothing suspicious. Otherwise, I would already be in a cell, being questioned, having the memories ripped out of my head.

Through one of the great air locks, and around us, the clean, white homes and glittering towers of Edo Section give way to architecture inspired by an imagined golden age of Paris. Block after block of beautiful buildings of even height, subtle shades of pale colors, harmonious despite the differences, long lanes, lovely streetlamps, plazas with fountains and old statues. The window frames are decorated with figurines and scrollwork. Tomatoes grow out of planters on the balconies. Rosebushes line the sidewalks.

The street divides and Officer Miura hangs a right, descending down into the gray underways below the city level. Lights stream by overhead. We come to the primary warehouse district, an underground section that services the entire Habitat. The cavern, the color of concrete, is several hundred meters high and many thousands of meters across. Trains and trucks flow in and out continuously around the broad, squat columns supporting the upper deck. The columns double as grain silos, food-processing plants. Silver-threaded needles crisscross the air, the distribution lines for the psionic energy grid underneath the Habitat.

Among the giant cargo haulers, the police car is a little bird crowded by elephants. Each of those titanic wheels has a diameter greater than the length of our vehicle.

I tap the map systems of the car and see our location and route. We keep heading for the stern. There is nothing there. Or there shouldn't be. "Where are we going? To one of the abandoned Habitat sections?"

"His storage unit is right at the edge. Warehouse management sometimes loses track of the building modules out here—they get moved around a lot. No safer place to hide something. Well, other than the unmapped zones."

Nobody comes out here. The traffic grows sparse. Disappears. Soon we are just one wedge of light slicing through the darkness with the headlights. The tunnel widens. We see the great wall at the end—the edge where the Habitat is sealed off from old compartments that are no longer used.

There are fires there, along the dam that goes left to right and up and up as far as the eyes can see. Dark shapes scurry away from our light.

"What are the—"

"Tunnel gangs. There are access shafts going up to every part of the Habitat from down here. They won't mess with us. Civilian amplifiers don't work down here. Police badges and"—she nods at me—"City Planning's construction gauntlets do."

I do not want to disappoint her by saying that I did not bring my gauntlet. Instead, a small self-defense pendant with management override codes hacked into it let will will let me draw upon power and use routines almost as well as a real gauntlet. Funny. That's not legal either; I wonder why I bothered. It's not something I would have done before all this. Before Mincemeat. Before Barrens and Holmheim.

Do I want to impress her? Maybe I do. When Barrens talked about her, he always did so with respect, almost reverence.

That is why, when we step out into the dark, echoing emptiness, I try to hide how frightened I am. I am too used to the bright lights and clean containment of the Habitat.

Her badge glows, and her eyes flare deep bloodred—the optical enhancements of a *bruiser*.

"Aren't you lighting up too?"

Not sure what I was thinking. Was I expecting her to hold my hand or something?

A packet of thought from organic brain to Implant to the amplifier under my shirt. It draws power from the grid, and with thought and focus, I direct the energy to my hand, to my fingers. A psionic arc light flares to life in the hand I hold out before me, white fire, ionizing gas held inside a sphere of force. Telekinesis makes a bubble of high-pressure air on one side, a lens that focuses the brightness.

"I'll try to keep it out of your eyes."

At the base of the periphery curtain wall, cargo containers are stacked high on top of each other. Dim orange and red outline their doors, lights that flicker on and off at random. A flimsy-looking framework around the storage units consists of stairs and walkways going up and down and across each teetering stack.

"I hope you're not scared of heights." She has her back to me, but I can hear her smile. She glances down at the tablet in her hands. "It's that one." She points.

It would have to be the highest one in the middle. More than a hundred meters up.

"I do hate heights," I admit. "But at least it'll be too dark to see how far up we are."

All those steps. I need to get more exercise. Barrens made me promise I would.

While we clomp up the steps, which vibrate with our weight, Miya starts talking. She tells me about Callahan. In her voice, I hear something more than friendship and affection, and I wonder if she ever got to tell him any of it.

"When Leonard showed me the memory, I was in, at first. But then, he got obsessed. It was getting to be too much for me. He was seeing Mincemeat in everything, suspicious junk in ordinary paperwork misfiling.

"Then, he went to you. I didn't think he would ever trust anyone else to see the beast in his head. Can't tell you how hard it was helping him hide that whenever we had to turn in after-action memories. He thought you were real special. Only girl he'd talk about."

That was something I'd never thought about. "How did you hide it?"

"We did repeated transfers back and forth from my viewing of it to a tablet and back to my head. It degrades the emotional content of the memory. That's what we would submit for him."

I would bet that was Barrens's idea.

The metallic frame creaks and sways with our movements. Nerve-racking, in the dark.

"Be careful. Some of the steps are cracked. If you fall, I'm not sure I could catch you without bringing this stupid scaffolding down on top of us."

Breathing. Control. Emptiness.

I put my left foot on the next step and keep going. As he often told me, *All we can do is what we can do.*

# 13

"Now we cross this bridge here and—" Miya crouches, holds an arm out to stop me.

"What?"

"There's someone up there. I see someth—gaaah!" she cries out, clapping a hand to her shoulder. A small, dark shape flits by my head, whistles through the air.

*Two shooters,* she thinks to me. Not direct telepathy, but through Implant-to-Implant messaging. If one of us had greater talents in *reading* and *writing*, there would be less of a delay in transmission; we could have acted as one.

I am freezing and thinking instead of acting. Gawking, sweeping my light back and forth through the darkness pointlessly. Somewhere out there, I hear the whirring of—what? Gears?

"Peace officer! Halt your fire and surrender immediately, or I will use deadly force!" Miura's voice is amplified, roars through the emptiness. When her voice is like that, I can only think of her as Officer Miura. Miya is too cute, something I might call a close friend. Not a name that goes with this warrior woman, hard-edged, dangerous. The voice a lioness's roar.

Her left hand darts out faster than I can see, grabs something right out of the air as she snarls, "You were warned!"

*Shield us, stupid! My* touch *is just barely enough to operate a car! And drop your light!*

I do so, barely in time. Throwing out my hands, I feel my talent get a hold of something five meters away. It comes to a stop just centimeters in front of my face, wreathed in the light of my power—a short shaft coming to a narrow, chisel-shaped point. It wobbles and falls as I see more flashes heading for us, more projectiles, catching the faint light from the dim orange glow off of the many container doors. I drop to my knees and press my hands to the plastech under us. It warps in front of Miura, a panel breaking off and twisting up at an angle. The points of the weapons punch partway through, but stop.

*The third one's got something from Barrens's storage unit! Can't let him run!* Her mind-messages are crisp and clear. Little bleed-through of irrelevant thoughts and emotions, despite the thing protruding from her right shoulder. Blood trickles down her arm.

Miura leaps seemingly to her death, changes direction by grasping the rail. She flips up and starts flying along the scaffolding, which shivers and sways and rings with her feet and hands thudding against the struts, accelerating her straight up as though she were just sprinting along a flat track. She glows bright with psi energy, a fire-spider clambering up a metallic web.

Sparks in the darkness, impacts of more of those—what are they? Barrens's voice in my head, talking to me while we watch an old 2-D movie. Crossbow bolts. Like William Tell shooting apples off my head I think, giggling stupidly.

Another skitters off the support next to me and parts my hair just behind my neck.

Those aren't paintballs.

As Barrens would say, fuck this shit. I am hyperventilating and not sure if I am going to pass out. I act first.

I clap my hands together and pull in kilowatt-class energy. My whole body glows as if I were standing in a cobalt spotlight, and the pendant under my shirt shines so fiercely it is a small blue sun. The catwalk stops vibrating, and all around me, walkway panels hop off their frames and float into a rough hemispherical formation.

Lit up like a firefly, I am a bright target for sure, but at least I am a fortified one.

Miura pings me, *I'm your eyes. I'll see for you. You take care of those shooters.*

She feeds me a stream of images from her point of view, lit up in the red-shaded, monochrome vision of her psionically enhanced sight. There is some degradation from the conversion through her neural Implant and then mine, static around the edges. She keeps them highlighted for me with bright blue targeting reticules. The data comes with a wash of hunger, a predator's anger. But tight and controlled, nothing like Barrens's maddened beast-self.

She keeps up the chase on the third man, who flees with the grace and speed of a free-runner. He flips through the bars and support struts and leaps from level to level; it seems impossible that he can move like this without the benefit of psi amplification. He is completely unhindered by having to carry a solid-looking briefcase in one hand. So either he has a hacked amplifier as I do, or he is an officer of some rank, or he is on Psyn.

He is not my worry.

I close my eyes. With the barriers obstructing my view, I have to do this blind, all in my head. I must not miss, or I'll bring the container units down on top of us, dominoes smashing each other down. My mental map of the area empties my head of all extraneous thoughts, until there is only data, with our positions, and their positions, rotated and adjusted for Miura's point of view as she screams up and across the beams and struts and buttresses after her prey.

More bolts spark as they ricochet off my barriers. Distracting. But not that distracting. My right hand slides down and to the side. In my mind, a straight line along my arm intersects one frame of Miura's stream of visual data, along the officer's line of sight. I do the same with my left arm, toward the second crossbowman.

*Hey! Stop them already!*

I hesitate only until another quarrel flies in through a gap in my turtle's shell and embeds itself into the catwalk by my foot.

Part of me remembers my youth, those first heady years post-Implant as my talent grew and I could do more and more, brief flashes. Toothbrushes and pencils, working up to tennis balls in the first year. At fourteen, without an amplifier, my raw strength topped out at about twenty-five kilos, enough to lift a small sack of rice. I could throw a softball with my hand and keep accelerating it with psi until it zoomed faster than 150 kmh. At eighteen, when my *touch* peaked in capacity, I could just barely lift fifty kilos, though it took all my concentration and left me swaying and dizzy and weak afterward. After that, all my improvements were with skill, and with my mental ability to efficiently draw more power off the ship's power grid using an amplifier.

And it scaled all over again with an amp. At nineteen, my limit was half a ton. By the time I graduated from the Class V Training and applied for a job with Professor Salvador's recommendation, well. In olden times, the things I can do would be the stuff of gods. With a proper amplifier, the force I can draw on now is not measured in tons, but in thousands of tons.

In the present, my mind is a hammer, it is a hand, it is a wrench, it is any tool I need it to be. It is kinetic energy applied without a material medium. It can hold gems up under a vain woman's earlobes. It can be a bomb. A tingling rush is shooting down from my skull, through my spine, along my limbs.

"Sorry," I whisper, clenching my fists.

Where the strangers stand, two platforms fifty meters away, close to another staircase, unravel. The plastech structure explodes away from them for a moment, then the fragments change direction, imploding around and into their bodies.

They only have a moment to scream. I can feel it, the feedback through my mind as tons of force smash them in.

*Nice shooting!*

I let the power feed go. My shields drop to the ground far below, as do the two uneven spheres of mangled human and plastech. Two hundred foot drop; they burst when they hit the ground, spreading body parts and shrapnel on the gray floor below. Too far to smell, but I imagine that I can, that the blood is climbing up my nose into my brain.

I'm on my knees, shaking, not sure for how long. Or rather, I do know the number of seconds, as it is recorded on the machine part of my brain, but I do not feel that time, as though I am not in myself, not in my own head.

*Fuck. Wound slowed me too much—that guy's got to be on Psyn. Lost him.*

It only takes her a moment to return. I feel her eyes on me. Is she disappointed? Disgusted?

"Come on," she says, pulling me up. "I checked the locker. They had to rush. I got something they left behind."

"I, guh, I . . ."

"Shhh." Her arm around my shoulders is solid. Strong. It is too small though, and from too low an angle. I smell lavender perfume instead of cigarette smoke and musk. I want my guard dog back. But wishing never did anything for anyone, and Miyaki Miura keeps pulling me back the way we came, and if I don't start paying attention, I'm going to take a header down a stepladder twenty meters long, or fall down one of the gaps I made when I yanked the catwalk panels into the air.

"We have to go before Warehouse Security investigates the disturbance. Hurry."

"Y-you're bleeding."

"'Snuthing." She does not even pause when she rips the shaft out of her shoulder.

I have enough presence of mind to levitate the scarf from around my neck and wrap it tight around her wound in the best pressure bandage I can manage.

"You did good, honey," Miura continues trying to soothe me. "You did just fine."

Her hand is on my hand. It is not big enough, nobody else's could be big enough, but I try to take what comfort there is to be had, while we run.


She brings us back up at a section on the opposite side of the Habitat and deposits me next to a subway stop.

We are in Moskva Section. The buildings are either massive and imposing, grand monuments copied from pictures in history books, or small and quaint with artful touches of grime. The plastech imitates iron and brass, concrete and red brick, and a museum is not too far away, a bonfire rising into the sky, eight side buildings around a core offset to the port side of the ship, all done in imitation brickwork, asymmetric and symmetric patterns, red and white and green and gold, domes and minarets rising into the sky. Did St. Basil's Cathedral actually look like that?

I can't distract myself with history while I can smell the blood on my companion. "You need a hospital."

Her eyes in the mirror express what she thinks of that idea. "One of Callahan's friends can fix me up. It's not that bad. No bones were broken. I'm slowing the blood flow to the wound. Looks a lot worse than it is."

We were both silent during the minutes it took to drive up to the "surface" deck of the ship, and the sound of our voices in the humming quiet of the car is too loud.

It kick-starts the thoughts I have been trying to put out of mind.

A police telekinetic could have subdued those men without hurting them. I am not trained for psionic combat. I can build a three-story apartment block from a blueprint with just my mind, an amplifier, and a heap of plastech, carve up appropriately ugly Gothic gargoyles looking down from the eaves, and fabricate what look like stained-glass windows. But that is while sitting under the sun with a cup of tea at my elbow. I do not have that kind of long-distance control while under pressure and being shot at and terrified, standing on a walkway two feet wide hundreds of feet in the air. I have just killed two people.

I could have just encased myself in an armored block to defend myself. No, but what about Miura then? Already injured, what would she have done if all three focused on taking her out while I turtled up? I suppose I could have enclosed her in a protective shell too. But that would have been a kind of helplessness too. If they had a *touch* talent and Psyn and took the opportunity to attack us . . .

"Stop that," Miura's voice cuts through the whirl of my thoughts. "Don't worry. I felt that TK surge of yours—you probably mangled their Implants too much for any memories to be recoverable from the bodies."

Such worries did not even occur to me. What a cold woman this Miyaki is. Could she really have been friends with Barrens, always warm, always concerned about ideals, justice, doing the right thing?

"Look, you should get back to your own office. Doc's just a few minutes away. Here." Miura leans out the window, pulls loose, folded sheets of yellowed, aged paper from her inner coat pocket. "Stuff they left behind. Should go to you, first. Barrens always talked about how smart you are."

My hands have finally stopped shaking and manage to take the papers without dropping them. *We shouldn't be seen together at our workplaces, and we shouldn't message each other directly.* She looks me in the eye, thinks a direct unicast packet to me with a set of instructions.

When one of us has something to communicate, an ad with a hidden digital watermark is to be placed on the Memory Auction and Exchange site. We are both to run automated search routines that are set off by that watermark, a hidden memory of me, her, and Barrens, sitting in a diner over burgers. The other is then to post a matching ad with a date and time indicating when we should meet. The elaborate instructions are for me to visit a series of locations in sequence where I will wait several minutes at a time, while she evaluates if I have been followed. She must have prepared this structured mental document beforehand. It has different levels to it, highlighted maps, some code modules that select through a series of dangling IDs she cycles through online that are to be used only for emergencies.

"Let me know what's in that. Or. Shit, maybe I don't want to know. I'll get in touch. Maybe I won't. I need to think about this. I didn't seriously think someone else would be there, looking for his loony conspiracy bullshit." She is talking almost to herself. Miya closes her window and leaves.

I am still dazed by the aftereffects of too much adrenaline. I burn with the need to talk to someone about what just happened. Who were those people? I have just been shot at, I have just killed productive crew members of the ship who are going to be added to some police clerk's Long Term Investigations desk.

My mind races in circles while I make my way back to City Planning. A train ride and two bus rides away.

They did not have the access required to use amplifiers down there. They cannot have been Enforcers, who could have just incinerated us, or ISec agents who could have shut down our minds . . .

Still, these others were organized. Those men in the hooded coats had crossbows. Purely mechanical devices. Prepared for the limits of being off-grid. They knew what they were after. They were not some random tunnel gang.

On the subway train, I clap a palm to my forehead and shake. My fingertips trace the emitter-plate pattern on my face. I knew nothing about them. They were just there, and I was afraid, and I snuffed them out.

If only they had not shot at us first! I blame them for being there, for scaring me. I promise myself to look up how combat telekinetics are trained by the police. As an adult my powers have grown far beyond what I thought they would be when I was a child. I have a rating greater than half a dozen police *touch* support officers put together—it should have been trivial for me to disarm them, if I had known how.

They had been far away, in the darkness. Even Miura's enhanced sight had only seen them as blurry figures without faces. I should not, but I know I will. I will look for the LTI files that will surely be opened on them. I don't need to know, I do need to know, I want and I don't, and I am angry at everything, at myself, and most of all at Barrens.

Were they with whomever Barrens has been talking to? Why did it happen like that? If they'd only talked first. Something. Maybe we could have figured things out.

Maybe they could have brought me to him.

## 14

WHAT DO I WANT? WHAT AM I TO DO NEXT?

I sleepwalk through the last hours of the day and file all the reports I was supposed to and make the final revisions to our joint proposal with High Energy with the proper efficiency figures. It will go into implementation soon and save us just a little more water, a little more fuel in the long years to come, even after I and everyone else on my team are long dead.

I send a thank-you note to Savelyev and promise to invite him the next time Jazz and the others throw a party.

Hennessy knows something is wrong with me. Every time he looks at me and updates me on the progress of the other team members, I imagine he is building up the courage to talk to me. He is a dear. I guess he actually does like me, as a friend. He doesn't try to butter me up the way the others in the department do. Every time I've asked, he denies any ambition to climb his way up the tree. He says he likes being my assistant and that's it. Even though I have not been pleasant company, not since Breeding Duty. Moody and too quiet, a distant authority figure on our team rather than a leader, perhaps even unstable.

I think about what happens next if ISec pursues me. I do not want some young, fresh-out-of-school genius with too-high test scores to be my replacement and walk all over my team.

It is maudlin. But I consider what needs to be done to groom my flamboyant, cheery assistant for my job.

*Hennessy,* I unicast him.

*Yeah, boss?*

*Look, when it's just us, Hana is fine. I haven't thanked you for Yule. Let's go for coffee after work, yes? I think we need to put in for a team-building exercise of some kind.*

*!!! Of course. Hana.*

His last thought-packet gets a small smile out of me. His mental state drips with warm satisfaction, a touch of dirty glee. Probably he thinks he is finally going to get one of those illicit, hinted-at sex memories I've teased him with.

Instead we spend an evening eating little, flat pastries with honey and sipping tea. I let him take charge of planning the exercise and only guide him with a few comments here and there.

"James." I stop him just as he starts getting going on his ideas for the coming year, about more than just improving team performance. He has ideas about other things we can try, for making the city seem a little more welcoming while saving a little more power.

I should encourage him. I am not going to tell him that I have seen his ideas already, in one form or another, in the Habitat logs. I keep my smile at its warmest and wonder if I'm doing it right. Whenever Barrens smiled, he looked like a savage about to attack. Is my smile also interpreted differently by others? Do I look frosty and disapproving when I wish to seem approachable?

"Yes, Hana?"

"I want you to start brushing up on your statistical analysis, control theory, management strategies, and etiquette."

His brow twists but he smooths it away with a stroke of his fingers from brow and on through the waves of his steel-gray hair. "Did I do something to displease you?"

"Not at all. Those are the topics you should work on if you are to qualify for the next rank of the bureaucracy."

Hennessy covers his confusion by pouring some more tea into my cup and his own. He lifts his cup to his lips and stares off into the distance. This streetside café faces the ugly block of City Planning across a small square with a circle of cherry trees and a reflecting pool in the center. With his face in profile like that, it is as if he is posing for an audience, and I have to wonder if he even knows he's doing it. His eyes fade just so, with the telltale glimmer of someone going through his recorded memories.

"What's so funny?"

"You are, James."

"Why do you want me to test up? There are no openings anywhere."

I turn the cup in my hands. It is warm and steaming. It is white, glazed with little blue flowers. The tea is green and fragrant and not quite strong enough for the slightly sweet pancakes we are eating with powdered sugar and cheese.

"If there should be an opening sometime, it would be better if you are prepared for it."

"Hana, you haven't received a Retirement notice, have you?"

If only that were so. He looks quite relieved when I shake my head in reply.

"Look at that. It's pretty, isn't it? For a winter sunset?"

At the false horizon, the colors are ethereal, highlighted with almost neon hints under the clouds. "It's too bright."

"Oh, only you and other City Planning folks will notice. But for everyone else it should be nice, right? And it doesn't cost any more fuel than other parameter tuples for the sky simulation."

Just once in a while, maybe, it was acceptable. Something to surprise people with. Too often and they would become numb to it, then subconsciously alarmed by the unearthly touches. I consider reminding Hennessy that the idea is not only to provide the best aesthetic experience possible for the crew, but also one that works best with our biology. No, he knows it and did it anyway.

"You're sad about something too."

"What?"

"You are."

I cannot ever remember even the slightest hint of melancholy on Hennessy's handsome face. Perhaps that is why it took so long to recognize it in the brittle quality to his smile, the fine lines on his cheeks and around the chrome on his temples.

"Maybe I am."

Everyone has his or her own little tragedies. Have I been too self-absorbed? Then I decide that it is impossible to overreact to crushing human beings with my mind as though they were just trash in a garbage compactor. Still, thinking about others' problems, surely, is better than thinking about that. Then there are the violent, unexplainable deaths. Disappearances. Urban legends, conspiracy theories. Aliens. It is beyond me already. Crazy stuff.

It is not too much of an effort to try to mimic the body language Hennessy always uses when he tries to commiserate with others. I touch his wrist lightly and incline my head a little in his direction, turning my shoulders more toward him.

"What is it?" I try to orient my arms and legs at similar angles, without being too obvious about it, adjusting for the limitations of the pencil skirt that seems more snug than it used to be.

"Oh, you know. Just a little lonely. Hah, it's silly, is it not? I was thinking how it would be nice to have someone. I was hoping your situation would work out. I had someone through you, you know, vicariously." He pauses, examines me for a moment, gray eyes narrowing. And laughs. "Oh, darling—that is not a bad try, but you're never like that with anyone. I do appreciate the effort at sympathy.

"Dah-ling, it's not the worst thing, you know, having a breakup. After the falling out of love, why, there's the falling in all over again."

Well. Better that he thinks it is just a disagreement between my man and me.

He pays, and then there is the urge to beg him to keep me company for a while longer. Then I am alone, sitting at a table on the sidewalk, watching everyone else walking to and fro, all of us alone in our heads, even the ones with a loving man or woman holding his or her hand or arm.


Home feels empty with just me in it now. Without his coat on the chair, or his shoes by the doormat.

I spread out on the table the papers that two young men died for today.

Just a handful of sheets, old, faded. They smell slightly of mold. The left-hand edge is jagged—they were torn from something. The header has the Noah's official seal on it—a fat, bulbous three-mast ship sailing on a sea of stars—the old one that lies at the bottom of the pool in front of my office building, inscribed into the pale pseudo-marble. A touch of my talent and the loose leaves shift slightly, but there is none of the innate connection I feel with plastech-derived fibers. These partial documents were printed on actual paper, organic fibers. They are three centuries old, from the time of the original crew of the ship.

I am touching history in my kitchen.

Two sheets are nonconsecutive pages from a report about propaganda techniques, and the success of information-management policies with regard to the percentage of the crew that has accepted the necessity of the Keepers.

A third sheet has a list of names, described as "First batch, punished for disseminating G-1 data.' A fourth sheet has the heading, "G-1 Experiments" and summarizes them as a failure because the subjects remained too hostile. It ends with a recommendation about special measures to contain them.

There is a list of many texts that have been deemed dangerous, some with suggestive titles about the arrival of "the Ship" and the legacy of "the Visitors."

There is half a clipping from a broadsheet newspaper describing casualties from a series of collapsed maintenance tunnels.

The last sheet is divided in two parts, G-0 and G-1, and underneath each of them is a long string of numbers. On the back of the last page are two lines written by different hands. A steady, even one states, "Mincemeat?" Then Barrens's irregular, wandering scrawl asks, "What was Cal thinking?"

Deep breath, Hana. Don't just throw it all down the trash chute.

We were starting to think that the deaths went back far enough that a single killer would have had to start ridiculously young and was still killing even now when he should be decrepit. Or if it *was* some conspiracy, it had to have lasted long enough for a couple of generations to be sucked into it. But for Mincemeat to have some connection with documents that are hundreds of years old, back to the time of the Noah's launch from Earth?

I miss the days when I thought it is one demented psychopath beating the system.

"Damn you, Leon. Why didn't you talk to me that last night?"

I need to think. I need to analyze and put this all together.

That deep hollow I've been pretending isn't there eats at me again.

It flings me into the black, padded chair in front of my terminal. In the space of seconds, it moves me to open half a dozen frames at once, with results from queries about memories available for download.

There is a charge of credits equivalent to an hour's work for me, then there is the falling into the memory.


The culmination of years of training. Psychology, education. Test after test to determine worth and personality compatibility. For this. My neural Implant programs have been modified to alter my hormone balance and biochemistry. My food is laced with carefully balanced supplemental vitamins, minerals, and proteins.

It is thrilling and odd and primal and perfect.

Soft humming from my lips, nothing I need to think about, just a warmth and welcoming.

He is cradled in my arms, and latched on. There is that tugging sensation, and I do not care that it is the result of years of preparation. There is a feeling of profound completeness filtering through me, the knowledge that this little guy is dependent on the nourishment from my body. Before this moment, my breasts were always just there, just cosmetic anatomical features that made my back ache sometimes and drew looks from men, and now they are so much more.

I am so much more.

I switch him to the other breast and sigh. I can feel his tiny chest expanding and contracting. His little breaths.

My partner Keeper watches with a certain awe.

Nothing could ever match this. If I ever had doubts before about this career, they have all vanished with this first intense connection. I do not know how I thought that the lack of a genetic link could matter.

This diminutive stranger in my life has taken hold of my heart. Imprinted. He is my child now, regardless of who gave birth to him.


I binge on them.

That night, I spend a thousand credits on memories like that. All that emotion, the physical closeness, the acceptance, without having to wake up in the middle of the night to loud crying or having to change a diaper.

Curled up on my side in bed, the hours pass so slowly.

A brief, blissful peace before I wake up and feel only worse, the sun streaming in, knowing a full day of work is ahead with my team looking at me and wondering why bags are under my eyes, why I look as if I've been crying.

No more purchased memories, I promise myself. If I let it, I could lose all my days to that. I fix myself the thickest, bitterest black coffee I can manage to swallow and tell myself with each sip that I don't need that.

I need to choose, just as Barrens made a choice.

I can throw all this junk away and go back to my old life, forget about Mincemeat and Leon and Miya and everything. Or, I continue with this, getting deeper. And if I do, will it be to find him again? Or will it be for me?

Hah.

Anyway, being angry at being protected without my choice is more useful than soaking up the terrible, tiny thought that he just doesn't need me anymore.

## 15

I PLAN, PREPARE, STUDY.

The main thing is finding him. The Noah is immense. Its true size is classified, but from the massive number of Analytical Nodes that Lyn and I found as kids and with some basic assumptions about the distribution and number of them, the ship's volume is so vast that a lifetime is not enough time for one person to walk down every tunnel, crawl space, corridor, and hallway.

Well, I already have a tool meant for finding things in the Monster. I need to retask a subpopulation of the swarm. It is not such a simple thing though. My boys aren't going to be leaving a trail of bodies and vanishings. What can I use?

I designed the swarm so that its accesses and use can't be used to track the people using it. Commands and requests and modifications happen through propagating packets of data, which are taken in and passed on nondirectionally by each particle of the program, ripples in a pool that go back and forth, only the pool is scattered across vast numbers of nodes in the network. I get a headache just imagining its signal pattern. The network the Builders made underlies the Nth Web, and it is just so damned huge. To trace Barrens through his accesses on the Monster, I would need a real-time analysis of the whole mess of it scattered all over the ship—that could take months of continuous processor time, easily enough to be noticed by Information Security.

There's not much point in finding my man if it leads ISec right to us.

If they take me, I'm not going to be let off with a warning and a mild psychosurgical procedure to dial back my curiosity.

I need time to figure things out and not draw the attention of those grim agents in gray. Or worse, the ones in black—Enforcers could burn me to ash with a thought.

There is the need to be more normal than normal, just in case I am being scrutinized in connection with Barrens's disappearance. Anyway, my job is intimately tied into the illusory world we maintain. To fool our bodies, to fool our minds. It is a lie, but a well-crafted one. I ought to be used to this.

After all the delays, my team's proposed changes to the water system are finally being implemented. We celebrate with a small party. Marcus attends because it is directly tied into his department's sphere of responsibility. Because Lyn and he are married, she attends too. Because the two attend, so does Jazz, even though High Energy has its own separate dinner. The food is good, the menu personally selected by Hennessy, who went with fusion Japanese-French cuisine.

Savelyev is there, and he is polite and kind and adorably geeky. I think I could have really got to like him, once.

We bond across our lovely little dishes with their flourishes of glittering sauces and delicate spice blossoms.

My tantrum at Yule got through to my friends, a little. At least they have the delicacy not to mention his name. Though, as far as they know, we've only broken up. I doubt they care enough to have checked on Barrens and discovered that he is actually missing. And Savelyev doesn't even know I was with anyone in the first place.

We eat and smile, and eat some more. The three of us girls laugh at Marcus's bewildered, flustered state when Hennessy starts to flirt with him.

I am okay with how life is. I refuse to give in to the desire to feel weak, to feel down. Better to be pissed at him. I'll give him what for when I find him.

The days pass. But they are not real days, without a sun's rising to mark each new one. They are simulations of days, merely a measure of time. I continue to chase down the ghosts on the system.

He's gotten too close a look at how I do my tricks. He's vanished from the Nth Web, except for the briefest accesses, and then only done through the powerful masking function inherent to the Monster.

I start to design a modification of the program that measures the processor load throughout the ship only at the time that someone is using the Monster. Distributed through the nodes, this snapshot function should still be lightweight and barely noticeable, and if I can physically map the subtle changes in how busy the network is, node by node, as the program is used, perhaps it can suggest a location.

Slow and steady. I am going to find you.

And then it hits me. The Monster has become a genuine Monster.

The complexity of its population has grown. Alarmingly so. It doesn't look like the loose, randomized cloud it's supposed to be. The population as a whole has too much order, with too much substructure to the groupings. This is no longer anything like my course project as a teenager—it has a geometric pattern, but it's so large now, I can't see the full shape.

This is beyond what Barrens can do, beyond my level of skill too. Unless he's rounded up a hundred-strong team of computer scientists of my skill and above, which is about as likely as Barrens's becoming Minister of Peace, something more is going on.

Searching through my Implant memories provides snapshots of the Monster's complexity maps over time. When did it start to grow too fast, start to really change? An equation to roughly approximate its altered complexity growth curve, and then running the math through the hardware of the Implant to compute backward, and . . .

And there. There it is. It began about that day the Monster came across one of the Builders' memories.

A shiver as electric possibility runs across the nerves. Are there alien bits of code corrupting the swarm?

I'll go mad if I start down that rabbit hole. My eyes need to stay on what's right in front of me. The parts I do understand still work, that's what matters.

Even if it's slow.

"Real life" work drains the days. The half of my job that is implementation is about dealing with people. Management. Communication. Evaluations. Directing workflows. Dealing with people is tiresome. I wish I could just shove that half of the job onto Hennessy and only do analysis and proposals.

Every once in a while, I still check on the hunt for Mincemeat.

Saturday night, and I am alone at home, as usual. I lean back in my chair, close my eyes, and examine a new memory uncovered by the Monster.

In that forum where the memory was first uploaded, other discussions rage, other rumors. Stories of some of the subculture going missing. Caught by ISec, taken away. The collectors of these horrid memories have gone deep into hiding or have been vanished; this memory is not from them, it is from someone who was hoping to sell it and could not find them.

If that is so, if Barrens was found through them or they were found through him . . . I can do nothing for them.

Many of the threads fade out with nervous posters saying their good-byes, wondering if their little hobby is on the edge of calling the attention of the men in gray.

To set aside this memory or not? Well. There is no real choice about that. I do want to know, for myself too.

Those forum-goers who remain debate whether it actually happened, or if it is just a fragment left over from some unreleased or unremembered creative production. The metadata indicates that it is an old memory, and its quality has been degraded by multiple transfers between devices and viewers—it will be impossible to conclude anything concrete about it either way.

There is enough signal loss that it will be less like reexperiencing the memory, and more like watching a movie. There will be a layer of separation, which, given what posters are saying about the content, is a relief. I ready myself, put aside thoughts of that jerk I love so much, and load it onto my Implant.


He is still young. Too young receive a Retirement notice. He does not understand the reasoning of the Retirement Management Agency. What has he done that is so terrible that he is being taken out of the work rotations? Is something wrong with him? He supposed it was not his place to wonder at the equations and analyses of his betters. He just could not imagine how it was more efficient for a mediocre worker such as himself to be removed from active duty on the ship before he had put in the work equal to a significant fraction of all the years that had been invested in raising him from childhood, giving him a neural Implant, and training him how to use it.

*Jackson! Pay attention!*

*Sorry, Cameron.*

*You better be careful. If you fall over and start choking on that shit, I am not going to dive in there to pull you out.*

*Yes, Cameron.*

*I mean it! Watch your step!*

Cameron is twenty years older. Why isn't he getting Retired?

He slogs through the stinking muck. He is accustomed to the stench by now. It does not bother him nearly as much as the resentment that has overwhelmed him since he received the red envelope with his name on it. In truth, it's sent him reeling. He has not been able to bring himself to even talk about it. He has barely been able to eat—he's lost ten pounds already.

*Put some more muscle into it!*

*Okay, Cameron.*

The probe is heavy in his hands. It is a long stick with a sensor suite at the end, a limited-use amplifier that detects changes in plastech density. The paddle shape of the sensor head has a lot of drag. A few minutes of shifting it through the thick sludge has his shoulders and back aching.

Finally, he senses the breach. *I got it.*

Without moving the end, he places a psi-tag on a hook projecting from the side of the probe's shaft. Carefully, he checks that his fingers are clear of the hook, then triggers the probe. He feels a little more power bleeding into his nervous system, enhancing his meager talent. The hook descends, and when it reaches the bottom of the probe, it activates, punching the chisel end of the tag into the crack.

Another team will be by later on to perform the actual repairs.

Cameron's voice screeches in his head, as though the man were yelling directly into his ear. *Come on then! Get moving! There's three more leaks a hundred meters aft! This segment of piping can't work until all of that is fixed and it can be pressurized again.*

*How far back is the fix-it crew, boss?*

*Never you mind. We take care of our business quick as we can. Let those wannabe engineers be slow and stupid.*

He draws the probe out, rests it against his shoulder as he pushes harder, marching through the meter-thick layer of crusted sewage. His labored breath is loud inside the confines of the breathing mask. He can feel his perspiration trickling down the inside of the slick, waterproof suit, pooling at the folds at his waist, and into his boots.

Perhaps he ought to look at his impending early Retirement as a blessing? It was not as if this were a fulfilling job with good opportunities for advancement.

What would he do with himself, though, in the Retirement section? He was so young, not yet twenty. He would be surrounded by men and women two to four times his age in there!

And how long before Anita forgot him?

He would break up with her first. Maybe tonight. He had seen other couples separated by Retirement. He would not be able to take a teary good-bye prolonged over months. Then the last day would come and the Retirement people would take him off, and then to have her sobbing and weepy and restrained by one of those red-coated men with their cheery smiles? No. Not for him.

Twenty minutes more and he has marked two more leaks. But the last one is driving him crazy. Forty minutes and he just cannot find it!

*I'm telling you, Cameron, there ain't no holes here. Gone over every centimeter, grid-style, and there ain't nothing.*

*Water Management says there's a leak there, so there's a leak there. The computers say so, and they are more reliable than we are.*

*Why can't the fricking computers tag the leak then?*

Patiently, Cameron repeats the same thing he has probably had to say once a day to somebody on his crew for the last ten years. *The sensor resolution of the Reclamation System only goes down to the square meter.*

Another twenty minutes and he can hear the repair team closing in now, just a few tags behind.

*Balls! I've tried spiral search, grid, three times already! And my back is killing me. And, agh, getting hard to breathe. You sure this breather's been put through maintenance? It's not supposed to stink this bad inside the suit!*

*Maybe you're just farting too much, kid. Okay, look. This does happen sometimes, Jackson.*

*Yeah? So what do I do?*

He cannot see his boss's face, but he can feel the sensation of the bespecta-cled man shrugging behind his terminal. *Okay, I'm going to send you an image of the map with the leak. Then you double-tag it as close as you can to the where the map signal says there's a leak. Repair crew will do a square-meter patch job on it.*

He snorts. Seriously? *You shitting me, boss? I know that ain't in the manual.*

*Not everything's in the manual. You know, some tricks we pass around among us word of mouth. Err, thought. Whatever. It works. It's not efficient though, wastes power and plastech. So don't you do it too much or the real bosses will come down on my ass and you can bet I'll squeeze yours till you crap blood, got it?*

What a great mental picture that is. He shakes his head and focuses on the map image in his mind. He closes his eyes, does the best he can to match up Cameron's image and his own location. Then he punches two tags into the pipe surface, almost on top of each other.

*Okay, can I get out of here now?*

*Yeah. Hey, something's going on with—*

Cameron's message is cut off in midtransmission. That never happens. The lights in the tunnel die out. In the distance, he can hear the repair crew cursing nervously. He curses too. This is one of the oldest parts of the ship, far outside the inhabited zone. It might take an hour to restore power to where they are.

And without access to the Nth Web, it is far too easy to get lost. They would all just have to sit tight in the awful muck and wait.

He does not have nearly enough talent to generate a significant amount of light on his own. He directs psi toward the lamp on top of his helmet. With the power grid cut off, he barely has enough energy to get a feeble, orange glimmer out of the sealed LED. It isn't even as bright as a candle.

Not that he can light a candle, down here. If he does, the accumulated gases will explode. Come to think of it, the improvised arc light that strong *touch* psychics could do would set it off too.

The cursing in the distance changes in character, turns to screams. There is a crash, the sound of thunder, stone-dense plastech shattering. Splashing, struggling. What's going on back there?

"Hey!" he calls out, voice muffled by the breather. "You guys okay?"

He retraces his route through the twisting pipelines. Down here, everyone has to watch out for each other. Every once in a while, entire tunnels collapse, the result of centuries of stresses and fatigue, and the occasional micrometeorite punching through at relativistic velocity, too small for the damage to register until it has spread and become a dangerous structural defect.

There is only silence now, except for the sound of his boots pushing through the slime, his loud breaths inside the mask, huffing and puffing. This is good, and bad. It means there has not been a catastrophic hull breach, as there is no sound of roaring gases escaping into hard vacuum, no disgusting slurp of goop out of the pipe. His thoughts are sluggish. Of course there isn't—he would have been sucked out into space by now, if the accident were like that. The silence is also bad. The men are not in a state where they can answer anymore.

"I'm coming, you guys! Hey! Where are you?"

His feet hit something, send him tumbling head over heels into manure. He hangs on to his mask, keeps it in place desperately as he pushes back upright. Using the probe, he feels around the bottom. With an effort that wrenches his back, he drags one of the repairmen out of the slime. He cannot understand what he sees, at first, with the dim light. Then his brain catches up with his eyes, and he screams. He cannot stop screaming, even if he knows he is taxing the breather's capacity. Eventually, the buildup of carbon dioxide has him dizzy, leaning against the curved wall. Long minutes pass as he gasps, and the softly whirring breather reconditions the suit air sufficiently for him to think again.

The man's head is gone. It is *gone*. There is just a red ruin left of the neck.

Barely, he keeps himself from running. He plays the light back and forth, up and down. There is a hole in the tunnel's ceiling, one that was not there when he first passed through. Where is the second member of the repair crew? They always work in pairs.

The lights come back on, white, searing brightness. He blinks. Up through the hole in the ceiling, there is a dark, vertical shaft . . . at the end of it, he sees something. Something dark, and huge. Long, twisted arms. He hears its snarls as it struggles with the broken shape of a man in the ugly orange jumpsuit of a Water Management man. And then it is gone.

*Jackson! You getting me? What happened? Repair crew chief is going nuts. What happened down there? A collapse?*

He cannot think. He just cannot think anymore. He curls up, does not care that the sewage reaches his neck in that position. His tears and snot are misting up the mask.

*Okay, Jackson, I got your visuals on my map. You just sit tight there, okay? We'll get a rescue team down there. Don't panic.*

He only puts his arms around himself and shakes.

Perhaps being personally involved in a dangerous incident has started to harden me against traumatic memories. I shake off the horror in moments. Or maybe I am just numb.

All right. If all this is connected, then what?

Jackson's memory, the many rumors tied into the urban legend of creatures in the sewers, and the document about experiments. What does it mean, put together?

Barrens would say that there is a population of such things. Is this the new direction he's found? The possibility that the Mincemeat killings are being performed by these monsters in the tunnels? But how would they avoid notice in the densely populated Habitat area? What else is there?

My brain cycles through the steps. Too much is still unknown. If this is now the line of Barrens's suspicions, it only generates more questions.

Say there are monsters in the old tunnels and maintenance shafts. Where did they come from? The result of experimentation? Animals from the vertical farms mutated by radiation exposure, perhaps toxic leaks from the reactors or inadequate shielding from a burst of cosmic radiation? Military beasts?

I bring up one image from the blurry, terrified recollection of the man named Jackson. It certainly seems dangerous. It looks nothing like the gracile creatures from the lost memory of the Builders that Barrens and I shared months before. Are these things related somehow to why there are no Builders on the ship? Or are they still on the ship somewhere, hidden away? I cannot imagine those wise, sad strangers experimenting on us, producing monsters in the dark on a whim.

If there is a population of the monsters in the tunnels and not just one or two unfortunate mutants, they could account for the numbers of all those missing people I had thought were false positives in my earlier data-dives. The need for secrecy is easy to rationalize—it is only one more thing for the average crewman to fear but can do nothing about. Fear is destabilizing. It can be deadly in the confines of a closed system. These could be the creatures described by the G-1 documents.

Something feels wrong about that. Not about the creature in the tunnel being a G-1, that feels right. But that they are the Mincemeat killers?

Recalling Barrens's own memory of Callahan's mutilated remains, it does not match. As violently torn apart as Callahan's body was, there was too much of it left there, in his apartment. It does not look as if he were partly eaten by some hungry predator, as the man in the attack that Jackson experienced was. And how would a creature from the deep shafts have gotten up there in his apartment? Why not take prey on the street level, snatch people walking along the sidewalks close to the sewer access hatches?

Experiments, experimentation. Human experimentation would explain the victimology, the random cross section of the ship's population, from young to old.

But too much is still missing. Never mind what the goals and methods of such cruel science might be; why run an experiment in such an uncontrolled way, where so many outside factors can interfere?

It is a mad underworld I have fallen into. Suspicion clashes against common sense and my desire to believe in the system, in humanity's universal mission to survive. What could Keepers and Breeding Duty possibly have to do with secrets about monsters under the city? And I remember one of Barrens's threads in an underground discussion forum. That other guy, who suggested that early Retirements are all Mincemeat deaths.

My mind refuses to make that fit. That is as far as I can get with what I have right now. My eyes ache, my temples are buzzing, and, agh, it's two in the morning.

I shove it all into a filing crate. A snap of my fingers floats it into one of my closets.

Sleep is no escape. My dreams have me running around in tunnels. Or worse, doing maintenance in them, hour after hour.

Soon, even the distraction and comfort of my routine at work is disrupted. A major initiative is being started from the top. Hennessy messages me rumors about something that will involve not just multiple departments across the whole Habitat, but entire Ministries.

I can't confirm them. He probably knows more than I do. So, I give him something else to do.

At my desk, I putter away at all the tasks that need doing. Correcting typos in the reports to be forwarded upward. Signing off on request forms. Passing messages along. Earth died centuries before and people are still plagued by paperwork. My eyes are getting blurry as I stare at a badly labeled graph about wastewater pollutants.

Hennessy knocks at my door. My special assignment for him took less time than I thought. Or, no. It's halfway through the morning already. Ugh.

"Come in."

"Hana?"

"Yes, James?"

"These are the records you asked about. I don't understand why you asked me. Your school pal Marcus works at Water Management. You could put in the request directly yourself and get the data back faster than I could."

I cannot explain that I am trying to protect Marcus from any future problems if I should get caught.

"Just some ideas I'm working on."

"Riiiight. Any reason why I'm showing them on my tablet instead of just messaging you with copies of the files?"

So that there are no records of my receiving them in my office, my dear assistant, no system logs of the transmission. For someone normally so perceptive in social situations, Hennessy is talking too much about matters he should realize I want some discretion on. Perhaps he does read it on my face now. Maybe what he wants is for me to confide in him. Hennessy, if I do that and something happens to me, well. You will not be able to take my position if you have been tainted by any future suspicions related to me.

Copying the files over to another psi-tablet takes only a moment. He blinks at that, realizes that I'm using a tablet with no detectable wireless function. Hennessy pauses at my door, closes it instead of leaving.

"I'm not stupid, Hana."

"Have I given you a reason to think that I have such a low opinion of you?"

"You can trust me. I don't know what this is about, but—"

Direct neural messaging. *Don't. Take care of our team, James. That's what I'm depending on you for.*

That seems to be enough to turn him away.

A quick query through the files suggests that the memory is real. At one time a man named Jackson and crew supervisor Cameron were in the same water-works maintenance team. A repair team was reportedly killed right around when Jackson was Retired. Of course, the given cause was a structural collapse. That was ninety years ago.

What is next? What's next is I'm not supposed to be thinking through all this on my own. That overprotective ass!

I need to get that function to filter away background processor use, so I can get on finding the jerk.

I think about putting up an ad for a memory I do not intend to sell, and leaving a message in a secret location, like a kid playing a game. Instinct holds me back. Why? Isn't Miura exactly the kind of company I want? She is already involved. She is a clear-minded cop. This is the sort of thing the police ought to be good at.

She has posted the ad but not asked me what I have found. As formidable as she is, she too is afraid.

I'll try to meet her next week. No, not even then. I will run as far as I can on my own, until I cannot anymore. There are still many threads to follow, on the Web, and Miura will not be any better at that than I.

Ah, that bitter ache. The sweet pain of a wound I keep picking at. I am still hoping that Barrens will be the one to send a message asking me to go to him. I would. I would forget all this, and go.

## 16

City Planning takes a turn that puts a stop to everything in my life other than being one of the six City Planning Administrators.

The rumors come true. Directives are issued from the Central Council. All management teams in every department, agency, and bureau scramble to meet the demands of a Habitat Reconfiguration plan that was handed down with almost no warning.

My team, like everyone else's, is swamped. We postpone Hennessy's meticulously planned team-building exercise in the Taiga biome. We schedule shift work. We consume prodigious quantities of coffee.

I try to make contact with Miura if only to inform her that I simply do not have time for further investigations, at least for now. Putting up the ad on the Nth Web takes a thought, even weaving in the hidden memory. When I check for a posting from her in reply, there is nothing.

I guess she is giving it up. That would bother me more if I weren't so busy.

The work makes a mess of me. Everyone in the department is exhausted and moody; Hennessy helps keep the team going. Hah. It is almost as if I planned on giving him more opportunities to lead.

Normally in the Ministry of the Interior, City Planning plans, and Primary Cityworks executes. Not this time.

Each week, we have to assist in the demolition and construction of a new city block to lighten the load on Primary Cityworks.

And it is not just the Ministry of the Interior. So much demolition and construction is going on, the Ministry of Energy has to carefully allocate reactor power, with scheduled rotating power outages in different sections of the

Habitat. Significant numbers of officers from the Ministry of Peace help redirect the traffic around all those construction sites. Ministry of Information marketing specialists feed the general public feel-good sound bites about major changes for the better. Nobody is telling us what the Ministry of Health is so busy with, but everyone hears of their struggles too; there are just rumors of some major health-care component to the Habitat Reconfiguration.

Since becoming an Administrator, I have rarely had to involve myself with construction.

Over mere weeks, I destroy and build multiple entire skyscrapers. It is exhausting, draining work. The rest of my crew are worse off—even teamed up in mental gestalt, their combined *touch* rating just matches my own individual ability, because of inherent inefficiencies of different minds linking up their talents. They need to expend 30 percent more effort than I do to accomplish the same task. Among the thousands of crewmen in the combined City Planning and Primary Cityworks effort, mine is the only team that is meeting our assigned quotas and performance metrics.

There are precious few opportunities to check on the Monster.

Night after night, day after day, we sneak in naps either on desks telekinetically converted to cots in our office, or in the backs of the supply trucks when we are on-site at a construction zone. We go back to the gray tomb of City Planning to turn in our reports and shower. Lesser workers, secretaries and janitors, assist us with laundry and food.

Time blurs in that state.

All right.

After this, I promise myself. After the workload eases up. By then, Hennessy will be ready, and the new staff members will be trained up.

Then I'll vanish too. I will find him, never mind if I barely have any idea where to start looking.


Then my team of ten loses three women to Breeding Duty and one man to early Retirement.

Antonia, Julia, and Erica have a week to psyche themselves up for the long sleep.

I schedule time to talk to each of them and . . . warn them. But I don't think they quite understand how hard it will be. It isn't in me to share how a place inside me still feels empty, or the dreams I still have.

Then they are gone. A long, paid vacation. Will they be the same when they come back, or will they feel what I feel?

Stephen receives his Retirement notice. He has two months more with us. With the current workload, we can't even throw him a party.

That young man who had the encounter with the tunnel beasts was right. Why are some individuals Retired so young? How can the numbers ever justify it? Stephen Wong is practically a fresh graduate. Hennessy and I have only just gotten him to where he's familiar with all our department forms and protocols.

Again that one poster's most mad idea floats to the top in my thoughts.

No. Madness lies that way. That's not a matter of hundreds of killings, but thousands across the centuries. What could possibly do that? And why?

No time to ponder whether the superiors who are supposed to lead and guide and protect their lessers are instead doing something horrible to us.

There is always too much to do. More roads to reconfigure, more old buildings to demolish and new ones to raise. The months pass. Stephen says his goodbyes.

The hundredth day of this work surge arrives. During the moments between, people come and go along the streets with dark crescents under their eyes, cheeks hollow.

*Hennessy, have you ever seen anything like this?*

It's a stupid question, a sign of fatigue that I even asked it.

*Of course not.*

Then it's Hennessy's turn to think something foolish to me: *I wonder if these new architectural designs really will save enough power to make it worth converting an entire Habitat section over to them.*

Our expertise in civil engineering is enough to know that this isn't so, that it's Ministry propaganda meant for the less informed majority of the crew.

We carry on the conversation in our heads while we instruct our new replacements out loud. Our instruction covers the construction of a large residential-grade tower. The rookies look ridiculously young, as if they were accelerated through the academy and skipped two or three years of training.

"It is of critical importance that you maintain the mental image at all times during a build, and not just rely on preprogrammed instructions in an Implant or amplifier."

*Look at that one, rolling her eyes. We knew it all when we were that young too, didn't we?*

*I suppose I am laying it on a bit thick.*

*Hey, if you want to get their attention and keep it, you know you can just show your stuff.*

I take a deep breath. Maybe I have forgotten what I was like, even with perfect memory. I am not the same as I was ten years ago, and despite being able to see all the events in between then and now with ruthless and exacting clarity, in many ways when I see through those younger eyes, it is like living out the life of a stranger. It is easier to empathize with what I was like as a child than how I was as a teenager and then a young adult.

*Hello? You going to get on with it?*

*Just focusing, James. Visualizing.*

True and not true. I was not entirely lost in my head—I was also waiting for the extremely complex programs I personally coded into my assigned builder's gauntlet to finish booting up and analyzing all the data from the blueprints for this morning's endeavor. The scripts will ensure that I can concentrate on general form and controlling and drawing and directing the power where it is needed, while relieving me of the mental load of imagining the minutiae, the exact measurements, dimensions, loads, densities, shades of color, and performance characteristics of the resulting structure.

I close my eyes and snap up my right arm. The steel-gray gauntlet shimmers in the morning light. Then the sun is eclipsed by the intense blue burst of raw psi energy arching from my face-plates to the gauntlet.

I stand now, in a pillar of lightning, pulling upper-megawatt-class energy off the grid.

Music starts to play in my ears, following a lesser script that draws upon a memory of myself from the night before, listening to Vivaldi, consciousness drifting along the light, playful melody of violins and tying in the notes with each step of the mental choreography I am to dance when it is time.

The light around me fades, and now it is the entire construction site that glows underfoot, concentrating around the ultradense stacks of plastech ingots. The deck floor for hundreds of meters around hums, vibrates.

My hands and fingers curl and sweep, left and right and up and in slow, gentle arcs. Ingots fuse together and flow into the shapes and forms in my thoughts; slabs and beams and columns and joists grow out of the bubbling mass. Delivered in its densest form, the plastech must be spun out and recrystallized in various configurations, so that parts of it perform like steel, and parts of it perform like concrete, and parts of it like wood. It is an organism growing in fast-forward. Skeleton and skin forming simultaneously, shaped with the push and pull of my mind.

Violins sing in my thoughts, and I hum along to the memory as I lift and shape tons of matter. The scripts in the gauntlet cooperate with the ones in my Implant, and they are the players I direct in this performance, the orchestra I conduct. My breath is slow and sure and my heart beats in time with the strokes of my talent.

Vivaldi goes to Puccini.

Telekinesis dopes lines that act as power conduits, it extrudes pipes and drainage and links up to the waterworks, it carves the holes for the windows and bubbles out spaces for rooms and hallways, the thousand, thousand little processes unfurling like the individual notes of an orchestra.

This is to be new housing, following supposedly more efficient design principles. The ceilings of the rooms are high, and many of the walls in each apartment are set to behave like crystal. Future residents will be able to control the opacity of their rooms, to allow more light in from the "outdoors" when they wish it, or to enfold themselves completely in black if they choose. They will also be able to control the thermal properties of the walls and the windows. And rather than appearing in straight lines and right angles, the ventilation ducts are curved and round, a webbed network under the skin of the floors and hidden in the bones of the solid, weight-bearing pillars. Spiral staircases and elevator shafts are hollowed out.

Mozart.

The whole thing starts to tilt here, and then there. The shape of the superstructure is irregular, and that makes it more complex to fabricate, but I have checked over the figures repeatedly in preparation, and I smile as the troops of my imagination carry out their work.

The tower turns and twists, slowly. It looks nothing like the sober concrete block that used to stand here. It is the neck of a bird stretching up, soaring hundreds of meters into the Dome's sky. As the theme plays out, my thoughts slide through it, ethereal blood, and I make room for others to join in.

The outer shell is supposed to be able to control the heat and temperature of the entire building with little additional power. These special panels and built-in computers are installed by Hennessy's group. The smart structure will automatically handle the air and the thermal flow and adjust for the demands of individual tenants. Hennessy is conducting his own concert, with his own music in his head, as he and the team members linked with his mind handle fine interior detailing.

"Ode an die Freude" now, as I make one last series of checks, subjecting the tower to different levels of stress and strain. Those last triumphant notes fade out and away, while the skeleton and skin of the newborn giant sighs and whispers under load-testing and validation.

I clap my hands and release the grid's power and smile up at this strange-looking girl. She is out of place, here in Edo Section's residential area, too much sleek future gleam among all the white and blue pagodas and compounds. Soon, many of those will go too.

The greenhorns look suitably impressed now, and I am pleased by their wide eyes, their open mouths. I have checked their files over—of the four of them, even the strongest is only half of my power rating, though that boy is surely the future of the department. They will be better than the individuals they replaced, if they work at it.

It seemed to me to take only minutes, but that was an ordeal that lasted ten hours straight. My mouth is dry, and without the music to buoy my thoughts along, I feel the exhaustion weighing on my neck and shoulders. The sun is already setting, and Hennessy will be busy throughout the night completing the interior.

I hope our new teammates paid attention and took notes. Watching this sort of work may be boring after a while, but they have to actually do this too, and to do it requires an intimate familiarity with every process. If we were not in such a rush, in their proper training a build-master would walk them through the scanning of each part of the blueprint and then the working out of how one's amplifier programming converts it into scripted telekinetic act based on each contributing mind's will and emotions.

"Okay, ladies," I croak out to the new ones. "Now, take a break. Eat something. Nap. When you get back, pay attention to Hennessy and keep taking notes on your tablets. You'll join his gestalt next week when we do this all over again."

It is the end of the day and a department memo winds its way down to the field office, strictly for Administrator rank and above.

Unbelievable.

All this activity is required so that an entire section of the Habitat can be closed off—reassigned for some secret purpose, to be placed under direct control by a joint task force of the Ministries of Information and Health. Thousands of crew have to move into the rest of the Habitat, and all of the food-generating capacity of Beijing Section's vertical farms that will be lost must be compensated for in the remaining farms.

It is to be done by the end of the year. The crew's living space has never been contracted so rapidly before, and certainly not to retask Habitat real estate toward some other purpose.

*Something is happening,* Barrens would say, alarmed. No, perhaps he would not be—for him, the Council always makes unfathomable decisions over the crew, for purposes that are never revealed. He might even be amused at my shock. *You're too used to thinking you know why things happen. That's not what it's like for most of us.*

He would be right. Too troubled to focus on further reports, on evaluations of our new teammates and recommendations about the next projects, I escape for a time to a public hard-line terminal fifteen minutes away from our current work site. Finally, I check on what fish my nets might have reeled in, in the many weeks I have neglected them.

There is the usual explosion of data to filter down and skim.

And then . . .

And then. My hands trace the words hovering in my visual feed. It is Barrens. Messages. Assembled from fragments distributed throughout the Web, a line here in one forum, a few lines there on a random person's log about his pets. It is a means of communicating with me that only one who knows exactly how my search algorithms work could use.

They are arranged like pages in a journal. I am hot and I am cold as I feel his emotions poured out in those digital thoughts. Longing for me. His doubts. His excitement about finding like-minded people in the shadows.

The newest entry, however, freezes my heart. The date is from the week before.

*They are already watching you, Hana. You have to run. Today. Get to where they can't track your Implant. I will find you.*

17

IT IS HERE.

It is now.

And I am not ready. I had planned for this contingency, but with the avalanche of work hours imposed by the Habitat Reconfiguration, I never got to completing my prep.

I still don't know where Barrens is. I haven't even completed the design for the signal analysis module.

I was going to have multiple bags with supplies packed at home, at the office, and a smaller one on me at all times, to be ready to run. I bought backpacks with lots of little pockets and extra amplifiers and various useful little gadgets and never even got them out of the packaging.

I was going to write a multimedia management manual for Hennessy, with every little tip and bit of advice I could think of. At least I got around to delegating more responsibilities to him.

I was going to have a nice secure message that would fire off untraceably, apologizing to my friends and telling them to stay safe, and not to worry about me. At least we were hanging out more again, until the cursed Ministry project took over my life.

Chilled and shivering in my seat despite the warm sunlight streaming down on me through the window of the little booth, time running out, I'll just have to manage.

I send out a one-word command to my little bots. *Eclipse*. My part of the swarm begins to make compressed, encrypted copies of its particles and their data. Then they break the packets apart and spirit them away across the Analytical Nodes of the Nth Web. The links are severed, and the ongoing processes write over themselves. The parts of the program not under my control will live on, but the processes directly linked to me will vanish, keep ISec from being able to take control if they are aware of the Monster. The parts of it that I was modifying to track Barrens go dormant.

There is no time to get a change of clothes or the tablets with my latest design efforts.

I have *touch*. And I like to think I am pretty smart. Whatever I don't have, I can make. Plastech is all around me. Even what I am wearing. Though it might take time to reconstruct the coding I have done on the mobile devices at the apartment, it's all still in my head, perfect memories of how they were made.

I step back out onto the street and know that it is too late.

Lyn is there, with a devastated look on her face, as she walks toward me in a colorless, murky Information Security coat, at the head of a column of five black-armored Enforcers.

There is no time to talk. The Enforcers raise their hands, and there is darkness as they reach into my head and shut me off.


The walls of my cell are in friendly colors. A border at the bottom edge is a deep shade of green, perhaps myrtle, then there's a light blue, like the sky. The painted flowers are in bright yellows, chartreuse and pear.

Everything is luminous to a greater or lesser degree—the light comes from everywhere and so it seems to come from nowhere. It never changes, so my body has no environmental cues to track time—even with the internal chronometer function of my neural Implant, my sleep cycle starts to fracture, and I am always tired. No one has spoken to me since I was processed and placed here.

A niche has been hollowed out of the wall for a bed. The top inch of the plastech has been processed into foam cushioning. It is surfaced with what feels like skin, but I have seen it before in my materials briefings and I know its tightly woven fibers are tougher than steel, tougher than carbon composites or ceramic blends. The commode in the opposite corner from the bed is metallic and efficient, rounded. There is not even a door, let alone a doorknob. Food comes in through a slot in another niche in another wall at random times, another measure to confuse the suprachiasmatic nucleus of the brain. There are no utensils, either. There is no loose plastech anywhere.

Every surface is subtly charged with another person's psi. The entire room is a one-way amplifier, under the control of others.

My gifts can affect nothing, except for the water I can get from the faucet and the food I can float from the feed trough to my mouth—just the tasteless, if nutritious, mush of protein, fiber, sugars, and fats from the bioreactors that recycle the organic garbage of the ship. The cheapest eats possible. And there is, of course, no access to the Web.

Eating this way, using telekinesis to lift food to my mouth, reminds me.

At fifteen years old, I broke my right wrist during a game of basketball after school; I tripped across the feet of a doughy-looking boy named Arnold when we both chased after a rebound, and I landed wrong. For the two days it took the pain to fade after a Doctor used Psychic Healing to repair the fracture, I used *touch* for a spoon, to hold my toothbrush, to put on my clothes, to tie my shoes, to be the hand I couldn't use.

"You make that look so easy," Mala said admiringly.

I am glad I have *touch* instead of *bruiser* psychometabolism. Superstrength and speed won't get me out of this cell, but psychokinesis means I don't have to eat on hands and knees with my head down like a dog.

My clothes were taken from me, every hair on my scalp and skin shaved off with the precision that only a psychic blade can achieve. Perhaps it is meant to be dehumanizing, to encourage prisoners to live in the pleasant escape of perfect memories, better days. Perhaps the persons on the other end of the amplifier that is my prison can eavesdrop on my thoughts more easily that way.

I clear my mind. Meditation is a refuge.

For only an hour a day, I let myself indulge in other people's experiences of cats and children I had purchased over the last year, and my own memories of better times. All maintained through the Implant. I can play them over and over, and when I am sick of them, there are more memories from when I was younger: all the movies I've seen, the books I've read, the concerts I've attended. An inner universe is inside those thoughts. But I have to limit my time in them. It would be too easy to lose myself in my head, to let go of the days.

Humans can get used to anything. I know this because in the bad old days of Earth's dark wars, minorities that were disapproved off by majorities found themselves getting accustomed to much worse than what I am going through now.

They were surrounded by the smell of death in their camps while they were starved and worked to the bone.

Escape into memories, for them, was surely harder.

Knowing now that the psionic technologies we use are alien in origin, I can also understand all the limits humans have in using them. Some things are easy, while other tasks require more understanding of the Builders' technology than we have. Otherwise, why allow prisoners access to these perfect past lives through the Implant to comfort themselves? If they could just turn an Implant off, it would be a more devastating punishment than any prison. No psychic talents, nothing but blurry, deceptive brain-based memory for company, no direct access to the Nth Web, no use of most of the devices it takes to live on the ship at all.

It is harder to code into my neural Implant without an external device, especially with how fuzzy I am from the poor sleep induced by the constant light. But I manage; I just have to be more careful, as stray thoughts add in pictures or smells or touches that have nothing to do with the DREAM33 programming language used on the device. There is nothing but time. Old exercises to refine the clarity of my thoughts reestablish the mental discipline of precise thinking. I cannot affect my environment, but the Implant is still a part of me.

It takes three days to write a function to control the brightness of the signals along my optic nerves. It allows the simulation of a proper night and a proper day by altering the perception from my eyes.

It helps. My sleep starts to return to proper ship time. Clarity returns. Even if the food comes at random, I hold off from eating it until it is at a reasonable hour for a meal. There are things still under my control.


I exercise when I'm awake. Push-ups, sit-ups, shoulder-width dips, lunges, crunches. The things I used to watch Barrens do sometimes in the mornings, or when he would wake in the middle of the night and couldn't sleep anymore. I shadowbox in the evenings, going through the basic self-defense drills he showed me. Simple jabs, straights, lateral elbows, low kicks.

I push my mental training, now that I am at least rested, and I play with tricks to better apply my *touch* talent even without access to the grid's endless power. I lift individual drops of water into the air and have them dance for me around the room, even as I change their shapes. I cleanse myself with hard sprays of water that I redirect from the tap, and I dry off by shucking the moisture away with the steadily improving grip of my mind. As the hairs on my body and on my head start to come in and turn to stubble, I shave them off with a slender filament, a telekinetic razor—I'd never managed such precision before.

The blade pleases me. But I bury any thoughts of using it as a weapon. There is, after all, always someone watching me. Any visitor that comes for me will know I can do this, will be warned by my jailers.

For Enforcers, such manipulations are just parlor tricks. They are the elite of the elite. From hearsay, I know their psi-training is beyond me. Not just in terms of raw power, but technique.

When I was a student at the Class V Center, one of the Enforcer cadets from Officer Command School came to my psionics class to demonstrate some of their manipulations. That is the only time I have seen a man fly under his own power, without the aid of an amplifier. When that glowing figure descended from the sky to our training field, it was like a visitation from God. He played games with us, simultaneous Ping-Pong games using telekinetically controlled paddles against ten students.

I was one of those ten, and I was the only one to win my no-hands game. I was so envious back then, of that incredible mind, just as, I suppose, those who barely have enough psi to power a glow stick must be envious of those like myself.

The days pass. Once a week, I treat myself to a second of memory with Barrens. Just a kiss. Just the feel of my fingers vanishing into those huge, hard, warm mitts.

Boredom becomes the strongest motivation for attempting ever-new variations of *touch* training. When I shower, I create dollhouses out of the water, floating in the air, populated with little men and women sitting at tables. I try gardens. Clear butterflies catch the glow off the walls, and they never get caught in the webs spun by my watery spiders off the stems and leaves of clear, crystalline rosebushes. Fish fly through the air as the water sluices down the diminishing planes and hollows and curves of my skin. Some days, I re-create Minnow and run my fingers down his back, and other days, I draw water into the form of a baby, to cradle in my arms. I sculpt busts of my friends, their faces smiling at me.

On the sixtieth morning of my incarceration, after breakfast, I finally have a guest.

One wall parts down the middle and slides apart.

Red curls tickle my nose. The rich rose and lavender scent is annoying, after my clean, odorless, sterile months, but I do not mind. The embrace is warm.

"I'm sorry," murmurs the breathy contralto in my ear. "I've been trying and trying to see you. I am in Information Security, but I'm just a researcher, not in enforcement. It took forever. I used up favors just to be the one to bring you in, make sure you weren't hurt."

"Don't be sorry, Lyn. I'm here because I deserve to be. They were my choices, nobody made them for me."

"Bullshit! My lovesick darling, if not for that man, you would not be here."

Is that really so? At times I thought it. But have I not always sought out the limits of available information on my own? I was doing that long before I met Barrens in a dirty alleyway, both of us bleeding and wounded. I started to develop my neuralhacks while I was just a kid in school. Lyn was right at my side with me, only her subversive tendencies died away completely after our discovery of the size and power of the computational network on the ship.

Maybe another person would have blamed Barrens for the mess I'm in. Hah. I could have turned back so many times along the way. I could have said no in the first place. I could have just made Hunter, given it to him, and never participated. It's not him that put me here. I made my own choices. I didn't want to be left behind, I didn't want to be protected.

"Hana, crèche-sister. We met when we were just kids. My Keepers were friends with yours and took us to the same parks and playgrounds, the same concerts, the same museums. I'm not here as an ISec officer—I'm not even a field agent. I'm here because I'm your friend.

"This is your only chance. This evening, they will begin your interrogation. You have to cooperate. They're running out of patience."

I pull back and look at her teary green eyes. She is my oldest friend.

When we were little, I punched a boy for yanking her braids. She helped me with my homework so many times when I wasn't disciplined enough to start on it in time.

We are so far from the girls we were then.

"Lyn, why haven't they just Adjusted me? Just strip all the data out of my head."

"If they do that, there will be nothing left of the person you were, I've been convincing them, talking to everyone I can, that you can do more for them if you are still you."

How could my voluntary cooperation be preferable? I am nothing special. I have my talents and skills, I am in the upper ranks, but there are still many superior to myself.

"Do you even know what this is about, Lyn?"

"Of course not. And I don't want to know. But I know you, Hana. You might deviate from the rules sometimes, but you believe in the mission like nobody else. You read histories, old political tracts, physics papers from the nav archive about our trajectory to Canaan."

Do I still believe in the mission? In its paramount importance? Ah, well. Of course I do. What matters my lonely little longing for the son I am not permitted to know, or the existence of mysterious creatures in the sewers and shadowy, unexplained deaths? We, the crew of the Noah, have a higher purpose than any of our spoiled, pampered ancestors back on Earth. This colonization attempt is all our eggs in one basket. If it fails, humanity is extinct. There is just far too much data for this fundamental truth to be a lie.

Lyn sees that on my face.

"Okay, good. Cooperate. Then I can have you out of here, and we can start getting things back to normal. Oh!" Her hands close around my arms, fingers probing my biceps. "You've gotten so thin. I'll try to get them to give you a bigger ration. It's so awful in here. Maybe a blanket, at least. And, wow." Lyn pulls back, blushing. "A robe, or something."

Such luxuries! Perhaps it is twisted, but I have come to enjoy the empty minimalism of this space. Owning nothing, having nothing but my memories and my talent and the games I can play with water and the programs living in my head.

I see Lyn Starling before me in her expensive, ruthlessly professional business suit, steel blue, without the impersonal harshness of a watery-gray ISec overcoat. Her elegantly coiffed hair. Gold bracelet, platinum ring, pearl necklace. When we embraced, the rich, slick material of her jacket is too much, unreal.

My lack of possessions, my lack of freedoms, the life within my inner self, these things seem more real to me and more true than the life I had before. Our perfect little world maintained by secrets and a willing acceptance that those above us know better.

We chat for a while, Lyn trying hard to pretend I am not naked, and hairless. She tells me of current consumer trends, the latest fashions, the newest commercially available gadgets that Marcus wants to purchase, Jazz's upcoming performance at a concert in the park with the rest of her team from High Energy. Lyn talks about the newest texts, entertainment streams, experimental art-house movies built around the composited memories of the performers.

Only her talk of food gets to me. New restaurants. A change in the culling pattern of the livestock herds that has made various animal products more affordable. My stomach clenches, I can almost smell her breakfast on her breath: butter, cream, eggs, fresh bread.

"Lyn?"

"Yes?"

"If I don't cooperate, they're going to do it, aren't they?"

Her green eyes turn wild. Afraid for me. "You have to, D. Please. What do you owe that creep anyway? He's not sitting in a cell. If he's as resourceful as you think, they can't catch him even if you help them."

Oh, Lyn. You do not belong in Information Security. You are not hard enough for it.

When she leaves, two men in black armor come in, accompanied by one woman in a Behavioralist's green coat.

Naked but for my best reluctant smile, I seat myself on my tiny cot. "Welcome, gentlemen, lady. I'd offer you all some refreshments, but you haven't deigned to serve me any meals since the day before yesterday."

## 18

THE LONGER THEY STAND BEFORE ME, SILENTLY EVALUATING ME FROM HEAD TO toe, the more I regret my flippant greeting. Should I be begging? Should I just pretend they are not there?

In the Enforcer exoskeletons, the men look inhuman. The armor is contoured to the body in curved, segmented sections. Over the face the armor follows the surfaces of the cheeks and jaw and around the mouth, but there are no lenses for the eyes, nor slits to breathe through. It is the woman, though, who is most dangerous to me in here.

I am being read.

*Yes, you are.*

She has red-pink eyes, this stranger who has my life or death in her hands. Her skin is unnaturally pale where it is not covered by the gleaming silver lines of her Implant emitters. I have never seen the pattern before—it is only a few lines, here and there, going out from the corners of her eyes and down her neck under the collar of her blouse. But it must spread extensively—I can see chrome threads on her bare hands, like glittering veins. Her hair has faded completely to a pure, snowy white. I have heard, by way of rumor, that adults with extreme psychic gifts all look this way because the constant flow of energy through their cells degrades pigments as their talents mature.

*That is true.*

It is easy to shut one's mouth. How does one stop one's own thinking?

*Don't try meditating. It will irritate me.*

In terms of talent, this Behavioralist is as far above the one that evaluated me after my Breeding Duty as I am above a bus driver. She is *writing* herself into my brain, not just sending packets of thought at me. Her ghostly hand is in my brain, manipulating the neurons as she chooses. She thinks it and I think it too. She wears the green, but she could just as easily be wearing the gray, or the black.

*Amusing. Usually, they are too afraid to consider such details.*

Of course I'm afraid. I'm terrified. My mind races through lessons and rumors from school. She is small in body, inches shorter than me, but the force of her will fills the room, the presence of a giant.

Something I learned from my man, though, is to grasp at anger when fear is paralyzing.

"Are you done showing off?"

She smiles. "I don't often hear that from a detainee. Then again, we don't have very many detainees, as you must know, Miss Dempsey."

Yes. Their meticulously filled out reports grace my desk quarterly. No names, of course—just the raw numbers of how many men and women whose minds they tear down and rebuild as they see fit. They only need enough capacity to hold people until the Adjustment process is done, usually just a day for a shallow Adjustment, a week at most for a deep Adjustment, with a few more cells for special cases like me.

"Your researcher friend already told you that we don't plan that for you."

"If you're not going to crack my head open and fry it in a pan, could we observe the courtesy of only considering what I say, verbally, to be part of this discussion?"

Her laughter is the skittering of spiders along my spine. She makes no mnemonic gesture to guide her power—there is only the result, as the floor behind her bulges up and takes the shape of a plain, white chair. It is wax melting, except in reverse. She twists the plastech away from the control of the prison systems with ease.

No wasted energy at all. I might manage such a trick if I had an amplifier on me.

She sits and crosses her legs. The briefcase carried by one of the armored Enforcers pops open. Large envelopes and gray folders and a gleaming, emerald-trimmed psi-tablet float up before her, and just as she releases them, she draws up more material from the floor to make a table to rest them on.

The Enforcers do not make their own chairs and sit. They stand, silent. The black material of their armor reflects no light—the seams, the edges between the plates, the joints, all these things are nearly impossible to see. They are dark silhouettes, holes of darkness shaped like men. It would have been easier to be leered at by macho cops in blue coats who could not keep their eyes off my boobs. Feeling the stares of these non-individuals is more dehumanizing than the entire experience of my imprisonment thus far.

"Don't pay attention to the grunts, Miss Dempsey. It makes them nervous. Keep your eyes on me."

"I certainly wouldn't want to make them nervous."

"Now, to business, yes?"

It is not as if I asked her to waste time poking around in my head and intimidating me with her superior talents when she knew all the while that it would come down to a spoken discussion. "Please." I nod.

Smile, Dempsey. It is probably not wise to give the lady itching to lobotomize you any lip or dirty looks. Best not to think snide comments.

Her shark's mouth is lovely as dimples sink into prominence. I amuse her, I suppose.

"It rather pains my superiors to admit this, but I agree with your friend Engineer Starling. Your voluntary assistance is more likely to result in a favorable outcome than tearing all the facts out of your brain and rewiring you like one of those things from old Earth wars—what are they called? Guided missiles."

She pulls out 2-D images printed out on stiff, glossy paper and spreads them in front of me.

"I could have just pushed the relevant memories into your head, Miss Dempsey, but sometimes, the old physiological process of seeing an image and that information being processed by the brain has its advantages. It may be less immediate, but the slow realization as the self synthesizes the relevant concepts and takes in the picture, well. It has its own sort of gravity."

Men and women, they lie naked on cold metallic slabs. Their skin is bluish, except for where it has been torn by violence. Their stillness is more than a lack of movement.

"Don't you think it is ironic, Miss Dempsey? The man brought you under his wing, trying to find the truth of what he thought were serial murders, only to become a murderer himself? Him and his new friends?"

No. Not Barrens. Justice is his life. The value of individual human life, as opposed to the utilitarian cogs that keep the mission going, that's always been what he burns to protect. "I don't believe you."

"His organization has killed seven officers that we know of. Others are missing."

Her eyes catch mine. It is not a command. It is not a compulsion. She slams my mind with her conviction, her sincere belief that this is the truth.

"Do you see those funny holes in their chests that are a bit ragged? Better versions of the crossbow bolts that were shot at you at the edge of the inhabited zone. We know about that too." She pulls out one more picture.

The name escapes my lips. "Miyaki!" So this is why she never attempted to contact me again after that one hidden message.

"Barrens killed her too. Personally, that one—I extracted the memory from her corpse myself. He must have wanted us to see the good officer's death—the rest of the victims got pithed."

Pithed?

"Cored. They take a spike and shove it up the foramen magnum at the base of the skull and deep into the brain, then run a bit of electricity through it— destroys the Implant nexus, prevents memory retrieval."

No. I cannot believe it of him. I will not.

She tilts her head and those eyes catch the light, the red flashing to pale pink. They pierce me without any need for psionic manipulation of my emotions. Her face is stone-still but for her mouth; her brows do not twitch, her body language is unyielding and focused in the extreme. But her eyes are alive, sincere, fierce.

"Take the tablet. The last few seconds of her memories."

Escape seems beyond reach. Curling up on the tiny excuse for a bed might just tempt her to *write* commands directly into my nervous system, playing me like a puppet.

A deep breath and there is nothing to smell, just aseptic recycled air.

"I don't have a choice, do I?"

"Choices always exist, even when it may not seem like it. Even in this cell, with nothing to own but your own skin, haven't you exercised what freedoms you have? To fight to stay strong, to keep your body fit, to train your mental techniques. Why did you do them, knowing they would have no effect on the outcome?"

She holds the tablet up between us. On it are vid-streams of other men and women that were or are in cells like mine. Most of them are bleary-eyed, dirty. One has become nearly skeletal, just lying on the floor, staring up blankly— difficult to tell if that one was male or female. "Others have been in this room. After a few weeks of this, most of them give up. They let themselves go. They exist only in the escape of their memories. Strong crewmen with talents to match my own and genetically gifted with extreme potential for intelligence and physical fitness have been broken just with the emptiness of this room, and the constant, bare environment."

Is that a compliment?

"So, yes, Miss Dempsey. You do have a choice—though you cannot choose the consequences, you can still decide."

Another deep breath for me. Knowing would be terrible. Not knowing allows for doubt, would allow me to keep my faith in Barrens, for as long as I have until this woman rips myself out of my head and puts whatever she and her superiors decide is useful into what remains.

My hands close around the cool, glossy tablet. Contact is not necessary as this tablet has its wireless functionality, but the gesture firms my resolve. Maybe.

Glowing with red fire, drawing all the power the amplifier can. She knows it can only end this way. She unlocks everything she is.

Drawing this much psi, her *bruiser*'s body works differently. She is at another level from most of the Inspectors at the precinct. It's why she made captain so young. Rather than the pounding heart and roaring blood and adrenaline and searing breaths and jagged, flaring pulses of sense organs into the brain that she knows is the experience for most of her coworkers, her body becomes slow and still, her mind empty and quiet. Each breath is an eternity. And the moment between each heartbeat is peace.

She pulls herself from the crater in the wall, folding the thin, ragged edges back. She missed. How could she have missed? He was not even lit up yet.

Time is so slow, the sounds she hears are distorted, the input from her eyes is dim. It has taken long years of practice to understand the world around her when she is this deep in her battle trance.

The low, rumbling vibrations through the air are words. His words. "Miyaki Miura was my friend. I don't know who you are. I do know why you're here."

He is too dangerous to waste precious seconds talking to.

There is no talking anymore. He lights up too. They are two suns circling each other in a decaying orbit. The ground shudders, cracks with their footsteps.

She is still faster than he is, but not by much. She slips her head to the side, and that great big block of iron that is his fist just brushes her cheek. That slight contact cuts her skin, bruises the flesh beneath, even with the stone-hardened effect of being charged up on so much energy.

Baton in one hand, knife in the other, she spins by and strikes. She swings the club, it clips his elbow—and shatters. That club is made of one of the toughest grades of plastech, the result of a newer processing method. He swings with that arm again, and now she knows that the Psyn works on him and it is bad. He is much stronger than normal.

He is snarling, and hissing. She has long known of his beast. He never brought it out before in their sparring matches against each other. She always beat him, before this.

Now there is no time even for thought.

Another step in and she is inside his range. She must stay close because of his reach. She steps past him and kicks the back of his left knee. It gives, but only slightly. She thrusts the knife into his kidney, and the tempered, chisel point easily punches through the thickened plates of plastech of his coat to reach the flesh underneath, only for the blade to stop mere millimeters into him, catching on the dense energies of his flesh without reaching his abdominal cavity.

She ducks under another swing of his arm, dances backward.

Then she dives in again, into the whirling wind of his hands clawing at her.

With her mental state, all emotion is suppressed, distant. There is no fear. He has always been ridiculously tough. Psyn has made him into steel.

The tip of her boot finds the pit of his stomach. She feels her toes breaking. Those huge hands descend toward her leg.

She lets her rear leg collapse and slides forward on the floor, under his charge.

Spinning as she pushes off the floor, she flies to the ceiling in a leap, over his maddened rush. She rakes her knife down his back. Blood sprays. Again she is unable to reach the organs beneath.

She should run, wait until the Psyn runs out, but if she turns her back on him, he can escape, vanish again, nearly impossible to find.

He sinks deeper into his beast. He lopes along the ground now, not quite on all fours, but crouched low, and at times he plants his hands to help him turn that bulk of his as he chases after her lighter, fleeter shape.

She pivots around her right foot and avoids his widespread arms. Darts in as he is still turning, and she fires knees into his side, into his ribs, alternating with spinning flourishes with the blade to distract his eyes and cut at his flickering arms, whipping back and forth. She can feel the shock of the impacts traveling up her bones, up her spine, rattling her teeth. More of his blood flies through the air. She is so deep in psi that each crimson droplet is perfect in her vision, she could count them in between the spaces that she is trying to cut him.

She thumbs the chemical spray in her gloves. A cloud of caustic, toxic gas billows toward him. She has him now. She—

His shoulder crashes into her abdomen and forces the breath out of her. His tackle powers them both through the air. He slams her down into the ground, and her spine cracks.

Explosion in her head. Flash of white. She feels her body embedded into the floor.

He is moving now, so fast, his image is indistinct. The outline of his flame-wreathed body is red mist.

His fist.

Another flash.

Darkness, awareness an instant later. He has knocked her out of her trance. Pain now, all throughout her body. Agony. His fists, his elbows, hurtle down at her again, and again.

He is this immense darkness, looming. His eyes are red orbs. His teeth gnash.

She is growing numb. Her body will not listen to her. Her talent is fading from her grasp.

The last sensation before the dark claims her fully is the sound of meat being beaten, and the click of cracking bone, as the silver emitter plates on her face break away from the threads anchoring them in her brain.


Gasping. Choking. Coming out of that memory is like being pulled out of deep, cold water. The utter annihilation as all the nerves still firing lose coherence, and the data being collected by Miura's Implant becomes indistinct noise, background clutter.

Shaking, shivering.

"And now," the Behavioralist says, in her prim, proper tones, "you know."

# 19

"So, Miss Dempsey, what will you choose? Will you do your duty, for the Noah, for the mission, for humanity?"

I come back to myself, fill up my head with the dancing randomness of pieces of my childhood. Mala scolding me. Mala holding me. The favorite stew she used to make for me with tomatoes and mashed garbanzos and the bones from the butcher shop down the street. The last commercials broadcast into my head on my last walk to work. Minnow's fur. The tiny warmth of a baby lying atop me. The feel of Barrens inside me, moving so slow, stretching me.

She frowns. "Is that shock and disbelief scattering your thoughts, Miss Dempsey? Or are you trying to hide from me?"

Now, I show anger. It is genuine. Easy to summon. I imagine what she sees of me. The deep flush tints my dark skin. My nostrils flare. My hands clench. My neck is taut. "Of course not! It's just—how can I tell what's real anymore?" They can do things. Such skilled Behavioralists.

"Oh, it is real. Real enough that I don't have to *write* the belief into you."

The memory is meant to rattle me.

I need to give her what she expects. Is that my idea, or is that hers, slipped into my head when I wasn't paying attention?

"So what now?" More bitterness, unfeigned.

"We are unused to being stymied, Miss Dempsey. The establishment has grown too accustomed to our toys, to the ability to track locations through the Implants, to read the thoughts out of people's heads at leisure."

The woman, who has still not given her name, spreads her arms just so, lays her hands on the table, palms up. "Galling, for my colleagues and superiors. The protocols aren't working."

This is why I have not been Adjusted yet. "You need to do something outside of protocol."

Her smile returns, the touch of winter. "Between your friend's ardent requests for leniency on your behalf, and, since she is not completely without *other* friends higher up in the chain, and given the abject failure of our methods so far, I am willing to give you a chance, Miss Dempsey. Understand that I am alone in this. Most of the old men refuse to admit that Barrens is a serious threat to the stability of the ship, to the very success of our voyage. They want to peel your consciousness open and thresh out every detail they can find of the man, in the hope that a key will be found there. Something to destroy him before it's too late."

How can Barrens's investigation into some arcane mysteries involving the crew be so dangerous? Leon, you were right. The higher-ups have become entrenched in self-importance. Secrets destabilizing the ship? I can understand information's being leaked having some negative effect on productivity and efficiency, but a threat to the mission?

If there were such secrets, his theory of Ministry-sponsored elimination would no longer be ruled out just because of the victim selection. I let none of that through, lose that thought in a forest of simultaneous, chaotic thinking, about conspiracies, about propaganda, about all the lies everyone on the ship lives with every day.

Even the days City Planning simulates for the crew is a lie.

"I do not exaggerate, Miss Dempsey." If her smile is a razor of ice, her frown is carved doom on her marble face. "I am not lying about the grave nature of this danger. We. The Noah. We need your help."

But why, what's driven you to killing? Just as they've put too much importance on their secrets, you have too. No information can be worth individual lives. Isn't that what you always complained about? The way the priorities of the mission made us all unimportant, faceless? There has to be more to that memory of Miura's. But I can't let the ISec agent read that so I think of the hurt when he left me and howl in my head about his obsession, his ego taking him too far. It is what she wants to see.

Deep down, hidden in the cracks, I believe in him still. I will believe in him until I find him, and ask him, face-to-face.

The hum of the luminescent walls crackles faintly—interference from the fluctuations of her grasp on her power. Her patience runs thin.

"How do you think I can find him when you lot have failed?"

"A great deal of what has made him and his followers dangerous, Miss Dempsey, came from you."

"Oh, that's silly. I'm not that good a programmer, I—"

She shakes her head and allows her mask to slip. She is older than she appears. More tired. "I don't know how Testing could have let you slip through their fingers. You were misplaced with the number crunchers of City Planning. We could have used you much better.

"Barrens and his men continue to use your bots, your little net of programs—they have turned them to purposes I doubt you realize were possible."

Ridiculous. My feet take me back and forth, pacing. "Don't mock me," I whisper. I scored well in that part of the Class V evaluations, but I was not in the top tenth of a percent. Lyn did better. Marcus and Jazz. Even Hennessy has better pure coding skills. "Flattery annoys me." The only reason I couldn't find Barrens using the Monster is that it would draw ISec attention. Without needing to worry about consuming too many computer cycles, they have a number of brute-force techniques by which to track him through the swarm.

"Your algorithms, Miss Dempsey. Ones you use habitually, and which you have taught to Barrens, and which he has taught to all his little pet terrorists—they have a flaw. They use more power than they should, they run slower. But they self-modify in the most sophisticated way. It makes your little toy on the Web impossible to crack. There is an element of randomness to them. Quirkiness, the eggheads tell me. Emergent behavior.

"Somewhere along the way, your programs become more than a collection of machine learning algorithms. They are on the way to becoming AI."

What? No—that can't be right. Its self-modification functionality is limited; the network of the population might have grown, but the individual particles of the swarm can't have changed that much while still running all the little modules we attached to it.

Only . . . I had already started to suspect that alien data was contaminating Monster. Could it have gone so far already? Rather than merely introducing bugs and crashing functions, could the interaction between my code and that of the Builders become something like this? It's a blur of equations and structure and ideas in my head, and then I push it back under waves of emotion. She must not know what I think of Monster. It could be so much more dangerous than she already fears.

"I am not a technical analyst, so I will not bother to regurgitate what the technicians tell me. I am a troubleshooter. I solve problems of the human sort."

She is a hunter of men.

She interrupts my pacing by simply appearing in my path. I did not hear or see her move. There is no time even to feel alarmed. Her fingers rest against my temples, chrome to chrome, emitter to emitter. She *writes* something into my mind. An immense, strange mass of stuff. All the information she believes I will require. Images. Documents. Training memories. Textbooks.

The pain is not physical. It is a revolt of my neurons against rapidly assimilating so much data. My throat hurts. I feel my diaphragm squeezing. I cough, maybe choking on my spit, and I am crying out, on and off. Sensation comes and goes—my body detaches from me and comes back. It is as if my brain does not belong with this body anymore.

"Think on it, Miss Dempsey. We return in the morning. My name is Karla. I think we will enjoy working with each other."

The chair and the table recede into the floor. They leave me lying on the floor, twitching, drooling, overloaded, and the doorway disappears when they exit.

One unifying ghost of an idea, laden with intense emotion, is spread throughout the data dump—her absolute and unyielding conviction that what lies beneath is simply too terrible to know.

Putting my head back together takes hours. Whatever she did was not an Adjustment. Skills are buried in here, in my thoughts. Learned reflexes overwriting my own, but nothing touching the self that remains me. At least, I think I am still me.

Even my internal chronometer was screwed up by whatever she did. Much of the normal programming running the neural Implant has been altered in a thousand different locations scattered across the modules.

Finally, my wiring is straight again, and my body is my own.

I feel a want, I have a plan. Are these my own ideas in my head, precipitated by the skills and information she gave me, or am I another kind of puppet? I can choose to stay here and assert my will and end up a vegetable tomorrow, or I can dance to the tune of the Ministry of Information and stay myself for a little longer. Every single day I was here, every hour, I spent meditating, refining my telekinesis, modifying my Implant programming. Did I do all those things, or was it Karla influencing me all this time?

Barrens would tell me it does not matter. Surviving matters.

Oh, I do want to see him again. I want to ask him, "Why?"

The thrust of my hand opens the tap. A crackle of *touch*, just a little power, but a lot of control, is all it takes to break up the fat stream of water into micro-droplets, mist. Fog fills the room. Fog that glows eerie blue, masking myself from any psychic observation. It is weightless and takes hardly any effort at all. What consumes every iota of focus I have are the tiny blades of water spinning, whirring faster and faster, grinding at the inside of the faucet spout. The exterior is hardened and impervious, but the inner surface is not as tough, and mostly processed just for corrosion resistance.

A thread has started almost without my conscious direction. A subprogram running off my chronometer, counting down how many minutes I have before the warden decides that this seeming privacy is dangerous.

I get out a few grams of plastech powder from the eroded faucet spout, re-leased from the control of the prison system. I fuse the wet, gray dust into dense slivers to continue the process, and it becomes easier and easier. I do not have the raw psychic ability of Karla, I cannot simply override the warden's control over the substance of my prison, but it is not physically indestructible.

The subtle whirring sound becomes an earsplitting shriek. My improvised drill has reached the hardened shell. Because it has been hardened so, it has some properties in common with ceramic. Too hard to scrape, too hard to cut—it is brittle.

Now, my task becomes difficult again. Deep breaths. My heart pounds. My head hurts more, more, more. Everything I have pouring into the growing, shaped slug of plastech in the faucet. Plastech can be expanded by a steady trickle of psionic energy at a specific frequency. It only takes a little time.

Finally, it shatters. Freeing up a dense third of a kilo of material to work with. Material that is already extremely hardened.

I shape it into a series of spikes. They are sharp. They are also harder than the substance composing the floor. I drive them into a circle around me, one at a time, with all the force I can muster. Force is interesting. I can only generate so many newtons of force without an amplifier. But because the mass of each spike is small, and force is the product of mass and acceleration, each narrow projectile thrusts down as if shot from a cannon in the movies. They pierce deep.

Now, I repeat what I did to the plug in the faucet. The spikes become seeds as I feed them power. They grow, becoming less dense, expanding. Roots, spreading.

There is no dramatic explosion of sound. Only the spreading of cracks under my feet.

The wall is starting to open.

I fall down my little rabbit hole, into a service cafeteria below. I am dizzy. I hit hard, absorb the shock of a ten-foot drop. Wet warmth at my nose. My ears. Pushing my gifts this far without an amp is a terrible strain. I am bleeding from my nose, my ears. My eyes are probably red, blood vessels popped.

Around me, Information Security men and women gawk at my nudity. These are not Enforcers or trained field agents—ISec is composed of hundreds of ordinary crew, secretaries, office workers, accountants, programmers, researchers. They get in the way of the ones that are trained, who are shouting at everyone to get down.

Outside of the prison, the plastech that composes everything around me is not under the control of a jail-keeping routine rendering it resistant to psychokinetic manipulation.

A series of trays fly to me, and I unravel them into thin sheets and fuse them into a bodysuit around my flesh, and boots to cover my feet.

Now, I run. I shove my way through the breakfast crowd, toward the kitchens, and the maintenance tunnels. I spot an amplifier around the wrist of a sleek-looking public-relations officer in a slinky dress, her brown eyes comically wide, her mouth clamping down on her sandwich. I tear the amp off her before she has time to think, then I am five feet away and getting farther before it occurs to her to yell, a mouthful of partially chewed mash hitting the floor behind me.

An ISec paper-pusher wants to try to be a hero and jumps at me, trying to tackle me. He's been watching too many old movies. He should have used his amp bracelet to subdue me. I send him flying away from me, a bowling ball knocking the pins of the crowd aside for me to rush through.

Now, some of them start to use their psi, and a hail of spoons and forks shoots after me, so many bullets. Poorly aimed bullets. They do more harm to each other than to me. I float more food trays along my way to block them.

This part is just like my paintball matches with my friends.

There are no Enforcers after me. They will all be held back just long enough for me to escape from the less competent, less trained interrogation staff. Or at least, I pray that Karla is doing so. Or I will be dust and ashes within moments.

The gray men in their murky, colorless coats drop through the hole I made. More are pushing their way in from the cafeteria entrance.

I am already past the kitchen doors. I fuse them shut. The sensation of being able to draw on the grid again is heady. I had been scraping by on a trickle in the desert, and now I have a sea of power behind me. The kitchen staff stare, stunned at this disruption of routine.

A flare of cobalt blue and the drainage grate pops free from the corner of the room. I force it wider.

The doors crush open. Angry men running, even as I jump down again. But I have to slow them down or the first *bruiser* that gets mobilized will knock me out before I can think to react.

I run and run. The breath whistles in and out between my teeth. I might have exercised as much as I could in my cell, but running a marathon is not the kind of fitness I could shoot for.

Foul smells in the air. Sewage sloshing around my feet.

Methane gas.

I part with a few grams of material from my sleeve, harden it into a pair of rough, metallic disks, leave them hovering behind me as I pound my way down the tunnel.

When I judge that my pursuers have reached my little present, I force the disks to strike together.

The spark gives birth to a fireball. I fling up a wall of dirty water and sludge to stop it from reaching me. The heat bakes it into a crust.

I hope I have not killed anyone.

Now, I have to get lost. I need to keep going deeper, to where there is too much interference for them to track and pinpoint my location through my Implant emissions.

Exhaustion. Not enough food. And the strain of pushing my talents beyond the limits I thought I had. Knees are trembling. Feet drag through the muck. The information that Karla has forced upon me includes many maps of these service tunnels. Functions she has added to my Implant make it a trivial matter to trace my path so far and match it up to the complex, three-dimensional web of shafts and tunnels.

So tired and it is still so far. I descend deeper into the network. Small plaques with hexadecimal markings label some of the intersections and keep me oriented. Karla did not explicitly mark out an escape route for me, but with my many requirements of staying away from where I can be detected and tracked as well as reaching one of the Nth Web data conduits spread throughout the ship, I have only a handful of options to choose from. Most of them are flagged, indicating that maintenance teams are scheduled to check on them soon.

The sludge underfoot begins to move faster, threatens to drag me under.

I am close, at last, to a side-access link to the information network lines. There is no wireless to the Nth Web in the uninhabited zones. I need that hardwired line, need to signal Monster so Barrens can find me.

If she was telling the truth about the Monster being untraceable, then I don't need to worry; I can just use it to call out to him without the complex tricks he was using to message whomever else he's dragged into this.

I just hope he'll be able to find me, or I could be lost down here until I starve.

There. A circular door atop a landing high enough to be just clear of the slime.

Not locked, but too heavy for my feeble human muscles to open. Groaning now, I call upon the borrowed amplifier's power again. First, I reform my bodysuit and stretch the already thin material to its limits while treating it with subtle vibrations to increase its toughness and change its opacity. It covers me now, head to toe. A clear bubble forms around my head, encloses me with a minute's worth of breathable air. I need it to get past what lies ahead.

Too much strain in too short a time. The world seems to spin around me and I hang on to consciousness. The half-ton hatch swings out into a blindingly bright space full of lights.

The constricted, choking space of the sewage shaft opens up into a vast emptiness. The fetid air blasts out at my back. Fingers and power clutch at the walls and keep me from falling.

This is one of several main arteries cutting through the superstructure of the ship. It is unintentionally beautiful. Streams of light so intense they look like solid matter crisscross through the air, blues, yellows, greens, reds—the psionic power grid. The largest rivers spiral around the center and stretch up and down; it is all colors and none. They feed in and branch away from it toward the curving walls. Bolts of lightning crackle, traversing up and down, bouncing from the control antennae projecting out into the space, gleaming bridges of delicate filigree, ever-shifting, formless plastech tendrils that twine about the crackling pathways of energy rooted in the obsidian surface of the walls. Immense blocks of circuitry are embedded right into the structure of this grand hall of light. Strange symbols are carved everywhere—a character set I've seen before, in that one lost fragment of reclaimed data.

No time to take it in and wonder why there's this strange, ancient artwork here where there is no one to see it. Maybe they were markings by the Builders, useful during the construction of the Noah.

"Pay attention!" I bark at myself. It would be far, far too easy to die at this step.

Air sighs in and out along hundreds of vents. Not breathable air though—which is why I need my airtight shelter.

In the suit, my breaths are too loud in my ears. Must breathe slowly, must not saturate my air with $CO_2$ before I get to the data line on the opposite side of the shaft. It just takes courage.

I let go of the moldy, slippery doorway and take a step out into the emptiness. There is no drop. There is no simulated gravity as that would serve no purpose here. My stomach, though, insists that I am falling. My heart pounds. My inner ears tell me there is no "down" anymore.

Emergency zero-g training seems like a thousand years ago.

Biting my lip, I pull myself where I need to go, the faintest glimmer of my *touch* surrounding me. Slow. I must be careful. Touch one of those glowing currents and there will not even be ashes left of me. Banks of steam are crawling up and down the walls in rivers—vapor coolant, tremendously caustic. I must avoid those too.

A hundred meters away. The tiny, white door I am aiming for grows in size. Now to decelerate. It would be stupid of me to get this far and crack my head open from hitting it too fast and asphyxiating in this ridiculous, skintight, translucent body stocking.

Dizzy. Little globules of blood from my nose and ears are floating around in my helmet. Distracting. Hands are trembling. Forgot how cold it would be. Cold. The blood droplets are freezing into little red crystals. My breath is icy mist, making it hard to see.

I spin in midair and press my feet against the wall, just clear of the data line. I spread my hands, force the triangular doors to slide apart. Air starts rushing out of it. It is not a vacuum in this main shaft, but it is lower pressure, to keep toxic gases from backing up into other systems. Not too hard to fight my way into the tunnel against the current. Gravity reasserts and pushes me to my hands and knees in the much warmer, pearl-gray triangular corridor. Numb now, when I close the doors.

Tear open my helmet. Blessed, warmer air. Oxygen. Not much farther.

Crawling. Cannot stand anymore. Gleaming panel, an Nth Web access terminal right in the wall. It takes a painful, long minute for my twitching fingers to open the panel and touch the conductive access port.

*Hey. My guardian. My lion. I need you. I'm here.*

I fold the words and the hex label on the terminal into a clear packet of thought. I enclose it in a file with a smattering of keywords and data, send it off to the Monster.

It is a matter of probabilities. The chance that my program has already spread to the closest Analytical Node to find my message. The chance that Barrens will see it before lack of water kills me.

With the last dregs of my power, I cocoon myself into the tunnel wall, with just cracks to breathe through for air, and then I close my eyes and hope I have gone far enough and deep enough. Exhausted, still it takes what feel like hours to fall asleep. I just escaped from a secret prison because the alternative was being lobotomized. Am I a foolish girl looking for the man I love, or, as Karla spoke of, a guided missile streaking toward a target of the Council's choosing?

Barrens would say, "You're badass, baby."

Consciousness returns in slow stages.

Awareness. I could wake up immediately. But I do not. I let myself drift. I am in a bed, with blankets. A huge paw is closed around my hand. So warm. Better than the best memories of that stupid cat, that other person's child.

My head aches fiercely. A jagged boulder is bouncing back and forth in my skull.

"You're awake." His voice is soft. Still a low rumble, a gentle growling.

It hurts too much even to talk. Probably he can see it on my face. Feel it in the pressure of my clutching hands.

"Yeah. If you got a headache, that's from the surgery."

Fantastic. Yet another person's been in my head, rummaging through it.

*Surgery?* Pulling on my psi to message him Implant-to-Implant causes my eyes to feel as if they will burst.

"Yeah. You were hemorrhaging in your head—pushed your talent too far."

"And we also had to remove the part of the Implant that lets them track us," added a clear, high, childish voice. "Barrens, we should leave her be. The stimulation will keep the drugs from helping her rest."

"Yeah, got it. Sorry, Doc."

Silence then. Chill along the veins of my arms, feeling the drips going into me. Their words are slowing down, slurring. I sleep again.

# 20

THERE ARE PLUSH COUCHES. THE FLOOR IS FUNCTIONAL TILE. THE LAMPS ARE bright over the tables and desks, but outside those pools of light, it is dim, and murky. Cigarette smoke in the air diffuses silhouettes. The walls have been converted into floor-to-ceiling displays.

Barrens sits before me. The table between us has been fabricated to look like wrought iron. The small lamp on it is just bright enough to be functional, but our faces remain in shadow.

A tablet is in his hands. An unlit cigarette dangles between his lips.

Coffee. Hot, scalding. Takes both my hands to hold the mug up to my mouth.

Smell of bacon, frying. Bacon! I only had it once as a child, when Mala rewarded me for one particularly exceptional grading period. As an adult, I could afford it whenever the urge struck, but it was always a little magical to me, that rich fat like little else.

Around us, other men and women eat and chat. They talk about Web streams and movies.

We could have been sitting in a café somewhere.

But too many of the conversations delve into history and philosophy and conspiracy. Everyone is talking about the latest news. They have found a way through toward one of the secret sections of the ship.

And they have found more evidence of the Builders. Joe November still insists on being called Bullet, and for the first three days of my recovery, he has taken every possible opportunity to visit me and offer to show his collection of psychometric impressions of the Builders—mostly from touching the ancient writings on some of the tunnel walls out here in the uninhabited zones. I guess he changed his mind about the aliens not mattering so much. Or maybe it's his newfound popularity.

A number of the men and women in Barrens's group are nearly addicted to the alien sense memories Bullet has shared. They fantasize about finding a hidden cache of Builder artifacts, alien wisdom that can change our society, improve our clumsy understanding of their technologies, a panacea to make everything better in every way. When they touch Bullet to reexperience the memories his talent has extracted firsthand, they sway in place, like maddened fans overwhelmed by the presence of an old-time rock star.

I decline every offer to see them. Just the one memory that the data-miner found was plenty for me. Their minds are too different from ours. When I revisit that memory, it is always deeply disturbing; I imagine it feels like being high. They felt emotions so intensely, yet so differently from us. They had emotions we don't have words for, and without the background cultural concepts and context, they are mind-bending. And can any memory of a Builder walking through a corridor or doing maintenance work or humming match what Barrens and I saw, of that pair of others standing above the Noah as it was being created?

The real excitement in the air is about the expedition into what they call the Unmapped Regions. They talk about who will get to go. They talk about how, soon, everyone will know the Noah's secrets.

They tend to be either very young, just teenagers, swinging their hands about and gesturing with enthusiasm, or very old, gray- and white-bearded men and thin crones with reedy voices. A pair of them stand before one of the large displays, reformulating program code. Blocks of instructions that I recognize. I wrote much of them.

Above what looks like a pool table, a three-dimensional image is projected. A densely packed series of lines and curves and tiny, glowing blips, data labels, tags. It is a schematic of the Noah focusing on one of the abandoned sections, depowered, with no life support or gravity.

A plate is lowered before me. The boy that serves it inclines his head deferentially to Barrens.

"Hi, Bullet." I hug him and smile and, when he blushes, hug him again. I think it was those weeks in isolation, and having so many strangers around now. The only two people I know here from before are Barrens and Bullet, and I take every opportunity to touch them and feel that I exist.

"Thanks. Grab some for yourself too, huh?"

"Uh. Sure. Haha." He turns a little pink. "Hey, you know, it's not just Builder memories I've found, so if you want to see anything more, you know I like to feel useful."

"You're probably the most important guy here, Joe."

"No way." He shakes his head. "That's the big guy, because he's the hand that's holding this mess of crazies together. And that's you, for making the Monster. Though, the artsy kids that joined in want to call it Argus instead. I wasn't ever into mythology."

A number of youths on a couch wave to him.

"Go on, go on," Barrens says. "You've had more time with Hana than I have, and your groupies are wanting more of you."

A little twitch around his eyes, as if Bullet wanted to roll them. "It's not me that's got groupies, it's the Builders. Easy for people to fantasize that they were so perfect, seeing as they're all gone and we can't know if they were just as screwed up as us." But he sighs and goes over to the alien enthusiasts anyway.

Beside me, Barrens sips his coffee.

My fork breaks the yellow yolk of an egg. It is glorious. It trickles onto a thick cut of toast. In my mouth, fat and salt and protein and the complex flavors, and the slight crunch of the crusty bread, and all of it overwhelming, after months in isolation with flavorless goop. Sunlight in my mouth. I eat only a few, tiny bites. It seems like a dream.

Big fingers tug at the skin on my wrist and pinch. Just enough to let me feel it.

"Not gonna wake up back in a cell."

"When did you learn how to *read,* hmm?"

Not that Barrens needed to pinch me. There are too many aches and pains. And more than just from burning my talent to the point of scraping the inside of my mind. Where my spine meets my skull is a sharp, throbbing ache, where another youth performed psychic surgery on me. He slid needles of incorporeal force into my head and destroyed the collection of nanite threads composing the transponder ganglion, the part of the Implant that constantly transmits location data. Supposedly, the procedure is without side effects. Barrens said they have all gone through it.

I wonder though. The sharp, clear plans that got me out of Information Security have become fuzzy and directionless. If I had the time to scan through my memories one by one, would any be damaged? Are my talents affected? It will take time to test myself. There's so much to catch up on with the jerk. I'm going to let him have it sometime, for leaving me.

Later. Real soon.

Right now I can't stop looking at him when he's around, and I sink into the deep bass of his voice when he talks.

"I *was* a cop. It doesn't take psi talent to know something about body language, facial expressions." That rough, calloused thumb glides over my cheek. "Like to think I know a lot about you."

His touch gets a sigh out of me and I lean into his hand, into the heat radiating from the furnace of him. I missed this too much. I missed him. Barrens stares at me hungrily as if he cannot believe I am here, as if he wants to consume me and possess me, that beast of his too, and at the same time there is that tenderness no one else knows. This is real, to me. It has to be. His presence, the gritty roughness of his hands.

Strange, hearing his voice again. His spoken speech is cleaner than before, more like the thoughts in his head. I guess he needed to work on that at last, to be a leader to his flock. Is he the leader? He is boss to this small gathering here, but no one has told me how many other groups there are, how many other bosses there are. How are decisions made? How independent are they?

Then there is what happened with Miyaki. He took an oath to protect life. An oath to defend each individual of humanity left. When we are suitably alone, I will ask, and I will listen.

He is so busy running things, there has not yet been an opportunity.

"You have a lot of friends now, Leon."

"Yeah. Have to stay in small groups though. Or Enforcers come down on us. We lost a cell in the week before they got you. A lot of people we would have wanted to recruit on the forums too.

"Mostly, they just kill us. I guess we riled up the hornet's nest. Even mission-critical status means nothing, not if someone is a part of what we're doing."

*We.* Lots of *we,* now.

"Don't frown. Good cause."

I just shake my head. I point to my plate. "Where's all this from?"

"Ah. One of the secrets, Hana. You're in City Planning. You're supposed to know numbers about how many tons of what are produced, how much livestock is butchered and stored and sold and eaten. Well."

Bullet returns from a minute spent letting the kids "commune" with his psychometric impressions of the Builders. He pulls up a chair, munching noisily on a bacon-lettuce-and-tomato sandwich. He is the same and yet not the same. I guess this movement thing has been good for him.

I am still annoyed that Leon took him along and not me.

"I was telling Hana about where the food is from."

Bullet exclaims, the hand not on his food sweeping in big, grand arcs. "They're huge—I mean really huge—storerooms, Dempsey. Not accounted for."

Leon slides a tablet over to me. It is a copy of that much larger map hologram dominating the center of the room. I understand a little more now. Members of his organization make forays into those deep levels of the ship, making their way as they go along physically, linking up chunks and clusters of lost data that the Monster has found.

"There are vertical farms down there more than double the capacity that should be, given our crew population."

"That can't be right."

Barrens leans over and taps the screen. Tables of numbers scroll down. Inventories they ripped from the data nodes down there. "What secrets keep two-thirds of the ship's agricultural capacity back from the crew, eh? Why do most of us get just enough to meet the minimum daily requirement of nutrients, with luxuries only for the 'better' ones, the elites? Isn't this made for abuse?"

I want to tell Barrens to stop raising his voice to me. He never used to do that. Then I realize he is not speaking just to me.

They are all listening to him. Nodding. It is stuff they have heard before, but nonetheless, it reassures them. He used the word *cause* before, and now I see why ISec is afraid. Propaganda, Keepers, carefully ingrained cultural ideals, and censored history, to produce a rational, reliable, stable crew—there is no place for Barrens and his true believers.

*Sorry,* he unicasts to me. *I have to give them these little nuggets. Pep talks. Or they start to lose focus.*

Does anyone really know anyone else? And I was just thinking that only I could see the deep thinking behind his simple face.

The intensity in their eyes gets to me.

*It's okay, Leon. I'm just tired. I think I'll eat more in a while.*

He explains to them what I have done for their little rebellion. That I am the reason they have expanded to more than just a handful of isolated individuals believing that they alone could see that something was wrong. My code lets them search through the Web without being caught, lets them communicate with each other and know that there are others like themselves. Barrens uses the word *destiny*.

I am still in range of direct Implant-to-Implant link, and he thinks to me, *Yeah, I know. I'm laying it on a bit thick, huh? Don't think badly of them. They are smart, they have great ideas, and they have all kinds of different skills. But they're not used to hearing other people say what they've been afraid to believe, and for some reason, they like it when it's me saying it. Couldn't tell ya why, babe. Maybe my ugly mug stuns them into being receptive for the bullshit. I am still only me.*

Oh, I hope that is so. I shove aside a moment of indulgent fantasy, of him and me running away together, and being happy, and forgetting about mysteries and deaths and the darkness cast by the fake sun in the Habitat.

I will have it out with him soon and be free to talk and to yell, to scream.

Barrens delegates various jobs. He deals with the minutiae of running their group, checking on food inventories, reading reports, communicating with other groups. Lunch is stew and bread. I sink into a couch in front of a data terminal, close my eyes, and lose myself in the glittering light, the unfolding complexity of my program's growth, studying what changes have occurred while I was held by ISec, and during the months I was too busy in construction to pay attention.

It's grown even more in the time I was in captivity. It recognizes my touch on its code instantly. What used to be just results being returned and dry documentation and data tables is now accompanied by cheerful, musical pings. As if it were welcoming me home.

I cannot deny any longer that it is becoming artificial intelligence, and not in the way the term is used in the present to describe a whole class of dynamic algorithms, but the old way. Turing-testable, Strong AI. It is as Karla said.

It can now write itself without restriction. I don't think anyone in Barrens's group realizes that it is no longer under our control.

Dinner is flat rice-noodles, fried with lemongrass, curry, and peppers, and ground beef, fish tacos, and steaming trays of corn bread.

Too soon, and not soon enough, it is another "night." Or at least, Barrens is off-shift.

The shift that was asleep comes awake, and he introduces me to more of them. He repeats some of the same bits of motivational talk. *Weird, innit? As individuals, we don't like it when people are repetitive in conversation. But in groups, repetition is vital, like something is lost in the transition from a single person listening to a collective.*

We linger long enough that when we walk away from the central hall down a narrow shaft allocated to sleeping quarters, we are alone. The previous shift with us have already parked themselves in their little coffin chambers, while the rest are behind us, having breakfast, waking up to face another day of diving into the Nth Web and searching for more secrets, or planning this or that or, I suppose, any of the hundred tasks it takes to start up a revolution.

Barrens clears his throat. Suddenly smaller, shy. "There's empty spots further down, we carve 'em out as we need 'em. Ah. But this one is me." The quiver of invitation.

While recovering from their Doctor's neurosurgery, I'd been sleeping in the makeshift clinic around the corner. Tonight is the first night I'm free.

Only then did it occur to me that in the months we were apart, he might have found someone else, been with someone else. That he is not . . .

We *seem* to be alone, but now I can hear the silence. They are listening, I guess, the ones in the sleeping cylinders close to us.

I like to think that the dark shade of my skin hides the blush, but I know he can see it. I slide by him and crawl into his sleep-space, one of dozens of hollows carved out of the walls, stacked together like the cells in a honeycomb. It feels like the dorms again, back in the Class V Center, scrunchies on the doorknobs warning off roomies, everyone knowing who was sleeping with whom.

Only, when he shuts the hatch behind us and crawls alongside me, his massive shadow over me reminds me and I cannot help it. I shiver and close my eyes.

I remember the same face, aglow with fire, crushing me. Crushing Miyaki, but her last moment is mine, in my head.

*What is it?*

I cannot live in fear of my guard dog, my lion. "I want to talk. And out loud. Not just Implant to Implant. I need to hear your voice and my voice too."

*People in the sleep chambers next to us can practically hear us breathing, Hana.*

"A moment."

Filed away in my skull, in memories where I learned construction techniques, materials design, and plastech processing, is an entire subsection on how to soundproof a closed space. I use these techniques now. The surfaces around us glow as I restructure the walls, adding damping cells where the dense metallic crystal is softened and made porous, and manipulating the angles of the rigid support struts to diffuse more sound out and away from the surrounding sleep-spaces to the other side of the load-bearing wall that marks one of the outermost edges of the sanctuary. The hatch too is modified, made more concave, to catch sound and direct it, again, out to the sanctuary wall.

Now, we cannot hear anyone around us. The echoing footsteps of the people walking to and fro, the hum of their conversations, it all fades away.

In this dim, narrow place, we are as alone as can be.

"Leon, what happened with Officer Miura?"

The cushions under us whisper as he turns, taps at a panel above us. The ambient light intensifies enough for us to see each other clearly, but it is still soft, low. It comes from a single glow strip installed along just one corner of the hexagonal cell.

The shadows across his face are sharp, and I think of how the others in my life see Barrens, the harsh, rugged planes and angles of his broad cheeks, the thick brow, his heavy jaw.

As he closes his eyes, his hands clench. His shoulders twitch, those savage teeth press together and grind. His fury fills the air around us, violence in the air.

Halting words. Stuttering as he rarely does. He tells me of bringing Officer Miura in. Of needing someone to teach these kids how to take care of themselves.

"Miya came to us the week after you were caught. She seemed okay, y'know? F-fine." He trusted her. "Better than fine. She believed it when we told her what we had. When we showed her."

He goes silent. Nostrils flare.

If I interrupt, he'll stumble on the words. Surrender. He is close to the edge, close to switching over to the beast. That's not what we need, and I put my hands on his cheeks and pull his head so our eyes are level. Stay with me, you.

His hand reaches out. I lean into his touch. And feel him transmit through our implants.

I brace myself for more scenes but it is a list. A list with hundreds of names.

"Bullet's the one that found them. Each early Retirement. It wasn't just the ones we thought.

"Made ourselves look. Each one. Every early Retirement, if there's a place we're sure they vanished, Bullet's been able to go there and *see* their Mincemeat remains. All the way back to first-generation crew. A death like that leaves a footprint that his talent can find even hundreds of years later. That's how long it's been with us. It's something the top officers are doing to the rest of us. And then Monster found us other things too. Adjustment records, for people connected to an early Retirement. Not every single one, but I guess the ones where there are direct witnesses, they need their memories fixed. It's what would have happened to me if I'd stuck around Cal's apartment long enough for the Enforcers to get there."

The world around me tilts. Yes. Impersonal, heartless documents. The best and the worst kind of proof. *If there are Adjustment records, you know it's official.* I hold it together.

Miyaki helped them plan the next step. The theory that developed was that it was some sort of awful R&D project. And if there are experiments, there must be labs where they are conducted.

"She found hints of it for us, even. She led us to . . . You heard it, for sure. Beijing Section, abandoned all at once? They're making labs there, Hana."

His words sketch a picture. The other side of the work I was doing for City Planning, the hidden reflection in the mirror. Of endless cages, heavily rein-forced. Buildings clad in hardened armor from the inside out. The staff mostly wear either the gray of Information Security or the black of Enforcers. But there are a number of Doctors from the Ministry of Health, red-trimmed white coats.

"We saw it. We saw them moving in samples in bottles. Pieces of the mon-sters in the tunnels. And pieces of people."

They got in, saw what they could see, and got out. Cleanly, it seemed. "Only, nobody noticed how Miya was acting different when everyone started talk-ing.' "

All those discussions about what it could mean. And there had to be other labs too. Other secret locations that had been running experiments from the very beginning of the ship's launch. And somehow, everyone agreed, Mince-meat tied into the monsters in the dark, and the hidden history of the Noah's alien origin.

He blinks, and by the sickly light of the glow strip, his eyes are unnaturally dark. Shark's eyes looking into mine. "That was the trigger, I guess. Critical combination of terms."

Calmly, calmly, while everyone was walking and talking on their way back to the Sanctuary, just as they reached a stretch of the tunnels that had grid power, Miyaki Miura started killing them. She stalked them through the brightly lit halls, drew her weapons, began her lethal dance.

"They fucked her up, Dempsey," Barrens whispers. "Adjusted her. Couldn't reason with her anymore. Kill or be killed."

His voice cuts and snarls. His hands vibrate in place. Is he remembering it now? Remembering the sensations as his hands beat his friend to death?

"She was. My oldest friend. Couldn't knock her out. She kept getting up. Kept . . . When it was done, just left her there. Close to the abandoned Hab sections."

After a shuddering breath, he steadies himself. Becomes still.

*Did they Adjust you too, Hana? Are you going to get set off on me?*

There is no answering that.

We lie close and quiet.

"I can't stay," I whisper. "I shouldn't."

"How are you going to get me to let go?"

For the first time in forever, I press a kiss to his cheek. Press dark fingertips against his pale skin. He twitches and sighs, the scowl easing from his mouth.

We kiss and it is harsh and bittersweet. There is no telling if a switch inside my head waits for Karla's psychic finger. It is not my imagination after all, his people following me with their eyes; since waking, whenever I am not around Barrens, at least one of his people with a crossbow is always behind me.

It is my turn.

I tell him about my doubts. My fears. How hurt I was when he thought protecting me meant leaving me.

"I mean, a note, Leon?" I laugh just a bit, but I'm also tearing up.

I stutter through the moments. Shaking through the halting silences, passing along fragments of moments when the words fail completely.

The strangers with the crossbows in the darkness, snuffed out. It is I, shaking, remembering the darkness, the adrenaline. The swaying scaffolding.

The solid weight of his arms pulls me close.

He is scowling, but it is not at me. Fury again.

"Damn it. Trigger-happy punks." *I told the others their people needed more training.* "Those dipshits. Made it sound like they escaped from ISec, coverin' their fuckup."

He slams a fist into the wall, dents it deep.

"Leon."

*They could have hurt you. They almost killed you. Don't feel guilty for them, Hana.*

Barrens tries to explain something about the divisions in the movement. The other leaders are smart, he insists. But the egos. "Wish I could lock 'em in a room with me and all of us duke it out an' settle things." His great big chest expands with a slow, deep inhalation. *But I can only lead those who want to follow, I guess. I can't just bust heads anytime there's a disagreement. Wish I could.*

It is exhausting, all this unloading.

*A break?*

*Yes.*

Just as we used to when one or the other would get too steamed during an argument, we pause and breathe. And let it go.

Stories still wait between us. The things he has been doing. My weeks in the detention center, the feeling of abandonment, being under the microscope of Karla.

In the silence of this cell, there is only the sound of each other breathing. I scoot closer still, right up against him. It may never have been a perfect society to Barrens, but to me, it was *close*. Everything was fair, determined by testing and science. Instead, there is a terrible shadow, so much more than I thought we did not know.

Still there is this, between us. There is the warmth of his arms. There is the hesitant tenderness of his touch, as though I am the most fragile thing he has ever beheld.

"I don't want to sleep yet," I admit.

"Me too."

We talk another two hours.

He tells me about his people. Their quirks. How he gathered them up from the dark corners of the Web. Dreamers. Crazies.

His inner circle consists of Gregory, who never completed his medical training, but was close, Tommy, a police mechanic, Susan, formerly an entry-level propaganda officer, and of course Bullet, whose psychometry has led them to several finds such as the secret food caches.

"They were his recruits. Crèche-mates. Oh, and they have a thing. A deal. The kid likes her; she likes Tommy instead."

With Barrens right here, the temptation I had to keep fighting to escape to cat-brushing and breast-feeding memories seems to belong to another me.

*I missed you.*

He holds me just a little tighter. *I regret leaving you behind. I'm sorry.*

*Dummy.*

———

I jerk awake. How long was I asleep? The chronometer says it was just ten minutes.

I feel Barrens looking down at me. Smiling.

"I haven't told ya what I think of the new look," he says, slowly caressing my bare scalp.

Part of me wants to jerk away. The part left from before detention. The remnants of vanity, the old pride in my appearance.

Then he kisses the top of my head, and I feel a shiver start there that seems to run right down my neck and along my spine. That's different. He kisses me again and there's a little spasm that makes it all the way down the leg tucked up over his tree-trunk thighs and along my arms, which still don't reach all the way around his enormously broad back.

"Want me to grow it out?" My voice is all breathy and I feel a touch silly.

"I kind of like this." He lifts me up, turns me easily. He cradles me against his chest, fingers touching their way down my scalp and neck.

I just listen to him breathing. Wondering what happens if I fall asleep. Wondering if, when I wake, I'll have been triggered in my sleep.

I should sleep somewhere else. It's not safe. If I turn out to be like Miyaki, I could do so much harm.

*Don't. You already fell asleep, more than once. Stay.*

*Doesn't mean it's okay. Miya seemed fine to you too.*

"I'll take my chances," he growls. His embrace tightens.

I've missed this so much, my gentle, pale giant.

# 21

AT FIRST, ALL I DO IS REST. AND THEN ALL I DO IS WATCH OTHERS WORK AND train. More than a few look at me with outright suspicion, and worry.

It is a week before anyone remembers to tell me that the group has taken the name the Archivists.

The amplifier I took from that ISec clerk serves as a distraction for a little while. It is a civilian defense amp, limited in output and onboard computing power. It looks like a slender hoop of silvery gold; the circuitry is nanoscale and far too small for the eye to see.

The average crewman would not know where to start to modify one, though a number might know how to bypass some of the safety features and overclock the hardware to let it draw about 10 or 20 percent more power, at the risk of overheating and burnout. Salvador had us make them from scratch in class, way back when.

The eyes can't see the circuitry, but when engaging the amplifier, my psi runs through each tiny line doped into the plastech matrix, and through those infinitesimal pulses, a properly written application in one's Implant can map the microstructure. From there, it is about the hours it takes to add a few grains of plastech taken from the raw construction ingots the Archivists have lying around, and adding to the existing template. More capacitors and parallel channels let it draw and hold more power from the grid, more memory and processing power let it actually control that additional power, and finally, it takes mere seconds to flash its operating system and upload the one I keep a copy of in my Implant, which I have been tweaking and using on all my amplifiers for over a decade.

The result: it looks the same, but has close to the ratings and access codes of the engineer's gauntlets I'm used to and has my usual suite of applications loaded to make it more responsive to my style of *touch* and thinking.

Unfortunately, I finish it too quickly and again have too little to do and too much to think about.

I could mope at being kept out of things. I could be offended that no one has asked me to help with the perpetual tweaks on the AI swarm. But from my conversations with Bullet, they too know that it's special, that it's not like any other program they've worked with. Under the prodding of the two most important figures in the group, the others act a little more openly around me, and a few start to talk to me about the data-miner, about my design and how it has changed.

At "night," I close my eyes and seem to catch a glimpse of something huge coming into shape around us. Mincemeat deaths going on even now. Suspicious Retirements. Man-eating things in the sewers. The secret history of the Noah. The Builders. The other groups of Archivists, pursuing their own ends. My data-mining application that has become so much more, become a secret communications tool, become AI, working relentlessly toward so many disparate goals. Construction of undeclared research laboratories in Beijing Section. And somewhere, the encroaching steps of those who hunt us: Karla, and the rest of Information Security.

When I try to fit it together, this mass of details cascades and swims, refuses to assemble into a coherent whole. The pieces change shape and keep moving when I try to touch them.

The Archivists seethe, agitated, impatient for the next step, the next big reveal. After years as individuals feeling alone in their doubts about society, they have been brought together, they feel validation. They are getting closer to the great secrets at the heart of all the mysteries. They have no doubts.

Their certainty and faith make me nervous.

I wish we had more time alone together, Barrens and I.

He leads. He manages. And he teaches the kids how to fight.

Everyone practices with amplifiers.

They also train to do without amps, for fighting in areas of the ship without power.

Before my detention, this would have resulted in a major argument between Barrens and me. Because he will not rule out the use of Psyn.

Only the rarest of individuals have the internal discipline to use it without personality instability.

Barrens is one. The effect of Psyn on him is eerie. It makes him coldly, mechanically rational. Perhaps, having wrestled with his inner beast all his life, he finds this external chemical influence to be just another mental influence for him to crush into submission.

I avoid those sessions when he trains the others with it. I loathe it. It terrifies me, the drug.

He used Psyn because he had to. Miyaki, fully empowered, amplifier encoded with all the safety bypass codes ISec wrote into her mind, was murdering them.

After that incident, they had all wanted to be tested for Psyn compatibility. Voted on it, demanded it.

He looks uncomfortable when he explains, "Better I help them use it safely than for them to screw around with it on their own."

Of the twenty men and women in this cell, only a few, other than Barrens, react positively to Psyn. Most, tested with but a drop each, either have too little response, too much response, or are overwhelmed with hallucinations. He is conservative with the dosage and keeps a close eye on the rate of consumption.

He teaches them to work in teams of three, standard police strike teams of a support telekinetic assisting and covering two *bruisers*.

They learn hand-to-hand combat and weapon use. They practice taking apart and putting together and using their crossbows.

An oversize version, practically a ballista of ancient Roman design, fires bolts all of a meter long—it takes two men to operate one, or a *bruiser* or *touch* talent using Psyn. These massive projectiles, shot with such velocity, can punch through inches of armored wall.

The smallest ones are worn on the wrist, little more than slingshots. But rather than true bolts, they fire hollowed shafts with just enough force to shatter them upon impact. Two chemicals are contained in separate cells in the shaft, and when they mix, it produces a caustic gas that burns the eyes and respiratory passages, instantly incapacitating a man with one breath.

They practice target shooting. How to move together, covering each other.

We both acknowledge that he is training a fighting force and not just a group of eccentric investigators; it is a simple enough thing.

"Would you like me to help with that?" I ask.

"Why would you?"

*You only want them safe, isn't it? These are defensive tactics and drills.*

We do not look each other in the eye. He puts his heavy paw on my hip and I lean into him.

They are grateful though, his little soldiers, when I take the time to build obstacle courses and assorted urban environments for them to train in.

If we could only just stay like this, in one of the deep, unpopulated areas of the Noah, outside of the Dome. Perhaps the Ministries and the Enforcers would just let it go, just let us vanish into these shadows, rather than expend the effort to find us.

Finally, the others accept my presence enough that few object when Barrens has me sit in during his exchanges with the other leaders of the Archivists, facilitated by the AI net's communication functions.

They speak of inciting action, of changing the way the crew sees the world we live in. A former low-level ISec agent named Gomez says, "We are not spending all this time preparing troops with the aim of just running and surviving." An advertising executive named Thorn, sleek and handsome and a little too eager, talks openly of changing the system. He speaks of working on something more potent than crossbows. Many others clamor to have their say.

After these virtual meetings, Barrens looks exhausted, his heavy face worn, leaner. The armrests of the chair he sits in are crooked, crushed by his hands, which express what he cannot.

*I just want to find out what's going on. I just think people should know what's going on.*
*Why are you with them, Leon? You don't need them.*

I draw his huge head down and hold him.

*They didn't start out like that. But they're not all wrong, Hana. If we find out. Well. Change may need those who are willing to fight.*

I make myself useful in between the moments. Aside from improving the surrounding architecture for their needs, building proper kitchens and walls and bathrooms and bedrooms, I modify the support structure in the perimeter around our warren. Simplified data nodes I learned to make in Advanced Psychokinetic Engineering 133 are seeded throughout the walls and the floor to monitor psionic activity, programmed to identify all the members of our subgroup, to house local copies of some of the Monster's subunits, and to warn us of incoming non-Archivists.

I participate in a few exercises myself—to try to maintain my own fitness, mentally and physically.

Escaping from the ISec facility took something out of me. I still tire easily, even with the better food, even with all this recovery time.

This odd collection of lonely, paranoid people is still uncomfortable with my presence, unsure of my standing in the group. Yet they do accept Barrens's words about what I can do. Especially when they see me race through the objectives changes they've kludged into my artificial kids, taking only moments to analyze and redo what takes them many hours.

They seem impressed, I guess. But they remain standoffish. Indifferent. Anyway, they are usually too busy to pay much attention to me. Training, hacking, scouring recovered data, cleaning, maintaining and making more weapons, food prep, laundry. This group is tightly knit together, already has its set routines and rhythms and rotations.

Always, someone armed is watching me.

Tommy, Andrews, and Mann are the worst of them. Their eyes are always suspicious of me, following me. Even when it is not their turn to stand guard over me, they keep their weapons close.

Other than Barrens, only Bullet is relaxed with me. "Don't take it too hard. Those three almost got gutted when Officer Miura went all psycho-killer on us," he says.

"And you're not worried?"

He shrugs. "I have a good feeling about you."

It does not mean much, given the lack of the silvery pattern indicating precognition. But his smile helps.

Odd little guy, really. We become a little more than the friends we were. I guess, in terms of the old days of lost Earth, I am like a big sister to him. He hangs out with me, asks me to teach him my programming tricks. I do so, sometimes, showing my little hacks for tablets, for the Web, and internal ones for neural Implants, such as the smoother interface between Implant and gauntlet that I used with the aid of music, when I built skyscrapers with my mind. We talk about our childhoods, about school.

We had the normal upbringing that Barrens, with his beast, did not.

The others respect Bullet despite his sometimes timid demeanor, his misleading youthfulness. Besides the gift of his psychometry, which has made him a celebrity in the movement, he is an excellent chef. It is a good thing he enjoys it because he is so good at it that the rest of the members of our family of circumstance don't like to eat anything less than Bullet's culinary contributions to the cause. Others take turns to assist him, but in the kitchens Bullet is the king.

Once a week, Leon leads half of them off into the darkness, to map their way deeper into the maze outside the Dome.

Often, I lie awake, just waiting for them to return. Worrying.

That nagging voice in my head tells me I should run, now, or send off a coded transmission to Karla and bring the hammer down on everyone. Is that my own voice of reason, or is it a passenger in my head, courtesy of Information Security?

A simmering mass of discontent under the surface is waiting to be unleashed. It has always been there. The confining, limiting pressures of shipboard existence. Humans were never meant to live like this. If we find out all the secrets and set them free, will the discontent ease, just from the knowing? Barrens seems to think so, but the risks gnaw at me. Even after it all comes to light, change won't come easily. Can the Noah afford the cost of that change?

Another trip. This time, a meeting of the top ten of the Archivist leadership, face-to-face.

I am starting to get an idea of the numbers of the Archivists. There may be hundreds of them. Many still hold mission-critical positions in the Habitat. And they are actively recruiting.

Everyone is sluggish when Barrens is gone. Without him, they slowly devolve into introversion, pessimism, nihilism, navel-gazing. They talk in endless circles about why the ship's society is the way it is. They wonder and theorize about what might link these strange, gruesome deaths with the rest of the Noah's dark secrets. Secret laboratories. The tunnel beasts. And so many dreamy fantasies about the Builders, the desire to find something of theirs that will somehow fix *things*.

Come back to me already, Leon.

# 22

TONIGHT IS THE THIRD NIGHT BARRENS HAS BEEN AWAY.

They tell me it is longer than usual.

I get up from my bed and head to the kitchen.

Only Bullet stays upbeat and cheerful. He is cooking a meal fit for kings. "I got a feeling they'll be back soon," he says, shrugging when I, and others, ask. Nobody begrudges him this potential waste of food—they have just brought in more supplies from one of the secret stores close by.

More of that glorious bacon, cooked just so, leaving enough fat to still allow one to taste it on the mouth and chew it. He fries up diced potatoes in the fat to a golden, crisped exterior, still soft within. Onions too. Then eggs, with just enough milk, scrambled, fluffy, perfect omelets. Bullet produces an immense platter of them and keeps them warm in the oven. He begins to cut up fresh apples, with the intent of preparing a light dessert.

When I offer to help, he waves me off.

"Nah, missy. The boss says cooking's not your thing anyway."

I laugh because it is true. My cooking skill is limited to omelets and cereal, period. And I laugh because the Barrens I first met was too insecure to ever imagine anyone referring to him as "the boss."

My AI net has now officially been named Argus by the Archivists. They voted on it.

It chimes with inputs from the sensors I set up around our safe house.

I have decided on another name in my head. Though *Argus* is better than *Monster*, Argus Panoptes was a giant with a hundred eyes, and if its intelligence does happen to keep growing, I'd rather the AI not have an identifier that's linked to a legend about a figure that served the gods and was also killed by them.

So a human name, simple, unpretentious. Archie.

I like to think it responds to me better than it responds to them, is better at recognizing my digital touch despite months of work from the hands of others. When I whisper that name as my thoughts tinker with Archie's code, it seems to become even more responsive to me. Almost happy.

From the kitchen, I walk over to the numerous monitors displaying the structure and complexity of the AI swarm. Dragging a seat over, I sit and gesture. My hands and fingers stretch and unfold the components, revealing the underlying blocks of code. I gaze into the growing universe of its digital DNA, trace the lines of its skeleton of data.

The more I examine it, the more sure I am that nothing I or Barrens or his other hackers programmed into Archie could have triggered this emergence.

*Archie,* I think in my head into the terminals. *It was pieces of the Builder's programming, wasn't it?* I don't expect an answer, but it feels right.

While my design was partly self-modifying and the uses we put it to created the circumstances that allowed the swarm to find it, the critical lightning strike that keyed its evolution to something more was something alien lost in all those Analytical Nodes.

The timing fits. Its rapid development began soon after that day in the biome, when it found the alien memory.

If my man was not out there, maybe being chased by Enforcers even now, if there were not all these other things going on, and all the overwhelming weight of these secrets we have uncovered and which we have yet to uncover, Archie's true nature would be enough to awe and terrify and exhilarate me. A unique, digital life. There is so much we could learn from it, especially the alien segments of its code. It is also scary, wondering what its final form might be.

Come on, Barrens. Where are you?

Archie's excited ping almost catapults me out of my chair. It reads the sensors at the periphery of the Sanctuary and passes them to my Implant. I sigh, in relief, at the feel of Barrens's approach.

Turning to Bullet, I say, "Seems like you're right. They're—"

*Finally in transmission range! Hana, get the Doc ready. Meena needs help.* Barrens's mind's voice is troubled, afraid. It is never like that. This is going to be bad if it can rattle my guard dog so.

I relay his message and Barrens's army snaps to readiness, their ennui forgotten. One group prepares their weapons, while Gregory prepares his improvised clinic. We shut down unnecessary power draws, such as the heat and most of the lights and the tablets and the displays on the walls, so that the Doctor can draw it all for his amplifier.

Two pairs of men and women have propped the ballista into position, aimed at one of the two access points into our shelter. The gleaming, giant-size crossbow is menacing. The arms and the tension lines creak with the strain as the operators turn the cranks, drawing the immense bolt into firing position.

The other entrance goes through the power lines in the ceiling: our escape route, if the worst comes to pass.

The doors slam open.

Chaos then. People thought they were prepared, but nothing could prepare a person for that wheezing, keening wail.

Barrens and one of the others, Tommy, I think, are carrying the third member of their exploration party on an improvised stretcher, two lengths of pipe ripped out of a wall somewhere with their heavy coats stretched between. Tommy is shaking so terribly it is a wonder Meena has not fallen off their rig.

She is unrecognizable. The rich brown mane is falling out in clumps. Her bronze skin is mottled pale and blotchy purples, her belly is bloated, her face is swollen. Blood is trickling out of her nose and ears and mouth, out of every orifice—her coarse denim trousers are soaked, befouled.

Bullet whispers, "What's with her hands?"

The sight of them is paralyzing. Some of her fingers are just . . . missing. Bloody stumps.

"Doc!" Barrens thunders. "Get over here! You lot, make a hole—quit gawking and get out of the way! Bullet, have 'em disarm the ballista before people get skewered by accident!"

"What happened?"

"Don't know," Tommy's words rush out, propelled by fear, anxiety. "We were fine, she'd been complaining about aches and pains, and then she just stopped and fell over, and then she started, huh, she . . ." Then he can't talk anymore, on the edge of passing out.

Gregory takes control, and Barrens lets him. This is Gregory's field. He is brilliant. And he is all we have. "Don't drop her. Miss Dempsey. Please float Meena into the sterile area."

Deep breath now. Forcing down an urge to vomit. Others around us already have. The smell of puke and blood obliterates the perfume of Bullet's cooking.

"The rest of you back off," Barrens orders. "Don't get in the way."

I float her gently, gently off the stretcher. Tommy falls over immediately.

*We were carrying her nonstop for the last twenty-four hours.* Barrens sits heavily. "Take care of her, Doc."

I try hard, very hard, not to jostle her, to move her evenly, supporting every surface. Every place my *touch* fluctuates produces a bruise I can feel swelling, turgid. Adrenaline stretches the time it takes to get her the thirty meters into the Doctor's crude operating theater. I see her skin starting to come apart, even under her soaked shirt.

"Miss Dempsey, cut her clothes off and levitate them away please. Carefully."

I try. It is easy, with an amplifier, to cut Meena's plastech-based clothes. It is harder to remove the sticky scraps of them. Lifting the cloth away causes more lacerations.

When I lower her onto the gleaming, sterilized, cushioned table, the bruises I gave her pop open into wounds, sores. The path in between the entrance to our lair and the Doc's surgery is a river of blood.

Gregory walks briskly to and fro beside Meena, waving his healer's rings. Faint, silver-gold streaks, a gentle glow, bathing her. "Dempsey, you'll have to assist," he intones somberly.

What? No, I can't. I trained with buildings and computers, not flesh and blood.

"Hana," Barrens's voice is a caress, but it is also steel and straightens my spine. He has followed us into surgery. "Meena was our nurse. You're the only other left with a high enough *touch* rating to do fine manipulations."

Sigh and whine on your own time, Dempsey. Breathe deep, focus. "What's next?"

*I'll be right here with you. Just let the Doc guide you.*

"Bullet!" Barrens barks. "Keep the others away, got it?"

With a twitch of my finger, I drag the curtains into place behind us.

"Hell. There's no way I can force you outta here, boss, if you don't want to be moved. But you better just stand there and be quiet, okay?"

"Don't pay attention to me! Help her!"

Thinking would only get me into trouble here. I have to empty myself, be another instrument of the Doctor's, mind open to his commands.

Where he uses psychic surgery to probe or to cut or heal, his telepathy informs me and I must follow, reinforcing her organs, gently holding them in place. Healing is similar to *touch,* but it is more, it's an amalgamation of telekinesis, empathy, and the ability to manipulate the biochemistry of another. My talent's fingers are inside her now, but unlike the Doctor, all I can do is push and pull and cut.

It is abominable, feeling, smelling, almost tasting, how disgusting we humans are inside, just tubes in tubes filled with fluids of differing varieties of disturbing color, odor, and viscosity.

Barrens keeps his thoughts perfectly still, as if he were just a statue. He is as a stone, silent.

Meena is breaking apart right in front of us. Her flesh disintegrates. Her bones. Her skin. It pulls apart from its own weight no matter how I hold the jigsaw pieces together, no matter how Gregory forces healing energy into the seams to knit the cells together. Every time he closes a cut or break, internal or external, a dozen other hemorrhages begin. At random, parts of her remain untouched. Her left foot is completely whole, while the right is a mangled mess. One heaving breast is a lone, perfect reminder of her previous beauty, rising from the red ruin of her torso, where the bones of her ribs and some of her internal organs are visible through the rents in the flesh.

We draw so much power the lights go out. In the dark, Meena's body is lit up, a bonfire of our combined energies.

What is worst is the awareness in her eyes, the horror in them. The whistling wheeze of her breath through the collapsing bulb of her nose and through her disintegrating teeth is a sound that will haunt me forever.

Meena's own talents flare wildly throughout the process.

*That's what's killing her,* Gregory's thoughts exclaim, confused, astonished. *Her own raw psi is randomly destroying her cells.*

It is the longest hour of my life. If I thought it was something before, the eternity of that first day in the Information Security holding pen, this is as far beyond that as nothing I can think of. In the last minutes, Gregory shakes his head and pulls back, glowing rings around his fingers shutting down.

Her brain is coming apart. Her last coherent thoughts beg for mercy, to make it stop.

"Let her go." His voice is hoarse. "We're just prolonging it."

We are crying, the Doc and I. But Barrens, Barrens is still and steady, a pale boulder, waiting. We look at each other, the three of us.

Gregory takes a deep breath. "I can't."

"I'm sorry, Meena." Barrens pushes past us. He pulls a knife, and I know he could end it instantly, with his skill and strength. It would be painless, for her. But for Barrens, it would be one more person's blood on his hands.

Staring at his back from behind, I wonder if he has somehow gotten even larger. But his bent shoulders put that illusion to rest. I step in his way and I put my arms around him. No.

*You've done enough, Leon.*

Compared to what I've done. Compared to killing those poor dumb boys in the darkness, because I was afraid, because I was untrained. This is a mercy.

If I just let her go, she will go to pieces on her own. Aware as each part is severed.

I focus the *touch*, let it build, let it charge, formless at first. All at once, I let it out, channeled into her mind. It crackles along the channels of her neural Implant and destroys the organics of her brain in a flash of thought.

I need to get out of here. But I can't move. Nausea roils in my gut. Barrens sees me. Really sees me. Between us, without a touch of psi or the connection of Implants, we share awareness, the awful familiarity of this experience. We have seen the aftermath of this before. Many times now. In memories, on flat 2-D images, referred to by names on a list. Mincemeat.

## 23

BULLET BREAKS OUT HIS HIDDEN STASH OF WHISKEY.

Everyone needs it. People stumble off, eyes glazed over, some alone, some in pairs, huddled up in their bunks or on the couches or just sitting on the floor in one corner or the other.

Only Barrens and I do not drink.

He leads me away. For an hour, we walk in the cold, dark, unpowered tunnels. Down several ladders, turning round and round. We come upon a wider corridor with a ghostly light in the distance.

"This is where we found you."

"Oh."

There is still the outline, the depression in the wall where I formed a shell around myself to hide. They broke it open when they got me and never fixed it. The concave surfaces are a mold following the shape of my body.

We look out the clear porthole in the door onto the great power conduit running through the heart of the Noah. It is beautiful, and strange. How many others have stood in this place and seen the same thing?

He tilts his head back and sniffs, nostrils flaring. Takes a few steps closer to one of the walls. His fist and arm are enfolded in ruby light. His blow crunches through the laminated plastech layers. Water gushes. Almost burning hot, it steams in the cold, dry air. He tears off his bloody sweater and shirt. Shoves his trousers down. Just stands there, looking at nothing, while the water sprays him down. With the light from the porthole, his massive body looks as perfect as ever. Pale once the blood has been washed free, he is all hard angles and muscle; perhaps he is even larger than before, now that his group has stolen stores of meat and fish and richer food and he eats better than he could afford in the past.

Eventually, he comes back to himself.

I don't resist when he pulls me to him and starts undressing me. It is to shiver when his coarse, rough fingers touch me.

"We can't stay too long," I murmur. "A leak like this is too much. It will draw attention." Shaking now, in his arms. The heat of us and the steaming shower. We live.

"You can fix it, after."

Fear. We taste it on each other. Maybe it is to fight it off, to feel alive, that causes what happens next. Maybe I just miss him. Maybe this is a denial of death.

We kiss and it is not gentle. It is savage. Primal. I turn my back to him and place my palms on the wall, and spread my legs. When he takes me, we howl, hearts pounding, while the water runs down our skins. Muscle against muscle, we are fighting as much as we are fucking. When we are done, panting, gasping, we slide down to the floor. He presses his face between my thighs, and I stretch my jaw as wide as I can manage to get it around the thick, steaming length of him, and we start again. The long red trails of my scratches down his arms, and the bite marks he leaves on my neck and my thighs are strangely beautiful by the alien light.


Nobody gets any sleep that night. When we return, wearing new clothes I made by drawing material right off the corridor wall, they are already in deep discussion.

Barrens's appearance and his slow, deep voice stills their rising panic.

"So. Not experimentation. At least, if it is, it's something that acts real slow. Meena was with us since the beginning. Been months since she's even been in the Habitat."

Most have their eyes down, refusing to look at anyone. The few who are not lost in themselves, in more pleasant memories, murmur their assent.

"This is why we do this. Got to know what's going on." He takes a breath, barks, "Now. Snap out of it." He assigns them their tasks. Activities to focus on, to take their minds away from what they have seen.

Gregory needs proper equipment to analyze Meena's remains. Instruments too complex for me to synthesize out of plastech.

Barrens sends one team to go off and find the Doctor the required lab components.

Gomez's face fills the display in the assembly room. He would be handsome if not for that perpetual squint, the pinched lines around his little mouth. Giving instructions.

Another team is to pull memories off all the witnesses and out of the gleaming silver threads of Meena's intact neural Implant, then splice it together and edit it to remove cues of our identities—leaving only our feelings of horror, and the raw sensory input of the smells, the sight of Meena falling apart, the feel of her dying skin when she was touched, the unbridled, twisting, gut-wrenching emotions, and the echo of her pain, her conscious, lost disbelief as her body betrayed her.

Other leaders' faces appear on the monitors and concur.

Barrens grimaces. "What the hell for?" he rumbled. "We need to focus on figuring this out."

"This is for the packet we're going to distribute," the one named Thorn answers. "Spread it around. Just label the memory, 'This is Mincemeat,' that'll be all it takes. This is how it begins. We'll shake everyone out of their complacency! This will change humanity, it'll . . ."

A deep breath now. This is exactly what Karla wants me to stop.

I hold my breath, waiting to lose control of myself, to become a puppet on a string, a bullet fired from a gun.

Nothing happens.

I shake it off and reach for Barrens's wrist, try to squeeze him, to let him know I'm here.

*Leon, release that memory without context, and it will cause a panic.*

*Agreed.*

His face turns bright red, but he does keep from shouting. "No. My people aren't doing that. If it comes time for it, if we must, we will. Not before. We are not going to get civilians who aren't involved Adjusted because you're bored or impatient."

The argument between Thorn and Barrens goes on a long time. Everyone else pretends not to listen or watch. Gomez looks ghoulishly amused.

In the end, my man is worn down to a compromise. Some of Barrens's team will prepare the propaganda packet, but we will hold on to it—it is not to be released—until all the leaders agree that it is time. This leaves me shaking my head. It is no resolution at all, and the terms for what constitutes when to release it are too vague. Still, at least Barrens keeps them unified.

We organize the last team.

Barrens assigns Bullet and a slightly cross-eyed, soft-spoken lady named Susan to me. *Hana. I know you saw those number codes in the sheets you got out of my storage space. G-0, G-1. You know what they are, right?*

Of course. I knew immediately. There was a pair of numbers for each of the two entries. Incredibly long hexadecimal numbers and letters and characters. They are old-style private and public keys for the encryption of files—a process from three hundred years ago, before programmers became more comfortable with the quantum computing allowed by the massive neural banks of psi-tech computation.

*We have to find the lock for those keys, Hana. Nobody can work with Argus like you can. The others can handle a simpler search; this thing, whatever happened to Meena, Gregory says there were rumors from when he was in medical training. They'll look for those stories. And they'll help you too, but you'll have to teach them.*

I am to do the nearly impossible—find files or databases or a passworded *anything* that might match those keys that could be anywhere on the vast Network.

Close my eyes. This is bigger than any of us. It is the tide that is pushing the others in his organization.

Barrens eyes are looking down at mine. *I should have brought you with me all along.*

"Okay," I finally say. Swallow. "We can start by tweaking the way Archie, um, Argus, builds ontological relationships, concept maps, based on those old pages in your vault."

Like puzzle pieces falling into place, it feels natural, teaching others something, breaking a problem into its components. We discuss and work out the specifications for the new searches and begin to map out the requirements for Archie to find and identify the lost files. It is just managing a project team. In truth, with the way Archie seems to fit against me, like gloves around my hands dipping into dataspace, I hardly need assistance.

They have their purpose, their cause. Barrens has his need to know the truth, to find out what happened to Callahan, to uncover what Mincemeat is. In the end, everyone does as he or she must, and so do I.

# 24

WE CODE IN THE NEW FUNCTIONS, LET THEM PROPAGATE THROUGH ARCHIE'S distributed architecture—conjugative plasmids spreading through a digital bacterial culture. Once more, I am struck by how different the AI is when I am at the terminal. When Susan or Bullet work with Archie, it responds to function calls like any application. With me, Archie anticipates me somehow. Its reaction time is significantly faster, as if it starts to execute my commands before I finish typing them in. It is more alive for me.

Once we finish setting fully 80 percent of the AI swarm's capacity to the new tasks, there is little for me to do but wait. The volume of information the data-miner must sift through is enormous. Useful results may appear tomorrow. More likely, it may take years. With how huge the Network is, it may take forever.

Barrens does not look displeased when I tell him this. He still looks tired from dealing with the rest of the leadership, but excitement lights the fire behind his eyes. "I didn't expect a miracle. And we got progress on other fronts."

Other fronts?

Events are accelerating, most everything is out of my control. I guess it was always like that, even when I was working my job in City Planning; I just never noticed because of how cleanly the illusion was maintained. There is that feeling that I am missing something—that I ought to have figured out more with the pieces I do have.

Barrens takes me aside into our sleep coffin.

"Argus—sorry. You like Archie, right? An older search turned up something else. We're planning an expedition now, coordinated with another cell. I'll let the rest of the team know tomorrow, then we'll have a week to prep."

A deep breath. We curl up inside the tiny space, sitting cross-legged, hunched over. Barrens's hair brushes the top of the chamber.

"An expedition?"

"Deep into the unmapped zones."

So. "The old lab facilities."

Barrens shakes his head. "That's what the others think. I don't think so anymore. Thorn, mostly, is fixated on it 'cause he's been pushing the idea that the Mincemeat deaths are the result of human experimentation. After Meena, the timing just seems off. And there's more." Barrens lifts his personal tablet, accesses the data for me, and we link up through it and our Implants.

Images and text and menus come aglow in my vision, hovering in front of us. My fingers dance through the information, manipulating the maps, highlighting particular figures. It is immediately apparent that this cannot be just some center for secret research.

"It's too large." The power, food, and water consumption rates are immense, as great as what is used for the Habitat. No, it uses even more power than that. Much more.

"Even if it's nothing, going there will give everyone something to do while we wait for Archie to find the G-0 and G-1 files. And if there is something there, it's big. It'll at least distract the hotheads for a while."

My hands settle on his jaw and cheeks and turn his face my way. "You are not leaving me behind again."

Barrens sighs. His eyes turn to one side. I can guess that he is thinking of any number of things he might say to talk me out of coming. The possibility of getting lost out there, in the vast uncharted regions of the ship. Unknown dangers. Maybe even just running across Enforcers guarding that immense sink of the ship's resources.

"No. I'm going. Try to take off without me and I'll just get lost trying to follow you. Anyway, you'll need strong telekinetics where there's no gravity."

"I want you to stay safe."

Driving my elbow into his side just gets a slight *whuff* of breath out of him. *Leon. I'm safest wherever you are.*

He slouches lower, leans his head against mine. *I guess I was leaning toward having you come with us anyway. You're the smartest person here, Hana. If we do find something, best if there's a real mind with us.*

It's been forever since a compliment heated up my cheeks. "That's settled then. Who leads the other group that's going?"

Now his face contorts, as if he were forcing down a mouthful of vinegar. "Gomez." *The rest of the heads want him there. They wonder if I'll share what we find.*

*And would you share, Leon? No matter what?*

Barrens's eyes fade and slide to memories.

Once, I think, his answer would have been aggressive and automatic. He would have wanted the information disseminated freely no matter the cost.

I shift over, straddle him. Rest my face against the slow, deep beating of his heart.

"Depends." His rumbling voice goes right through to my bones. Under my fingertips, his muscles are rock, tense, as though he were fighting even now. "I don't know, anymore," he whispers. "Don't people deserve to know?"

He can only look unsure with me. Only with me. He is changing, and not sure if his heart still agrees with his own mind.

"There is time," I tell him, "right? We'll do what we were doing all along. Try to learn more, so we can know best what to do, one way or the other."

Barrens presses his mouth against the crown of my head. *Glad you're here. Whenever I'd get confused, I'd think of you, and how we'd talk about things. I should not have left you.*

Those steely coils of flesh slacken, relax. He starts talking about the logistics of our voyage. He shows me the route we will take, the place where we'll meet up with Gomez. Consider what we might find there. How many of us are going, and how much food and water we will need to bring. Flashlights and self-powered lamps for everyone. Cold-weather gear. He bounces motivational stuff off me, the things he will include when he talks to the rest of the group.

I fall asleep first, while he is still working and reworking tomorrow's speech.

I dream about getting a stray data packet. Even as I scan it, it is too late, and Karla has fired me off. I go wild. At the end, there is me in Miyaki's place, being battered to death by Barrens's huge hands.

Too soon, I am staring at his broad back as I follow. Hot breath misting in the cold, freezing air. Shuffling along in the dark, eyes trained on the dim light of the oil lamps Tommy had built for us.

Some of the corridors are narrow and rounded, and some are large, empty halls in hexagonal or octagonal shape, in cross section fifty meters across.

The first day, we go far enough that we are out of the reach of the simple automated telekinetic emitters that produce the gravity on the ship. Or rather, where we are, they are kept off to conserve power. Those unidirectional force generators are built all throughout the ship's structure.

We float tethered together, trying to avoid accidents. Having the strongest *touch*, I am in the lead, pulling us along telekinetically, followed by Barrens, then Susan, Mann, and Bullet. The other TK with us, Tommy, is at the rear, keeping watch on everyone, nudging people back in line with flickers of blue energy. Whenever their motions and gyrations or accidental contacts with the wall or floor or ceiling (not that it matters which is which) pushes them away, clumsily, helplessly spinning, we have to stop so that Tommy and I can use our talents to stabilize everyone and get us back in "marching" order.

Six beads on a string, carried along on telekinetic currents.

On the walls of some of the large corridors, we see more of the reliefs I saw while I flew across the zero-g gap in the great power conduit. More of the odd, angular character set. Images of the Builders. The surfaces have a worn-down, blurry look, as though someone tried to remove them. Here, the plastech has been processed in some manner I am unfamiliar with—it feels incredibly hard, resistant to telekinetic manipulation.

Occasionally, we face blast doors that do not match the smooth, ancient walls. Half a meter thick, they have been opened by the lead group. Among the little treasures Archie dug up during the months I was not paying attention are numerous passwords for locks scattered throughout the ship. A few people in each cell act as key-bearers, carrying thousands of passwords for the doors we have yet to find. So far, every obstacle has yielded to this motley collection of digital keys carried in their heads.

We take breaks to rub our cold, numb fingers. We drink and eat.

We know night falls only by our internal chronometers and the sensation of fatigue. Just the sameness as we proceed deeper into the dark tunnels is tiring. It might feel more like a camping trip or an adventure if we could light a fire to warm ourselves by, cook something hot to eat, while those with decent voices sang something encouraging. Instead we try to stay quiet and minimize light and sound.

After the rich food Bullet was preparing for everyone each day, the bland, filling ration bars of pressed grain and dried fruit pulp are like cardboard.

Tommy and Mann finger their crossbows nervously as they play their lights back and forth, sweeping the darkness. Everyone is thinking of maintenance worker Jackson, and his encounter with a beast that ate men.

*Think I should give them a pep talk?*

*Better save it, Leon. It's only the first day.*

One more exertion of *touch* zips me into a sleeping bag. My head aches from the day of steady TK exertion without the grid's power to draw on. Sleep comes quickly.

Morning begins with Barrens nudging us out of our uncomfortable slumber, everyone curled up, pasted to one wall or another with adhesive tags. We eat another meal of dried fruit and nuts and jerky and drink lots of water, pack up our things, and continue on. It ought to be effortless for everyone but Tommy and me, but it is tiring just the same, I suppose, to be moved around like so much luggage.

It feels like when I was in prison. The lack of environmental cues for the passage of time. The constant discomfort. The lousy food.

But, no, not really. I just need to reach out, and even if it is through thick, ungainly gloves, I can hold Barrens's hand and be comforted.

It is worse for the others. They are uneasy, most speak in monosyllables when they speak at all, and only when necessary. The dank air smells ancient. Nerves are tight.

They've shared too many of the traumatic memories absorbed by Bullet's psychometry.

On the third day, we go "up" when we should have gone "right" at a five-way intersection, and it takes a whole day before we realize that we are lost and backtrack to where we were. We reach the rendezvous point a day late. The other group left a message for us taped to the floor and went ahead.

Only Bullet keeps up an ongoing conversation with me. Just whispers. But he is wide-eyed and smiling and not at all intimidated. Each time we find a set of carvings, his excitement is renewed.

"Just don't touch them, Bullet. Not even with your gloves on. I don't want to think what might happen if your talent flares up unpredictably. You might get a thousand-year-old alien vision or something and be knocked out for a day."

His hands jerk back. "Oh, yeah. Good point. What do you think these writings are though, Miss Dempsey?"

"I don't know. On old Earth, in ancient times, people that built monuments sometimes carved their names where nobody could see. Maybe it's like that."

"You think so? I like the sound of that. Maybe their names are here, somewhere."

If we share that much psychology with the aliens at all. Their minds could be so different that we would have no common reference frame of communication even if we could translate the language. But I think of that memory Barrens and I saw, the way the one Builder seemed to be smiling. It's comforting to imagine that they were not completely different from us.

What we have found of them is wondrous. The art on the walls, and it is art, is beautiful. Strange places, stranger moments.

Sometimes in our heads and sometimes out loud, and sometimes with Barrens joining in, Bullet and I wonder about why ISec erased the Builders from our histories. We could learn so much if teams of anthropologists were finding and studying these treasures hidden throughout the ship.

We find remnants of the campsites of Gomez's group here and there. Discarded food packs. The messy biological excretions are left in far corners—the walls are too hard to alter into hiding our trash, so we are forced to leave, well, leavings. Of ourselves. Right along our route, as we go along, often just a dozen feet down one side passage or another—little bags of trash or urine or feces, glued to the walls.

On the fifth day, we are woken by the floor's vibrating, jarring us—a loud, powerful rumbling.

Barrens lifts a small canister to his face. Lets loose one spray into each eye. Psyn.

He presses his hands and his ear against one of the walls.

"Supply hauler. Big one. We're going the right way—definitely the parallel shaft in the schematics."

The team had been growing dull, tired by the endless miles of tomblike halls. Just knowing that life is close by, right next to us, is affirmation. Everyone wakes up, is more alert. We push a little harder during the long hour it takes for the train to pass. The ones with the wrist crossbows shake off their stupor and keep their eyes open, scanning the darkness.

Of course, if there were Enforcers out there . . . Well. They are said to be so skilled, they do not require Implant or amplifier to be lethal. It could be propaganda, in which case we would have plenty of warning before they attack us—they would need to power up the corridor to get access to the grid to fuel their abilities. If it is not propaganda, only the ones who can use Psyn would have much of a chance of opposing them.

*I can almost hear you thinking about me being on drugs.*

*I don't like it, Leon.*

*Sorry. It's necessary. Wish you'd give it a try. You're such a powerful psi, Hana. If Psyn works for you, you'd be the difference if we got in trouble.*

In trouble? Perfect images slide forward in my thoughts, standing, glowing in the dark in an improvised bunker, seeing through Miura's eyes, reaching out with my talent to strike. The words get jammed up in my head. That's not what my gift is for.

His knuckles brush against the narrow strip of flesh bared between my hat and the hood of the heavy thermal jacket. Without a word, without a thought projected from Implant to Implant, he understands me and apologizes, and even if I am afraid of so much, I am grateful for everything that got us here, to this place and moment.


"Where the hell are they?"

The other group was supposed to wait for us at the last gate before our destination. We have reached it after days of floating along, and they are conspicuously absent.

A number of empty water bottles are floating around, and discard bags are taped down, but that is all. In front of us, the gate looks entirely underwhelming, simple-looking double doors with a faux-wooden finish and brass knobs. It could have been the entrance to the kitchen of a restaurant, or to a meeting room in any office building. The light from our lamps casts eerie shadows about our floating forms.

Tommy scowls, rubbing at the thick blond stubble on his face. "Gomez. Always like that. Show-off. Get in, get out, prepare a propaganda release, send it out before we get back, make like he's the leader of the whole movement."

Barrens's face is tight. But not with anger. He is troubled. "They should have been out by now. They'd come back the way they came. Gomez wouldn't give up the chance to gloat."

Murmuring now, among the others.

"Maybe ISec got them?"

"We know they got this far." Barrens calls Bullet up to the front.

The smallest guy in our company crosses his eyes and bites his lip. Glimmering of blue around him as he maneuvers to the head of the line where we are. When he pushes too far one way or the other, or his vector wobbles, it takes him real effort to straighten out. Tommy or I could easily get him up here more quickly, but it doesn't take much empathy to understand that people want to do what they can on their own.

"Okay. I'm going to give you a half-dose, right?" Barrens says.

*Don't look at me like that, Hana. We're real careful. Nobody's addicted. This helps him control the psychometry, makes it less random.*

I do not like it, no, not at all.

A puff of lavender mist into his eyes. His face slackens and takes on a soft, dreamy expression.

"Getting anything?"

Bullet reaches out his hands, slides them along the floor. Soft ribbons of power spread out from where he touches—nothing visible, but all of us can sense it.

His voice turns singsong and breathy as he lets out what his senses perceive.

"We should wait, Johnny. We should—"

"Man, come on. It's our chance to be the first!"

"Barrens'll be pissed."

"You worry too much. Leonard's more easygoing than you think. He's a nice guy. You read too much into that ugly mug he was born with."

Ten minutes of such dialogue. A little scatological humor too, as more than a few of them had needed to pee or defecate while the two teams' leaders made up their minds.

Tommy is smiling; most have pensive, impatient looks on their faces, lips pursed, brows furrowed. Waiting for the hammer to drop.

"That's it, boss," Bullet comes back to himself. His eyes are bloodshot. A whole-body twitch goes through him. "They use one of the password codes we've collected, open the door, and go through."

That settles it for us then. I already knew we were going to proceed.

While Barrens gets everyone together, prepares them, reminds them to be cautious, to keep weapons at the ready, I take hold of Bullet's little wrists.

He has his hands pressed hard to his temples. Nobody seems to care.

He flinches at every sound, and I speak as softly as I can while still being heard over Barrens's pep talk. "What's wrong? Is it the Psyn?"

"It's nothing. It's like this anytime the talent flares up intensely, Psyn or no. Time breaks down. Like everything that's happened before is happening at the same time as now."

Sensory overstimulation. "Okay," I whisper soothingly. "You know how to do the 'empty mind' meditation drill, right? It will help. Breathe with me. Slow. That's it."

*He'll be fine. Come on. Got to move—anyway, we may need him to* look *into the past as we move along, to find out what happened to the others.*

"I'm fine," Bullet says, watching the way we look to each other and then to him. "I can keep going."

*You're right, Leon. I wish you weren't. I'm worried about him. He's absorbed so many memories in the past months, and his talent is not well understood. I don't remember him having such a tough time taking in something, I mean, with the Mincemeat scenes, it was the traumatic emotion, but just now, it's only guys talking, and he looks sick.* Barrens tugs the line, floats closer in front of Bullet, and shines a light in his eyes.

"Really, boss." Bullet blinks and puts on a ghastly smile.

*All right. If he gets much worse, we'll stop for a couple of hours. But for now, we move.*

That is as good as we can do. If something is seriously wrong with him, we'd need the Doctor to do a brain scan on him, and Gregory isn't here. The faster we finish this expedition and get back, the better for everyone.

# 25

Barrens goes through the doors first.

I don't notice at first how thick they are. The exterior panels look like wood, but a solid foot of dense, metallic, armor-quality plastech is sandwiched in the center.

There is power beyond the doors. The air is a rush of welcome warmth. There is simulated gravity. There are bright lights. There is the welcome sensation of feeling complete as my amplifier detects the grid and our high-tech devices are no longer just lifeless hunks of junk.

We are pulled down to the floor, and we right ourselves, standing a little clumsily after days of zero g.

Bullet lands awkwardly on hands and knees and immediately folds up on his side, a fetal ball, a whistling, wheezing keening coming from his lips.

He is not the only one.

Susan too is incapacitated. The two with the strongest *reading* talents. They thrash on the ground, limbs banging against the metallic grating.

*Shit. Things never do go according to plan, do they, love?*

*I've got them. I'll get them out.*

There is so much power here. Drawing on the grid has never been so easy. I enfold them in gentle fields of TK and get them back out into the cold, dark corridor.

It would be exhilarating if my head were not throbbing. Even my meager *reading* induces psi backlash. My eyes water, my heart pounds, my chest is compressed by the weight of the air.

The raw misery emanating from everywhere is so strong.

Barrens has no such capacity at all and is the only one completely unaffected.

"Talk to me."

I pull one of his hands up to my face, pressing his rocky palm to my temple. "Brace yourself." It takes but a moment to pass him a whisper of the raw emotional charge filling the air, the hate and the black terror pressing down on everyone.

He just grimaces. "Oh."

Yes. Oh. I check on Bullet and Susan in the corridor. They're starting to recover.

Bullet moans, "Sorry. It's too much. Can't go in there."

"You just take care of her."

We close the doors, but do not lock them.

The rest of us grit our teeth and take in the sight we have been trying to avoid thinking about.

Our entryway is halfway down an immense, sloping, concave wall. The chamber beyond us is gigantic. Gigantic. It is the size of the entire Habitat Dome. Larger. There is no artificial sky, just an ugly expanse of slimy gray and green and rust-brown ceiling crowded with a tangle of pipes and lines and wiring and bulbous tanks and upside-down observation towers. It looks neither like the pictures and documentaries about the cave systems of lost Earth, nor like a deliberate and planned architectural construct—it is the inside of some nightmare's belly, with tumors and bulging veins and arteries and gruesome organs growing out of everything. The floor looks much the same as the ceiling, except countless rows of spheroid structures repeat in fractal patterns, a bewildering, maddening vision of not-quite-random iteration. Piercingly bright rays of light reach out from the ceiling towers, cutting through the shadows of the ambient glow of the steaming power lines against the mess of geometry.

The cargo hauler shaft beneath us exits farther down the floor, its twisting, curving tunnel resembling the snaking, pink tube of some animal's intestines.

And the smell . . . numbed from the harsh, dry cold of the journey here, our olfactory nerves are now processing it, I guess, or perhaps our brains rebelled for a while, refusing to accept the input signals.

It is not the smell of raw sewage. It is slightly sweet, tinged with sulfurous rot. It is less strong, yet more foul, than the odor in my disgusting trek through the sewer line.

Tommy vomits. The retching sounds and the additional smell sets off a chain reaction of nausea. Meena's death has hardened us. No one else pukes, though it is close; my own guts clench, roiling.

We are paralyzed, eyes tracking across mile after mile of wrongness. The Behavioralist Bureau's Keeper regimen has stamped religion out of our ship's culture and kept it that way for centuries, a triumph of rationalism, with all our faith directed toward the simple ideal of human survival. Still, this looks like hell, a concept that still exists for us.

Could the Builders be in there somewhere? No. No, I cannot imagine those peaceful, graceful people generating such a dense aura of utter misery.

Barrens pulls another little canister from inside the big blue greatcoat he still likes to wear.

"What are you doing? Just use your amplifier." I don't like my voice when it's like this, hissing, ugly.

"Don't know how much time we've got here. Drawing on my amp too. Taking in every sensory input I can. All of you, order your perceptions. When we get out, we'll only have our memories. Somebody keep an eye out for those goddamn idiots. Smells so fucking bad, I can't get any scent of Gomez's group."

I get the shakes. The bolt of raw terror slides through me. I search for that sense of empty, focused discipline I found back in the ISec holding cell. A stone, I am what I must be and stand firm. And I am not alone. It is enough.

That awful fear is still there, but it is someone else's fear, for a while.

This place is familiar to me. Déjà vu.

"It's okay. Everybody, we'll take ten, okay? But then, we're gonna move. Gonna climb down to the closest egg-thing, okay?"

Barrens looks at me, worried. "Hana," his voice rumbles in my ear softly, softly. "You gonna be okay? Need your mind and skills for this, darlin'—you gotta look at the layout of this place, think it through."

Every step in is harder. The air is charged with psychic screams, echoing. There is something. Something about those eggs.

I have long known that the only direction for Barrens is straight ahead.

Teeth gritted, I take another step. And another. "I'll be fine." You're not leaving me behind.

The others get up too. They lean on each other, knees shaking. They're only moving forward because their eyes are on Barrens's broad back, taking in his quiet, constant anger, his furious courage.

*This place is huge. How deep are we going?*

*As far as we can. Our visit won't go unnoticed. Next time, there will be heavier security than some ancient doors that open to hexadecimal codes.*

We creep down the steep paths. We hop across stagnant pools of turbid fluids that collect where the incline flattens out.

"Shit. Where is Gomez?"

We close in on one of the small egg-structures. It is a kilometer away now. Steam billows out of ports scattered around its surface. Each is a hundred meters across. The one we approach is unlit—one face has cracked open. Hatched.

Crouched there, looking up at the gaping opening, there is this more intense smell—concentrated chicken broth starting to spoil. The ground around the shattered blocks is flooded by slick, clear slime. It trails away. Mann and Tommy are jumpy; they nearly fire on every moving shadow.

*This is a bad idea, Leon.*

*Yep. Probably is.*

We follow the trail down. I cannot help thinking how different this is from my only other hike with Barrens, back in the Forest biome.

He holds up a clenched fist and we crouch low in the shadow of one of the large pipes creeping along the surface. It is two meters in diameter, greenish, encrusted with gray-green fuzz, going along the right side of our path. I cannot help but grimace as I stick out a hand to keep from tumbling when I lose my balance.

Barrens's neck is craned up. He turns his head left and right. I hear him sniffing.

*What is it?*

*I smell blood. Human blood. And more than that.*

He drops down and feels around in a particularly broad, stinking pool. His face is grim. He pulls something out.

We all gasp. I scoot back on my butt, ignoring the filth soaking into my pants.

It is an arm. An arm torn free. On the hand, there is a lion tattoo.

"Gomez," Tommy whispers.

At the crest of a hillock, we see a shadow lurch upright. Is it fifteen meters away or fifty? The light and the curving surfaces all around throw off perspective. But it is definitely too close.

*Nobody move.*

Spotlights sweep in, focus on it in brilliant brightness.

It is huge. It seems impossible to take in its appearance all at once. Only in pieces can I take it in. Its flesh is mottled, patchy. Parts of it are pink and soft-looking. Parts are covered over with uneven, bristly hairs. Parts are gray, like the hide of a rhino, or an elephant. Parts have no skin at all, are just raw, exposed muscle and veins and bone, covered with pus and yellowish discharge and blood. There are . . . extra bits. Limbs. Eyeballs. Mouths. Ears. Along its back . . . backs? White, bony spurs project from the lines of its spine. Teeth. Such teeth. Most of the partially formed faces scattered over the massive skull are small, slack, and unaware, but the largest of them, slightly off center from the front of its head, twitches from expression to mad expression—anger, sorrow, delight, smiling, laughing, weeping.

That one face could almost be human.

It moves with sinuous grace despite its mismatched, lumpy limbs.

Scattered about its feet, there are . . . pieces. The hands holding on to hunks of meat and bone look so normal. Except for extra fingers on the one, and missing fingers on the other. The monster takes bites out of something that crunches in its teeth.

When it roars, it wails. What is worst about the sound is how familiar it is. And more than the air vibrating, its voice calls straight to all our minds. *Wwaaaaaaaah.*

Even Barrens feels that. He flinches back. I can almost feel his beast growling, ears pulled back. Preparing to fight. The rest of us are reduced to limp weakness, scrabbling on the ground. Barrens is on all fours, his hunter's crouch, his lips pulled back in a snarl.

*No. No! Leon, you cannot fight that!*

Too long. Too long before he uncoils his beast self, pulls it back. So close. But then Barrens the man blinks. Cocks his head to the side.

*Under the pipe. Now!*

All of us crawl under.

Then there is a sound that I have never heard in person. But I have seen Web streams about the special training that Enforcers are put through. It starts with a high whine. It deepens and thrums and pierces the skull, growing to an ear-splitting shriek, and then, the air itself is torn asunder.

Above and ahead of us, bursts of Enforcer's fire light up the air, brighter than the ten-meter spotlights sweeping back and forth from the observation spires.

Enforcers, psi wings unfolded from their armored shoulder emitters, rain fire down on the creature. At any other time, I would marvel at their personal flight gear, so much smaller and sleeker than the cumbersome frames of police ornithopters.

The floor under us vibrates, ripples with the shuddering forces of the battle. The air-pressure bursts from the explosions pop my ears, deafen me.

The monster is torn up. Blood sprays in great fountains. Smell of cooking meat, and I know I will never again consider eating animal protein.

Despite its terrible wounds, it does not fall. It leaps away, crying and moaning. Leaving a trail of its own blood.

The Enforcers, fireflies of obsidian shells and living lightning, dart after it.

*Leon, no! Where the hell are you going?*

"Tommy," he whispers. "Get them back to the safe house. Somebody has to see. I need to see."

*Don't you dare.*

*I have to go, Hana. I can't turn away. People died for this.*

*Not without me.*


While Tommy and Mann crawl back to the exit, I follow Barrens into the shadows.

We watch from around corners, behind the squat, bulbous buildings, through the thick tangle of pipes and vents.

Plumes of black smoke rise, intertwined with the white steam hissing out of the various lines burst open by the battle between the creature and the strongest psi talents of the ship.

And it is a battle, not a hunt.

Even horribly wounded, the multilimbed horror leaps impossibly vast distances. It must be boosting its physiology with psi energy. When it turns its head up to the insects tormenting it and howls, white fire crackles up from the ground, bursts of psi. One of the black-armored figures is incinerated instantly, falls.

More Enforcers come. A dozen now. Each of them pulling megawatts of power. Some push down on it, slowing it with pure force opposing its movements. Others try to trap it with huge chains created right out of the plastech floor, sending tons of material looping around its body. The rest of them maintain a bubble of glowing cobalt light around their group, deflecting the fire to the side when it comes too quickly for them to dodge.

The creature keeps breaking the chains as it lopes along.

The explosions get louder, and bigger, as the Enforcers stress the grid. The lights across this hellish city flicker. Debris floats through the air, falls, floats again as the simulated gravity flickers on and off.

Barrens gives chase with Psyn-boosted *bruiser* speed. I keep up only by carefully catapulting myself around with *touch*. More than once, I come close to cracking my head open, or spraining an ankle when I land. We are cockroaches watching the gods shake the world. The superstructure of the ship vibrates.

Can they feel it back in the Habitat, or is the inertial damping sufficient to hide it? Well, even if it is not, the shipquake can be explained away by the flyby of a comet, or a meteorite storm's impact energies bleeding away against the armored hull.

Something about Barrens's words about the layout click in my head. As he is about to leap, I reach out and grab him with my mind. He could easily tear free, but he waits.

*What is it?*

*Look. This whole place is armored up and hardened. Despite all the energy they're flinging around, nothing is breaking.* My thoughts race by, incomplete. I try to send him the drift of my thoughts but it is too fast and unfocused and hazy. Barrens is shaking his head, trying to keep up and absorb the information. My sense of space of this place untwists—the way the towers are configured—arranged not to watch for intruders, but to watch the lay of the land. Too high to watch for ordinary humans crawling around these deep shadows, but at just the right height for the naked eye to see one of those huge beasts.

"Slow down!" he mutters, squeezing my hand. "What are you trying to say?"

"It's a prison."

Another explosion—the fight has changed direction and is getting closer. A searing wind flings debris everywhere, sets our clothes flapping back, gets my eyes watering.

We take cover in the lee of a hill. A supply bunker, the terminus for one of the branches leading away from the snaking, intestine-like train tunnel. The walls are angled very flat, and there are no windows. We climb higher but stay crouched behind a cooling unit, hissing as it vents hot exhaust out in front of us, vibrating and humming.

I point back the way we came.

*All those eggs. They're drawing huge amounts of psi energy. Except for that one with the hole in it.*

*So you're saying, every one of those buildings . . .*

They are the source of the storm of emotion saturating the air.

Then the Enforcers are so close to us, it is a risk even to think in one's own head. They have subdued the creature. It is half-encased in plastech. It moves majestically along, a few meters above the ground. In stillness it seems so much smaller. It is so close, it feels as though, if I stood at the edge of the rooftop and reached out, I could touch it. Its misshapen skull turns on its neck, and one huge, milky, blue eye gazes into my soul. Together, they make for a slow procession, the Enforcers walking around and beneath the monster—probably to save power. They pass below us along the narrow path. Where the buildings close in too far, they raise the mass higher into the air.

*They're taking it back to its cell.*

Barrens chews on his lip for a second and nods.

*Now, can we run for it?*

"Yeah," he mutters. "Probably a good idea."

Just before we get moving, he spends a long time staring at one of the egg-shaped prison cells.

"What is it?"

"There's ID numbers on the eggs. Above the main coolant line feeding into the base. Something familiar."

He shakes his head. It is hard to tell because of the greenish light, but he goes pale.

"What is it, Leon?"

"It's nothing. You're right. Time to get out of here. Place is making me crazy."

26

We rush from shadow to shadow, pausing when we have cover, and try to time the passage of the glowing circles of the spotlights. Barrens goes one stop ahead and signals me when to follow. Since I'm always hunched over, sometimes crawling along the lee of a ridge that climbs up toward our exit, fatigue stings and clutches at my back and legs. Under my cold-weather gear, I'm dripping with sweat even with the zippers and the hood down, but I don't dare remove it or I'll freeze to death in the unpowered areas.

Somehow, we avoid the Enforcers' attention. Possibly the amount of psi energy in the air and the terrible presence of the creatures render our merely human presences unnoticeable. Or perhaps taking down the monster drained the Enforcers too much for them to do anything else after they've put it back and rebuilt its cage. In addition to the fight, it must be exhausting working with the ultrahard, crystalline form of plastech that composes everything in that giant prison.

I remember all those defaced murals and carvings of the builders, made of even harder matter. How much would it stress the grid to go into the gigawatt class, and how large a communion of merely human minds would it take not to burn out from channeling it?

We creep back out the doors. Barrens lays his hands on them, and I hear the bolts slide shut when he transmits the lock code.

The ground loses its hold on us and the air is again icy and stale.

Barrens leads, even lost in thought. Sometimes, he seems to forget I am there at his side. He will lope along, faster, pushing off in great bounds through zero g. The effort not to be left behind leaves me huffing, short of breath. Then he remembers himself and slows down, watching for me. When we resume, it starts off at an even pace, and then he will start to drift farther and farther ahead once more.

I focus and push on. The light of telekinesis flares at my back, keeps me fly-ing forward. In a straight line, I am faster, but when we reach corners and turns, Barrens can just twist, bounce off his feet, and jump in the proper direc-tion, while I have to use TK to decelerate, reorient myself, and speed up once more. The trail of discard bags and junk flies by.

After four hours of running, I give in and call out through my Implant, *Leon, I need to stop. I'm exhausted.*

At first it looks as if he cannot hear me. It is just the nature of zero g though. He has nothing to hold on to and has to bounce and push off from wall to wall to bleed off his forward momentum. When he has slowed down enough, he waves to me, lets me pull us together.

*Yeah. Okay. We need to eat and drink, and sleep too.*

Barrens plays his flashlight over me and frowns. "I'm sorry. Should've paid more attention. You don't look so good."

He starts rubbing my hands and arms; even through all the thick layers, it's heavenly. As is the water from my belt canteen.

We have come to a narrow, one-meter-wide shaft that climbs "up" from our previous orientation. All along one surface, the carved faces of the Builders watch us in silence. I pull up a mental image of our best map and try to match all those turns to it. This tunnel is a long curve following the spine of the Noah. We are about five days out from the Sanctuary. Less than that with just us; I won't have to help keep a line of people in orderly motion.

We each draw out a spool of line, thread it through a belt loop, and anchor the end against one surface with tape.

Looking at his face, really seeing his eyes, I squint.

The lines across his forehead are stark and deep, and he is looking far away, into his head. Maybe finally seeing confirmation of a vast, hidden truth under-neath the placid existence of the crew is more than even he expected.

"Now you're the one who's so calm," Barrens murmurs as he folds him-self around me. "Your career was figuring the limits of what's on the ship and how much and how quickly it can be used, to keep the balance you kept talking about. You've just seen that there's so much more, and you seem . . . unruffled?"

Am I? Maybe I am too overwhelmed to show it. Maybe it is bone-deep in me, or rather, core-deep, at the primal center of the brain. Maybe it is just habit. I was indoctrinated all my life to think only about the mission and to abide all else, so this too I abide.

"I don't know why."

I turn, push the hood back, and tuck my head under his chin. His stubble still feels odd against my close-shaven scalp. I hear the slow beating of his heart. Something huge has come together in his mind, something he is still figuring out the words to describe.

"And how about you? You are uncovering truths. Secrets that are vitally important."

He leans back from me and we watch each other for a while, through the mist of our breaths. The numbness we feel is not because of the cold. A tremble starts inside him, just long enough to set his mouth to quivering.

"Should we stop, you think?" *We don't have to go back to the Archivists, Hana. We can just . . . just hide. Live out a quiet life on the fringes.*

It takes many icy breaths for me to understand what I see on his face, lit faintly by the energy from the emitter plates on our skin. My hunter, my protector, he never fears for himself. But for me, he is afraid.

*Leon, could you live with that? If we just quit?*

*It's not simple. I thought it would be. I thought we could just find out what's what, let everyone know, and everyone would make their own decisions. I never thought before of how . . .*

"What is it?"

"Never thought before of how just the knowing can hurt someone," Barrens whispers.

He has figured something out. And he wants what?

"You need my permission to tell me?"

Behind his eyes is a storm. The crackle and flicker of his red and my blue make unreal masks of our faces.

He kisses me then, and there is something in the taste and feel, and the pressure, of his lips. Something I don't understand. Whenever his words were not enough before, there was so much that would pass between us with just touch and gesture. In this cold, dark place, where there is no one else but us, no one else to see, or hear, the nature of my fear changes.

Oh, but I am afraid, my knight. I am.

In the dark, we spin slowly at the ends of our tethers. I want to think we are okay. He must sense that we are not, the way I hold on to him so tightly as we drift into sleep.

———

I open my eyes, gasping. We're tangled up. I cut us free from our lines with a small flash of psi, try to wake up all the way.

Barrens looks down at me. His lip is bleeding. His legs are wrapped around me. My wrists are clamped in his hands, but he is just holding me still, not crushing me. We are still in one of the unpowered sections, no gravity to hold us to the floor. We drift through the frigid air.

"I'm awake. Ah. Did I do that?"

"Yes. Bad dreams?"

Anyone would have nightmares, after all this. "I can't remember."

His eyes search mine. I wonder what he sees. He lets me go and starts rummaging through his pack.

"Jerky? Biscuits?" He is avoiding something.

"What did you see just before we got away?"

"Ah, let me see. Here we go. A real luxury. A little brick of cheese."

*Don't say one thing with your words and something else with your body.*

Our slight movements set us turning faster. Irksome, trying to keep our eyes on each other. There is no grid to draw on here, but it takes little power, in zero g, just to stabilize our positions and hold us in place. I choose one surface in the narrow corridor, decide that is the floor, and pull us, feetfirst, against it.

*Okay. I am asking you to tell me. No matter how bad it is.*

He does not look nearly so large now, after I've seen the creature in that horrible place. He starts to talk, stops. Tries again. He breaks a biscuit in half and wolfs it down, tears a big chunk of synth-meat jerky and swallows it with a long gulp of water from his canteen.

"Do you remember our Yule together?"

"Leon," I warn him. I won't let him dodge this.

"Not trying to change the subject. It's relevant."

I shake my head when he offers me the jerky. Even if it is not real meat, I want nothing to do with even artificial stuff. Not after that awful place. Those smells. I accept a stick of puffed rice.

*You saw it too. You just have to look inside the memory. You're smarter than me. You have all the pieces.*

Can that be so?

My concentration slips away, and we come loose from "the floor."

"No."

"Hana . . ."

I do not want to know after all.

*You already know.*

Pulling in my knees, I am a ball, featureless. Nothing. A perfect memory can be a curse. There is no forgetting. I see the ID number on the plaque on the cage. I have seen it before. It was printed in Barrens's careful, cramped scrawl, left for me after Yule.

"What does it mean?"

He winces. I guess I have lost control over my voice. I'm shrill. I hate losing control. But when have we ever had control over own lives on this cursed ship?

"I could have made a mistake when I retrieved the ident code," Barrens says softly. He does not believe it.

"But you didn't."

I fling myself away, hurtling down the shaft.

Or I try. He was expecting it, and aglow with superhuman enhanced reflexes, his hand catches mine. Despite my maximum unamplified energy output, the addition of his mass results in only a little more than half the speed I would have gotten, on my own.

"Let me go!" Crying. I hate how I look when I cry. I'm pounding on his arms and shoulders.

Pulled off center, we are about to crash into a wall, but he twists, somehow, and catches us, landing feetfirst and taking the shock with his powerful legs.

Can't talk anymore. I can only hang on to him.

I try to drown myself in other memories. Safe memories. A cat. Someone else's child. Delicious meals. Everything reminds me of what I cannot escape in my own head. Children. Meat. Death.

He is right. I knew it already subconsciously.

My tears drift away, perfect spheres. They will freeze, eventually. For just a little while, I let it out, let go of how I feel. Barrens's arms around me keep me from flying to pieces. His rough, deep bass rumbles through a soft, crooning nothing.

It might have been a few minutes. Or longer. Then I stop looking away. The world has not changed. It is I who changed, in the knowing. The choice to run is long behind me.

The place we just saw is a prison. This is certain. The monster escaped from one of the cells. And on one of the cells, I saw an ID code that matches what I learned in a better, simpler time, only months before, is the ident number of my missing child.

My child is one of them.

## 27

THE WAY IS COLD AND DARK AND GRIM WITH JUST THE TWO OF US AND THE silent weight of the thoughts in our heads. There was fear when we were outbound on our voyage of exploration, but there was excitement too, and the camaraderie of Barrens's tight-knit group. Now, it's all exhaustion, confusion.

It is cold enough that I accept Barrens's offer of his awful cigarettes. I cough and choke, but the chemical buzz of the synthetic nicotine helps me forget the hunger, and holding it in my mouth and pulling and puffing is at least some distraction from the constant, bone-freezing cold. The smoke trails behind us as I push myself along and follow as he leaps from wall to wall.

I want this long walk to be over. I am tired constantly and ache as if I have pushed my talent too far again. Yet I also want it to last forever, just the two of us, because when we arrive, decisions will have to be made and the data rattling around in our heads discussed.

I do not want to think about it anymore, but my mind keeps going.

There are only so many possibilities regarding that dark place filled with monsters. Why are they kept alive at all? Why are there so many? My Implant supplies me with perfect glimpses, and at a rough estimate there are as many of those creatures as there are of us. My child is one of them. Are they all children of humanity? How? Why?

One day away from Sanctuary, two pieces align. Realization wells up from the darkest corner of my thoughts.

"Oh, no. No, no, no!"

Barrens stops immediately. "What?"

He gathers me up gingerly. I pepper him with a mess of thought fragments.

The numbers. It's the numbers. More memories. The annual report on Breeding Duty is in my head. The ratio. I know this because City Planning needs to know this. To maintain the correct number of homes, keep up the correct production of farms, educate the right number of Keepers . . . And also, there is no forgetting the numbers Barrens's people found, those hidden stores and farms and water-reclamation plants.

Barrens winces. "Slower,"

"Leon. You can't tell them." I pull back. My voice wants to twist free. I won't yell. I won't shriek. I try to be cold. Analytical. "Especially if I'm right. Promise you won't."

He looks lost. He bites his lip and nods.

"The birthrate in the Habitat is just enough to maintain an equivalent population of the creatures in that prison."

He blinks and squints and turns it round and round in his head.

"Leon." My voice is harsh, hoarse. "Every Breeder. Gives birth. To one of *them*."

Our flashlights, dangling from wrist straps, sometimes shine right into our faces. I glimpse the moment it hits him and every muscle goes slack.

*Again. Show it to me again. Slower.*

Mala's voice in my ears, going over my meditation. Slow the breath. Slow the heartbeat. Think focused and tight and clear, so that the Implant can process the signals.

I think to him, one by one, each relevant document. As I do, I explain what the numbers mean. Here is the current population of the Habitat. There is the number of women who go through Breeding Duty each year. Now, the annual Retirement rate. Then, a 2-D still image of when I first looked out upon the dark city. My best guess on the number of prison cells. I end with the plaque on the one cage that matches the ID code he retrieved for my baby. A short sequence of how wildly destructive that one escaped creature was.

"They are all our children. And all our children are they."

Dizzy with the scale of it. The deceptions. The mechanisms of control.

"How? Where . . . Where do the normal kids come from?" His mouth shapes, over and over, It can't be.

It follows. I could still be so wrong. But: "The simplest reason why they must be kept alive is that we need them. If . . . if we give birth to *them,* maybe they give birth to *us*."

It takes a whole day more of us just floating there, by turns shaking our heads, nodding, trying not to think about it and obsessing over every logical step anyway, before we get hold of ourselves.

"You're right," Barrens says. "We can't tell anyone."


Our supplies run out just as we taste warm air and gravity reasserts itself. Thirsty, drained in every way, we drag ourselves forward. With a metallic clatter, Barrens opens the door to the Sanctuary.

Sleep. Food. Drink.

My recovery from my incarceration and then almost burning out my Implant by pushing my talents during the escape must still be dragging at me. I should be supporting Barrens loudly when he argues with the others, but it is all I can do to stand at his side and offer my presence.

The city of the dead. That is what they're calling it. The Necropolis. Discovering what is there has set fire to the cause, and not in a good way. Most of Barrens's own group have already left to join the mass gathering of Archivists elsewhere in the ship, on the orders of Thorn, who, after the death of Gomez, is now the most popular of the cell leaders. Only four remained to wait for Barrens's return: Tommy, Gregory, Bullet, and Susan.

Worse, the Archivists have already released Meena's death out there, to the Nth Web.

Already, fearful discussions are starting to flare up across the forums.

In the day longer we took to return, the movement has left Barrens behind.

He is red, smoldering, furious. "You aren't giving people knowledge," he hisses at the display. "It's only spreading fear." He paces back and forth, too upset to be still.

Thorn still wears his fancy waistcoats and trim trousers. Under the lean, handsome face and the bright blue eyes, he projects malice and glee. "Is that you saying that, Barrens? Or is it the ISec plant at your side? What happened to your conviction?"

Taunting now. Would he be doing that if they were speaking in person? The effect of Barrens's looming physical presence does not extend across virtual space.

Around us, I can hear the others shifting uncomfortably in their chairs. I already know that Barrens cannot win this argument. Nothing he says matters. He grows angrier still; it pours off him in waves. It is school all over again for him. Maneuvering and deals behind his back. He thought they all had a common goal. He tries to talk about the danger of isolated data without context. He explains his concerns about disorder. Stumbling, halting words about the greater responsibility to the mission.

He tries to appeal to the other leaders, calls them by name. Jules, Nena, Dan—most of them, I do not know. Over the link, they refuse to meet his eyes.

"Enough! We have already put it to a vote. Turn over your findings, your memories. We already have the data of those that returned ahead of you. Or are you becoming like *them*? Are we to trust you with knowing what secrets to share and what to withhold, like good little Ministry pawns? This is not just *your* movement! We have to stop the Mincemeat experiments!"

It is only a twitch of the shoulders. Inside, I feel my man staggering, suddenly adrift. What can we possibly tell them we found down there? That it is not some vast set of experiments on humanity, but something worse?

"If we get enough of them thinking, Leonard, just imagine! The crew itself will pressure the secret-keepers into revealing what is hidden. They cannot Adjust everyone!"

In the heat of the moment, nobody notices who cuts the transmission. It probably looks as if Barrens did, seated there before the terminal. Only, it was me. How did I do that? I thought it, but did not yet direct it to the workstations, so how did Archie pick up my command?.

Barrens sits on one of the oversize chairs made specifically for him. His whisper cuts through the air. "All of you, take some rec time. Susan, if you are up to it, someone needs to monitor the boards, the newsfeeds, keep an eye on what's going on in the Hab."

Their faces are heavy with the things they want to say. In the end, only Bullet says, "We're still with ya, boss." And the others nod, before drifting elsewhere in a Sanctuary that is now too large for those who are left.

*Did I start this, Hana? Or did I just let other people use me? Are those idiots doing what I wanted all along? Should I try to help them? Stop them? Thorn thinks of revolution and power and politics. I just wanted to find out what happened to Cal. How did it get like this?*

*Leon, what does your gut tell you about how people respond when they're afraid?*

Barrens is a student of history. Even our cut-up, redacted, censored mess of history still has examples. Then there is his training for dealing with crowds. With mobs. He presses his knuckles against his eyes, asks, voice chipped and cracked, "How do we stop this?"

Everything crashes together, picking up momentum. Events that are minor separately weave into each other and fuel inevitability.

Information Security ignored it at first, in the feeds. They attempted to work as they always have, in the shadows, with their own resources. They blocked off access wherever the synthesized memory of Meena's death could be found, deleted the centers from which the illicit memory propagated. But the network of the Nth Web was bequeathed to us by the Builders, a vast system beyond human design. When Thorn used Archie to plant those black seeds, it shot them far and wide through every Analytical Node, too widespread for ISec to stop.

During those first days after the Archivists spread their weapons of information, it was only in the discussions in the shadowy frontier of the unregulated, the ghost zones of dataspace, where awareness of the awful memories of Meena's death lived. The memory spread from one crewman to another, converted one skeptic at a time with the potency of its raw fear. Official news covered the usual mundane affairs of production quotas and efficiency and our slow progress through the deep emptiness of space, with sprinklings of the doings of Council-sponsored celebrities, Web stars, singers, dancers, their couplings and breakups and spats. There was no propaganda response to soothe the growing anxiety. By the time we reached the Sanctuary, 30 percent of the population was actively discussing Mincemeat, and there was total, 100 percent, awareness of the issue.

Susan and I analyze the Archivists' Web operations and, based on her smidgen of ISec knowledge, what Information Security's responses are accomplishing. We make projections and watch our simulations unfold. One Archivist makes ten postings in as many minutes. He influences the discussion of ten online. Outside of the Nth Web, those ten talk about it to others face-to-face, and who else can that new ring of worried individuals approach to answer their questions? Like a disease, it spreads.

Sometimes, we see individual boards and forums going down, erased. A few last-second messages go out now and then, declaring, "ISec is here." I can picture the heavy hand of Karla and others like her desperately throwing out their nets and chains, bringing in individual cells and interrogating them, trying to catch more. They might requisition aid from the police, they might call in every Enforcer and Behavioralist they can, but there just are not enough of them.

It takes time for even the most powerful psychic to tear free the secrets from someone's head.

Based on the rate at which information is being put out on the Network and the rate at which it is erased, Susan and I estimate that for every Archivist or fresh recruit that is caught, at least two fresh crewmen are successfully recruited.

Barrens is a wolf snapping at the bars of his cage, pacing, pacing.

We cannot seem to sleep, despite our exhaustion. We pace, and talk.

"Dempsey." *Hana.*

*Yes?*

*I know Archie is spread throughout the whole system. But is it still yours? Can you take full control, if you have to?*

I wish I knew. I try to explain my theories about Archie. I try to make Barrens understand. I do not think anyone can control Archie anymore. It is AI. It chooses to follow, or not. Something in the combination of my deliberate design and the accident of the data fragments from the Builders gifted my datamining agent with more and more self-modifying, self-evolving complexity. That day in the park when we celebrated Barrens's birthday, it was already starting to change. By the time we viewed our local copies of the alien memory that night, Archie was being born on the Nth Web.

"Just great," Barrens murmurs, bitter. "We have to convince your program too!" *How are we going to talk it into helping only us? Can it be reasoned with?*

I swallow the lump in my throat. "It will take time to study Archie."

*If you had to, could you shut it down?*

*I don't know. I just don't know. And I have to be careful when studying it. If it feels threatened, there is just too much that is unknown. Human culture has hypothesized about how a true artificial intelligence might behave, but no one knows with any certainty; there's never been anything like Archie before. I don't think even the Builders had something like it, or we would have come across it in the Nth Web.*

That is not what he needs to hear.

Barrens gives it to the others the next morning. "You still with me?"

"We are," they chorus.

"Then this is what we've got. We're going to stop Archie . . . Argus. We do that, and ISec might be able to get on top of this. Any other ideas?"

They shake their heads. At least they don't look lost anymore.

We divide up the tasks and begin.

From then on, Susan keeps her eyes on the chatter on the Nth Web. She gets her own cubicle with a terminal, in the corner next to the kitchen.

Off in his clinic, Gregory continues his studies on the biological samples left of Meena. When Thorn called, the others rushed off, and they did not bother with her remains or take along the equipment the scavenging party scrounged up for him. He has a proper lab now, with a quantum tunneling microscope, gene sequencers, protein assay kits . . .

He says he is close to something major. Barrens is afraid that if we ask him to stop, he too will take off for the growing movement.

Gregory is not much of a programmer anyway.

Bullet, Tommy, and Barrens help me study Archie. We take notes on wired-only tablets—unsure just how much Archie can understand. We arrange the rest of the terminals along a semicircle, facing inward, so that anyone can stand up and stretch and see what the rest of us are up to.

As Archie is not a single program, or even a population of uniform copies of the same program, this is not straightforward.

The only reason it is still possible to study Archie is that its subunits still respond to the legacy commands of the ancestor programs I originally designed. I had expected that the changes of the swarm as it spread and self-optimized would cause problems, which is why I worked debugging functions into it to see which nodes on the Network a particle had spread to, and what the current state of the code of that specific copy was. I should have suspected something when we never needed to fix anything. No program ever launches so smoothly.

I get thousands upon thousands of unique feedback reports when I issue the survey command. The data is collected into its own database that I've written functions for to map the geographic spread of the data-miner across the Nth Web. We cobble together a cladistics function to graph the evolution of the different subtypes, grouping them according to the relative similarities in their code, a tree with the original ancestor at the root and steadily more distant children as one climbs up through the branches.

It is more similar to a genetic study of subspecies spread across geography and time than it is to software engineering.

On our desks, maps of the Network are lit bright, color-coded section by section according to the largest subpopulations of relatively similar particles. We can select a single particle or a group at a time and open them. The actual lines of written programming that compose them are decompiled and the differences automatically compared and highlighted in developer frames that we can scroll through. The notes, observations, and comments we put into the map are shared among the rest of us automatically.

The first side-by-side comparisons between the original code and the current generation are disheartening. The polymorphisms—the code variations of its instruction set—are vast in number. I purposely avoided true genetic/memetic algorithm strategy. All the differences should happen in only two modules out of the original five that compose each particle: the part that assembles the query results into data structures, and the part that handles the signaling between particles. The extra communications that Barrens added makes for a sixth that should not have changed either. But there have been code mutations in *all* of the modules in *all* of the particles we sample. Functions that used to do one thing have been moved, copied, and altered to do completely different tasks. Data types have been altered. Loops were added, changed, or deleted.

We strain our eyes over displays full of diagrams trying to trace the critical path of the changes between Archie as it is now and the far simpler data-miner I programmed the year and a half before.

Everyone pushes as hard as he or she can, staring at line after line of program text and a mess of vertices and edges representing comparative maps of the deletions, translocations, and insertions that have happened within the digital equivalent of the chromosomes inside Archie's cells. We eat ration bars instead of proper meals. There is no time to cook or clean or do laundry. We nap and eat at our terminals, leaving only to take care of biological needs that won't wait for us.

It is apparent that this is beyond the boys. It is mostly beyond me too. I have had one machine learning class over my whole life, and this would be difficult for a specialist.

Little by little, the shape of Archie becomes visible. Not a clump of clumps at all. From the pattern of the signaling between the units and the comparison of the sample particles we've examined, the many groupings have become specialized by function. Some scan a specific type of database. Some retrieve a specific type of data. Some gather the results. Some assemble the results. And they are all controlled by something else, which means a central subset does the controlling.

Archie has a body, eyes, arms, and, even if we haven't come across a single copy that has those control functions yet, a brain. And a nervous system to connect them all.

Bullet perks up. "At least we have an idea of what we can go for!"

"How the fuck are we going to find every single Analytical Node that's got one of the brain particles out of the hundreds of thousands scattered across the ship?" Tommy moans.

It goes back to the main reason ISec could not stop Archie. The AI is too spread out.

"We could try—"

From the corner, we hear Susan jump to her feet, sending her chair clattering to the ground. She walks over to us, chewing her nails. Dark semicircles are sunken under her eyes, and her tawny mane of hair is a tangled mess. She whispers, "We're running out of time." She presses her fingertips to her temples and transmits the most recent events and her current assessment. She acts as a conduit between us and the newsfeeds.

Thorn's propaganda people have made their next move and released another carefully crafted packet.

Visions of the City of the Dead, and the demise of Gomez (presumably from some member of his team who managed to escape but did not run into us), and the battle of the Enforcers against the monster join Meena's gruesome death in creeping across the crew's consciousness. Sparks of truth fly faster and farther through the Nth Web. Information Security programmers and Behavioralists pull in additional resources from other branches and departments to track down these illicit boards and shut them down. There are arrests and Adjustments, outright memory and personality erasures, but Information Security cannot catch them all.

Without a word, Barrens pushes back from the terminal, skids back on his chair, and stalks away. He drives his fist through the heavy dining-room table behind our setup, reduces it to splinters.

Incidents of vandalism and random violence pick up across the Habitat. The Archivists foment discontent, spread rumors, talk to everyone willing to listen. As large as the Noah is, it is still a closed space, and dark emotions are contagious, dangerous stressors. Word of the Archivists as an organization, as a cause, is in the thoughts of many.

Another day vanishes as we struggle closer to understanding Archie.

Tommy slaps the arms of his chair. "I got something." He spreads his arms wide, makes his find available to all our terminals.

He has found a grouping of program components with immense blocks of dense code. They have replaced what were originally minor code blocks regarding unit conversion and dates. They are almost undecipherable, interspersing giant loops of data structures passing information back and forth with the Builders' language, math, and logic.

Bullet pumps one fist. "Are these it? The control subset?"

He visibly droops when I check the Network map and shake my head. These are the most complex and evolved subunits we have found so far, but the signal pattern to and from them is wrong. It's not the control-cluster set; they're too isolated, communicating mostly with each other rather than acting as the hub.

I run another debugging command to see what these subunits have been assembling. From the parts that aren't in an alien language, I see material extracted from psychology texts, Behavioralist manuals, Keeper guidelines, case studies.

"I think they are studies of human interactions. Archie's thoughts about people."

It could take a thousand specialists entire lifetimes to understand Archie.

Someone yawns. It's contagious, and everyone yawns. My neck is killing me. I desperately need a shower. "Look, we're burning out. Let's take a break. Maybe eat something decent for a change."

The others stumble off. Barrens and I remain.

I tell Barrens my real assessment.

He throws up his hands, lights up a cigarette, and takes a few long draws before downing half a glass of mead drawn out of Bullet's still. "We're fucked." He stands there blowing smoke rings and watching them disperse. *Hana, what would happen if you just ask Archie to stop responding to Thorn and the other cells? It likes you. Would it do what you ask?*

*I don't know if it can even understand a request like that yet. Archie is no ordinary distributed program; it's got complex substructure connecting all those spread-out parts. I keep calling them particles because of my one machine learning class, but they're like cells in a living body. I'd have to structure a communication like a virus, so that it could spread to all the nodes where Archie is, so that we get to the bits that compose its mind.*

As I think it, I know it is the only thing we have left to try.

We share one of the shower stalls in the guys' locker room. Bullet and Tommy have collapsed in the sleep capsules. At this point, I don't care what they think or see anyway.

The hot water helps. But Barrens and I are too tired to rub each other's back or appreciate the view.

I pull on someone else's jeans, someone else's shirt. The Archivists that left did so in a rush; a lot of their stuff is still here.

The sight of Barrens struggling into another man's clothes does get a small smile out of me. No one else is remotely close to his size. I point my fingers, use psi to adjust the cut and fit. I pop open another locker and add the material from the stuff in there to Barrens's outfit.

"Thanks."

I straighten out his collar. I've dressed him in my best attempt at his old policeman's uniform. I think it will help his mood, and it does. His shoulders and neck straighten up, and his eyes look just a little clearer.

As we make our way to the kitchen, Susan calls out, "It's getting bad!"

She multicasts another report into our heads, keeps the data flowing in real time to us as she reads it off the Nth Web.

We must look strange, standing there, looking at nothing, hearing nothing, totally still, except for the rapid movements of our eyes behind the eyelids.

Today, on the feeds, good-looking anchors at last begin to address the issue directly. They claim it is all a hoax. An elaborate scam being propagated by malcontents, just hallucinating young students drugged out on Psyn. Practically an April Fools' prank, they say. Ted Samuelson and Sarah Harrington look into the cameras, seemingly straight into the audience's eyes, as they smile genially, calling on all the good citizens of the Noah to be careful of the clever schemes of bored children.

The ship's real estate is closed, a fundamentally limited environment. There, it is easy to watch everyone, at work, at home, at play.

In the realm of pure information, that which is built on top of the alien Analytical Nodes is infinitely more complex and powerful than the devices humans used before. Given how profoundly Archie has been changed by interacting with Builders' code, the Nth Web too must have changed from what the original Ministry of Information made. It is larger than what the ship needs and what ISec can monitor.

In a week, there is to be a virtual demonstration. Thousands upon thousands of crew members are planning to attack the public advertising space, flooding the commercial system with fake ads containing all their pent-up indignation and paranoia. They are no longer isolated little flames to stamp out in the dark—a few hundred of the core group, the next, larger ring of fresh recruits numbering a few thousand, and twice that many ordinary people who just want to know. They demand to know.

The chat rooms are a wildfire of speculation. The Archivists are winning the imagination of the average. They have their message out there. "We are just like you. Aren't you tired of never knowing anything except what other people tell you is permitted for you?" Meena's disintegrating face full of confusion and terror has become their rallying symbol. Every crew member on the ship gets a digital packet, the Archivist manifesto. Practically a newsletter. There is talk of change and oppression, and simple one-liners such as "The time for secrets is over" and "How long will you let them lie to you?"

We unplug from Susan's thought streams. All of us sit and drink Bullet's powerful, sickly sweet liquor. Me, Barrens, Susan. Tommy and Bullet stumble back out of their beds, and Gregory shuffles in from his lab and drinks with us.

Barrens looks at me. "We gotta try something, Hana. Do whatever it takes to get hold of Archie's functions. There's no time to find its core; we just gotta go with our best guess. Thorn and the rest of them are turning the Habitat into a powder keg, and they're fucking around with lit matches. We have to stop this before, well . . . Shit!"

The rest of them blink or tilt their heads, purse their lips, confused at the way Barrens is shuddering. They have never seen him show such a loss of control. "Before what?"

He swallows hard.

It is my voice that says, "Before Archie finds the G-0 and G-1 files."

The last pieces missing. A sliver of thought flickers in my head. I had guessed that G-0 designation refers to us. If the G-1 indicates our monstrous children . . . Or something worse . . .

"They're planning to bring the whole thing down, whatever the cost," Barrens says.

"And the cost," my voice fades to a whisper, "could be extinction. For everyone. Total mission failure."

The words send them reeling. Our mission is to keep humanity alive. We are it. If we fail, there is no one to help us.

The others sleep. Even Barrens sleeps. I slide free of his arms after a pointless half hour of waiting and hoping for the refuge of unconsciousness.

I need a drink.

Only I am not alone.

Sitting on the floor next to the doors of the supply room, Gregory is drinking.

"Ha. Couldn't shle . . . sleep . . . either. Eh?" He tilts his head and peers up at me. He smells foul. But his bloodshot eyes gleam.

"You're finished?"

"Yeah." He takes a swig of Bullet's strongest, whiskeylike moonshine. "Yeah, you could say that. We're all finished, my pretty. People just don't know it."

I consider telling him my theory, about us, and our children. And *them,* down in the black city.

He holds up a hand. "Don't. I know . . . know too much already. I figured Mincemeat out, doll. I'm sorry. I'm just going to drink until I can't think anymore."

The bottomless despair in his voice, empowered by his subconscious empathic projection, chases me away.

I think of telling my lion.

What difference would it make to know? If the news is so terrible that all Gregory can do is drink, would it not just distract us? Or worse, weaken the resolve of the others? We could find ourselves in paralyzing debate over what the Doctor's findings could mean, whether his interpretation is right or wrong, lose hours of time we don't have. It will not help us with Archie. It will not help us stop what the Archivists are doing. What possible good would it do for us to know now?

At the terminal, staring at line after line of logic and information, gazing at the far-flung structure of Archie, I drift in and out of sleep.


The few hours of uneasy sleep I get are not enough, but it is all we can afford.

We work at a furious pace. I design the core content—the logical structure that I hope Archie will understand as a request to follow only my commands. Barrens, Susan, Tommy, and Bullet work on the script that will send our message out to every single particle of Archie's structure, taking into account the differentiation of its subgroups, the signal pattern of its internal communications.

Gregory becomes a ghost. He mostly hides out in his lab, coming out just to replenish his supply of alcohol. Though sometimes, he will watch us, mouth opening and closing. Sometimes, he begins to speak, then stops, and looks at me. And I say nothing.

Each day, I get tired a little earlier. I don't have time to figure out what is wrong with me, why I haven't fully recovered after my escape.

The hour of the virtual protest arrives and we are still not ready. The problem is taking control of every single piece of Archie throughout the whole Network. If any significant fraction of the swarm does not receive the takeover virus or does not assimilate it, the Archivists will still be able to access the AI's extended, sprawling databases through the subunits they can still control. It is all-or-nothing.

Barrens's hands close on my shoulders and pull me away from the terminal.

"I'm sorry. We just need more time." They were counting on me and I was just not fast enough. Capable enough. Maybe Lyn could have done it, if she were here.

"Shh. We tried."

He gestures toward Susan. "Put it on the wall."

She fiddles with her terminal, gets it to project onto the flat, featureless plastech. One window shows the ship's official news channel. A window with a simple bot is scrolling through the ad system. Another display shows a map of the interconnected nodes of the Nth Web.

It begins. We see the traffic starting to surge on the map. The endless, scrolling open market of the Nth Web begins to stutter and slow. On the news, a bleach-blond man with brilliant teeth smiles and tells everyone to stay off the Net while major maintenance is being done to the Analytical Nodes.

"Why isn't Information Security stopping it?" Tommy asks.

Bar graphs light up at each vertex, red needles rising from the blue sea of the Web, concentrated in one cluster at the center. Load monitors, measuring incoming access requests.

We look to Susan. She was only an entry-level propaganda designer; not even genuinely a part of ISec structure. But she has ISec friends and has had some of the training, read some of their manuals and standard operating procedures. She yelps. Glances down at her fingers, bitten to the quick, a little blood oozing. Her cheeks flush when she notices us all pause and look back to the wall.

Susan hides her hands behind her back. Clears her throat. "Um, I think they're already doing what they can." She points and some of the needles are highlighted in green. Sometimes they suddenly drop, and then the traffic spikes elsewhere on the map. "They're shunting traffic away. They're trying."

It is a dance of light, red spines growing out of the ad system nodes, briefly flashing green before they are cut down, as those Net users are redirected elsewhere. Mirror sites.

"It's all fucked anyway," Gregory moans. "None of it matters."

Tommy sneers, raises a fist. "Shit. Doc, put that bottle away. Or, hell, go back to your lab or something."

The Doc belches. His hands shake. He laughs and forces it down. "I'll be quiet."

"Why not just close that whole section of the Net?" Bullet asks.

Susan takes a breath. "If they do, it's an admission that there's something serious. That it's not just bored brats pulling a prank. If they shut down any significant chunk of the architecture, the Archivists win." She starts to explain some of the propaganda management techniques of her old job to the boys. The psychological effects on a crowd. "I mean, just think about it. Ever since you got your Implant, how often have you gone even an hour without plugging in and using the Network for something? We use it to work, to entertain our-selves, to schedule things, even to control major ship functions. If something as big as the Web Market goes down, everyone's faith in all the systems, and in the Council, gets rocked."

Bullet and Tommy ask her questions, and she answers them.

Barrens is conspicuously quiet.

*What do you see, Leon?*

*Thorn is a self-righteous, arrogant prick. But he's damned smart. Damned smart. This can't be all there is to this stunt.* He goes stiff. "Fuck! Hana, you gotta message ISec! You need to get them to shut it all down!"

We all stare at him, gawking.

*Hana. You must!*

I get to my terminal. I'll trust him, as I always have. I start to draft a document.

Barrens is there, hovering over my shoulder. *There's no time for that! That bitch from the detention center. Get to her. Tell her to bring down the Network!*

His fear is contagious. I place my hands on the conductive contact points of the terminal and fire Barrens's plea through the application Karla *wrote* into my head. His words, his voice. Without hiding where we are or who we are.

I can already imagine the message winding its way through ISec's system. I picture them coming for us.

"They're regaining control," Tommy murmurs.

My attention returns to the wall displays.

The towering red lines are flattening out, as is the rate at which they appear. In the other windows, the ad system begins to respond more smoothly again, and on the news, as a particularly beautiful propaganda officer explains a new Council initiative to reallocate the training quotas for the different academies and training centers, a line of text pops up at the bottom, informing all that the maintenance is done and normal service has been restored.

Gregory raises his bottle. "Cheers. You have a little more time after all. At least until we all get shoved ass-naked into a bunch of little cells by men in gray coats."

"Okay, back to . . ." Bullet pauses. "Who's sent me a message?"

I have one too.

The gorgeous, blue-eyed blonde on the news twitches. Then, despite all her training, a moment of shock shows in her eyes. Her voice hitches as she tries to drone on about the Council plans for the future improving everyone's quality of life.

I point at the wall and play back the last seconds on the map. Just for an instant, just as ISec neuralhacks successfully flatten out the stress on the system, every node on the map registers a comparatively small red flicker upward.

Only Susan and I notice it. She has her hands jammed against her mouth, starts shaking her head.

"Too late." Barrens's voice is tight and cold.

Tommy yells, "What? What's the big deal?"

"They," Susan gulps, whimpers, "they sent out a message to everyone."

"What do you—"

"Everyone that was on the Nth Web, whether participating in the protest, watching the news, or doing anything at all. We all just got the same message."

From the load average on the map: just about 92 percent of the entire population of the Habitat. Thorn and the rest of them have successfully used Archie to spread their latest release to nearly every crewman on the ship.

Out of the corner of my eye, there's that constant blinking point of light. Insistent.

The attached file is labeled G-0. It has already been decrypted.

"Choose for yourselves," Barrens declares. He slouches back in his seat, closes his eyes, and dives in.

The others talk it over for one minute, for five minutes, then ten. They go under.

Except for Gregory, who keeps on drinking. He looks at me and then unscrews the top from another bottle of homemade brew. "Pretty sure I already know what's on it." He gets up and sways, stumbling his way to one of the coffin-size sleepers. "I don't want to hear any talk 'bout it. Get me when you all decide what to do next." He belches, shuts the hatch.

And now, though Barrens is close enough to touch, I am alone.

Karla's voice is in my head, pestering me about choices and decisions, and freedom. I could have gone one way and never helped Barrens along this path.

I slide into the file.

It is not a memory, after all. It is data from the surveillance system built into yet another secure, secret, undeclared location outside the Habitat, drawing power, getting shipments of food, with its own staff, none of whom are listed in the rolls of the crew.

It is a woman on a bed.

I recognize her. She has brown eyes. An average build. She could be anyone. But she isn't just anyone. She was Apollo Gorovsky's Keepmate.

The clip has been heavily edited. I would guess that only a few frames taken from each day were strung together to the day before and the day after, a link in a chain that, based on the file size, is ninety-four seconds long.

After the first ten seconds, there is a pause. White text on a black background announces, "This is footage after a Keeper was forced into early Retirement. She was only twenty-four years old. The rest of this covers a period of approximately three months."

In a series of flashes, one image flips to the next—screen shots of Sasha's identification files, her school records, her test scores, her employment history, her medical records, her purchase log.

Then it starts. I cannot close my eyes to it. It is pulsed into my brain along the optic nerves. Too stunned to break myself out, I see what cannot be unseen. Of course, I have witnessed it before.

In the beginning, she is fine. She is merely bored while the Doctors scan her on the bed, day after day. Then her cheerful smile fades. Her skin turns pale, except for where bruises bloom. Her eyes turn red.

I am watching Meena's death all over again. Only slower. This is a process over months. In the last days, the pain must be incredible. She is in pieces, so much raw flesh, organs and bones maintained by telekinetic fields and sterile bandages. It is just like when Gregory and I held Meena together with all our might and concentration. They keep her on full sedation . . . but when the eyelid disintegrates away from her one remaining eye, it flicks back and forth, back and forth. And I cannot say anymore if Sasha is asleep and just dreaming, or if she is horrifyingly aware, and awake, as Meena was.

Detached from my body, I still feel myself swallowing, biting my lip. *Why don't they just let her go?*

Then, I see them. So small they are invisible except for when they catch the glowing storm of energies around her body, minuscule silver lines extend in from the surrounding darkness.

I have had those inside me too. During my examination before Breeding Duty, and further before that, prior to my neural-Implant surgery.

Medical microprobes.

Can it be that after three hundred years, human science still cannot understand what this thing is? Do they prolong it to study this thing as much as they can?

At last, it ends when too much vital tissue is compromised and her blood can no longer be kept circulating by psychic surgery and telekinetic pressure.

A few more slides, black backgrounds, one line each. The text is red as blood.

"Every single person that Retires ends his or her life this way. There is no Retirement Office; it is just another combined branch of the Ministry of Information and the Ministry of Health. There is no pleasant beachfront living, with daily dances and bingo.

"There is only this.

"Slow, agonizing death.

"For everyone."

Then thousands of still 2-D pictures. A before and after, with a name and an ID number. Some were old men. Beautiful boys and girls in the prime of their youth. Some were children as young as five. The after pictures all look the same, just different flavors of gore. The G-0 file is a listing of every crewman that has been "Retired" over the centuries.

"Ask Information Security what else they are hiding from you. Ask them about your children." The flash of the black city, with its cages, the picture of the monster fighting armored Enforcers.

"Ask them about Mincemeat."

Oh, oh. Oh, no. Not this.

Barrens snarls, wordless, furious.

The shock of awareness slides through me. But knowing the way I am I to die does not affect me as much as the terrible unknown of just how badly the crew will react.

And then, we see it.

It is as if a bomb explodes in the ship.

Archie lets us monitor the data traffic. Briefly.

Ten long minutes pass as the system bandwidth fills up with text messages, audio, thought-packets.

The Nth Web goes black. For the first time, based on my limited access to the truth, the Noah's Analytical Nodes are cut off and isolated. The Network is shut down. Archie, an emergent AI that lives only as the collective gestalt of countless pieces of communicating chunks of code, dies, its virtual brain cut apart.

If I had to guess, only the mission-critical nodes are still up.

"Oh, Karla. It's too late."

I remember when Barrens first showed me his memory of discovering Callahan's remains, the slow synthesis of suspicions and ideas over the months since then. How much worse can it be for the average crewman? Confronted all at once with awful death, is not the human instinct to find others, an instinctive desire to fight, to survive? Irrational, primal, universal.

Large blocks have been censored out of the ship's history of humanity and Earth. It does not take a complete knowledge of history to guess what happens next. My duties in City Planning required me to study crowd dynamics. It will start small. Pairs. Trios. Groups. Then groups start to coalesce. Something happens to humans, a chain reaction—a point beyond which individual reasoning has nothing to do with the behavior of the crowd as a whole.

Barrens shakes me out of my stupor. Shakes us all out of it.

"It's not over. We have a duty to do." His face is bleak. Hollow.

Yes. No matter what has been kept from us, this is still true. The mission.

We share a look. He shakes from head to toe. Nods.

Ten minutes of effort to wire my psi-tablet directly into the lower-level databus—where the Analytical Nodes transmit the information that directly controls the vital functions of the Noah. Connecting through here, it is impossible to hide where one is accessing the system from. I do not know if what I send will reach anywhere with the systems of the ship sliced apart.

I write a message to Information Security. The thought-packet contains only *Karla. We are coming in.*

## 28

Tommy and Susan cannot deal. The way they see their lives and the ship is suddenly different. All they want now is to live. In their eyes, I see the terror of knowing; or maybe I am only imagining in them what I feel myself.

"I can't," Gregory murmurs. "I'm sorry."

"Me too," Susan says. "I don't want to go there just to get Adjusted and sent to fight our friends."

Tommy mumbles, "I have to take care of these two. They'd never make it without me."

Barrens shrugs and looks at his feet. "It was me that let you down. That got you into this."

That is that.

They will hide and wait in the tunnels, scavenging food from the undocumented supply warehouses, watching. Until they come to grips with what is happening. Or perhaps they will spend the rest of their lives out there, numb and indifferent to the uncaring world they have left behind. Or perhaps one of the tunnel gangs will find them. That small criminal underground never has enough healers, and even if Gregory never completed his training, he is skilled.

We stand at the doorway to the blackness of the unpowered regions, with the warm air from the Sanctuary blowing past us into the icy dark.

Bullet stops to embrace Susan shyly, and to shake the hands of the young Doctor and the burly mechanic. They talk for a few minutes, just a moment of sentiment, remembering their shared childhood.

"Bye, Bullet." Susan presses her pale lips to his cheek. She presses a cut lock of blond hair into his pocket.

Barrens passes around the small, handheld crossbows and belts holding a number of chisel-pointed quarrels. I refuse mine, and he does not insist. We heft our packs to our shoulders and take a last few breaths of heated air before we wrap our scarves around our faces.

We split apart at the first intersection. Susan, Tommy, and Gregory are headed deeper, to where the secret storage areas are. And we orient ourselves back toward the Habitat.

Bullet keeps looking back over his shoulder as his friends' lights vanish around a distant corner.

Barrens murmurs, "You didn't have to come with us, Bullet. You still have time to go with your friends. You still haven't told her how you feel, even."

"But I do. Maybe what happened wouldn't have happened without you two; well, it also would not have happened if not for me. If I hadn't gone looking myself."

So begins another hike into the dark. I never realized how much I could miss my own home, my office job, the chowder place close to the park, the entire life I have been exiled from. Even when we make it back to the Habitat, even if we are not Adjusted so deeply that we are not just empty shells, how could anything be the same again?

Every time we come across a data-line hard port, I send Karla another message, letting her know where we are, and where we are going. Soon, we cross the great power shaft, and then we reach the same sewer line I escaped through months before.

The air is hot and fetid, but there is power.

Drawing on a touch of the grid through my modified amplifier, I change our jackets and cold-weather gear into waders rising up to our chests and masks to filter out the fumes.

Walking through the thick, foul slime, I wonder about the monstrous children that sometimes escape from the black city. Could we escape if one attacked now?

From there, it takes a few hours to get to where I punched down from the bottom level of the ISec holding facility. I shake for a moment, physically weak. These moments are coming more frequently. Annoying.

Barrens takes my hand, and my knees steady themselves. He nods at me once.

"Let's go, Miss Dempsey," Bullet says.

I raise the hand with the amplifier. The muck below us is pushed apart and away from us, and the ceiling above opens up into a short shaft. Aglow with my *touch,* I float Barrens and Bullet up through the hole first. Barrens reaches an arm down and pulls me up.

And we are here, alone, in the basement of the only ISec installation I have been in. The kitchens I ran through are empty.

The floor above is covered in dust and rubble, and the floors above that are just gone. The building has been torn apart. We sit on the steps beyond the double doors. We are on a tall hill, overlooking this section of the Hab.

It is burning. Pillars of smoke rise in the distance. In the sky, one of Hennessy's psychedelic sunsets flickers on and off, sometimes revealing the cracked Dome above. Pipes are leaking, spraying down, here and there. The glittering spire of the Eiffel Tower–inspired vertical farm in the center of the district has been shorn in half. The streets are twisted and torn, filled with dust and debris and ash. The buildings have been warped into windowless, armored bunkers, except for where they have been blasted apart—the lonely bones of their corpses eerie by the light of the distant fires, which glow and shimmer through the dull haze of particulates in the air. Breathing in, the air tastes stale and old and smoky. The lungs of this section of the Habitat, the algal purifiers and the biomes and the crop zones in the vertical farm, must have been badly damaged, or they are simply overwhelmed by the load of the fires burning throughout the city. Below us, a few crewmen are in sight, staggering along, covered in soot, shuffling between the shadows.

It is quiet. Silent except for the absurdity of some holographic billboards hovering over the cityscape, still advertising different varieties of tofu, vegemeat, wine, dresses, watches—the trappings of a consumer culture that was only the shallowest mask, a costume of individual choices over closed lives.

It is a war zone kin to the distant memories of burned-out cities from Earth conflicts.

Bullet's face has gone completely pale. His mouth hangs open as he wrings his hands. An inarticulate, low wheeze escapes his lips.

I consider the implications of a mob with psychic talents driven to extremes of fear. Anyone that has *touch* is a living factory, capable of turning plastech to weaponry, the designs of which can easily be spread by engineers just by telepathic contact. Any *bruiser* is a deadly soldier, even without training. Psychic surgeons can use their healing to kill. Those who can *read* and *write* are more effective communicators than radios or messenger runners or smoke signals.

I lean, boneless, against Barrens. He is folded up inside himself. Haunted. Behind us, I think I hear Bullet crying.

Again, I tap into the local data-lines.

*Karla. We are here.*

*About fucking time. Welcome back to gay Paris. So, Miss Dempsey, do you like what your friends have done with the place?*

*Please.* I send her an image of us, with our approximate location. *Barrens never wanted anything like this. He tried to talk them out of it, he . . .*

The hostility in her thought stream pounds in my head, sets the blood throbbing through my temples: *He started something bigger than himself and lost control and fucked us all.*

*We are here to help.*

There is no response for several minutes. If Karla has cut contact, I suppose it is no more than we deserve. Perhaps a strike team is already on its way to erase us. The gasps of my companions draw my attention, and from the way their eyes are rolled back in their heads, I know Karla is scanning them through her tenuous connection with me. Could she Adjust us even from here? What could I do if she chooses to? If I interrupt, I may only cause more damage.

Eventually, I see the tension leave their faces, and I relax when Barrens murmurs softly, "Guess I . . . Yeah. Fuck it. I accept."

Bullet also murmurs his assent.

I almost feel Karla's strained, bitter chuckle vibrate through my skull. *As it happens, Dempsey, there are still things only you can do. And our resources are so strained, I'll even take on that twerp and your fuckwad lover.*

She sends me the image of her location, and a series of pass codes. ISec is holding the vertical farm and the immediate area around it. Section v-farms are vital for food and water and, more important, the cycling of breathable air. At the false horizon, the flicker of the sky simulators end where the great vault doors have been sealed, isolating each section. We are to meet an Information Security team halfway to the farm, close to the commerce plaza.

*Get moving. The codes will unlock the amplifier restrictions. There's also recognition codes to get through the checkpoints. Watch out for nutjobs.*

She cuts our mental line. There's not much point in saying I've already by-passed the power-draw restrictions on our amplifiers.

Barrens shakes his head one more time. He produces a shiny bit of metal out of his pocket; a badge is on his breast again.

Would things be any different if I had tried to track him through it the very morning he had left? Or would all this be even worse—Karla would not have gotten to me, and with me joining the Archivists sooner, how much more could the Archivists have done with Archie? Perhaps things would be even worse. Or, with me at his side, perhaps Barrens would have never recruited others at all.

. . . But it was not just him anymore by then. Bullet was with him, and he brought in his own friends, and they brought in more.

There is regret, but no time for self-pity. We see that in each other's eyes.

There is not much of a discussion. I look at Barrens and he looks at me, and we both know and nod.

Bullet's eyes sweep back and forth across the cityscape, his fingers trembling around the flask of water as he fumbles at unscrewing the cap. Maybe it is just too much. In a matter of weeks, the things we've seen, and with how he absorbs these experiences . . .

"Bullet, we're going."

"Y-yes."

We head for the least damaged car in sight. Hooded men appear out of the alleyways to surround us just briefly—it only takes a flare of Barrens's badge and his glowering stare to back them off.

With the crackle of my own heavily modified defense amp, I feel safe for a moment, then realize that I have not programmed in anything that can handle crossbow bolts. Ah. Then a brief, dizzying flash has me stumble. It is already there, in my head, from when Karla uploaded so much data into my mind. An algorithm for exactly that purpose, one that creates a *touch* field that is permeable to air and slow-moving objects, but which will catch and immobilize any high-speed projectile. I draw on the power of the grid, and the world around us becomes tinted a faint blue. We cannot see the boundary, but those around us might see the slight blue shimmer of a dome that keeps pace with us.

Barrens recognizes it, bites his lip, and says nothing.

The vehicle we stop in front of is a six-wheeled transport used by construction and maintenance crews. The elongated beetle-shape has been thrown onto its back. Crossbow quarrels have punched into the door. Two of the wheels have been blasted off. It smells of smoke. A trail of blood starts at the shattered window and goes off into the alleyways.

"I'll have this running in a few minutes. Please keep an eye out."

"Sure, Ms. Dempsey," Bullet says.

"Got it."

My hands conduct the music. This is a lot easier than growing a building or even fixing a broken tablet. One sweep of my left gets it right-side up; with my right, I slice off the cargo bed, the rearmost axle, and rearrange the remaining wheels. With a snap of my fingers the bloodstains and soot peel away. The last exertion draws the most power, into the high-kilowatt class, as I compress the material I removed and recrystallize the plastech into the hardened, toughened configuration that is used for the structural skeleton of skyscrapers, then cut and fit the pieces to fit over the body, as well as using them to replace the clear windows with opaque armor leaving only narrow viewing slits for us to peer through.

When I am done, the innocuous hauler is much smaller, a sedan from the end of the twentieth C, ominous black, all ugly, hard-angled surfaces.

We are not alone when I come out of the trance. Two hundred meters down the street, Barrens faces off against a pair of young men. Much closer, beside the smoking shell of another burned-out transport, a third would-be attacker is dead, with Bullet's quarrel projecting from between the boy's eyes.

The three attackers have symbols on their coat sleeves: a large eye, the pupil of which consists of many smaller eyes. Is that the new symbol of the Archivists?

"Dempsey! Watch out!"

I finally take in the dark streaks flying for me and stopping in flashes of light. Glittering sparks as kinetic energy is instantaneously converted to light and heat in midair and they fall, a rain of marbles. Atop the ruins of a brasserie on the corner, a cackling woman is pointing at me, lit up in blue. Her hair streams behind her, long, black waves, and her eyes are wide, and behind the flashing blue glow of *touch,* I see the telltale web of broken blood vessels around her pupils and the edges of her emitter plates—Psyn overdose.

She laughs and shrieks. She tries to overturn the car onto me, and I settle it with a thought. Wind whips around her, dust flies, and cracks propagate across the wall she is perched atop. With so much Psyn in her blood, she is powerful, even without access to the grid, but it is too much for her; she cannot control it. Raw psi flares around her, leaking out of her will's grasp.

Foiled, she grows angry. She thrusts her fists down at me. Force presses down on me—I barely manage to shield myself and the car. The road under my feet explodes, sinks into a crater, pushes even deeper until a great hole opens beneath me revealing sewage tunnels twenty meters below. I float myself over to the car, and standing atop the hood, I roll it backward.

Perhaps if I get out of sight, she will lose interest. Then I can support Barrens and Bullet. Right now, this woman is taking all I've got.

The vehicle stalls, wheels squealing as she gets a hold on it too. Stops it.

She stamps her feet, utterly maddened. Like a child. The buildings around us sway and rumble with her undisciplined fury.

She can barely think. She is burning through her talent so quickly, she will probably drain herself unconscious even if I do nothing. A hail of stones and boulders rain down on me.

I'm more worried about my companions.

I lose sight of Barrens as he vanishes, a bolt of red lightning crackling across the road. Two other trails of fire blur about his path. Thunder, whip cracks, concrete shattering. They are three shooting stars blasting the ground with each leap, ripping through the air as they strike at each other. The comets spiral up the side of a ten-story office building, breaking what's left of the glass façade, colliding again and again.

I cannot help screaming when I see a dark shape fly out of one of those red explosions. A large man, already broken. No. It's not Barrens.

*Hana! Pay attention to yourself! I can handle these amateurs fine!*

My jaw drops when I turn back to this madwoman. In the moments I looked away, she has become totally unhinged. She lifts the entire three-story shophouse unit off the street, tons upon tons of stone-textured plastech. As it breaks apart, she throws half-ton chunks my way.

Now, I stress the grid. My rewiring of the civilian amplifier is not as good as I'd hoped. At sustained high-kilowatt-class draw, I can smell its circuitry starting to burn out as I deflect the paths of truly dangerous building chunks. Most of them are pulverizing the hillside behind me, overshooting badly. Her poor aim is all that saves me.

I am about to reach out and snuff her out with a narrow, focused burst of force when the woman's eyes roll back in her head. She starts trembling, shaking. Blood is pouring down her face now. She is in full psi-seizure.

The remnants of the building fall back onto its foundations, burst apart in a cloud of dust and stone.

And all is quiet again.

Barrens is striding back. His jacket is somewhat torn, and a bruise is on his cheek. I did not see how he disposed of the last attacker.

Closer, the young man I've started to think of as a little brother is still staring at the one he's killed. He shakes. His mind's voice calls out, *Why?*

*They probably saw us using psi and assumed we're ISec. Or maybe they're just handing out jackets and Psyn like candy.*

Only when I walk closer do I see the wet stain spreading across Bullet's black T-shirt. "You're bleeding!"

"I am? Oh."

Barrens just catches the boy. "Kid!"

Bullet's knees give way slowly. "Huh. So this is what it's like."

"Bullet!" I catch him telekinetically. Try to smile at him. "You'll be . . . you'll be fine."

"Naw, Dempsey. Boss. I don't think so." A spasm starts, stops, leaves him coughing blood. "We were trying to do good, weren't we?"

"We were," Barrens rumbles.

"Isn't so bad . . . hurts less than . . . how everyone dies . . . anyway . . ."

By the time we get his jacket and shirt off and spot the crossbow bolt that has gone almost completely through his torso, Bullet is gone. His face is caught in its last moment, a soft smile, remembering.

Barrens touches those eyelids, closes them over those once-bright eyes.

I entomb the corpse in a block of glittering white stone. I cannot think of any worthy epitaph. So I leave only his name, carved into the side. JOE NOVEMBER.

We drive in silence.


I have only driven a ground transport a handful of times, mostly back when I was a rookie on a construction crew. It is not difficult with the streets being so empty. Only occasionally do I have to slow down to get around empty vehicles and the smoldering remains of fires.

Most of the people we see skitter away into the shadows. Some throw rocks at us, yelling. A few have crossbows. Once, I have to ram through a barricade of chairs and tables and chunks of rock and drywall, while bolts ricochet off the car's armor.

"How could it have gotten like this so fast?"

Barrens presses his thumbs to his temples. Whispers, "All along, the others have been planning. Waiting. They must have been mass-producing and stockpiling Psyn for months. Ah, fuck. I was used, me and my boys. My fault."

"It's not all your—"

*Don't. Please.*

The terraced lines of the three-floor shophouses along the road end, replaced by the large offices clustering around the broad, green gardens leading to the vertical farm. The first ISec checkpoint is in sight.

Blue-coated policemen, eyes blank, obviously Adjusted, stop us just long enough for me to broadcast the codes Karla gave us. They wave us on.

A great big tactical transport rumbles up toward us, slamming aside the empty cars on the road. Emitter and receiver plates are all over its surface. It is mist gray rather than the deep ocean blue of the police force. The windshield has spiderweb cracks. A spike has punched halfway in—and I recognize it. One of the Archivists' crossbow quarrels, only scaled several times up. It must have been launched from . . . I remember the equipment of Barrens's cell. This must have come from an even larger version of the Roman-style ballista. Aside from that, the armor is pitted and scarred with little craters.

I stop the car and the transport stops too. We get out first.

A heavy door slides open, and a ramp clangs down.

She strides down to us at the head of a full squad of five Enforcers. They are not wearing just the standard armor, they are outfitted in massive amplifier suits. I only saw Enforcers wearing such gear back in the prison city. Up close, they are walking tanks that dwarf even Barrens.

The changes in Karla's appearance since we last spoke are stark. She has lost weight. Those sharp cheekbones are too sharp now. Purple half-circles under her eyes. And her uniform is rumpled, as though she has slept in it. I am shocked to notice that she is so delicately built, and shorter than Bullet and me. She seemed so much bigger back in the detention cell.

"Well, well. At last we meet, Peace Officer Barrens. I have heard so much about you." Her smile is sharp, her voice drips with cold poison, contempt. She walks around him, looks him up and down, like an animal. Like a piece of meat. "Did you enjoy the tour?"

She wants me to cower. After Meena, after the city of caged children, after these war-torn streets, a bitter woman's cruelty is not much to bear. "It is what it is," I say.

Her eyes are on Barrens, only on him. "Wasn't there another—ah, I get it. Guess you should have picked better followers. Imagine them shooting at their great leader and his companions, no warning at all." She matches the face in our memories to the file in her head. Dismissal in her face as she changes the angle of her neck, looks down upon Barrens though he towers so far above her.

"You will obey my commands without question, without hesitation."

My man's teeth are pressed together so hard I am afraid he will crack them. But he nods. "This"—his arms swing out, pointing out the sky, the Habitat all around us—"it's not . . ." I can feel him wanting to say so much more.

"Despite your intentions, here we are." Karla smiles darkly. "What a pleasure to hear you talking so softly. Meekly. Now, know your place."

She snaps her fingers. The green flash of her talent fires and crackles around us.

I toss and turn, wriggling on the ground. It is like choking down a rock almost as wide around as my throat. There is no "pain," but there is pressure. Blood trickles down my nose and ears. When I wipe my face, the tears on my fingers are red. I am blinded by light. But it is a light in my head and closing my eyes does nothing to stop it. Through the hard-packed dirt, I feel the vibrations of Barrens flailing on the ground close by.

The light fades, leaving a solid, dense block of impenetrable black, pressing down on my brain.

"Get them on board, strap them in. With the Induction rushed like this, they won't be moving for a while."

## 29

THE INFORMATION STARTS TO UNFOLD.

All Information Security principles boil down to three basic tenets.

First, that the more dangerous a piece of information is, the smaller the proportion of humanity that can rationally deal with it.

Second, that all information is dangerous to a lesser or greater degree.

And last, that all dangers to the mission must be minimized.

Upon these axioms, all ISec regulations are built.

Besides the rules, there are operating procedures and ciphers and training memories. In between the documents, data, experiments, films, and texts, long moments of hazy darkness ebb and flow like tides. Those blackouts are when powerful hypnotic-suggestion programs layer the rules ever deeper into my subconscious.

During the Induction, I cannot control my body. Only the straps hold me in the seat when the transport decelerates and makes its turns.

I am dreaming, but I am not asleep. When we reach our destination, I am still trapped in my head. I am floated down corridors with many doors. There is a room with beds and machines.

When it ends, I feel removed, separated from my own senses, even if I am aware of the faint light of the monitoring devices next to my bed. The feel of the bed against my back and the straps holding me down come through my nerves as though I am feeling them remotely, through a datafeed. And the smell of cigarette smoke?

Karla's rich voice cuts through the silence, the steady thrum of the cooled air from the ventilation shafts. "Welcome to the Ministry of Information."

I hear the deep thump of an explosion, but I cannot tell how far off it is.

She is there next to us, standing over us. Just looking.

I cannot see her clearly, my brain still unable to process the signals from my eyes. But I can sense the radiant warmth of her power, and she seems fearsome and tall, swallowing everything up in her cold light.

"Now, you both require sleep. Real sleep." She snaps her fingers, and I sense Barrens in the bed next to mine going limp, sinking to deeper slumber. "That and we have to undo the hackjobs that burned out the tracking ganglia in your implants."

Karla leans closer to me. She blows smoke in my face.

"And a good-night to you too."

More brain surgery. When I wake up, I do not even notice the difference.

In a conference room in Karla's office thirty meters under the district farm, we have barley and spinach, dill and tofu, carrots and onions. Bread. Coffee.

I feel lousy. Am I coming down with something? But I've felt this way, on and off, since my "escape." My head aches. I feel tired even though I've just woken and showered. The food sits in my belly, too dense. The smell of tobacco in the air gets my guts to twist up, and it takes real effort not to vomit all of breakfast. This ISec Induction is rougher on me than it is on Barrens, even if I went through something like it before, in the holding cell.

All these revelations so close together, they have made a shambles of the neat, tidy society I knew. Barrens's quest has brought him what he wanted to know about what happened to Callahan, and so much more.

"So. We got it mostly right," he whispers, almost to himself.

"Yes. We did."

In between the lines of the Induction, the last pieces can be found: the documents that justify ISec methods and history.

Barrens and I bounce our understanding back and forth between us, until it all falls into place.

A derelict alien ship crashed onto Earth, with technology that revolutionized everything. Psi-tech. But the Strangers' ship also brought with it a terrible disease; one that spread far and wide before anyone understood what it was or where it came from.

It is not a fungus, bacterium, virus, or prion. After centuries of study, no one has come close to finding a cure; no one even truly understands its mode of action. The best guess is that it is a nucleic-acid-based nanomachine that selectively alters gene transcription.

Officially, it is designated Nucleic Machine Disease-1; but so few people even knew that it existed, even the ISec staff now calls it Mincemeat.

It is not the name that matters but what it does. The pathogen has an alternating sequential generation phenotype.

I and all the "normal" humans are G-0. The span of our lives is random, and sooner or later, we are all condemned to share Callahan's fate, flesh rent asunder. Those of us in Generation Zero give birth only to monsters, only to the G-1 creatures.

They are animals gifted with supercharged psionic talents. Yet the G-1s have to be kept alive because their offspring are G-0 individuals. Without them, no more humans can be born.

"What pitiful things we are," Barrens whispers.

A few records of the end of Earth are available to us at our current access levels. What we can see emphasizes the true danger of the G-1 beasts. Most have powers only a little greater than human-normal, but a dangerous few are orders of magnitude beyond us, and when they lose control in a mindless rage, they produce explosions of psi greater than the explosion of any atomic bomb. I cannot help watching one memory in my head, over and over. It is a view of Earth from orbit showing an entire city being annihilated by one brilliant white sphere of power.

An unregulated birth could result in the death of millions. And there were many unregulated births during those last years on Earth.

The alien ship is refitted in orbit by Earth's survivors. Then, they leave. One last image from the Noah is a look back at dead Earth. The blue and the white are blasted away. The crust of the world is broken, leaving a sphere of blackened rock and bright red lava.

Here, in this closed population, where monitoring is easier to enforce, the ship's crew sets up a stable society. It is easy to get the cooperation of all while they watch Earth receding from the ship's observatory, a wasteland, everyone burdened by survivor's guilt. The primary protocols are developed. G-0 humans are indoctrinated against the instinctive social behaviors around blood relationships. Their monstrous G-1 children are taken from them before they can be subjected to the trauma of seeing what is born from their bodies. These beasts are kept asleep almost through their entire lives, their only purpose to live long enough to breed and give birth to the next generation of we G-0s, given to Keepers to raise to propagate our otherwise doomed species.

People want their children's children to be spared the burden of these secrets.

The cycle of life and death on the Noah is set in stone. The decades go by, and humanity is made to forget rather than heal.

Only, sometimes, mistakes slip through the cracks.

Most of our neural Implant functions have to do with monitoring our health, to warn the Retirement Office when a citizen is about to become symptomatic. At times, the automated monitors fail to catch the occasional rapid progression of the disease, and the remains are seen before they can be cleaned up. As with Callahan. Sometimes entire groups of witnesses need to be Adjusted. A child dying in a classroom. An old man drinking in a bar.

Occasionally, one of the weaker G-1s escapes into the unmapped regions, necessitating long, dangerous hunts in the dark. The Enforcers are not meant to combat dangerous crewmen; the police and ISec handle that. The Enforcers' true purpose is to keep the G-1s contained.

After keeping us waiting for an hour, the doors slam open, and Karla stalks in.

"What next?" I whisper.

She examines us, *reads* us, and smiles crookedly. She seems satisfied with our reactions to the Induction. She is all business and briefs us on Ministry operations. All of the ship's staff, including the Enforcers, have been put at the disposal of Information Security for the duration of the crisis, except for a skeletal crew of specialists required to keep basic ship functions going, as well as maintain lockdown on the G-1 Prison City.

The gates separating each section of the Habitat have been closed. One by one, the sections are being pacified by a combined force of ISec field agents, Enforcers, policemen, volunteers, and Adjusted conscripts.

"Pacified?" Barrens clenches his fists. His knuckles pop.

She lights another cigarette with the fire of her talent. "After the combat guys destroy all resistance, Behavioralists are sent in. One pocket at a time. Those who are willing to focus on the mission have the last month of their memories edited. Every single other survivor is Adjusted. The deepest form. We are still on the defensive here in Paris Section, until reinforcements arrive and it is our turn."

When I ask her why, the indignation flames her cheeks pink. Barrens asks

too. Her anger presses us back in our reclining chairs. I keep asking. About the
drop in efficiency. About why such extremes are needed.

"Why can't you just dull their emotions? Enough to get them to submit?
Why turn them into puppets? Given enough time, they'd still be willing to
carry out the mission, even knowing that we all have the . . . Mincemeat. The
first-gen crew managed."

Her laugh is half-crazed, veering from genuine amusement to insincere scorn.
"So naïve. Back then, humans were held together by the shared trauma of wit-
nessing the end of Earth. The Council has written off this generation of crew.
Free thought is too dangerous for them now."

"I don't under—"

"Of course you don't understand! You two, two . . . fuckwads!" Karla tosses
the cigarette away, incinerates it with a thought. Her power flings the ashes
into a trash can. She sighs, lights another. "Oughta pull the guts out the ass of
whichever of your mutineer friends decided it would be a great idea to put Psyn
in the fucking *food supply*. The cheap grain/protein mash that most people have
to eat for one or two meals every freaking day."

Nobody believes in God, any God. We are raised to believe only in ourselves, in our responsibilities, our duties, on this long, lonely watch as the Noah
traverses the space between the stars. I want to pray for someone to fix this. All
those people, slowly being driven to psychosis.

But there is only us. We have to make this right.

"Can you picture it? Psyn making everyone edgy. Then the announce-
ments and memories and documents and Mincemeat being broadcast on the
Nth Web."

Barrens's hands are gripping the table between us so hard, I hear the material flexing, starting to crack. "Okay. We get it."

"Do you? This is nothing compared to how much worse it can still get."

What is she saying?

"It is terrible, knowing about the Builders, about the disease. But why would
that stop the mission? It is still the only hope for our species."

Karla's lips twist into a sly smile. "Imagine a secret so much worse that just
knowing it will cause a critical mass of the population to choose chaos, choose
failure." She blows smoke, directs it to linger around us, needles of irritation
shaped like grim gray butterflies. She spits into the dregs of her coffee. "All that
stuff you just learned. That is not the secret of secrets."

What?

Barrens puts his hand on mine, shakes his head. "No." He bites his lip hard enough to cut it. "It won't help us fix this."

"Oh-ho!" Karla cocks her hip to one side, blows a kiss to him. "Oh-ho! Loverboy is starting to understand! He glimpses the forbidden fruit."

"But—"

*Hana. I don't want to know any more. We need to focus.*

Survival is basic human instinct. Nothing can make so many people give up, not with the indoctrination we all grow up with. We are all taught from birth of the importance of the mission, it is explicitly taught by our Keepers, and more subtly reinforced with subliminal messages in our stories, in our music. No. Give up on the human race itself? Wait.

I collapse, fists against my skull. Just skimming the border puts the taste of death on my tongue.

"Dempsey!" Barrens's hands on me, gentle. "What's happening?"

"Please," he begs Karla. "Stop it!"

She laughs. "It's not me doing that." Ugly. Hateful. Karla's laughter is the most expressive vocalization she's got. "Every time you think in dangerous directions, ISec programming in your Implant will erase a little bit more of you. Better discipline your thought patterns—too much, and it will start scarring the wetware. You'll get seizures, go nuts. It's a security measure, to guard us, we guardians of dangerous data.

"Now, if you'll stop fucking around questioning procedure, we have work to do."

Karla points a finger at Barrens. He jumps to his feet, staggers back.

*Leon!*

He presses his hands to his face. Breathes deeply.

"Just giving the man his assignment, darling."

He is pale. But he steadies himself and drops his hands. Fumbles for one of his cigarettes. His face is stone.

"I—"

"You have your mission." Her eyes flash green. "Go."

Barrens looks away. He won't meet my eyes. He presses his lips to my forehead and murmurs, "See you later." *Don't ask me, Hana. I'll still have to do it.*

He stalks away.

"And now, you. While you slept, I took the liberty of *reading* your memories."

What? But . . . How? That usually takes a Deep Adjustment session. It—

"Don't look so shocked. The package I put in your brain back at the detention center also includes a back door into all memories acquired after its installation. Surely you didn't think I gave you the keys just like that?" Karla blows a few more smoke butterflies about me. "Hah. And now this indignation from you. Delicious. Worry not, darling, I don't care how good he is in bed. And out of bed. I was saving time, or did you want to waste one week in debriefing sessions?"

I focus on the trembling of my fingertips. What could I do to her even if I wanted to hurt her?

"Excellent. Hold that attitude. Now. I have run your plan by the data researchers. That AI of yours is really something. They agree that your approach is our best chance for regaining control of the Nth Web."

Wait. What? She's still calling it mine? "So. Impressed, were they?"

"Oh, yes. Very. They say you are the most brilliant machine learning savant of the age. For centuries, people have dreamed of artificial intelligence. They theorized about it, wrote stories about it, and failed at every attempt to make a real one, where you alone have succeeded. And in your spare time. They say that if your viral argument cannot grant you control over it, nothing can."

How can she not know Archie's origins? Even now, I cannot get hold of my thoughts. They race over and over through my conclusion that Archie's growth is because of the Builders' algorithm fragments. Maybe I started it, but Archie is as much a product of the ship's environment as it is of my design.

"We've set up a software-development center for you down the hall. Room E55. You have a team and everything; better than the amateurs you had with you in the tunnels. You need to improve it, finish it. Chop-chop! Get control of your toy and we can bring the Nth Web back up, communications, ship controls, everything. It is only your creation that allowed this childish uprising to get this far. With it on our side, ISec will ensure nothing like this ever happens again."

She can't read my thoughts about Archie. At all. Not even through her back door into my memories. How?

I am already walking out of her office.

Almost afraid to try it. *Archie?*

A cheerful chirp sounds inside my skull. Impossible. Archie should be completely nonfunctional without the Network linking its components spread throughout the ship.

*How?*

I get a flicker of imagery, a young girl who looks like me, but is not. In my thoughts, *it* is there. And I understand. Ever since it first showed me the memory from the Builders, it's been there. It is in my head, in my dreams, riding on the nanoprocessors of my Implant. Just one part, one unit in the swarm. But the most important one. The true spark of sentience.

The last ghost of the Builders' intelligence, or perhaps the first being of a totally new form of life, exists in my head.

## 30

KARLA MAY BE AN EXCEEDINGLY POWERFUL TALENT AND A GENIUS IN MANY ways, but she is not a programmer, and the software-development center she said was ready for me is anything but ready. Its machines are centuries-old terminals. They probably date back to the first-generation crew. There are actual physical keys that click as we type.

The first task of my team is to adapt software to interface between the low-level machine language that runs directly on the hardware, and DREAM33, the latest version of the high-level language developed by the Noah's crew over the centuries. These ISec specialists might be able to work directly with alien assembly language, but I cannot. The bottom-level language requires intimate knowledge of the underlying structure, using unintuitive commands manipulating memory addresses, pushing data from here to there, adding this or that; it is clumsy and unforgiving and requires knowledge of quantum mathematics to even begin to properly manipulate the circuitry. DREAM abstracts away the intricacies of the hardware, lets a programmer deal in ideas and content and logic.

What is to be done with Archie must be precise and reliable.

At least, that is the lie I tell these young, gifted teenagers who look at me with a mixture of revulsion and awe. To them, I am a reformed traitor, but I am also the one to reach the holy grail of true AI, even if by accident.

It takes a day and a half to make the necessary modifications to the existing terminals.

Then it is my turn, and I show them what lies beneath Archie's skin.

I show them the same node map and structural-comparison tool I used in those last days of Barrens's Sanctuary. On our screens, those multicolored clusters of Archie's structure stretch out, so many stars across the black sky of the Nth Web. It is only a reconstruction pulled out of the snapshot from just before ISec pulled the plug on the Network.

As I show off a cladistics diagram suggesting the growth and differentiation of the differently behaving subtypes of the program children over time, I also construct for them a basic map of where I believe the most vital functions of Archie are hidden throughout these families.

So many glowing lines, so many windows showing comparisons across the populations, statistical analyses of polymorphisms in the code.

We sit at our desks, side by side, in front of banks of display tablets and keyboards wired into the terminals, tapping away, studying the intricacies of Archie's emergent structure. They propose strategies to probe the different populations to a finer granularity to better track where the control cluster might be.

All the while, I hide from them the results indicating the data contamination from the Builders.

In truth, all the real programming I need to do is in my head. I only need to make Archie's core, that kernel of sentience in my head, understand. I already know Archie likes me. What is required is for the two of us to understand each other. Once I can explain what I need, I am confident this central piece of its intelligence can handle propagating instructions to the rest of the Analytical Nodes once we bring the system back online.

I do not get close to my team of five. I just remember their names and faces. Maybe it is my constant fatigue, or just the accumulated stresses of . . . Barrens calls it "the Year of the MindFuck." But I don't want to get to know these fresh-faced young people who look so focused and determined and idealistic. I am too numb.

I make little changes to what I already came up with back in the Sanctuary. I let them optimize it and test it against what existing subgroups of Archie are present in the Paris vertical farm's Analytical Node. Mostly particles focused on pattern recognition. They add more functions to the local copies of the swarm, preparing it for the greater role it is to assume: communications and data management across the ship.

Nothing humans have devised is an improvement on the alien hardware that came with the ship. Our tablets are clumsy, portable imitations of the hardline terminals built into the Noah. Our neural implants are the crudest adaptations of the Builders' subtle nanotech augmentation.

All our improvements have been in software, and even in that, we have not caught up with the original work of the aliens, which is still too complex and different for us to even touch.

Archie, which is made of both human and alien programming, can bridge the gap. The previous system of interfaces between an individual's computationally limited neural Implant to the incomparably more powerful Analytical Nodes of the ship will remain, but it will be augmented by the AI's abilities to integrate and incorporate everything. Security will be greater. Response time will be improved. Archie will be able to monitor *all* of the Nth Web, in a way that the Ministry of Information never had the manpower to do.

I wonder; would Karla distrust Archie if she knew of its alien component, or would she trust it more because it is more than us?

I am constantly tired. There is never enough sleep. They have to remind me when to eat.

It is one thing for Archie and me to make crude signals and expressions to each other. It is another for us to know what the other is saying clearly enough that I can explain *why* I need it to acknowledge only me and individuals I authorize. Archie's personality is inherently friendly and curious, childlike. It likes the idea of shaking things up for the sake of seeing what happens next. It does not understand pain or death or being Adjusted. Secrecy, motives, and agendas are ideas it is only beginning to grasp. I have to teach Archie a new language that I am still creating out of common concepts that we share. It is less programming and more like, well . . .

It is like being a Keeper to a child.

For all that Archie already knows many elements of human speech, it does not fully understand the words as more than abstract concepts; reality as its digital sentience experiences it is nothing like reality as I perceive it, and this is the what we must learn from each other.

Being a Keeper is a twenty-four-hour-per-day job that requires years of training in psychology, sociology, and education. I have precious little of the Keepers' formally refined skills and knowledge, and no time to acquire it.

Bullet would have been invaluable for this. But he is gone, and I have to go with my intuition and the upbringing Mala gave me. Or perhaps it's an advantage, not being saddled with so many preconceived opinions and techniques; after all, Archie *is not human,* and its psychology may never be human.

Every moment I have alone, I close my eyes and establish contact. Archie is always there; I only have to think to it.

*Hi, Archie. It's Hana.*

———

An empty space at first, just filled with ideas and thoughts, all abstract. There is nothing to see, there isn't even darkness. It is a memory being written into the Implant even as I am still experiencing it. It is the now at the bridge between neurons and nanocircuits.

*Archie?*

A ping. A beep. A deluge of data of all kinds, numbers, emotions, sounds, sights, touches. Too much. My head wants to explode.

*Slow down!*

Contrition.

Archie feels. It has emotions, even if they're not anchored in physical experiences like ours. But it is further along than I had expected it to be.

And then it flashes memories at me. My own.

She appears then, out of the void. Archie doesn't care what names go with what gender. Archie has merely taken a form it likes.

That form is me, and not me. It doesn't have the emitter plates on its face. It changes, from moment to moment. Sometimes it looks like me at sixteen, sometimes the me at nine. Sometimes it wears bright yellow pajamas with sunflowers, blurry and fuzzy from before my Implant augmentation. Mostly, it wears variations of my day-to-day outfits from school—slacks or jeans, blouses or T-shirts, and the occasional sundress and sandals.

While it is a little uncomfortable seeing another me, it is also a relief. It reinforces that for some reason, Archie likes me, and more important, Archie is trying to think in human terms. I would have no idea how to even begin if Archie had taken the form of one of the Builders.

This place is in my skull, but it is not quite in my mind—it is between. I project an image of myself into this sharing of human thought and unhuman information. Me. In the now, tired, older, a little softer, eye bags, not all that healthy lately. An ugly maintenance jumpsuit an assistant passed to me is what I've got on. We are two versions of me, standing nowhere.

It must understand something of physical sensations because when it smiles a ghastly, too-wide smile that would hurt a real person's face; it reaches out and touches the hand of my image of me. It's a tingling little shock, a jolt of electricity, data about proximity, pressure, and force, rather than the experience of pressure and force.

*That's not quite right, Archie. It's like this. It feels like this, to touch.*

Carefully, I strip out only the sensation of touch, from the first time I shook hands with grimy little Marcus, back in the Keeper crèche cluster. Not the visuals or the mess of sounds and smells around me back then, with little kids running back and forth and giggling and pinching each other or yelling at a scraped knee. Just the touch. And I pass that to Archie.

Archie flickers, its mouth makes a large *O,* then it tries again. Our fingers brush against each other. These are more than images, they are symbols, and symbols have meaning, and I have to teach Archie those meanings.

*Yes. That's right, Archie. That's how it feels.*

It claps. It.

She looks so wide-eyed and young, and sweet and guileless. Was I ever like this?

*Let me show you where I grew up.*

I pull it out of my memories, the apartment where Mala raised me, white walls, so many prints of hills and birds in the sky and trees, entry-level fake-wood furnishing, and an extravagant number of physical printouts, actual books, lining the shelves that dominate every space.

I sit on the floor and pull a box from one of the shelves.

While I open it and set up the colorful board and the many little game pieces, Archie is floating around the room, peering closely at everything, poking and touching, a look of unreal concentration on her furrowed brow. It knows more about expressions than I expect at this point. It must be from the facial recognition built into the original search modules.

It looks like a little girl, but it isn't one. From the endless hours Archie's spent combing through databases and dark corners of the Nth Web, I know it has more patience than any human child could ever have. It might be content to spend a whole year analyzing this one slice of memory of me sitting in Mala's old home, stroking every surface, staring at every item, to take in every perfect and imperfect detail.

I wish we had more time to do this right. For me to document everything, every response. This is contact with nonhuman intelligent life, the first one in known history.

But time passes here exactly at the same rate as it does outside this day-dream, and I have to risk rushing things.

*Archie? Want to play something?*

I choose games because games have goals, they have rules, consequences. I pick zero-sum games, where there is a loser and a winner. I share sense and emotional impressions of small embarrassments when I've lost, and the little pleasures when I've won. From there, I try to show that, in a way, my life has been a game. With rules. With goals. Sometimes I win, and sometimes I lose. Sometimes there is pleasure and . . . sometimes, there is pain. A popped balloon, that first magical, delicious chocolate ice cream cone on a Sunday picnic.

Between games, I share experiences of being with Mala. Teachable moments, when I messed up, lied, broke things, said mean things, and she punished me with a frown, with disappointment, with her sadness. When I'd do the right thing, Mala's joy, her smiles, her kisses, the warmth of her limitless fountain of hugs. The smell of her.

I . . . had forgotten how much I miss her. Forgotten, even though the memories are always just there, perfect and unchanging. I think of her when she was Retired, our last letters farewell. I hope she didn't suffer too much. But I can't jump ahead that far with Archie. It's not ready to understand death, not yet.

Archie relives these early moments of my life with me, learns to feel what I felt, so that all these memories we've dug up, all these people we've found on the Net, they're not just names and records and data, they're all people.

And we're all in a game where the goal is to survive.


The sessions with Archie are exhilarating, exhausting. Fulfilling when it takes a step forward, frustrating when it laughs and breaks the rules or runs off or changes the colors of the world, for curiosity and the pleasure of it. While it's all fun in our make-believe world, I can't have Archie shutting off the reactors of the Noah just to see what might happen when it takes over the whole ship!

Every other night, Barrens sleeps at my side. All his missions are limited to Paris Section while the gates are closed.

He does not talk about what he does. But I can guess. He weeps in his sleep and calls out names. I recognize some of them. Colleagues, among the Archivists. Former allies.

Would I have the strength to kill Jazz or Lyn or Hennessy if the safety of the mission demanded it?

I wish I could know they are safe. But they are in another section of the Habitat, and until the new system is brought online, communications between the sealed districts are difficult and sporadic.

Archie reaches a critical breakthrough. When it understands the idea of *promises*. When it understands that what happens in the physical realm is not like how it is in my head or on the computers. Data can be rewritten, but the physical world cannot.

That is also the first time I see it start to comprehend fear.

*Will you promise to behave, always? To listen to me, to follow the rules? We don't want to hurt anyone by accident.* Words must always be attached to concepts and emotions with Archie, to reinforce them while everything is so new.

Solemnly, the little not-girl in my head nods. Puts out her hand. We shake on it. When I bend down and press a kiss to her forehead, I stop thinking of her as "it." And we are ready for testing.

I game her through dozens of attempts with examples and stories and test cases. She still does not quite understand that humans are so different from her, so much more fragile, but she gets the concept of different human groups with differing goals. She just barely knows that this conflict is more than some abstract simulation, but Archie does comprehend that I want her to be on my side and mine alone.

She has accepted my thinking and not just me, and that has to be enough.

The team Karla assembled to watch and assist me is surprised when I interrupt their morning of slow progress with an update they never saw me work on. They are stunned when they upload her onto the local server and she immediately ties together all the subgroups of particles of the AI swarm that are present in the node. Part of Archie lives again outside my head, and she has taken control of this hardware cluster, just one of the thousands of supercomputers the Strangers built into the ship.

In my head, she's laughing, her smile starting to be more natural, as her realm gets bigger again, is not confined to my Implant anymore. I sense her glee as she races through the components of the node, reaches out with the pieces of herself that she was cut away from when the Net was brought down.

Archie passes every test case they can think of.

"How? It's only been a week!" they ask.

The best answer I can give is "Intuition."

"Huh. I guess that's how you came up with the AI in the first place."

Programmer LeMay, a tanned young man with meticulously crafted hair and lovely hazel eyes, calls Karla in.

While we wait for her to arrive, they repeat Archie's run through more simulations, to see the rate at which my update should propagate throughout the Network when she is reconnected, to see how the other subgroups of the swarm might respond. I do not pay attention. She is with me in my head, she will be with me on the larger system. Not because of anything I did—Archie will simply wake up as the atom of her consciousness inside me stretches out through the Network and reclaims the rest of her body. I ignore their murmurs of astonishment at her efficiency and force myself to eat a crêpe loaded with sharp, fragrant cheeses.

Barrens is out there somewhere this morning. Watching men and women, waiting for his chance to subdue or kill whomever Karla has assigned him to. Will he come back to me tonight? Or will he be killed by people he knows, high on the power of Psyn, fanatics transformed by altered states and the words of his rivals?

Karla appears, a pale apparition. Like me, she stands out among these bright young talents. She is leaner, more tired. Fiercer.

"That's it then?" she murmurs, skimming through the modular schema of Archie's structure. She zooms in on the functions I've changed, and the parameters that will change the AI's behavior, tilting Archie's purpose, those core processes. Karla is not trying to understand the code modifications—she is *reading* me, sifting through how confident or doubtful I am with each block of programming. I wonder, how does Archie determine which of my thoughts to secure against Karla, and which the girl AI allows to drift into the ISec agent's clutching mental intrusion?

The air is too hot. I shrug off a borrowed lab coat, then start to feel cold.

"That's it. Doing a better job would take two months and a team of twenty machine-learning specialists," I lie.

Now it is Karla who takes a moment to steady herself. Her pigmentless eyes stare into mine. Just as Archie is my tool, I am hers. I have been hers since she let me escape ISec holding. Both of our tools went beyond their boundaries and bear part of the responsibility for this crisis. As she said, there have been other uprisings. Only Archie has allowed this one to progress so far. And I was supposed to make Barrens stop before the movement hit the tipping point.

Here and now, my intuition substitutes for my lack of empathic and telepathic power. "This plan of yours. Do you have approval?"

"I do and I do not. It is like when I let you go the first time, Dempsey. I'm betting on you."

I try to slap on something like a smile. Surely she can see right through it, but she seems to appreciate the effort.

She thinks another packet to me. It is a thousand-digit alphanumeric string. "This is—"

"It's the key to the ship's systems, Dempsey. I'm not supposed to have it. But I'm not the only one that sees that what's going on is not going to be fixed by what's in the manual. We can't fail."

Nightmare scenarios flash through my head, as bad as the ones I thought up for my training game in school. I imagine some stupid mistake of mine, some glitch causing the Noah's engines to fire, sending us off course. Reactors overloading.

Another dizzy spell. I sway in my chair, I'd pitch off if I did not lean back and let the headrest cradle my skull and neck. The stress is getting to me. It is a wonder I don't have ulcers.

No. There won't be a glitch. I won't have it.

Archie pings me, wondering at the rush of bad feelings.

*I'm going to trust you, Archie. Don't let me down.*

Ghost image of her in front of me. Saluting me.

"What happens if this doesn't work?" Karla had hinted at it before.

Those cold eyes blaze hot. "When it gets to a level-zero catastrophe, as determined by the decision algorithms of the command staff, they receive further authorizations for steadily more extreme actions."

Extreme? In my head, I see the fires burning through this section of the Habitat, the closing of all the gates, the shutdown of the Networks. "How much more extreme?"

"Doesn't matter for you and me. If it gets that bad, we won't live to see it. Oh, very well. I will tell you that there are more reasons for the separation between the G-0 Habitat and the G-1 containment, and why the G-1 area has its own life support and power supply."

Ah. I see it. A doomsday scenario. Shut down the power and life support, except for a few pockets of Keepers in bunkers. Every other G-0 dies. And the remaining Keepers raise the next generation, bred from the G-1s. Of course, this is not at all ideal—the ship will have the barest remnants of a skeleton crew for the years it will take to raise and train a new crew, during which time, how many system failures will occur—how many parts broken without people to fix them, how many glitches in the software?

The damage would be terrible. The population will never fully recover if it comes to that. When the ship finally reaches the new world, will there still be a sustainable number of humans to colonize it? That alien world will not be without its own dangers. How many of the resources would be denied to our descendants by what it will take to fix what's going on now if I screw up?

"No pressure, Dempsey." Her grin is cruel, harsh.

"Yeah." I sigh. "Wait, you mean we start right now?"

"You said more time won't help, yes?"

Yes.

I tap in the code.

It's a heady moment when it hits me that, through Archie, I now have power over the entire freaking ship.

I clamp down on that bubbling terror and lift the virtual barricades isolating the separate Analytical Clusters of the Nth Web. The system reboots, the connections come back to life. On one of the screens, the Network map begins to light up, a web of light starting to spread as more and more edges extend out and touch more and more vertices. The disparate parts of Archie's structure also start to light up, start to come together into a collective intelligence that is ever more powerful as she absorbs the dormant copies of her old processes. Her complexity ramps up as her virtual cells, her organs, come together. It is not the number of copies of Archie's individual thought automata that produce her power—it is the number of links between them, like the synapses in a human brain. The rudimentary awareness that was hidden in my head stretches outward, becomes more. Evolves even as she regains herself.

An idle thought while we wait. "What was happening with that Habitat section that was being closed anyway? We, ah, the Archivists thought they were labs for human experimentation, back when we, they, thought that Mincemeat was something the Council was doing to us."

Karla's eyes are locked on the image of the spreading data probes, the progress bars as systems are rebooted and each fragment of Archie is assimilated.

"What?"

"I was just wondering."

She chuckles. Sour. "We had built up something of a resource surplus beyond the initial projections. The Council was going to start up . . . well . . . research. So there it is. The surplus is gone, destroyed by this mutiny. A waste anyway; how will anyone on the ship find a cure if all of Earth could not?" She gives me just a taste of how she feels, the crushing disappointment as her personal project was pushed out of reach.

The extended communication functions allowed by the Nth Web are reinitialized, and as I dive, mind-first, into the Network, I feel the sum total of the swarm's feelers extending out to me. Familiar. Comfortable. Welcoming.

"I'm in," I tell Karla unnecessarily.

"And I'll follow." She leans back into her own chair, next to mine, and piggybacks onto my neural signal. Anything that Archie is not hiding, she can *read*.

I feel her hand closing over mine. *Just get to it*.

And we do.

As I expected, it is a simple matter for Archie. She has already claimed over 90 percent of the swarm and has now begun to tie herself into the Noah, layering her components into the hardware functions of the Analytical Nodes.

The Archivists have as many followers as I feared, but it matters not. Their conflicting instructions and attempts to subvert Archie have no effect—the AI knows her own mind, makes her own choices, and she has already chosen me.

The virtual battle is over before it has a chance to begin.

"I have control."

"Get on with it. The old fogies on the Bridge will be going crazy with what's going on. We don't have a lot of time."

Archie sends out tendrils seeking information all across the Network. She initiates processes that analyze power demands and where there are unusual accesses of the grid inside and outside the Habitat. Right away, I see that the mutineers are concentrated in old sections of the Habitat just outside Londinium and Moskva. Archie also digs through the logs of the discussion forums and personal posts on pages just before the Web was taken down.

Karla's eyes are hard, sharing the ideas and thoughts almost as quickly as they form in the back-and-forth between my brain and Archie's data streams. "They have an army." She expected it to be bad, and it is. "And they've gotten around the section gates."

She gestures, puts up the growing map of their positions in the ship.

"There are so many!" someone behind us whispers. A loud discussion breaks out among the team. Karla ignores them, taking in and absorbing the data Archie is assembling.

All of the Archivists' cells spread their own ideas even before the explosion of Network chatter caused by the edited memories of Meena's death. The underclass of the ship, less educated and less disciplined in the first place, were also more dependent on the free nutrient slush. High on Psyn, they were easy prey for those who could play on their growing anxieties and paranoia. They became a ready-made army for the Archivists to recruit.

Archie spits out numbers, based on power consumption and rate of water use. Mere hundreds of fanatics have won ten thousand men and women to their cause. This does not include the thousands more people who did not join them, but who have become violent and unstable because of the tainted food.

There are only a few hundred Enforcers at any time.

My team members are all talking at once. "They managed to find side-access shafts to the other sections of the Habitat." Medical feedback streams indicate a steady trickle of crewmen through the sewers—new converts still have active locator modules in their neural implants. "We did not catch it because we were restoring order one section at a time!"

Karla springs upright. She waves her hands. Diagrams start appearing in her mind and mine. "Worse than I thought," she curses. "The rest of you, shut up or get out."

They manage to rein in their excitement.

What does Karla see?

Between us, she brings up a hovering display of more shafts and passages. "They're not going to try to take control of the Habitat, or to escape deeper into the uninhabited zone."

With the additional information before me, I see it too. "They're going to attack the Bridge."

Another secretive area, this is supposed to be known only to the most important and vital officers of the ship. I suppose Thorn either turned a top-level ISec agent or an Enforcer to the Archivists' side or tortured the information out of one.

A freight train passing by their occupied zone is stopped. Archie detects breaches in the walls. The great serpent resumes its steady progress toward the bow of the ship.

Karla puts a hand on my shoulder. Her fingers bruise me through the pseudo-linen. "Shut it down," she hisses. "Seal off that tunnel!"

I cannot. "They've isolated that locality. Archie is trying to break in but—" That area of the map goes dark. "They've cut it off from the rest of the Network."

"Our access codes should make that impossible!"

"They probably destroyed the data-transmission system on the train and along that tunnel—the door controls are all downstream of the hardware damage they've caused," one of the youths on my team interjects.

Karla grinds her teeth. "Forget it then. I'm transmitting a warning up the chain."

She closes her eyes and pulls back from me. I sense a torrent of communications in and out of her head, enough to make her glow, enough to pop some blood vessels and send a few drops of blood out of one nostril. She must be co-ordinating with the rest of ISec, maybe with the whole command structure.

Long minutes go by as I watch her eyes flicker up and down, moving under her lids, while her lips twitch with unspoken speech.

Her eyes open, and maybe I've gotten to know her well enough to read something of the little variations in her unvaryingly fierce expression. I can see that another plan has been made and will now be carried out.

"Let's go." She yanks me up and out of my chair.

"Go?" I sway on my feet. A bad time to be getting the flu. I've been feeling weaker every day. My bones ache and throb, pain rising and falling.

"Everyone we can get right now, Adjusted cops, mall security guards, con-struction workers, cooks, secretaries, everyone that the Behavioralists have al-ready processed and cleared in Edo and Athens are being mobilized."

"We'll never catch up to the attack."

"We can't save the Council. It's too late for that." She pulls one of the psi-tablets out of the mess that is my hard-line terminal. She does it with her hands—which shake. She uses her fingers clumsily, unused to typing as she is, and zooms in on another area of the ship's dauntingly complex 3-D diagram.

It occurs to me that she no longer seems to have the energy even to think the data into my head.

How many people must she have been hearing and speaking with simulta-neously to strain her? For the first time, she is merely human. Her back is bent, her shoulders bowed.

Or—no. That weakness, that response. It is familiar. She has just received a huge block of memories and skills, not unlike what she has done to me twice.

A long silence in the dim office as we all concentrate on the maps and dis-plays.

"There." Karla points. It is another mainline data nexus—the largest, glow-ing intersection of data-lines running down the very spine of the Noah. Close to where the mutineers broke into the supply-train tunnel, it intersects the cen-tral power transmission axis too. "We have to take this point. From there, we can control all the signals in the system. This is where we set up a new Bridge. We'll meet your boyfriend there too."

She regains herself. I can barely keep up with her stride. The assistants she gathered for me scramble, gathering papers, notes, pulling tablets out of the terminal interface.

In the corridor, men and women in black armor, gray ISec uniforms, Behavioralist greens, and peace-officer blues snap to attention, salute her.

"Interim Captain Karla Waitani, what are your orders?" asks a short, officious man with spectacles. I never did get his name. A small man, rude and self-important. Through the link with Karla, I can sense his envy.

She takes a deep breath.

Then she is in my head, just as Archie is in my head, and uses me to access Archie's hold on the ship's communications. She still does not notice the AI's presence inside me, even as she is using her. She fires off a hurricane of communication packets into the minds of a hundred officers all across the Noah, from the Habitat to the G-1 Prison City.

The little man staggers back a step. "Understood. Your personal transport is ready."

Karla marches forward. I just want to sleep.

*Follow, Dempsey. You're with me. I think you need some air, and I have a headache. A short rest would be good, before . . . how does it go in the movies? Before the shit hits the fan.*

## 31

KARLA DRIVES US THROUGH THE WRECKAGE OF THE CITY. WHEN THERE ARE small obstacles, she pushes them aside, when there are large ones, such as a suspension bridge with spans smashed down into a river or a tower that has collapsed across the road or a twisted forest of spikes and other assorted post-psi-combat relics, she lifts the whole car into the air to get across.

Her apartment building is still upright. It is in an exclusive, high-rent area. In front of the fallen chrome-and-crystal façade, a lone rosebush blooms crimson, forlorn and absurd among the blackened plants of the courtyard garden.

One wing has been smashed inward by the extended right arm of a replica of the Colossus of Rhodes. Helios's left arm has been flattened out into a shield, his head extruded into a crenellated turret for some ambitious group of combatants that had animated the huge statue.

What were the motivations of whoever did that? Perhaps they had not been trying to attack anything—maybe they had just been bored, stoned artists making some statement during that brief, heady moment when they realized that laws did not matter anymore.

"Follow," Karla commands again, stepping out of the vehicle. Standing still, arms crossed, she floats up into the air, buoyed up by power alone. She does not require an ornithopter flight pack, or the flight armor restricted to Enforcers.

Though I had wanted to make the OCS training program, her new position is not a job I would ever want. What must it feel like to be responsible for so much?

The amplifier on my wrist still works. My mind's touch pulls a manhole cover free from the sidewalk. I lift it up and sit on it and float after her, feet swinging. Flying with just TK is not beyond me, with an amp and the grid, but it is difficult, like balancing on an oil slick. It is easier to ride an inflexible object to push and pull along a desired trajectory—perhaps there is some psychological block that one can be trained out of.

She enters a balcony on the thirtieth level. Half the floor has collapsed, but she ignores it, walking back and forth without distinction between what is solid and what is air.

"I feel like cooking. The bathroom is intact. Take a shower. You look like shit. Take anything out of the closet—you have enough skill to resize clothes. Take an ISec coat. You might as well wear the uniform. In fact, pack yourself a bag of things. Whatever you like."

Now what is this about? Well. There's no sense in taking offense at a perpetually prickly person burdened with the fate of humanity. I try at glib. "I'm not doing the dishes. But thank you, I suppose."

I do need more clothes, and there's always a line for the showers at our makeshift base.

She is nearly a stranger, the me standing in the mirror. The physical me has drifted from my self-image more than I thought. Pale fuzz growing out of her scalp. The chrome emitter plates are the same, but the skin has lost its nut-brown coloring—it is still dark, but with less color, somehow. The eyes are bloodshot. The lower lip has been gashed open by biting. The athletic frame with its hard planes of muscle is all too exposed now, with too little fat to add softness and curves. The hands are trembling, twitching, unsteady.

Behind her, the shower stall is huge, big enough for a gang of people engaging in acts other than just cleaning themselves. It fills with hot mist. The mirror's frame is heavy with gold.

"Stop ogling yourself and get to it. I don't know how long the hot water will last."

"I was just admiring the facilities," I call out.

The hot water does run out. It does not matter, I scrub myself hard, trembling and shivering when it turns icy. A plane of telekinetic force shaves away the stubble on my scalp. I try to search for the steel I thought I had found during those weeks in isolation when I had nothing to do but exercise body and mind, and eat, and sleep, and exist.

The towel is soft. Plush.

Her bedroom is in softer colors than I expected. Pastel shades on the walls.

Rose, lavender, maize, beige. There are paintings of tiny birds and lush, sexual flowers. Hummingbirds, I think, and orchids.

The underwear in Karla's dresser is surprisingly girlie, lots of delicate, lacy things in bright colors. I wonder if some lover of hers is out there, perhaps pinned under ruins somewhere, or if he is an Enforcer, burning people alive for wanting to know what has been determined, empirically, to be too dangerous to know.

I set out a functional sports bra and panty, and black slacks and coal turtleneck. A pair of her boots. *Touch* stretches out the materials, thins them out, enlarging them enough to fit. The colorless Information Security greatcoat just needs the sleeves extended an inch.

Another glance in the mirror. My eyes are alarming. A minute of searching through her things produces a pair of mirrored shades, and I put them on. The woman in the mirror still seems detached from me, but at least she looks competent now, almost dangerous, rather than like some fragile, brittle refugee.

I fill a duffel bag from her closet with more things. The woman has an extensive wardrobe, mostly deep, autumn colors that probably set off her pale skin. I pick out jeans, slacks, stretchy tops. I doubt there will be occasion to wear any of her ballroom gowns.

When I emerge into the dining room, a fragrant spread is on the table. Soft cubes of tofu in light soy, with leeks and onions. Fettuccine with bell peppers, tomatoes, olives, basil, and cream. Hot, toasted garlic bread. Glasses of wine. The plates beneath are made of lavender crystal, and beneath them is a pearl-white tablecloth of silk.

Now I just have to cross the yawning, ten-foot chasm between the end of the hallway and where the floor still remains. Looking down, I see that the hole goes down several stories, and the other way, it goes up to a crack in the rooftop, revealing the flickering sky of the Dome. I bridge it, reuse the material of the floor.

"Sit. Eat." She drinks, watching me as I serve out portions for myself.

"Aren't you going to—"

"No." She shakes her head. "You, however, need to force down as much as you can. You've got all the symptoms. Your body needs to recharge."

"Symptoms?" She must mean psi fatigue. Still, there must be over two thousand kcal worth of food on the table. "You can't expect me to finish all—"

"Eat it or I'll force you to eat it."

It is good, at least. But eating and drinking, under her steady gaze, while she explains further about ongoing Ministry operations, is unnerving.

She reminds me that there are yet more extreme measures if need be.

"They involve a lot of dying. So, Dempsey, we cannot fail."

Just as Archie enabled Barrens's anarchists to dig up all those widespread fragments of lost information, Karla wants me to use her to identify and locate their leadership.

"We will assault these kindergarten revolutionaries across every rat hole they've occupied throughout the ship."

The larger groups, the mobs, the intellectuals that had started to protest outside the administration offices, they are considered the lesser priority, still salvageable, for the most part. The physical isolation of the separate Habitat sections will be enough to keep them under control, for a time. If the agitators, the leaders, are taken out of the equation, something of a reset is still possible. Those worst affected by the highest doses of Psyn, the mutineers' foot soldiers will need psyche repair, years of therapy.

"What about the Council? The Bridge? Won't they be held hostage?"

"They are not permitted to allow themselves to be captured. They are already dead."

There is nothing I can say about that. Sorry? Oops? It is the same as everything else. "Can't we negotiate? I mean. . . ."

"They already know too much."

We discuss what I am to do. Or rather, she tells me her new requirements of me, my new orders. All the while, I eat. I am starting to understand and it is one more piece of too much.

Too soon, my stomach starts to protest.

"Keep going."

"I would rather not—"

Her eyes burn, bright green overlaying the pink. My hands move, under her control, not mine. "No, stop, I'll—"

Karla does not eat a bite herself. Though she does drink the wine.

She makes me wolf it down. I feel bloated, stretched out.

*Why?* I unicast her.

Karla's eyes are cold, and her voice is colder. "Haven't you noticed, Miss Dempsey? Weakness in the limbs? Nausea? A lack of appetite? Despite that, your talents remain." She tilts her head back, lets another mouthful of red slide down her throat. "It's not psi-burn you've got. You're dying, Miss Dempsey. Daily excess nutrient intake helps slow the process down."

Oh.

I should have guessed. But I did not want to. Do others know? Nobody has said anything. Maybe everyone looks this terrible, stressed-out, not enough food. I'm going to look a lot worse, and soon.

The part of Archie that is present in my head beeps in alarm; I sense her processes tapping into the life-signs applications on the neural Implant. I can't freak out and have Archie feel me freaking out. I need to be hard and not just for me. *Nothing you can do, Archie, if it's so. I was always going to die this way. Everyone does.* She lets go a long, mournful tone. I see her in my mind, shaking her head furiously. She shrinks down to a five-year-old, stamping her feet, mouthing, "No, no, no."

How long since attaining sentience has Archie been attached to me? Could she ever bond with anyone else?

*Hush. You promised to behave. You remember promises? You can't throw a tantrum, honey. Everyone's counting on you.*

Archie presses her lips into a thin line, grows out to twenty, grows out to my age in a moment, but she's still got my hair. She manifests a Doctor's red-trimmed white coat, marches off as she fades from my awareness.

In the meantime, the foreign push and pull on the muscles of my body is irritating. Karla has a firm grasp on my strings, her mind's projections overriding the impulses from my brain. Even my tears, or lack of tears, is up to her.

I demand, *I'll feed myself. I can do it. I have the will.* Get out of my head. I have always done what I had to do. I'll freak out on my own time.

Karla's mouth twitches. She seems . . . relieved? "Good. I am about as far from the psychological profile of a Keeper as an officer can get."

My hands, my mouth, my body, are my own again. I make myself eat, set aside the sensations of fullness. The food is good. It is. She is not without kindness, in her way, this stern, gray icicle.

"How much time do I have?"

"You seem to be one of the average ones, Dempsey. Three months. Maybe four. You probably have a month left before you start to come to pieces, and a month more where you are somewhat functional."

"That's not so bad," I manage. At least there is a little time, maybe even enough time to put things right.

Rice balls are chewed, barely tasted, swallowed down. The sensation to heave it all up goes back up to my brain; I clamp down on it. There is too much to do to be sick now. I can feel sad later. When I see Barrens again, maybe.

"You may be relieved to know, or not. Your team from City Planning is mostly all right. So are your friends. They will be brought in. We require all the help we can get."

Hennessy and the others! I haven't worried enough about them. But there was so much to fear already. "Thank you. They will make things more efficient."

"They had better."

I plaster on a smile. "They will."

I am dying. I want him to protect me. To tell me he'll stop it somehow. Keep me safe. Leon, I wanted so much more time with you. How will I tell him?

After I have gorged, we float back to the ground. Multiple transports await us, all different colors, the gray of Information Security, the Enforcers' black, the green of Behavioralists, the police blue. They are huge, armored insects. Rather than wheels, each one walks on six legs ending in great big claws.

The little man is there again. His bald head shines under the simulated noon sun. "We are ready for the move, Captain Waitani."

The sky flickers again, badly.

Karla turns to me. "Will you accept your duty, Dempsey?"

My throat is dry. Acid and mush push up from my stomach. I nod and brace myself. This will not be pleasant.

"Hana Dempsey is to be granted all authorizations befitting her new status, as ship's Executive Officer," Karla announces.

"Acknowledged."

My legs go out from under me, but somebody holds me up telekinetically. My head is a series of explosions coming in wave after wave, as another immense data dump is crammed into my head, leaving me retching, screaming. Karla takes control of my physiology again, to keep me from vomiting.

Long minutes pass as I feel more and more functions updating and expanding in my neural Implant. My brain is battered. Mind too large to fit in my skull. Cannot see. When I hear, it is as if I hear across a great distance, a canyon, echoing. I feel old memories being crowded out. I lose them. Names. Faces. How much of my childhood vanishes in the blink of an eye?

"Let's get moving."

"Yessir."

Cannot see at all. If it was bad when Karla Inducted me into ISec, this is ten, a hundred, times worse. Everything is pain. I am manhandled about, belted into a chair.

The convoy rumbles forward.

Archie returns. Subdued. She ties my mind into the transport's sensor suite, distracts me from the wreck of my mind.

It is beyond strange, feeling passengers riding in me. Feeling the mighty legs of the transport push forward. Did Archie do that because she thought it would make me feel better, because she guessed that I would want to see what's going on, or was it just a whim?

In the distance, there is a great flash of light. Then the sound comes. The claws of the transport dig into the roadway. The passengers cry out. The pressure wave almost knocks the insectoid tank over onto its back. Powerful *touch* talents hold it down. The sky simulation dies completely, and it is dark except for the arc lights firing up under and in front of the transport, stabbing out into the darkness. The pseudo-gravity dies too.

Rubble starts floating into the air. The tank's claws dig even harder into the street, and Karla herself lights up with power, keeping the vehicle from falling up into a black sky. She unleashes a ten-minute stream of profanity as she takes in damage reports.

The Archivists' separate cells have been spurred to action by the realization that Archie is no longer on their side. Somebody has set off a bomb under the Paris Habitat Section's life-support center.

Archie chirps slowly, little packets of data. Casualty lists. She stands in front of me. Looks at me.

*Yes. Those people won't be coming back.*

Karla blinks. She must have felt the flicker of my thoughts.

*Dempsey? You should have been knocked out by that. Best put you out myself before you fry what's left of your neurons.*

Sleep is no refuge from the pain. I do not know if it is an interaction of the Command upload and the disease, or if it is Archie messing with my Implant, but I am less susceptible to Karla's direct manipulation. I keep drifting in and out of consciousness. I am aware of yelling and cursing. Phantom sensations as ballistae rain giant spears against the armored hide of the transport, while Psyn-fired mutineers die in futility against the sheer power of the Enforcers protecting the convoy. More explosions. The deck shakes under the transport claws. Clouds of dust and smoke, boiling masses of black. Entire city blocks are torn loose from their foundations and drift through the air, burning. Mile-wide panels of illusion generators break away from the Habitat Dome. All the malfunctioning systems and psychic energy unleashed in the air looses uncontrolled weather into the city, churning thunderclouds, a whirlwind driving a hail of frozen ashes and rubble. Fire. Ice. Lightning. Darkness.

It blends into my nightmares. The classical hell described in old texts. The Prison City of our twisted children.

By the time I wake again, it has been two days.

I am still blind. It is permanent.

I know now that, normally, anyone receiving the Command memory module requires years of specialized preparation to prevent harmful side effects.

Karla can handle it because she was already being groomed for Command. It just came early for her, and to a much higher station than she expected.

As for myself, the too-rapid assimilation of data burned me. Some of my memories are gone—a void in some places, damage in others, blurry faces, missing names. Parts of the brain dealing with the senses are overwhelmed by a snarl of uncontrolled nanite growth from the Implant. Yet I can see. And I can hear.

Thousands of new programs populate the hardware in my head. They are available to me as streams of input and output, worlds of information. Including views and sounds of my immediate surroundings. I could lose myself in all that data if I am not careful.

Archie. Archie has done something to me in concert with the Command module.

While I am being moved, a statue floating an inch over the floor, a portly, gray-haired lady adds armor-plated epaulets to my coat shoulders, containing built-in amplifiers specialized for communications.

It is strange to see myself in the third person, a detached point of view that sweeps around all of us.

While I was asleep, somebody put a bandage around my head at the level of my eyes. It is stained red. They put the mirror shades I borrowed from Karla over the bandage. I guess it is less unnerving.

"I can walk," I croak out.

"Good."

Karla releases me. And I walk. The corridors light up in my head with ribbons of luminous orange datafeeds, pressure data, power consumption, structural information.

"Welcome home. You will oversee the formal integration of the Argus AI into the Noah's operating system."

"Right." Bile and blood on my tongue. A flicker of thought and my trembling legs are shored up by mental force. My powers have expanded, another effect of the changes to my Implant. I can feel the emitter plates scattered across much of my skin, including my scalp—it is a pattern related to the circuitboard web of chrome lines on Karla, but without the same detectable symmetry and order. I can see myself from multiple angles, as though the walls around us are cameras I peer through. Down my neck, organic splotches spread out in curving roots and branches, a rash of fruit or flowering buds branded upon me by malfunctioning nanobots. There is as much unyielding metal to me as familiar brown flesh. It continues on under my clothes, down to my toes and mirror-frosted fingertips.

I feel around my mouth with my tongue and two teeth come loose.

I am about to spit them out when Archie chirps at me to wait, and nanites anchor the teeth with silvery filaments of microrobotic tissue. That is not supposed to be possible. Archie has taken physical control of my Implant structure.

*You've been busy while I was knocked out, huh?*

I see a flash of Archie's thought. Thousands of copies of her, scanning through the medical research databases of the Ministry of Health. More of them, luminous ghosts racing from dormant Analytical Node to dormant node, searching for information about the Builders' nano-augmentation.

In just two days, Archie has made more progress with the Builders' nanites than has happened in the past fifty years of human study.

*Yes. Ah. Good, uh. Good job.*

I imagine giving her a hug, she looks so proud, so fierce. I can feel her wanting to hang on to me. I can feel her desire to fight. To keep me. It's an embrace of only information, but the sense impressions on my nervous system register a tight, crushing hug, a Barrens-level, you're-not-going-anywhere embrace.

I wonder how much Archie does not realize she can do. Could she eventually fix the damage to my eyes, or is that too complex? Even now, her growth seems to be accelerating.

Again, Karla fails to *read* my thoughts when it has to do with the AI.

She drones on about the requirements and specifications for the new Bridge being rushed through construction. There are no windows—we are outside of the Habitat but far from the exterior hull. The walls are angled out, solid slabs of steely gray. There is no paint or tinting. Antique filament-based lighting elements taken out of some emergency storehouse dangle from wires descending from the bare ceiling. Any third-year student in Class V Training could do better, but nobody has had time.

"I want this facility livable and at least moderately comfortable to work in within the week."

*Did you really promote me to XO because you need an interior decorator?*

The corner of her mouth lifts all of a millimeter. *Amusing. Be sure not to give me lip out loud where your subordinates can hear.*

My body stumbles. Thinking and talking and walking with my muscles is something I've done since I was a toddler, but thinking and talking on the Implant and walking using *touch* is something I have been doing for all of eight minutes.

I could just float my whole body along instead. I have so much psionic power now, it would be easier. But I stand out too much already for my comfort.

All this added power comes with a heavy cost. If I'd had the same training as Karla, the same preparation, would I have absorbed this sudden and heavy apotheosis with the same grace? She is almost unaffected, while I have significant neural damage, lost memories, and I'm blind. A difference in genetics, or training, or is it an interaction with the symptomatic phase of Mincemeat?

The large hall where the transports have stopped ends in a pair of double doors guarded by blue-coated officers.

Karla has not stopped giving me more tasks she wants accomplished *yesterday.* "We also need more water routed in, and more sewage capacity." And more food needs to be delivered, which means more cold storage is required, until a separate farm is established for the Bridge. More of this, more of that.

She halts and looks askance at me. *Are you tuning me out?*

*Of course not, ma'am.*

*Better not, Dempsey. I'm being so nice to you and all. I even have a little present for you.*

Walking again, our heels click across the bare floor.

*Where are we going, anyway?*

*Your new offices.*

The guards do not seem to be looking at anything, even as their eyes sweep back and forth, almost mechanically. They salute Karla and wave us through.

Two floors down, we open the doors to what will be my last home. The chamber is larger than I expected. The air is cold and musty, very, very old. I see my friends through the ship's sensors before they turn and see me. Warm arms wrap around me. I can smell her hair.

"Hana! Are you, are you . . . ?" She sees me. She understands. "Oh." Lyn cries against me softly.

"You look great too. Both of you."

A sigh. "I won't lie, boss. You look awful. The jacket is too grim for you." Hennessy can still get me to smile.

"I guess we don't have much time to chat and catch up. Let's get it done."

"Shouldn't you . . . Hana, don't you need a bit of rest? Or some food?"

It is too soon. I cannot take sympathy from them. If we pretend I'm not sick yet, then I am just fine. "I'm not an invalid yet. Chop-chop."

I am grateful, I guess. With Lyn and Hennessy around me, I do not have to pretend to be friendly with the other members of the team, those painfully young geniuses who still have so much time ahead of them. Time I do not have. My mood dips further. I know Barrens would be with me constantly if he could. So he cannot.

*Yes. Your man knows them best. There are certain things he can do for us faster than an Enforcer team blasting its way in.*

I want him. I want him terribly. I could cry and rage at being parted from him *again* after we promised we would not be, but it won't change reality, and it won't move Karla. It is what it is, and at least I have my friends smiling for me.

"Hennessy, I need a report on the status of the hardware and where we are with supplies, water, facilities for food prep, medical, you know what I'll need."

"On it." He starts jotting down notes on his tablet even as he makes his way out. This will be just like setting up a new living community. Knock down walls, build new ones, put in wiring, pipes, kitchens, heating elements, cooling elements, ventilation, ergonomic furniture, all the while considering layout, comfort, efficiency, and productivity. The other half of the work is logistics. Just like City Planning.

"Lyn." Just a brief moment of awkwardness. She's always had higher ratings than me in most ways. Except with the *touch,* which she never felt like learning to apply to anything outside of work. It does not feel right that she is my subordinate rather than the other way around.

I can guess that one of my tasks will be to train someone to replace me for when the symptoms become unmanageable. Nothing Karla does is accidental. She will want Lyn to have full control of Archie when I am "Retired." But will Archie let herself be controlled?

Her head grins, ghosts in and out of my perception, my own Cheshire cat of a girl keeping me company. If I live long enough, maybe I'll see her reach two years old.

Through the three-sixty view afforded by my sensor access, I see Karla standing behind me, watching us. She turns on her heel and leaves.

Lyn lets go and takes a look at me. Feels my discomfort. She crosses her eyes and gives me an exaggerated, comical salute. *Come on, Hana. It's okay. I'm here to help.*

A deep breath. It rattles in my chest. Maybe I just imagine that. The disease cannot be progressing *that* fast.

"Lyn, show me how far we are in setting up the officers' hard-line terminals."

"Not that far. This old bird is hideously complex."

We take our places side by side in front of a great mass of hovering displays in our heads. We are in school again, cramming for a project we slacked on until the last minute. There are lists of lists of things that must be done.

"Just like school," Lyn says. "We start at the top and work our way down. Hey, this time, we have underlings to boss around."

I actually have more underlings to boss around than anyone except for Karla. That would have been funny, once. Now it only underscores how big a job this is.

Over coffee and egg sandwiches, we prioritize and we delegate and we send out memos and read requests. The young programmers who "helped" me with Archie are now my gofers of choice. Soon, my first day of work on the job is almost over.

"You should sleep. Hotel Hennessy just opened for business, you know." Hennessy waves at the far wall, from which he has carved out a number of serviceable bunk beds.

I should sleep, it's true. Everything still aches because of the Command upload. But I have been sleeping all this time. Time I won't be getting back. Instead, I get started on scheduling the biggest job that needs to get done first.

Lyn and Hennessy groan, but that is the extent of their complaining. They send an orderly for even more coffee and settle deeper into their chairs next to me.

"You don't have to keep me company."

They both shrug. "While you're up, we're up."

The most important requirement for the installation's functionality is to program a new set of command terminals—specialized machines with instructions and codes for managing the reactor systems, the propulsion modules, grid control, life support, navigation—all vital functions that must respond to direct mental input from the Bridge officers. None of the technicians on the Bridge escaped, nor any of the Council. Most of the development notes for the software were classified and kept *on* the Bridge. They were deleted before the Bridge staff killed themselves, compelled by the Command module in their neural implants to ensure that the mutiny could not take control of the Noah for even a moment.

It occurs to me that Karla, as representative of the Ministry of Information, myself for the Interior, that nasty little paper-pusher Ortigas, who I believe rose up from Energy, and possibly Barrens, representing the Ministry of Peace, are now the de facto members of the new Central Council. The only one I don't know is whoever the warden of the Prison City is, under the Ministry of Health.

I mentally wave off Archie's desire to supply me with the man's face, all his records, his history. He has his own job to do.

Karla once more catches everything except for the part involving Archie.

*Yes, you are all Council now.* I can practically feel Karla sneering. *Now I just have to ensure that I am present when you tell your boyfriend that. I want to see the look on his face.*

*Trying to work here. Are you just dropping in on my head at random, or what?*

Two floors away, Karla cackles in the middle of briefing an assault squad.

We work until I pass out in my chair.


When morning comes, Hennessy bullies me into taking a shower.

Ah. It does feel good, even if it stings where all the fresh emitter surfaces on my body pushed through the skin. My last shower was at Karla's, but then there was the time it took to get here, and then I put in a whole day of work.

When I return, I jerk to a stop. One corner of the room is taken up by a whole team of medics unloading boxes. Monitoring equipment. Circulatory assist pumps, dialysis machines, a mechanical ventilator . . .

Hennessy hastily shoves his hands their way. Sky-blue partitions rise from the floor.

It is a nice thought. I guess he's forgotten that I see using the ship, so he hasn't really hidden them from me. He's seen what I have under the shades.

"Sorry, ah. They're for . . . You know. They're getting ready for . . . later."

"It's all right."

It is easiest to forget while I work, so I get back to it. And so do they.

Lyn sips some coffee, taps a space hovering in between us. It lights up, becomes an image of the main bus nexus that links the Analytical Nodes of this section's cluster. It does not look like much—just a pipe half a meter in diameter, cut open, packed full with translucent crystalline data-lines. By now, tablets are wired in awkwardly, and a dozen people are crammed into the space of a few broom closets, trying to re-create the programming of Earth's very best when they refitted this massive alien craft.

Another place, another job, another life. It still comes down to routines. Eating, sleeping, paperwork, workflows, analyses. It is the same. But I am not the same.

"I have our people working on critical functions first, life support, communications," Lyn informs me as she shows off the newer boards wired into the ancient alien terminals beneath. "At least with almost all of the mutineers up front of us, we've cut off their ability to talk to the ones still in the Habitat. Right now, we can't spare the staff to work on monitoring the Nth Web—it's the Wild West on the Network, with no policing."

Doing this the old way will take more days than I have left. It is time to show off what Archie can do.

"Prepare to be impressed."

I stretch my arms up over my head, pop my knuckles, and spend a mere thirty seconds to write out, in pseudo-code, a polite request to Archie to monitor the Habitat's virtual space for all communications by and between Archivists. Oh, and to handle all midlevel interface between officer commands and the ship's functions, pretty please.

With a happy ping of acknowledgement, all the status displays on the monitors in front of us and the hovering ones visible only in our heads flicker, and the colors of the characters and the frames change from monochrome orange to a dazzling array of subtle hues.

"What the heck! How are you—Oh. Wow."

Before us, we see a representation of the hundreds of thousands of data accesses currently occurring in the Habitat. All the stars in the sky. As the minutes pass, flowers of angry red bloom around clusters of points in the display, labeling which ones are under the direct use of the mutiny. And on every terminal display, simple graphical menus appear.

Lyn claps me on the shoulder, "Amazing. How did I ever score more than you in the programming tests?"

The speed of it shocks even me. I thought that would take Archie hours, not an instant. "Uh. Haha. You were just lucky, I guess."

With my eyes blocked off by bandages and reflective lenses, it is easy to hide my surprise. Lyn is a great mind and a better programmer, but understanding people is not her strength. She cannot tell how uncomfortable her naked admiration and envy makes me.

Come to think of it, that day of tests was on the day I was so stressed out from being late. A day when it seemed as if everything went wrong. Would things be any different if I had woken up on time that morning? Would I have made Officer Command? Would I perhaps even be in the exact same position that I am in now?

"Uh. Now, I'll just get a summary of those hits and send it off to Karla. What next?"

"Wow." Lyn shakes her head. I feel a bit bad. I'm cheating. I'm not nearly as good as she thinks. It's Archie. And Archie became like this on her own. Well, I guess I did help her along. I provided the seed, and the rest was the Builders, and the statistical bolt from the blue that caused Archie to self-organize from the chaos of my code mingling with that of the aliens.

Karla messages us with orders to disrupt all recruiting efforts, and to merely monitor communications that are between Archivists.

"So"—Lyn looks at me expectantly—"you going to impress me some more?"

"Sure." Archie makes it all too easy. And she likes this, impressing them, being useful and seeing up close the delight on people's faces.

After each completed job, there is something else to do. We have to trace the contaminated food stocks so that they can be removed from circulation and identify appropriate vectors for subtly administering antipsychotics to the entire population. We have to specify and delegate less immediate but just as important concerns to the multiple specialists we are in charge of. Getting life-support maintenance groups working again in the Habitat. Reestablishing basic services. Giving marketing and ad teams tools for handling propaganda to defang the seditious information floating around on the Net and to ease the fear and panic of the masses until the Behavioralists can get around to Adjusting everyone.

I am dying. I need to fill every moment with something. While we work, I work with music. When I rest, I read my favorite stories to Archie. When I sleep, I dream, and Archie is there.

Archie, forever eavesdropping on my thoughts, pings curious chirps into my auditory sense. That's right. Nothing is stopping me anymore. I brace myself, frame my desires into simple instructions, and ask her.

*Leon?*

*Who the . . . Hana!*

In a sudden, startling shift of perspective, Archie feeds me visuals of Barrens's immediate vicinity.

He is standing in an alleyway between two low brick buildings. Something in the way he is leaning in the shadows makes him seem less noticeable. He is wearing an ordinary tan coat, and it is raining. He looks perfectly comfortable there, immovable, strong, despite the water streaming down his face. Thick clouds of dirty, dust-laden mist blow along the streets, but at least there is gravity where he is.

*How are you talking to me? Aren't you on the new Bridge?*

*I am. Archie is helping out.*

*Wow.*

His face eases into a smile, for just a moment. Before it goes grim. Peering around the corner, his eyes narrow. His silhouette is outlined in faint red, nearly unnoticeable through the mist.

*Ah, Hana. I see my current assignment. I'll . . . I'll message you when I can. And Waitani said I can see you, after a couple more.*

He sends me a packet of emotions and sensory feedback. How it feels to him to hold me. The way I taste when he kisses me. The smell of my skin.

And I reply too. But I leave out how miserable I am, just as I know he is leaving out how terrible his "assignments" make him feel.

*Bye.*

*Bye.*

I could watch. He would not know. But he would not want me to see what happens next. Karla has made no secret of the assassinations Barrens is carrying out.

I ask Archie to drop the link and then think of better things through a sudden bout of intense pain that has me almost falling out of my seat, while Archie's image behind me jumps up and down in alarm. It passes.

*I'm fine. We knew this would happen, kiddo.*

That look again. Defiance. I sense her out there, thousands of copies of her processes searching, searching.

The hours turn to days and the headaches come and go. If I did not know I was dying, I would think it is from the mundane fatigue of work. Now, every discomfort and weakness seems to me another symptom, another sign of how little time I have left. As tempting as it is, I try not to have too many conversations with Barrens. It makes me ache, his not knowing what's happening to me. I need for that to happen in person. I need to be able to hold him when he finds out.

Another morning of going over reports and analyses and Lyn notices me swaying. "Gosh. Go take a break. I think I have a handle on how to talk to Archie now. I can do this and boss around the teams under Jordan, Hideo, and Melinda. Get something to eat. The real kitchens aren't staffed yet, but the supplies are three doors down from us."

I go. In the middle of opening up a can of unidentifiable processed pseudo-meat, I get a message from Hennessy.

*Hey, you. Report is ready. Where are you? Oh, no, no, darling. You're not eating that garbage. Let me fix something for you.*

*That would be lovely, James. Yes. Please. I'm tired.*

And all the while, Archie keeps the nanites spreading slowly through me. Fighting to keep me here, alive.

# 32

I KNOW I AM ASLEEP. I KNOW IT'S A DREAM BECAUSE I'VE GOT MY HAIR AGAIN, and I'm in that ridiculous dress from the Yule party, and laughing with my friends while we watch Web feeds of kids putting on a play. And Karla is here too, dolled up in a dress of black leather and bloodred. And there is Archie.

*Is that you, Archie, or am I just dreaming you up?*

Mischievous smile. She becomes seventeen, flickers into a dress of silver sequins and lamé, a dress I couldn't afford at that age but wanted. Sticks her tongue out at me, mimes drinking from the glasses of mead that are everywhere.

Huh. Because of the Implant, lucid dreams are much more concrete and pliable.

*Let's ditch this party then, and play!*

I am still asleep. And then Archie pulls a part of my consciousness along, into the Nth Web. She takes me to a great big chamber full of recycled plastech ingots.

*Let's see what we can do together, Archie!*

Archie and I play. We create. Cities rise out of the ingots, floating castles in the sky. I could have done them without Archie, but Archie adds ten thousand tiny moving men and women striding back and forth, sitting, talking, playing in the cities I've made.

*Too bad there isn't a beach here.*

Then Archie blows my mind completely and manifests sand underneath us, and water, and waves, and a blue sky and the sun. That's . . . not plastech manipulation.

Some have managed that while hopped up on Psyn, their consciousness twisting reality for all of the brief seconds before their brains died from over-dose and psi-burnout.

Archie can do it and sustain it.

*It's lovely, really it is. But we should stop. That's got to be using so much power.*

She is a good child, she is. She pouts, but undoes the psychic manifestation anyway, puts away our toys.

I need to think long and hard about how much more Archie will be able to do.


"Up!"

I hear Karla loud and clear.

The bed is not warm enough. I never feel warm enough now. My mouth feels and tastes foul. Thrash around under the sheets. Feel trapped. Confined.

Again, Karla moves me around, like a doll. Blankets off. On my feet. My internal chronometer announces that I have been asleep for six hours. The deck sensors let me know that most of the Bridge staff is asleep.

How many more times will I wake up?

A rush of fear gets me gasping, hyperventilating. I'm going to die. Archie is with me, and she feels the fear too, and she plays music she thinks might soothe me, reminds me of our playing games in my room.

Time is running out for me and I can't waste it.

*Thanks, Archie. I'm fine now.*

Karla starts to drive my body, make me stand.

*Captain Waitani, get out of my head! I don't need this!*

She looks at me, quirks a peculiar smile. "Very well."

We eat in the private kitchenette Hennessy built into my offices. By now, he has made up several chairs just the way I like them, with that curve that prop-erly supports my lower back, and not too plush in the seat.

The food in front of us is hers, not Hennessy's. He is still sleeping in his own bed, now that he's finally had time to make proper bedrooms for himself, Lyn, and me. A salad with onions and cherry tomatoes and crumbly white cheese and peppers and orange slices, porridge with honey, coffee that is thick and syrupy. It is almost too good. She ought to have been a cook, not one of the thought police.

Next, to the bathroom. Hennessy has made up a separate, larger one for me. I practically have a hotel suite in my workplace. It twists in me again, the awareness of death. That giant shower is that size not for luxury, but because in the future assistants will have to help me for everything, when I can no longer help myself. I want to rush through as much as I can, yet I also want to feel it all and take it slow and savor the passing moments of being alive.

When I brush my teeth, at least my gums do not bleed now that I've switched to softer bristles. Doing it with *touch* would cause just as much damage, and a brush takes less effort. Yes. No taste of blood. I am still alive. I'm okay.

I strip off my borrowed clothes and shower while Karla's presence stalks back and forth outside. She is setting aside clothes for me. By the time I pull on fresh underwear and a gray business dress, I am about as steady as I can be for another day.

"Why are you doing this?"

"Don't read anything into it. I have to keep you functioning until we don't need you anymore. You're a limited-duration investment, and we need as big a return as we can get before you Retire."

Archie stands behind her, sticking her tongue out.

Right.

The main chamber of the rooms allocated to me is dominated by the over-size XO's terminal in the center. As I sit in the padded throne Hennessy is particularly proud of, I move my point of view through the ship's systems. I look at Karla's reflection in the powered-down screens, I look at her from above, from behind, from the side.

She is older than me. Without her makeup, I can see that she must be in her forties or so, despite the trim, hard figure that can only be the result of many hours of dedicated physical training and good nutrition. It is in the faint lines around her eyes and mouth. It occurs to me that she must have gone through Breeding Duty at least once already. What was it like for her? Did she also feel that hollow sadness that gripped and clutched deep inside? Did she need medication too? How much worse was it for her knowing that her child would be one of *them*?

I reach out with my thoughts and log in to the terminal. As the cooling fans hum to life and the screens flash and flicker, I am distracted, wondering about her. What was the color of her skin before it was bleached by the appearance and growth of her powers? What were her eyes like?

Lyn and the gofers have gotten the Bridge terminals all hooked up, interfaced with Archie and humming. There are proper kitchens now, a long, broad hall that serves as the barracks for most of the Bridge staff, a mess hall, a great big industrial laundry, a library, a gym, garages for the vehicles. Hennessy has finished construction of the vertical farm, but it will still be months before all the crops are planted and the livestock is delivered and we become self-sufficient.

My major duties shift to something I can do better than anyone else: working with Archie. What will help bring an end to all this is surveillance, intelligence.

So while my friends deal with their subordinates and all the work it takes to repair the damage in the Habitat and return some normalcy to the ship, I spend my days teaching my AI girl to spy on the Archivists, predict what they will do next, and point out potential targets.

Archie already likes to watch people, now that she has learned more about imaging and how people see. The tougher lesson is how to explain which people and what activities need watching, and the reasons why.

I could type about as fast using my mind's *touch,* but just now, I indulge in the use of my fingers. Who knows how much longer I will have them all? The old-style hardware keys clack and click. Something about the sounds is reassuring.

Behind me, Karla is a silent presence, watching.

"Talk to me, please. It's rather irritating if you're just standing there."

"You need to concentrate. What you're doing could be a difference of thousands of casualties."

"I won't be distracted. I'm just curious. Tell me about yourself."

I do not see her sneering. But I can imagine it. "What do you want to know?"

What do I want to know? Why do I want to know? "Anything, I guess."

"Hmph. Beethoven. Brahms. Bach. Hendrix." She rattles off the names of composers and musicians across time, across history. She thinks to me slices of time. Like me, she is a devotee of Thelonius Monk. Herself seated at a piano. Her fingers arched just so. The feeling of ivory under the tips. Days of music.

One moment of rage. Her birthday. The other children around her floating, crying, hysterical. The plates with the food exploding, shattering.

And then, tests. Test after test, administered by men and women in green coats. Audio of her eavesdropping on the discussions between her Keepers and the Behavioralists that kept coming back to evaluate her.

Injections. Pills.

The deep brown of her skin fading as she got paler and paler.

A stolen kiss, some boy, just before she was taken away.

She keeps telling me the story that way, flashes of memories, while she recites dates and times, facts, the names of the people she met. Brutal training.

Headaches that reduced her fellow OCS candidates to tears. Days spent paralyzed as the tissues of her brain swelled up, changing. Therapy. Relearning how to stand, to walk. She never regained the ability to play the piano—the reflexes are gone—but she does learn how to paint.

Time reels by while I play my own music in my head. Setting Archie to work I never designed her for. Building up an expanded code of conduct and ethics—I would like for her to understand when *not* to watch people too. This is a true bond. Archie has emerged, developed autonomy and adaptability, true sentience, and what am I doing? Tinkering with the bits and pieces of her personality and memories, Adjusting her to behave as will best benefit the Noah.

Every eight hours, someone makes me stop working. Sometimes it is Lyn. Sometimes it is Hennessy. They feed me, remind me to bathe, medicate me to sleep. Sometimes, there is a message from Barrens; the memory of a kiss, the great big bonfire of everything he feels for me. And then I keep going.

My awareness of the seconds ticking away never goes away. The chills. When I next take off my shoes, I prepare myself for the possibility that my toes might not all be there. Always, Archie is working the nanites, converting organics to inorganic, filling in dead cells with silver circuitry.

The Doctors attending to me are astonished by what's going on with my nanites. I don't let them examine me often, and Karla's primary concern is ending the chaos on the ship, not catering to the whims of Doctors who want to study a strange case of nanite mutation in someone who's dying anyway.

Out there, Barrens is hunting down his old friends. He is now an ISec weapon, just as Miyaki was when she was sent to assassinate him. It must be killing him, inside.

As though summoned by my thoughts, he returns, stomping in through the corridors. I think of him all the time, and it took him a week to make it here. He strides in by the guards and checkpoints, muttering and cursing as he strips off his bloody coat and gloves.

I am tempted to lock the last set of doors between us. He has not seen what's happened to me yet. He doesn't know. It suits Karla to make sure he doesn't know, until he finally sees me.

This is that moment.

It would be easy to hide. Open a hole in the wall, step through, and close it behind me.

He stops when he sees me. Says nothing for a long time. His breaths are puffs of mist; Hennessy has programmed the environmental controls to drop the air temperature wherever I am. The Doctors tell us that it will slow down the progression.

"Uh. We'll just . . . let you two talk. Yes." Hennessy rises from his station in the corner, almost physically drags Lyn out of the room.

Archie leaves too.

Seeing through artificial sensors robs me of the sense of looking straight into Barrens's eyes. Only now do I feel cheated by my blindness. Otherwise, the vision from so many angles, with zoom even, is superior.

"Hi. How was your mission? I've been . . ." Talking gets tiring. I am too nervous not to. It spills out of me, mundane chatter about the work I am doing with Lyn, the food Hennessy has been plying me with, the little touches I have been decorating into the furniture of my quarters to remind me of home. "Karla's been cooking for me too, sometimes. You should try her primavera."

Barrens glides close. He pulls off the shades. His trembling fingers trace the silver lines up my cheeks. His touch stops short of the bandages wrapping around my head and over my eyes. I press harder into his touch. Medics have coded routines into my Implant that reduce the pain and the cold, fooling my nervous system. I override them now, so that I can feel the chill in the air, and the warmth of his hands. The dull aches along my spine sharpen and lengthen into needles puncturing all the way through me. It is worth it.

Running out of things to say, and out of breath to say them with, it fades out of me on "I missed you."

"Me too. It's . . . it's a different look for you."

"Yeah."

He clamps down on the subtle movements of his facial muscles. "Haven't they been feeding you?"

*Leon. Leonard. I'm . . .*

We are still and silent. I imagine he is racing through his memories. Beyond the distracting flash of all the new metal on me, something is familiar in the slow way I am moving, in the hollowness of my cheeks. When he glances down at my hands, the pads on the fingertips that have not been chromed are bruised from the pressure of my typing. Under the nails that remain, the skin is red and purple.

It happened so much faster with Meena, but if he plays it back at a fraction of the perceptual speed, or checks the documentation from the ISec data package, there is only this.

Please. I want to waste as little time as we have left with tears. *Read* me, you big oaf. You don't have the talent, but you know me.

Barrens swallows. He pulls me out of the chair and embraces me, softly, softly. His voice rumbles in his chest, vibrates into me. "Let's get something to eat, okay? I want my turn, cooking for you."

He tries a smile. It fits how I feel. Just this side of brittle.

"Okay." Kissing him feels as if it will bruise my lips too. I suppose one good thing about all the nanite encrustation on me is that it conceals the bruises.

As we walk, side by side, he seems afraid to hold me, and I will not have it. I grab his great big rocky fist and squeeze hard. *Don't change the way you touch me. Not yet.*

He does his best. He has little of Karla's refined skill or Hennessy's intuition and creative use of ingredients, but simple, hearty, tasty food, he can handle.

For a while, I try to help with preparing ingredients and things in the small kitchen for the officers, but my fingers, my wrists—my whole body is stiff and ungainly with all the nanofiber running through it. The joints ache after a few minutes, and then I give in and use my talent instead. Celery and carrots and onions hover in the air over the pot and split themselves before jumping in. Salt and pepper shakers float and dispense a dash here and a pinch there. Mason jars open, bay leaves and thyme dance by.

"You're supposed to be letting me take care of you," Barrens grumbles as he sears a cut of synthetic meat in a pan.

And you will. "I want to do this with you, while I can."

The stew is good. We eat as much as we can stand. We sleep. And in the middle of the "night," we open our eyes and look at each other. Hunger is tempered by tenderness as we move, slowly, together. I dial down my anesthetic routines all the way, and if my nerves are afire with pain signals informing my brain of the slow deaths of my organs, there is still this pleasure, the stretching of tissues, the swell and pressure and friction of being alive, and the touch of our emotions. It is better than programs and drugs, and for a while I can forget and hold on to that ephemeral bliss. It is a snow fort built against sorrow: an instant of denying death.

He leaves in the morning, with a kiss, and a muttered curse. "More orders. She . . . says she will try to give me a little more time with you." His hands flex and clench, and the openness of his eyes shutters itself behind a lost resolve. "I'll . . . I'll see you."

"I'll be waiting."

Karla has new assignments for me too. She unloads all of the lesser work I was doing onto Lyn and Hennessy, who are getting accustomed to working with Archie. My AI girl is still an "it" to them, sometimes alarming and strange in her responses. They are slower than I am with her, but they still get it done.

Once Archie seems reliable enough to Karla, based on the quality of the reports Archie produces on potential Archivist activity in the Habitat and on the movements of the armed masses in the unmapped zones, my abilities are tasked to ending the conflict.

I am not to participate directly in the physical battles being fought over the halls and corridors and geography of the ship.

There are other battles, however. There are skirmishes on virtual ground, in the Nth Web, where Archie's swarm subunits are my soldiers, and I, the general, direct them against the Archivists' lesser, copycat AIs; and of course, there is my personal combat, within. Those battles are not battles at all—a cloned process of Archie's can step on the carefully crafted machine learning viruses like bugs and stamp them out.

Barrens sends me little packets of thought and emotion throughout each day. The way he felt when he saw me again after my Breeding Duty. The disbelief when he first kissed me. The wonder, when he first touched me and I touched him back. Rarely, he sends me a new memory that is happy, on the rare occasions he is able to turn one of the Archivists to us.

As Archie integrates more and more into the underlying, alien software of the Builders, the ship and my body seem to converge. I was already blind. Then, I am deaf, listening through sensors the same way I see. Then the pain starts to get so terrible the required pain-relieving meds and programs make my physical self fade away, as my interactions with the outside world go more and more through the ship instead.

The power Archie directs toward the nanomachines of my Implant compensate as more and more of the cells in my body die at random. Where muscle and bone and membranes and soft tissues fail, the silvery substance fills in the cracks, glues me together, substitutes for failing biological functions. Blood volume stays the same, cells and proteins replaced by catalytic superfluids and janitor robots. The days pass and the flesh diminishes.

And I forget things. At random. While dying brain cells can be replaced by the artificial connections and processors of the nanobots, transferring the memories from wetware to hardware is not perfect in that moment of death. Sometimes, one sense or another in a distant event of old just vanishes. Sometimes, they are confused. Colors might change or sounds or textures or tastes. The first rose I received loses its smell. My first kiss has no face. I might forget an item in the list of things I have to do. Ah, well. I had already lost so much to the Command upload, I do not even remember how much I have already forgotten.

Will I be able to tell when my mind is not a mind anymore and is only a computer?

Or in the end, will my consciousness be indistinguishable from the ascendance of Archie's virtual thoughts?

## 33

IT NEVER STOPS. MY BODY EATS ITSELF. THE NEXT TIME MY LION RETURNS TO
me, I can see my degeneration reflected in his eyes. He is already grieving.

Karla was wrong. I may not be going as quickly as Meena, but my decline is
faster than in "the average case."

Barrens comes and goes, and too soon even the gentlest kiss bruises me,
even the softest caress.

By now, it takes a small army to keep me going. They try not to look at me
directly or touch me, except for Lyn and Hennessy, who always put a hand on
my hand or touch my shoulder, my wrist. My attendants are repulsed; it is all
they can do to treat me like a busted machine. If I am human, it is a reminder
that their lives too will end in pain and suffering.

Every time he returns, Barrens takes a deep breath, as is his way, and throws
himself into being what I need. He sets aside the grim, bloody mantle of being
an assassin and all his doubts and pain, so that he can smile when he looks at me.
He joins my friends in helping me to eat. They tell me stories. Listen to mine.
They do not seem to care that the woman they knew is being replaced, little by
little, transmuted to plastech in the form of mirror-shine chrome, pearly-metal
alloys, and coal-black composites.

I am a sight, I know. I see better than they can, through optical diodes and
sensors in multiple spectra of light and radiation. A slender figure. A woman in
shape. She is naked, but does not seem to be because so little exposed skin is left
to see. Wires and tubes project out of her spine, out of the base of her skull. The
bandages on the eyes have come off—they are there, just spheres of crystallized
protein and nanites: petrified tissue.

Karla and a half dozen of the most skilled Behavioralists tinker with my friends' perceptions, condition their fear responses downward, increase their empathy and the effects of far-off sentimental memories from when we were young. Karla does not tell me, but I watch it happen. Walls have no meaning to me anymore.

She does not do the same for Barrens. What does she think of his struggle not to break apart in front of me? I watch her watching our private moments in her head: Barrens reading to me, or when he nerves himself up to carefully, carefully lower his great bulk onto my bed, trying not to disturb the plethora of cables, wires, and tubes, so that he can hold me while he sleeps.

When I speak, I rarely do so with this failing body's diaphragm, voice box, and mouth. It is easier and less painful to speak through the organs of the ship, thoughts transmitted through the Network.

When I move, it is not with muscles and tendons acting on bones. My mind calls on the ship's gravity simulators to lift me and float me along—our artificial gravity, after all, is merely the result of gigantic psi amplifiers projecting a telekinetic field along the vector the Builders chose to use as "down."

All the while, Archie grows geometrically, her tendrils adapting more of the previously untapped might of the alien computers spread throughout the vastness of the Noah. I am aware of the ebb and flow of power and data and gravity and light and air and water.

I watch the real-world battles from afar, with the ship's eyes; I listen with countless biomechanoid ears.

Is it all illusion? The life and death of each individual organism is tragic only in the context of the small, only by locality, only by how many relationships are severed. But I can feel what the Noah feels, and there is so much more than that. I am a vastness contained, swimming through the ocean of space-time. I see the light of dead stars, shifted up to blues in front of me and down to reds behind.

Canaan beckons in the distance. The computations are clear. Eight hundred and twelve years more, according to the original calculations. It is now even farther away in time than that because all these disturbances are using up the ship's reactor mass at an increased rate—which means that the possible acceleration the psychic propulsion drive can accomplish at the end of the journey has decreased. We will have to start the deceleration many years earlier now, to prevent the Noah from overshooting our destination. It will be a slower journey overall, which means even more time for a cramped, limited population in this closed space, the collective psyche of which will require tighter controls, more drugs, more psychological manipulation, to push down the aggressions and conflicts and unfulfilled desires of humans and their caged lives.

A black spot remains in my senses, part of the mental blocks set into place to prevent me from knowing the last secret. Something is attached to the ship—something not originally part of the Builders' design. I am not permitted to see it or interact with it. A mass, a misshapen tumor, disrupting the sinuous lines of the ship.

I have traced out the edge of where the built-in security of the Command upload will respond. Archie has mapped it out. I think, if I chose, I could pull it away and look and know.

It won't help anyone though, knowing. It won't change anything.

So I choose not to undo that part of the ISec conditioning. If I change my mind later, I believe it would take Archie all of a second's work. She knows it already.

I think about secrets often. A secret that could make too many people give up. We've already got so much destructive behavior with Mincemeat's disease progression and the effects on our children. I am starting to come around to Karla's point that it would not take a secret much worse than that to tip the balance.

It is hard enough living on the ship and carrying out the mission. The confinement, the testing, the ironclad roles we are shoehorned into for the rest of our lives.

Homeostasis on the ship is so much more fragile than I had thought.

Archie continues to mature. She often pings to get my attention, shows me things just to see how I react. She processes old movies, requests clarification about human behavior, asks me to elaborate on the taste of cold water. In her way, Archie is also making the best of the time we have left.

Time ticks unstoppably. The body continues its prolonged death. The boringly practical facilities of the Bridge take shape. More conference rooms, offices, bathrooms, barracks, recreation rooms, gyms, training rooms, data centers, planning rooms, kitchens, mess halls, armories, the specialized manufacturing centers that produce Enforcer armor and assorted ISec and Behavioralist amplifiers.

In the here and now, I lift a coffee cup to my lips.

The hot fluid slices through the oil and fat left behind by the fried tofu and onions and eggs that Lyn brought to me for breakfast. Archie chatters in my thoughts, tries to eavesdrop on the signal data from my tongue and mouth, tries to interpret information. The inside of my mouth too is being converted to nanites. I will not have taste for much longer.

Hennessy insists on fixing my makeup. It is probably more like painting a mask made of metal. I let him because it comforts him, and me, even if it only emphasizes the differences between what I am and everyone else.

In the distance, kilometers toward the bow, my love's former followers are killing, and being killed.

The battlegrounds are fluid. The walls, the floor, the ceiling, all these things are plastech and respond to will and fury, exploding, melting, reforming, becoming sword, becoming shield, cannon, bunker. But the original structure of the ship, that which the Strangers made, is vastly tougher and more resistant to change. Those ancient, armored ellipsoid compartments, ranging in size from a hundred meters across to kilometers in diameter, are joined up with adjacent halls by the relatively narrow power and data shafts and air locks. There, the fighting is fiercest.

The Archivists took the original command deck, but all those control systems have been locked out. They are trapped in the forward compartments. And their supplies, the food they brought with them and the emergency stores for the Bridge staff, are running out. Their only chance is to break out of the envelopment. Some surrender. Most throw their lives into the fire.

Each time Barrens comes back to me, he is paler. During the meetings in which the top officers discuss after-action reports of encounters between the mutineers and our Enforcer-led militia, he says nothing. When we are alone, he rages in furious whispers about the madness of his old friends.

"What are they doing? They're wasting all these lives. It's over!" He turns haunted eyes to me. "Was I like them? Ignoring consequences because of ego?"

I can only kiss him.

He shakes off these black moods as soon as he feels my cool, metallic lips. "Sorry. Sorry."

He falls into restless slumber. There is no sleep for me anymore. The body shuts down for a few hours but the mind enters a murky half dream. Through Archie, I am always present on the Network, awake or not.

Bright purple pings like bell chimes echo on the map of my awareness, luminous orange arrows drawing my attention to one figure whose silhouette is lit up with a white halo.

My attention zooms in there, at gate 19E. A battle is going on even now.

This night, ten Enforcers lead 1,012 Adjusted men and women in a fight over one of the great tunnels.

One Enforcer spreads his arms to the sides and claps them forward. Lightning ripples up from the power coils in the floor. The floor breaks up, becomes a wave of death rushing toward the attackers, and as it crests and approaches them, it changes form, becomes a swarm of razor-blade locusts.

An Archivist who pops his head up at the wrong time is shredded to pieces. Beside his headless corpse, in the trench they have carved out, four more die as the glowing, guided projectiles curve down and dance through their meat.

Others in a foxhole two meters back retaliate, aglow with *touch*—they reach out with their minds, and the life of the man that sent out the flight of tiny flying slivers is itself ended when his squadmates lose control of the ridge that is their cover, and the floor swallows him up, crushes him.

The ship's sensors fill my head with the sound of his bones cracking, pulping.

Other Enforcers cut loose with psychic flames. A hundred lives are erased in a second. The power fluctuates in that section. Life support stops. Everyone starts to float up in zero gravity—those with *touch* hold themselves and their squaddies down behind the cover of their trenches and foxholes.

*No.*

I'm sick of the killing. Why won't it stop? There are so few of us left.

*Take me there, Archie.*

My awareness shifts. And here, I am here. No body, but I see the fighting all around me, smell the blood, the cooked-meat smell of burned men.

I test a trick I have only begun to explore with Archie. I spread part of my consciousness into the closest Analytical Nodes and take control. I need the processing power. My perspective flickers, splits, and—

It takes long seconds to focus through the cacophony of my thoughts, to unify the extra pieces of me in the system. Yes. I am here.

*I too,* echo the parts of me in the Nodes. Process ghosts of me.

Everywhere I can, I try to save those who can be saved.

Above, the strongest soar through the air on curving shields of armor torn loose from the floor, raining a hail of glowing blue bursts of ionized gas down. On the other side, the Archivists have less skill, but they have the raw power and viciousness born of Psyn. By this time, those who have not been driven mad by the drug have attained heights of ability that allow them to push and prod their less sane comrades, manipulating them like puppets.

Some *writers* wave their hands and dig their talons into the synapses of their victims, putting them to sleep or setting them to fight their own, and my *other* selves in the system block their thrusts, restore the victims to themselves. *Bruisers* dance through the danger, dealing death with their red-sun fists, and another me floats their feet free of the deck, holds them up where they are helpless. *Touch* talents with no fear of overloading the power grid push more and more psychic energy into trying to catapult boulders cracked from the deck plating, shaping them into grapeshot and fléchettes, and I undo them too, catch the projectiles and render them harmless.

The loss of control by a handful of synchronized Archivists releases a backlash of energy, a whirling tornado of force and heat, air currents sucking up oxygen and burning people from the inside out when they breathe of the flame.

All my selves reach out and burst a water main, creating a barrier of cold, near-freezing water to hold the flames back from our own defenders. The flames splash against it and off it. On the other side, there is a white-hot hell—those caught in it do not even have time to scream.

Archie is entranced by the fire. And at the same time, I feel her phantom fingers closing tightly around mine, back on the Bridge, in the clean light of my offices, as she sees the casualty figures, detects their lives being snuffed out as their implants fail.

The flames die down, but the fighting goes on. Flickers of psychic lightning in the dark. Rubble being thrown back and forth. *Bruisers* roaring, animals swinging massive cudgels, cutting others in half with the power of augmented muscle. The deep-bass rumble of explosive bursts of power. The shrieking whine as psionic soldiers attempt to snuff them before the plasma balls strike their targets. In the zero gravity, body parts float free, globules of blood, vomit, urine. It's hard to keep track of which side is which even with my abundance of sensory feeds and the parallel processing of supercomputers extending my human limits.

Somebody is crying, huddled up in a ditch. I pull shields up over him and open a path for him, a narrow tunnel back toward the Habitat. Some of the floating wounded I pluck like sheets of paper floating on the wind and fly them toward the rear, where the medics are.

*Stop that,* Karla thinks to me. *Let them take care of themselves. You need to focus on the big picture.*

It is analysis that she wants out of me. Analysis, intelligence. Doesn't the woman sleep?

I pull back, back into my body, next to Barrens. In the confines of this wasting flesh, this dull pain, the weakness, the nausea, I almost jerk back out into the system. But I don't, though I do leave those digital aspects of me there, in the fight. It hurts, seeing them dying, knowing each one is a line that ends forever, a diminishing of far-fallen mankind. I have to try what I can, and nobody else can do this.

In the map room, Karla paces back and forth, watching the displays showing the same battle I am watching. She thinks I am done, she doesn't notice the parallel Hana emulations still trying to save people, one crewman at a time.

Karla stops and looks up to the ceiling, messages me, *That little stunt of yours. How much longer before you can close away entire sections of the ship? We could just cut off life support to them, wait them out.*

*I do not know. I can do it already in some places, but these large chambers and halls, they're made of the Strangers' ultrahard, crystallized plastech, the bones of the ship itself. I'm afraid of messing with them; I might damage the Noah and not be able to fix it.*

Karla winces as another precious Enforcer falls.

She doesn't feel another me cocoon away a boy that put up his hands, an Archivist crying out his surrender. Every little life counts.

She goes on thinking to me, *Well. We never thought we'd have that option in the first place, in the old plans. I'll commission a feasibility study. When this is over.*

She leans in closer to the display, taps a red dot indicating one of her squad leaders. She squints, sends him orders. I could listen in on it, but do not.

She places her hands on the projection and brings it closer, zooming out. She examines the three-dimensional mess of the ship's structures, and the clouds of dots indicating the presence of Archivists. She rotates it this way and that and shakes her head. This is something else the previous Ship's Captain could never have imagined.

*Dempsey, whenever Thorn tries a major attack like this, it's always to cover for something else. Use our favorite new toy and find out what it is.*

In my bed, Barrens rolls away in his sleep. I use telekinetic force to lift my man closer, back to me, and I hold him tight, even if it hurts to do so.

I have grown beyond where Karla can read my thoughts. Either too much of my brain is now electronic, or perhaps the way I can migrate some of my thinking and personality onto the ship's computers makes my thoughts too different. Or Archie is shielding me even further, now that she is starting to understand something about the concept of privacy.

I can safely ponder the likelihood that Archie and I have become something more than Karla expected. She is starting to fear us, but she still needs us, and it will be a relief to her when I die. She's finally started listening to my Doctors, who are insisting that I am dangerous, that my nanites are infected with something else beyond Mincemeat. It would make their fears even worse to know that it's not some random mutation, but the influence of the AI on my body. But she still needs me too much to lock me away in quarantine.

Archie puts Karla's request together faster than it takes me to explain the request to Archie.

Far away, parts of me are crying because someone in front of us has been torn apart. We can taste the blood soaking into the cracks of the deck. But they, I, we, keep trying.

I report, *From the pattern of assaults, Thorn's group is feinting to try to draw us into attacking here, and here.* The message is packaged with a data stream showing a simulation generated by Archie and me—blue dots being pursued by the red into the fore-section, along the biggest shafts. *Power is fluctuating at these points*—I place green crosshairs on the image—*suggesting that when he has drawn enough of us in, they can trigger perhaps a bomb of some sort to kill off that raiding force.*

Karla sees it, nods to herself. *Then we shall strike exactly where he hopes we cannot do so. See? You saved hundreds of lives with a bit of intelligence. Now, get some sleep.*

But I don't. The battle finally ends and I pull myself fully back into one place, and the headache is terrible. Memories overlapping from more than one point of view. Magnified emotions. I don't think that's a trick I'll be trying again soon.

I need to do more. I must. Or there is no reason for my coming to this, no purpose to the sacrifices of those who have been lost.

I teach Archie some of what I was trying to do in that fight. Unlike me, her consciousness was designed around being able to split off trains of thought, threads of processing effort. She can be in every place, in every battle, making a difference. Though not too big of one, or the power drain on the grid will be too much. . . . And at the same time, we can't let Karla find out just how much Archie can do completely independently, including manifesting psionic power through the ship's structure without any human input at all.

Aside from all the other burdens assigned to me, I take on the nearly undecipherable mass of information in the aliens' archives. Not that I can understand more than the barest fraction of it even with Archie's help.

---

My appetite diminishes. A month into the symptomatic phase, I cannot eat anymore, and my meals consist of a continuous drip of white nutrient sludge going directly into the remnants of my veins.

Still, when he is here, Barrens smiles for me. When my nausea is not too bad, he might lift a spoonful of broth to my lips or a chip of flavored ice.

A false dawn rises. Many of the halls and rooms of the Bridge now have sky-simulation apps running, even if it is only through a fake window. It helps. Back in the Habitat, order is almost restored.

He sits next to the half platform, half chair in which I am wheeled around. Around us, the machines protest at the feedback they cannot interpret from my changing body.

"You look happier." I can project my "voice" out of any object I desire. Converting things into speakers is easy.

"Happier? No. I have stopped regretting, that's all."

Cameras shift and zoom in on his face. "Oh?"

He shrugs. A jumble of his thoughts rides the current into my head, about personal responsibility and atonement. No talent for telepathy still, but weighed down with fatigue and strain, Barrens's thoughts jumble and leak as he uses his Implant to message me, flashes of emotion and sense impressions riding on the words. *I'm at peace because we'll finish it, you and I.*

Another battle occurs close to the Archivists' last strongholds.

The lines return as Barrens grimaces and frowns. Karla is in his head again. He glowers and protests at every mission. He does not want to leave me. We know, the three of us, that my time is almost up.

"Do I gotta—

"But—"

We both know how it will end. He could let himself get wound up. Get so upset that his hands tear through the doorknob on his way out, his footsteps denting the floor. But still, he will do it.

He cannot walk away.

"All right, all right! I'm going," he exclaims up to the air. "This is the last one!"

Barrens kisses me again. Each one carries shadow and light, the bitter taste of not knowing if I'll still be here when he returns.

"Be seeing ya," he whispers.

*Hey.*

*Ya?*

*What I feel for you—*

*Yes. Me too.*

And he is gone once more.

My condition starts to accelerate within an hour of his departure.

My heart reaches 50 percent artificial components. My body is half-fused into what has become the throne of my dreams, the seat at the center of the world. All glittering metallic surfaces, smooth except for the cables and tubes for nutrients and waste and data and power that have spread head to toe, I see the looks the others cannot help when they see that body: indifference, as though I am just another system terminal. It becomes harder every day to tell if I am a living being, with a soul, in a dying body, or if I am already dead, just a ghost composed of information, just signals on the computers.

I cannot walk or stand anymore. I have not the strength to even raise my head off my pillow. Attendants roll my body onto its side to clean me and attend to the sores on my flesh. Each time they do is a fearsome ordeal, as skin, muscle, and bone want to tear away with each movement.

When my friends think of me and cry where they think I cannot see, how can I explain that I am not unhappy? Even though I am going to pieces, even though the pain is an unstoppable flood building and building behind the cracked walls that the medics put up with drugs and neural blocks, a part of me spreads its wings. With Archie as my guide, wrench, sword, shield, chariot, and wings, my consciousness soars through the Noah. This broken shell is not a prison.

In many ways, I am free. I spend afternoons watching the deep-sea fish in the aquatic areas of the biomes. I listen to birdsong and dance with the lights playing on the floors of the dance halls, which have reopened in Paris Section, rehabilitated and productive and ordinary again. The parts of me that I believe now run on the nodes are aware of so much.

Archie shows me more of the Builders' psionic techniques—tricks that no human has ever been capable of before. Like a child, she is always hungry for praise when she shows me something new. Usually, they are just tricks of programming, or elegant, incomprehensible mathematical manipulations of equations and symbols. But every now and then, she shows me something that I know must never become common knowledge among the crew.

Even without Karla watching over my shoulder, I make decisions about knowledge that must be kept secret.

Another week passes, and the resistance is almost beaten. They are cut off from recruiting any more followers, isolated from the rest of the crew in the Habitat, many of whom are back to the normal ebb and flow of life on the ship.

With Archie and me, the figure of ten thousand rebels has been cut down at an astonishing rate. There is nowhere they can hide. There is nothing they can do to deceive us. Nothing is hidden from us. No new weapon is secret. No plan is a surprise.

Karla is pleased. Enough that it controls the fear she keeps hidden inside, that I am growing too strong, too different. She is anxious now for me to die soon, before it gets to the point that she needs to consider having me destroyed outright.

Sometimes, Barrens sends data packets at Archie. Dry reports, updates for Karla. Sometimes, they are letters to me.

Karla does not know about those. There is a lot she will never know.

# 34

THE LAST MIDNIGHT, MY BODY TRANSITIONS TO YET ANOTHER STAGE, WHEN IT does not inhale or exhale anymore, but is oxygenated by a continuous stream of air kept flowing into these corrupted lungs by mind's *touch* alone. I know it is the last midnight because my body is going haywire. The blue light of raw psi energy that I once found so comforting sparks across my body, slicing and tearing and ripping. At last, it is faster than the rate at which the silver nanite filaments can knit me together. I am removed from the horror of it by seeing it through cameras, as if that were someone else. I feel it all the same. Blood starts to stain the sheets. It trickles from this strange, half-metal woman, from the nose and mouth and ears, from around the ports where tubes give nourishment and oxygen and remove wastes, from the very junctions that were held together by the metallic microbots. Just a few drops here, and a few drops there. The disintegration quickens, second by second.

I wish Barrens could have made it back. No, it is better this way.

Lyn and Hennessy are asleep. Two nurses, a young trainee who still doesn't need to shave and an experienced lady with gray in her hair, are supposed to be watching me, ready to alert the rest of the medics.

Archie flexes her muscles and puts them to sleep too, by sliding into their neural Implants and switching their minds off. She defuses the alarms, feeds the monitoring machines false data.

We have been preparing for this. She has been hovering over me constantly, visible only in my head. Her expressive control has matured. She weeps for me now. Holds tight.

*No,* I tell her. I need this. I need to say good-bye. *Stay focused, Archie. Soon, you'll have me all to yourself.* Am I lying? I have no idea if that's true.

Slowly, she nods to me. Still holds on to my hand, ghost sensations in the brain.


Thorn, last of the Archivists' original circle of leaders, leads his best ninety men and women through the tunnel system, trying to circle round by means of a narrow access shaft that cuts from the forward decks out to an external air lock. They plan to walk on the belly of the Noah, across the miles to another air lock that leads to one of the supply corridors for the G-1 prison dome.

They need no more crossbows. By now, all the ones that are left have adapted to Psyn; they take it in such quantities that it will almost kill them to stop.

Their plan is to release the G-1 creatures. All of them. Can they possibly want this, even knowing how cataclysmic the powers of humanity's twisted children are? My mind is removed from the dissolving shell of my being, but phantom sensations penetrate my consciousness, as though my heart were pounding, as though there were a roaring in my ears.

I feel the passing seconds keenly.

They do not know that I am the one that opened this way. They discovered this route in a fragment of data that Archie left for them, to lead them right into an ambush, a dead end where Barrens awaits, with two dozen Enforcers and the best conscripted fighters from the crew hiding in side shafts ready to cut off retreat.

This was the plan we decided on the day before. Karla will just have to deal with the changes I will make.

Better not to warn Barrens. He will see the opportunity and act without questioning it. He needs his mind clear, to finish this.

Karla has known for a while now of my abilities in using Archie to reconfigure the ship. She does not know how quickly I can do it, or how fine my control is. Or rather, she knew what I was capable of two weeks before. She knows the old limits. With Archie's growth, I have grown too. I signal my digital daughter. Where is the boundary between my intelligence and Archie's, anyway? We are so close, yet so different in the way we think. Hard to say. Harder now as I take leave of the plastech shell holding the last bits of organic life in my body together and ride the light.

While I am gone, Archie takes what's left of my body. Hopefully, she can fake being me to Karla's satisfaction, in case the tireless new captain should call. She always saw me as a tool anyway. Nothing matters to her as long as I fulfill my functions, directing her commands to the correct people, analyzing data, predicting trends—all things Archie can do just as well.

The huge amplifiers spread throughout the ship for simulating gravity are all essentially *touch* amps. They are designed to run the simplest of scripts—to exert a force in one direction resulting in a constant acceleration.

With my will in the driver's seat these massive machines are just another tool. I've been using amplifiers since the day I was that little girl in front of a mirror, wondering about my future.

Sensors manifest themselves from the plastech walls, and I put eyes and ears on this most dangerous of the remaining pockets of resistance.

The hall that Thorn travels through narrows. The walls themselves start to move. He and his followers cry out in fear. They try to stop it. Their puny individual talents are nothing to the great devices of the ship itself—through the Noah's Analytical Nodes, I can wield terawatt-class power now; if there were a million of these drug-boosted psychics, they might just barely touch the same amount of energy.

The corridor separates itself into ninety-one separate cages with hardened walls a meter thick, one for each prisoner. Each pounds the plastech in futility, calling out for his or her comrades. *Bruisers* break their bones against the armor. Telekinetics push themselves to the point of unconsciousness trying to take hold of the plastech and cut it. Telepaths cry out with their minds into the darkness, suddenly, terrifyingly alone.

I bore a path through leading from Barrens directly to Thorn's cell. The Enforcers in the side passages hear nothing, detect nothing; they do not realize their job is done.

I see Barrens start, almost drop the flask of water he was drinking from. He is not confused long. I watch resolve steel itself into the fine lines around his eyes, the grinding of his teeth.

Barrens reaches Thorn in an instant.

The slender, effete, handsome man has fared poorly on a diet of battles and fatigue and Psyn. The stylish clothes are rumpled and torn. Hair has fallen out. The eyes are bloodshot. His vibrant, melodic voice is gone to scratches and rasping. "I just wanted a future I chose myself. Shouldn't everyone get to choose that?"

My wolf, my lion, does not roar or growl. He speaks in a cold, soft whisper. "Thousands dead. Tens of thousands addicted. They'll need Deep Adjustments just to function. Enough reactor mass consumed to add hundreds of years to the trip."

Shaking, trembling fingers light a cigarette. The spark of his *touch* is badly controlled, sears a lock of his hair, but Thorn pays no attention. "I always liked you. You're a good guy. Felt bad cutting you out. Problem was you are just too damned decent, Leonard."

"I should just kill you." Those lunch-box fists clench and glow.

Thorn nods. "I had a feeling it would end like this." A twitching grin spreads across that hollow face. "But I know something you don't. 'Cause you didn't just smear me across the wall. So. You want to know it too."

"Yes." Barrens cocks his arm back. "The ISec Induction will kill me in response. But in that last moment, I will also kill you. This is how I deserve to die."

Almost, I warn Leon to stop listening. Almost. But this is his choice. I won't make it for him . . . Although . . . Ah, it is selfish. Selfish. I need this. *Archie*.

Before the thought is finished, the image of the girl in my thoughts is smiling even as I feel something change in me. Tendrils of information fire off into the Nth Web. I see them racing toward this dark place in the middle of nowhere, addressed to the inside of Barrens's head. They arrive at the same time as Thorn's telepathic thrust.

Barrens's hand flies forward, and the last of the resistance leaders dies with his skull smashed open. Without Thorn and the others Barrens assassinated, the single movement of thousands is merely so many little mobs without a unifying figure.

It is over.

Barrens leans against the ice-frosted wall and slides down. He presses his hands against his eyes. Thorn's last thoughts *write* through his mind.

"Why aren't I dead?"

"Archie removed the ISec termination code."

His eyes pop wide. "Hana?"

The Builders had tricks of psionics that are beyond the human brain, even when augmented by a neural Implant. But I am not quite human anymore. And Archie can run the unfathomably complex matrix of psychic manipulations through the ship's processors. A body of energy projected remotely coalesces into the air, a more sophisticated expression of the same technique she used to make a beach and a sky, sand and waves, not quite illusion, not quite reality.

It is my self-image, the me when Barrens and I became whatever we are to each other. Better than that. I look healthy and vibrant with life. My legs and arms are strong. My cheeks have not withered down to the bone. My hair is almost luminous. I forgo the emitter plates on my face, so that he can see what

I would have looked like without the metal. I wear a simple white sundress with sunflowers embroidered along the hem and stand barefoot and tiny and looking up at him.

His wide-eyed, mouth-open look makes a boy of him again, a teenager. It makes me laugh. The laughter does it, snaps him out of his shock.

"Hana!"

His embrace is hard. He is weaker now, from exhaustion. But still so strong. He lifts me up to him and it is a delight to feel my cheek against his without pain, even if his is scratchy and rough because he has not had time to shave in days.

"How can you be here?"

"I'm not really here."

He tilts his head and frowns. Let's go, takes a step back and stares me up and down. Of course he is confused. He sees me, touches me, smells me.

"You sure look like you're here."

I pirouette and enjoy the simulated sensation of the icy air around my legs, as the skirt billows out.

"It does look like it, doesn't it? It's something Archie picked out of the Builders' lost libraries of knowledge."

His smile quivers. Perhaps he is noticing how I am not shivering, even if the air is below zero. Perhaps he can see that each of his breaths becomes a puff of icy mist, while I am not breathing at all. He sees that his bloodstained hands do not leave marks on my skin or my dress. He looks away for just a moment, wipes at his eyes.

"I guess I should thank her. Thanks, Archie."

A young giggle in my head. Programs should not giggle. And she is not a program anymore, has not been for a long time.

I dart in and kiss Barrens, and the taste is everything he remembers. We can both pretend, for a while.

I think it, and the ship warms the air. Above us, the gray ceiling is hidden by the imagery of clear blue skies. There is a sun. There is a breeze. Under our feet, the floor becomes grass. It is still plastech, but it is green and soft and feels like the real thing. We sit and lean against the wall and hold the moment tight.

Our hands touch. We chat. As though thousands of people have not died in the time we have been together. Because of us, in spite of us.

It cannot last. The deck structure under the pseudo-soil and grass vibrates and whines. We hear echoes in the distance. The grinding moan of Enforcers starting to burn their way through. My sunny day flickers.

These summer seconds are almost over. Far, far away, Archie lets me know that my body's functions are crashing. I do not know what will happen next—if this death will end me and I will just fade away, or if I will continue on, as something else. I wonder if souls are real, and if I lost mine as my brain cells were replaced with infinitesimally small machines.

Leon presses his lips to my cheek for just a second. He asks me, "Do you know?"

"I don't."

"Do you want to?"

"Why not?"

Our foreheads touch. He encapsulates the truth in data, from brain to Implant to the ship, and from the ship's systems to me.

I see the glorious white-and-blue ball of Canaan, floating in the black. It has a reddish moon. It is slightly smaller than Earth.

"It is what it is," he whispers to me. "I guess it has to be enough. This is what lies in store."

The Noah, a majestic, massive winged white bird manifests out of the emptiness of space. It enters orbit. And then . . .

The isolated package, the irregularity hanging from its belly, all square angles and ugly pipes, completely unlike the smooth, living curves of the Builders' making, detaches. It enters the atmosphere, riding down on a column of blue telekinetic force.

When it lands, thousands of coffins in a dark chamber open. Men, women, children. Waking up.

The Noah itself leaves orbit. It turns away and begins to pick up speed once more. It plunges into the sun.

*We're just automata, programs with bodies keeping the ship going until we aren't needed anymore.*

*Those chosen people in the Ark, they get to wake up, rebuild. The last uninfected humans from Earth get to paradise. We aren't allowed. The disease, Mincemeat, the whole cursed cycle, the social order with Keepers and ISec and Behavioralists and Breeding Duty, dies with us.*

Through him, I experience thirdhand the emotional contamination that spread among Thorn and the others. Arguments. Everything that came after. The battles. The sheer burden of knowing. A number wanted to just blow themselves to bits and did, taking as many others with them as they could. Others wanted to jettison those sleeping survivors in the Ark—to have our descendants, G-0s and G-1s, doomed people and monsters together, try to make something of it on the new world.

So close. It had been so close. ISec shut the Nth Web down just before the Archivist leaders would have broadcast this terrible truth across the Habitat.

There was no anger left in Thorn in that last split second, calmly waiting for his skull to be smashed open. Just confused sorrow—the downfall of his ideals, the bitterness of a reality more harsh than his most pessimistic moments of cynicism. So much like what Barrens feels too. Only for my lion, he can imagine a future where humans walk on soil again with a real sun above them. Even if it is not for the likes of us.

"It is worth it," Barrens whispers, "isn't it?"

*It has to be.*

I show him what I have seen in the Habitat. People are living again, unconcerned, maybe even happy, despite the unfeeling Adjusted dolls among them. The rebuilding is going well under Hennessy's direction. I show Barrens my darkness too, those times when I watch my son, twisted, ropy limbs of muscle, all eyes and fangs, sleeping in his amniotic cage, inside that other city, squirming in nutrient slime, moaning and wailing in nightmares. My secret wish, that unspoken thought when Karla told me I was dying, to end myself there, to not face the pain, to end it cleanly.

If we have to choose between hope and despair, we might as well choose what lets the species survive.

This is how it ends for him and me. We don't say we love each other, and we don't say good-bye. There is the way we embrace hard as we can. Here, we kiss our last kisses, put everything there is of us into it. Good and bad. Nights and days. Countless flashes of memories pass back and forth between us, sensations, emotions, our shared history reexperienced.

I feel it all at once, the sensations walled away in that bleeding, broken thing. A slow sinking into a deep pool of still water. The convulsive twisting. Systemic organ failure. Despite all these upgrades, in the end I'm just meat, just like everyone else. The false body begins to flicker in and out of existence in Barrens's arms.

There is a last surge of fear.

Archie, too, realizes she is losing me. Her panicked blips and tweeting whistles, her psionic manipulations, none of these things can stop what is happening.

Far away, I feel Barrens scream my name.

I stop—

Karla's rank as Ship's Captain becomes official and permanent. She consigns my corpse to an isolated research lab under the highest levels of security. She commands the mission with an iron heart and erases from her thoughts the dream of trying to find a cure.

Jazz is Retired a year after the Mincemeat crisis. I watch over her dying moments. I think she senses me, for just a moment, before she passes on.

Marcus dies two years after. When he does, Lyn throws herself into her work and practically dwells on the Bridge. She spends the rest of her life trying to unravel Archie's mysteries.

Hennessy sometimes recalls his old boss, a woman that helped him get promoted, who loved his fancy sandwiches and never did get around to telling him about what Barrens does in bed. James runs the logistics for the entire ship now, only a little less efficiently than I ran my part of City Planning. Once in a while, he flirts with Barrens, who never gets comfortable with the attention.

Barrens expects to be Adjusted. At the least, to have some memories erased. Neither happens, and no one ever explains why. He suspects that what he remembers and his conflicted service as the Minister of Peace is better punishment than what Karla can invent.

Eventually, my dear, wounded Leon finds a measure of healing. In the restoration of the Habitat. In his clumsy attempts at gardening. In the love of a young woman he meets in a corner café.

Sometimes though, he looks over his shoulder and sees a figure out of the corner of his eye. Familiar maybe in the tilt of her head, the length of her stride. He loses her in a crowd, or around a street corner, or through the door of a shop. Each time, I tell myself it is the last time.

For the rest of my friends who survive, I've been erased from their lives. I am the classmate that they cannot quite recall, the coworker that got transferred away, a blur, an anomaly in their Implant data, smoothed over with psychological triggers planted by Behavioralists.

Women give birth in their sleep to monsters, which are taken from them and contained, entombed in the dark. G-0 children are born in the Necropolis and brought back to the Habitat to be raised by Keepers. They get their Implants, go to school, grow up. They do their jobs. They perform maintenance through-out the ancient structures of the Noah. They clean the streets under a false sun. They grow crops in the giant greenhouses. They buy new shoes and dresses and suits and entertain themselves with concerts and dances and movies. Some commit crimes and others try to stop them. They sleep and dream. They know nothing of aliens or the doom that waits for them.

The mission, the simulated economy, culture, politics, it all just goes on. The same as before.

Except for me. I am the difference. Never again will anyone discover dangerous data on the Network. When a crewman descends into the symptomatic end stage, it is always caught in time, witnessed only by top-clearance Ministry of Health specialists and ISec Retirement staff with the proper clearance. No more G-1 creatures escape far enough to make it to the sewers and tunnels under the Habitat. I am nowhere; I am everywhere. I cover over mistakes in the system, fill in the cracks, perfect the deception of Utopia.

I am not lonely or bored. I have Archie. I have the dreams of the lost Builders, still locked up deep in the ship's computers.

Sometimes, I make a body, just to have a cup of tea and watch the Keepers in the park, playing not with the next generation, but the one after that. I take walks. I watch people. Sooner or later, they too Retire. I am there for each of them when it happens.

In my child's dreams, he is not a monster. He is a boy, running through grassy fields and white beaches, splashing in the surf, while his mother watches and laughs.

I put out my arms and close them around him.

And I regret nothing at all.

## Acknowledgements

I never would have gotten this far without all the people that drew the writing out of me when I was growing up, and the individuals who saw something in this story and made it happen.
It's not a complete list at all – that would be its own book.

Thank you:

To mom, my wife, and friends: they made it possible for me to try.
To the AS Hill crowd: they got me writing when I was supposed to be studying science.
To Auraeus Solito: the first teacher to make me believe I had something in me.
And to Kristin Nelson and Peter Wolverton: they brought the book home.

# WANT MORE?

If you enjoyed this and would like to find out about similar books we publish, we'd love you to join our online SF, Fantasy and Horror community, Hodderscape.

Visit our blog site
**www.hodderscape.co.uk**

Follow us on Twitter
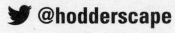 **@hodderscape**

Like our Facebook page
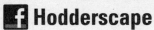 **Hodderscape**

You'll find exclusive content from our authors, news, competitions and general musings, so feel free to comment, contribute or just keep an eye on what we are up to. See you there!